Acclaim for *Sleeper, Awake*, by Bob Rich

"As the title suggests, this is a book concerns a person waking from cryogenic sleep far into the future. You may think this concept has been explored unto the point where nothing more can be said. However, the sleeper is just a small part of this tale. It is the introductory device that allows the author to show us his version of the future of mankind. This is a highly polished, well constructed work that gives the reader a glimpse into Bob Rich version of mankind's destiny. It is not a story high in action content—this is far more SF in the vein of Asimov where the ideas are all important than of Heinlein's militaristic aggressive style but with Asimov my favorite SF author I certainly wasn't complaining."

Steve Mazey, *The Eternal Night*

"In this story, Rich has fleshed out well-rounded, very human characters. Though of a different time and place, Flora's new friends bear close likenesses to people we encounter in our everyday lives. Sleeper, Awake contains insightful messages about living in a world where racial boundaries are nonexistent; about relationships between family members, friends and lovers; and, most poignantly, perhaps, it's about Flora's soul-searching journey as she comes to a new understanding about the cycle of life and death. If you relish thoughtful, imaginative speculations about what our future may bring, you won't regret taking the time to read *Sleeper, Awake* by Dr. Bob Rich!"

Jeanne Allen, *Ivy Quill Reviews*

"When beautiful, wealthy actress Flora Fielding had herself placed in suspended animation, she expected to be revived during the twenty-first century so that her breast cancer could be cured. Instead, she is shocked to find herself awakened almost fifteen hundred years later. Flora faces physical and mental challenges, but she is a somewhat passive protagonist because of her health. Abel, Kiril, and Tamás provide most of the action, and there are lots of thrills and chills as they and other male characters scale mountains, ride bulls, and navigate stormy seas. The women are strong and independent, loving and inspiring the men who may soon father their children. The story brims with fascinating, sometimes controversial theories about our present and future. Dr. Rich, who writes with compassion and irony, has fashioned a rather complicated plot, and the reader may occasionally feel as overwhelmed as Flora does upon awakening. Still, the tale moves swiftly and is filled with charm, tenderness, and excitement. And the scenic descriptions are fabulous."

Ilene Sirocca, *Running River Reader*

"*Sleeper, Awake*, a science fiction novel by Dr. Bob Rich, is a truly amazing experience. To step inside this novel is to step inside an almost alien, but totally believable, world. Dr. Rich designs the futuristic world of Sleeper, Awake with such compelling detail that one comes to the conclusion that this must indeed be the reality of our future earth. Despite its alien quality, the world of *Sleeper, Awake* is in many ways a vast improvement over the world today. I give this fascinating book 5 stars.
Marilyn Peake, author of *The Fisherman's Son*

"The author, through a descriptive narrative and well-developed characterization, shows a future where a great upheaval shifted the environment and altered landmasses. For example, a huge mountain formed where Chicago once existed.   In his fluid writing style, Dr. Rich creates a world of the far future where hunger, war, and disease are but a faint memory in the consciousness of humanity. The world of *Sleeper, Awake* is a fascinating read. I give it all my fingers and toes up."
Michael L. Thal, *EBooksNBytes*

"Ravaged by cancer, Hollywood star Flora Fielding takes the desperate step of having herself placed in cryogenic storage. She is finally awoken after fourteen hundred and thirty three years. Vividly written, Dr Rich's writing transports you into a world beyond comprehension, yet he presents it so well, it becomes plausible. Wonderful landscapes, incredible gadgets, love and a touch of poignancy, this book has it all. Like me, if you weren't a Sci-fi fan before, you will be converted after reading this book."
Barbara Tanner, author of *Hannah's Choice*

SLEEPER, AWAKE

BOB RICH

Winner of the EPPIE 2001 Award for Science Fiction

Modern History Press

Ann Arbor, MI

This is a work of fiction. However, it is based on 30 years of research in diverse fields, and it's more true than many a textbook. If you don't believe this, research it for yourself.

Library of Congress Cataloging-in-Publication Data

Names: Rich, Bob, 1943- author.
Title: Sleeper, awake / Bob Rich.
Description: Ann Arbor, MI : Modern History Press, [2021] |
Summary: "Flora Fielding tried to escape cancer through cryogenic storage, but awoke in an utterly different world 1433 years later. There are only 1 million humans, and having a child is a major reward. This gives women power over men, because they choose the father. She helps to deal with the first crime in over 1000 years, and we follow with her the intertwined   lives of people in a world of universal wealth but major personal   challenges"-- Provided by publisher.
Identifiers: LCCN 2020058698 (print) | LCCN 2020058699 (ebook) | ISBN
    9781615995561 (paperback) | ISBN 9781615995578 (hardcover) | ISBN
    9781615995585 (epub) | ISBN 9781615995585 (kindle edition)
Subjects: LCSH: Humanity--Fiction. | Future, The--Fiction. | GSAFD: Science
    fiction.
Classification: LCC PR9619.4.R53 S57 2021   (print) | LCC PR9619.4.R53
    (ebook) | DDC 823/.92--dc23
LC record available at https://lccn.loc.gov/2020058698
LC ebook record available at https://lccn.loc.gov/2020058699

Modern History Press   www.ModernHistoryPress.com
5145 Pontiac Trail   info@ModernHistoryPress.com
Ann Arbor, MI 48105

≈ 1 ≈

Flora

The voice came as if from far away. It was a pleasant, deep female voice, saying over and over, "Flora, wake up. Flora Fielding, wake up, Flora..." on and on.

I'm awake, Flora tried to say, but her mouth, her lungs wouldn't obey. Her eyelids felt too heavy to lift. And she was cold. Her body was ice. If she moved, surely she'd snap like an icicle — if she could move at all. Her skin hurt everywhere from the bitter, malevolent cold. Her bones ached, all over.

The voice stopped its endless chant and said, "I detect that you are conscious. Don't struggle. The machine is slowly bringing you back. You'll be OK."

So it worked. It must have worked, Flora thought, and a feeling of triumph lent her energy enough to force her eyelids open. The research she'd funded must have found a cure, and now they were resuscitating her.

At first everything was a liquid blur, then she found herself gazing at the sight she'd seen before going into suspended animation, before she'd been frozen. A network of plastic pipes descended from a pastel yellow ceiling. They were filled with fluids of different colors: red blood, creamy yellow food, a blue one, another with clear liquid.

"Move your fingers," the voice commanded. Flora tried, and after several attempts felt them twitch, then bunch up. The cold now felt less excruciating. She took a breath that made her chest rise. "What year's it?" she managed to mumble.

The voice answered, "Thirteen hundred and twelve."

This was meaningless. *I couldn't have gone back in time!* Flora thought in panic, but then the voice explained, "You've been in cryogenic storage for 1433 years. We now have a new system of dates, from the establishment of Control."

A feeling of unreality, of complete disbelief swamped Flora: *It can't be true. It just can't!* "I... I expected to be asleep for maybe ten," she said, her still-weak voice quivering. One-and-a-half thousand years! She turned her head slightly, looking for the source of the voice. She saw no one.

As if reading her mind, the voice said, "I'm Artif. I've been directed to resuscitate you."

"Artif?"

"In your terms, I'm a computer, sort of."

This was encouraging. Surely they had cancer beaten if their technology was this advanced.

A new, masculine voice spoke, a deep, musical baritone. "Welcome, Flora Fielding. Tony Califeri had records of several of your movies, and I've seen them all. You were marvelous."

The female voice cut in, chidingly, "Abel, Flora knows nothing of Tony. She has no more knowledge of our history than a newborn baby."

"All the same," the man's amusedly unrepentant voice answered, "I've seen the movies, and Flora was wonderful."

"Thank you," Flora spoke, a little more strongly now, and became intensely conscious of being naked. Her fifty-two-year-old body was not for a man to see. Or fourteen-hundred-and-eighty-something year-old body, if it was true.

To her surprise, the man said, "Flora, I'm not in the room with you, but on the other side of the earth, in the Arafura Sea. And don't worry, there are no visuals on. Judging from the records, we guessed you wouldn't want to be seen."

She could only thank him again, but then asked, "Are you a doctor? Have you got a cure?"

The deep voice sounded a melodious laugh. "We leave doctoring to Artif, it's more efficient. What do you want cured?"

"Cancer," she said in surprise. Wasn't that why they'd revived her now? There was a silence. Then he said, "My translator is looking."

The female voice spoke, "Abel, that's an uncontrolled growth of rogue cells. I've met four cases this year."

By now, Flora's body felt almost normal. She raised herself on an elbow. Black spots swam before her eyes, then cleared. She asked, "Er, Madam, what do I call you?"

There was a smile in the wonderful voice. "Actually, I'm not female, but the support system for the planet, the executive arm of humanity."

Abel said, "She's Artif. I believe that derives from your language. At least... was your language spoken in a place called Canada?"

"Yes," Flora answered. She became aware of a tingling sensation in her fingertips. Artif commanded, "Flora, move your legs and arms."

Flora tried, and to her relief was able to move almost naturally. She sat up and looked around. Her cocoon for a millennium and a half seemed to have remained unchanged since that time, subjectively an instant ago, when she'd last closed her eyes. Cool pastel blue walls glowed with indirect lighting. She knew that almost all the wall space consisted of doors hiding the equipment that had kept her alive without deterioration all this time: mechanical and electrical muscle stimulators, hygiene maintenance devices and the like. She'd been fuzzy about the details even when Dr. Martin had insisted on explaining them to her.

The room had no windows, only the closed, airtight sliding door that was almost indistinguishable from the rest of the wall. Her elevated bed occupied the middle, with the tubing descending from the low, cream-colored ceiling.

The only addition was a hovering ball that rose to be level with her eyes as she sat up. It was the size of a very large watermelon, Flora thought, only it was translucent, and filled with something resembling swirling white clouds.

A woman's voice came from the ball, not Artif's voice but a lighter, higher one. "Greetings, Flora Fielding," she said, "I'm Mirabelle Karlsen. I'll be your Advocate when you face Control."

Artif spoke, her voice also coming from the ball. "Flora, what you're looking at is something like a television set of your times. I've studied the records. Only, everything but sound has been turned off. Just tell me when you are willing to be seen and I'll give you vision as well."

"Control" sounded ominous. And something was very obviously not right. Ignoring Artif for the moment, Flora answered, "Mirabelle, what is Control? And why do I need an Advocate?" This ball thing confirmed it, she must indeed be in the far distant future.

"Control is the governing body of humanity. The name originally came because Brad wanted to ensure that Artif would always be controlled by people, not the other way around. Anyway, about the need for an Advocate, if I had my way, you wouldn't need one. You wouldn't have been disturbed except for Abel. Ask him." Her voice had a sharp edge to it.

"Now, now, Mirrie," Abel's voice was also located in the hovering globe, and carried the same lazy amusement as before, "you know we all agreed in the end..."

"Don't call me Mirrie! And yes, I agreed in the end, but..."

"But nothing. Agreed is agreed."

"You may not realize," Artif spoke over their bickering," but these two are the most powerful people on the planet. Abel is President of Control, and Mirabelle is Deputy President."

That's all I need, Flora thought, *to be caught in the middle of a power struggle.* The thing was to sidestep the issue for now, until she could gather more information. That had always worked in the past. So, she said, "I... I'm honored by your welcome." She was pleased that her voice once more held its usual resonance. "Er, Artif, these tubes... how can I..."

One flexible tube entered her abdomen, one each her two lower arms, one, with blue liquid, her misshapen right breast. And tubes also emerged from her lower orifices, removing wastes.

"Perhaps the two of you would leave us for a few clicklets," Artif said, command in her voice.

Abel said, "Certainly," at the same time as Mirabelle's "Of course."

"Lie down, Flora."

She did so.

"I've adjusted the chemicals going into you. You'll return to sleep. When you awake, you'll be free of the equipment, and free of pain."

Abel

Abel T'Dwuna rarely did just one thing. Currently he was doing three: fishing, supervising his twelve-year-old son, and participating in the awakening of the Fielding woman: proof of his continued ascendancy at Control. Of course it was the right course of action, never mind Mirabelle and her shrill-voiced faction.

The sea undulated to a slow, oily swell. The waves broke with a white spray on the distant shores of the coral atoll he could see every time his boat rose to a crest. Just visible in the corner of his eye to the left, his house dutifully kept station on him, at a set distance of two hundred meters. Her multicolored sails were half furled.

The early morning sun behind him rapidly ascended into the tropical sky. As so often at this spot, Abel admired the change of colors. When he rode high on a wave, the sea around him glowed a deep blue, and then the slow wave rolled out from under him, and the water turned turquoise green.

Abel thought a command at his lure, through the implant. It stopped its clockwise circling and started a lazy figure of eight. He didn't particularly care if he caught anything, but there was no point in doing a job inefficiently.

He now felt the heat on his back. "A bit of sunscreen," he commanded without needing to speak aloud, and a white globe rose from the locker, hovered over him, then sprayed his naked, almost black body with a fine mist.

He noted that Flora Fielding had awakened, and spoke a greeting. Artif relayed it, using a communication globe, since, of course, the woman didn't have an implant. Abel shuddered at the thought of the bleak existence that must mean. But then he looked up from the currently green depths, and as always his boat gave him a jolt of pleasure. It had been a major work of art, oh, more than forty years ago now, before he'd been selected for Control. It was such a wonderful design that over three hundred people had asked for copies, and he became the father of three of his children because of the fame the boat had brought him.

Well, they were all adults now, but young Tamás still needed care. Abel could feel the boy's fear as a background, and kept up a continuous, wordless mental hum of reassurance.

"Dad," Tamás said, "I need to do a wee."

"I know, mate." Being in a one-way merge with the boy, Abel had been aware of his need for a while and had been expecting the complaint. Even while taking part in the conversation in America, he said to Tamás, "Check if there is anyone under you." Of course, Abel could see that there wasn't, but children do need training in politeness.

"No Dad, no one within fifty K of the Tree."

Abel laughed, making sure it sounded both friendly and confident. "Then it's simple. Hang on with one hand, unfasten with the other, and see how far you can piss."

In the far-away Swedish Isles, Tamás took a deep breath. Shifting handholds, he slowly turned so he wasn't facing the immense trunk, but outward. The red ball of the late afternoon sun was actually below him, almost ready to set. His left hand welded itself around a branchlet the thickness of his wrist as he released his hold with the right.

"Hey, hey, boy, relax," Abel said to him. "You use too much energy this way. You're in no more danger of falling than if you were a meter off the ground." At the same time, Abel continued fencing with Mirabelle, who was trying to trick him into a premature disclosure to Flora, and watched a large, striped fish swim into view. He commanded the lure to flee, and the odlero flicked her tail and turned to follow. Abel found it necessary to exert considerable control to keep all knowledge of Tamás's escapade from Mirabelle, who'd be furious if she knew he was three quarters of the way up the Tree. She cosseted the boy too much. Twelve going on thirteen, and still treated like a child. No son of his could be allowed to become a soft no-hoper!

Mirabelle

She wore nothing but a flaring skirt that barely covered her knees, in her favorite deep blue. She was in her study, sitting cross-legged on a soft bearskin she'd tanned herself, after stalking the bear for a week and killing him with a single arrow. Her eyes were closed — she most definitely needed to concentrate on just one thing at a time, and presently that was Flora Fielding. Poor bloody woman. Mirabelle was furious every time she thought of the job ahead of her. At least, it would be up to bloody Abel to tell her the bad news. *I mean,* she thought for the thousandth time, *how do you tell somebody she was awakened only to have to argue for her life?* As she'd said over and over, it would've been far kinder to turn her off and be done with it. But no! That'd be murder! Instead, you awaken somebody into an utterly foreign world, so she can die slowly from some ancient disease, because you want her to speak for 122 strangers. Bloody Abel and his noble ideas.

Flora was awake now, and Mirabelle gave Abel a chance to greet her. After all, it was his idea, wasn't it? But when he stayed all lovey and honey-voiced with not a hint of troubles to come, she had to enter the conversation. *Just the right note of warning,* she thought as the woman took in the implications. And, as intended, she'd managed to bait Abel into climbing out from behind his all so friendly mask.

Artif asked for privacy, and so Mirabelle withdrew and opened her eyes. Her house was in the brittle red light of the sun, a great rust-colored ball underneath her, as it reluctantly set at last. Way below, scattered cirrus clouds had turned a dirty red. A storm swirled far off to the south, but she was too high for any turbulence to affect her. In fact, one of the topstores was almost directly above, looking enormous from here.

Mirabelle smoothly stood, uncoiling her long limbs. "A cup of chocken," she ordered without speech, through the implant, and the kitchen made a whirring sound. A globe emerged from it and floated to Mirabelle's hand. She slightly squeezed the cup, then sucked the hot, delicious fluid through the thin hollow tube that emerged in response.

"Tamás?" she called.

"Sorry, Mirabelle," Artif answered, "he's not available right now."

"What? But I'm his mother!"

"Of course. But he's with Abel at the moment, and they've asked for privacy."

Mirabelle made a hissing sound, blowing air out through her nostrils. She thought up an image of herself with flames shooting out of her nose, wide mouth agape with huge pointed teeth, black wings stretched to each side, and sent it to Abel.

Annoyingly, he laughed in response. He stood in front of her, dark and naked, then transformed his image into a hammerhead shark. "Two can play that game," he said. His mouth didn't move, he spoke in Swahili, but she heard him in Swedish.

Mirabelle dismissed the dragon image and stood in his boat, his admittedly lovely boat.

"What're you doing with my son?" she demanded.

"Our son," he answered, scuffing his bare left foot on the bearskin in her balloon, high above the Swedish Isles. "You know, I was thinking how limiting it must be, to be like the Fielding woman, without an implant."

"You're trying to change the topic. Where's Tamás?"

"Mirabelle, Tamás is a boy on the verge of manhood. He needs to train himself in acts of daring. You cosset him too much."

"I thought so. You've got him in some place where he's out of his depth." She easily adjusted her image to the movement of the boat.

Abel laughed, his eyes on the swirling of the faraway storm seen through the balloon's transparent wall. "Far from it! 'Out of his depth' is the worst possible description!"

"I see. The Tree. I'm going down."

"He's all right. Mirabelle, he's all right. I'm in a one-way merge with him, every clicklet. And it's not as if you'd never done anything daring."

"I wasn't twelve years old, with an old fool egging me on."

"And you didn't have an old fool holding you back either."

They glared at each other. Mirabelle broke contact and ordered her house to descend. Oh, she loved Tamás, more than life itself, but for Tony's sake, why did she have to choose Abel as the father? Back then, she'd pushed and cajoled and argued, but now she could no longer fathom why.

Tamás

It's not fair, why couldn't I have been born a girl? he thought, and not for the first time. There were blisters on both his hands now, despite the thin protective gloves, and his fingers ached. He'd scraped skin off both his knees, through the thick trousers. His underclothes were clammy with old sweat.

At least, Mother is too busy to bother me, he thought. He knew she found it hard to be in more than one place at a time, and that she was doing something with some Sleeper. Butting heads with Dad as usual.

He stopped a moment, studying the next few meters of ascent. He'd have to work his way over to the right, to that lateral there. He stretched, managed to grasp a handhold, swung on one hand for an instant then got the other one anchored. Leaning away from the Tree, he scrabbled with his feet against the rough bark of the trunk, and then had the branch under his chest. *Girls don't need to do stuff like this,* he again thought resentfully, then, *Artif, don't let Dad hear!*

"Don't worry, Tamás, you know I always maintain privacy," she answered instantly, and the boy was soothed by her voice, much more so than by Dad's constant reassurance. That was merely annoying.

He squirmed onto the branch, got his knees under him and stood, one hand steadying him against the trunk. He grabbed a thin, all too flexible branch at the new chest height. Dad said, "See the fork? You can sit down and have a rest there."

"Good idea." For the zillionth time on this climb, Tamás flexed his knees until he was almost squatting. He sprung straight up, grabbed a branch, swung, did a desperate chin-up, then squirmed like a snake until he was secure again. The nice, flat-bedded fork was now an easy step away. Tamás told his pack to move from the back to the front, and thankfully sat. He leaned his back against the trunk and looked around.

Level with his eyes, a small, fluffy pink cloud was motionless, no, very slowly swirling within. It must have been well after the seventeenth period, for the summer sun was setting at last. Above, a long way above, was the shiny little ellipse of a topstore. It looked about twice the size as from the ground. Tamás tried to look down without moving any more than necessary, but the network of green needles on brown branches obscured his view. He deliberately relaxed his body and closed his eyes.

"Have a drink," Dad offered.

Tamás opened his eyes, feasting on the early morning tropical sunshine. His body gently swayed to the movement of Dad's boat, and the salty breeze felt wonderful on his sweaty face. His climbing clothes actually started to steam a little, but Tamás welcomed the blessed heat compared to the cool air up the Tree.

A white grin split Dad's dark face as he passed Tamás a cup. There was blood on his hand, and he held the gutting knife in the other. The big odlero on the board in front of him was about half gutted.

Tamás accepted the globe, squeezed it and sucked. It was entirely normal that, at the same time, he was aware of his body back on the Tree, drinking from an identical cup.

Having sucked the cup dry, he returned it, saying, "I'd rather be doing this than climbing!"

Abel laughed. "You've got to earn the right first."

"I know." *And it's not fair. Girls don't,* he thought.

Something must have showed on his face. Abel said, "I was scared too, son."

"I can't imagine you, scared."

"Well, I don't have much to be scared of, nowadays... except for your mother of course." They grinned at each other. "But, when I was almost fifteen, I walked across the lava in the caldera of Mount Hokkent. And OK, you have the protective suit, but the problem is that if you rest your foot for longer than a couple of clicklets, it starts sinking in. Leave it long enough, and you are anchored. Forever. And halfway across, I got a cramp in my left calf."

Tamás shuddered. *I don't want to do anything like that, that's for sure!* he thought. "But what's the point?" he asked querulously. "So, you could have died, or had your feet cooked for life."

"Because a man needs to prove himself. Oh, there are pitiful sods who are too afraid to, but no woman will ever choose them."

Yeah, that's the problem. The girls have it all their way, and it's not fair.

Abel said, "Tamás, you'd better keep going or you'll get too stiff."

Tamás opened his eyes, way up in the Tree. He groaned as, one hand against the trunk, he stood. He casually looked up. A silver speck was rapidly growing, coming closer. At first, he thought in surprise that the topstore was coming down, then he recognized his mother's house. *Now I'm in trouble!* he thought.

There was no point, climbing further. Half thankfully, half-resentfully he waited. Mirabelle said, "Tamás, don't move. I can't do a job without you getting into trouble."

"I'm not in trouble." How dare she treat him like a child?

"No? You reckon you could climb another seventy meters, and then down again, in the dark? Down is actually harder than up."

"I've got a rope. I was planning to go down in drops."

"Tony be thanked you have a little bit of sense. Even then."

The house was now level with him. It stopped its descent, hovering about fifty meters away, clear of the wide spread of lateral branches.

"Come on, son. A hot bath and a massage for you." A circular hole opened in the balloon's glistening side, and a silver bridge extended toward him. When it got close enough, he stepped onto it, and a translucent silver web instantly enfolded him. The bridge retracted, and he could look down the immense distance to the ground during the swift ride home. *I climbed all that way!* he thought with pride.

When the door closed behind him, he looked up at his mother's furious face, and almost shouted, in the Swedish that was so expressive when used in anger, "I wish you'd just let me be like any other boy!"

"You're only twelve."

"I was all right. I was going well. Just let me be!"

Her eyes flashed blue lightning, and he knew when to stop. Besides, Artif was unhappy with him. He stalked off toward the waiting bathroom.

⚡ 2 ⚡

Flora

She awoke feeling rested, and hungry. For a sweet second, she thought she was at home, in her own place, in her own time. Her right hand actually twitched for the bellpush. But the bellpush wasn't there, and Millie wasn't there to answer it. She was dead, long, long dead, more than a thousand years dead.

Her mansions were dust. Her fleet of cars and planes were rust. All that wealth she'd accumulated was gone. Only this room remained, and presumably the underground installation it was a part of.

Flora opened her eyes. The blue room was the same, except that the tubes had disappeared. The ceiling was an unbroken, creamy expanse.

"Welcome back, Flora," Artif's deep, warm voice said. For a moment, Flora hated that voice, so sweet, so reasonable, so... foreign. It was the voice of this new, alien world, and she didn't want to be here. She wanted to be back home.

Artif continued, "I've never resuscitated a Sleeper before, though Tony's records are pretty thorough. Is there anything you need?

"I'm... I'm hungry. And it's very hot here."

It was. Now that she'd said it, Flora was aware of the humid, dense heat in the room. It was like the one time she'd gone on a guided tour of a tropical jungle in Borneo, with the air dripping water, a heat that had flushed her skin and coated it with sweat.

Artif sounded surprised. "This is the temperature people prefer. Oh, of course, the climate change. It didn't occur to me that, after all, you're from the Ice Age."

"I am not!"

"There is a meal by your side. Why don't you sit up and eat?"

Flora did so, to see a tray, hovering on no support. It held a fist-sized brown globe, a plate made of some kind of material that looked like plastic, and a knife and a fork. The meal on the plate seemed more like dinner than breakfast: a nicely browned steak and four different, unknown vegetables. The arrangement was a work of art, with the different colored vegetables placed in a pleasing pattern.

The communication globe floated beyond the tray. Artif said, from within it, "I'm sorry, I just couldn't decide what you'd want to eat. Hope this is OK."

"It is, it looks wonderful, thank you. Only, could I have a drink too, please?"

Artif laughed. "You've got one. Pick up that round object, and gently squeeze it."

Flora did so, gingerly. A short straw popped from the top of the globe, releasing a delicious smell a little like hot chocolate. She took an experimental sip, then enthusiastically sucked the container dry.

"How is the temperature now?" Artif asked. "I feel so limited in anticipating your wishes, since you don't have an implant."

What's an implant? There were so many questions to ask! "Much better, thanks. Can you make a breeze or something?"

Instantly, a cool airflow played over Flora's sweaty bare front. She cut into the meat and tasted it. "What's this? she asked, not recognizing the taste.

"Hippopotamus."

Flora tried a piece of mauve vegetable, and found it delicious. "Why hippo meat?"

"It's a very common animal. I farm them all over the place."

Flora thought while eating. "I think," she said slowly, "that relates to you calling my times an 'Ice Age.' And you said, people nowadays like it hot and humid. So, the climate's changed, hasn't it?"

"It has, and actually, you caused it."

"Me?"

Mirabelle's voice came from the globe, "Greetings again, Flora Fielding. No, not you personally, but the people of your times. You suffered as a result, but we're very thankful. It's one of the reasons you Sleepers have been kept alive, as the last representatives of times BT."

"Every answer leads to a thousand other questions," Flora said ruefully. "What's BT?"

"Before Tony."

Artif added, "Tony's records explain your way of measuring time. Your calendar goes back to the birth of somebody called Jesus. Ours is tied to the establishment of Control, but also we divide history in two: before and after the life of Tony Califeri. He is more important to us than Jesus was in your day, because, as I understand it, many people did not acknowledge His leadership. There were Muslims, and Buddhists, and Atheists, and other religions. However, every person on earth now reveres Tony."

Flora was well into the meal. She asked, "Er, Artif, do you think I could have another drink?"

"Certainly. Chocken do?"

"Was that what I had? Yes please."

"Wait a clicklet. I don't have facilities within this room. It's coming from the kitchen I've set up outside." As Artif finished speaking, the door slid aside and a brown little globe floated through, straight to Flora's hand. She pressed and sucked.

"How do you do that?" she asked, "making things hover in the air?"

Artif sounded surprised. "EGM. That stands for electro-gravitational modulation. The principles were described in Tony's records, so I thought you'd know about it. It's selective pushing or pulling against nearby large masses. I can show you the math if you like, some time."

Flora shuddered. "Technical things confuse me."

Mirabelle's laugh came from the communication globe. "You sound just like Abel when I try to explain some physics to him."

Flora put the second empty cup on the tray. The tray smoothly moved to the door, which slid aside, then closed behind it. "Things moving by themselves seem like magic to me."

"I'm not sure what 'magic' is, but they don't move by themselves," Artif explained. "The door has the original equipment, installed in your times, and maintained by me and my predecessors. And as I said, small objects are moved around with an EGM motor. I control all such things. There is nothing mysterious here."

But Flora had a much more urgent concern. "Artif, when I first awoke, you said something. You said, in the past year you'd found four people with cancer. What happened to them?" Her heart beat so hard she could hear it, and she found she was holding her breath, waiting for the answer.

"Three of them got better, and so far they've had no recurrence. The fourth decided to hand on."

"Hand on?"

Mirabelle explained, "It's how most people die. Oh, occasionally people have fatal accidents, especially men out to gain credentials." Her voice was full of some sort of strong emotion, and she paused for a short while. "For some combination of reasons, a person decides she's lived long enough. She tells Artif, and the woman on the top of the List is notified. There is—"

"Whoa!" Flora interrupted. "What list?"

"The List. The next women who can have a child."

"I... I just can't cope." And suddenly, without warning, surprising even herself, Flora started to cry. Great sobs shook her, and tears covered her face, and she leaned forward, hugging herself like a lost child.

Through her own uncontrollable sobs, she heard Mirabelle say, "Artif, let me go to her."

Artif answered, "Yes. I'll cover her up."

And then a light, gauzy cloth that was not cloth wrapped around her bowed shoulders, draped over her bare, shuddering body.

An instant later, strong arms held her, a warm hip pressed against hers, and long, straight golden tresses swung into her field of view.

Flora looked up, into concerned blue eyes. Mirabelle was much older than Flora had expected from the voice, and yet she was beautiful. Her strong, lined face was triangular, with a wide forehead, high cheekbones, and a pointed chin with a cleft. Her nose was straight and prominent. Her skin was much darker than Flora's, a deep tan almost hiding a sprinkle of freckles.

To Flora's surprise, Mirabelle's top half was bare, revealing small, still shapely breasts with prominent nipples. A blue skirt covered her thighs. Her skin was puckered into goose-bumps all over, although the temperature still felt too warm to Flora.

"My dear, I was afraid of this," Mirabelle said softly. "I just knew the flood of new information would be overwhelming. But do you think I could make anyone listen?"

Flora snuggled into the comfort of the strong, supple body next to her and sat up straighter. "Oh, I'm so sorry. I don't know what came over me. Artif, do you have tissues in this time?"

Artif answered after an almost imperceptible pause, "I have found the reference. No, Flora, we have very little that's thrown away after use. I'm getting you a handkerchief."

The door slid open and a tray came in, bearing a neatly folded cloth square, which was red, with wonderful floral patterns all over it. When Flora unfolded it, she found it to be much larger than expected, more like a child's diaper in size, and with a fluffy, soft feel. Thankfully, she wiped her face and blew her nose. Then she turned to her neighbor.

"Mirabelle, thank you for coming. It's, it's really lovely."

"My pleasure." The woman's voice came from the globe beyond her, and her lips hadn't moved.

"Only, how did you get here? Where were you before?"

Mirabelle pulled away slightly. "Now, Flora, don't get upset, but more information overload is coming."

"I know. I just have to accept it."

"I'm not really here. What is here is my image, projected by the communication globe. And—"

"But you *feel* real! And I can even smell you, it's not unpleasant, but..."

"That's right. It's complete sensory projection. Oh, it's nothing as good as if you also had an implant, but it's what we use to go someplace where there's no one nearby. That's the primary purpose it was designed for. Also, we use it if we need to interact with animals. We communicate with other people directly through the implant."

"I guess I need to learn about that."

Artif said, "Apart from Artif 1.0, that was Tony's greatest invention. It's the essence of humanity now, and makes my work possible. For over twelve hundred years, every week-old baby has had a tiny thing painlessly inserted under the skin on her scalp."

"Look, here is my spot," Mirabelle said, took Flora's hand and placed it on her own head. Flora felt a little bump through the hair.

Artif continued, "This thing is like a seed. It's programmed to grow and develop, and becomes an integral part of the person's brain."

"What's it for?"

"Think of it as a gateway. At any one time, much of your brain is unused. The implant taps into your brain, and, how can I put in your terms? Makes use of this immense power as if it was a computer. And also, every mechanical device on the planet has a computer within it, for example the kitchen just outside. And every computer, whether it's an implant in a person or an inanimate object, can communicate with every other computer on the planet. They can all send and receive encoded energy, just like your TV sets and radios and telephones used to."

"And that's what Artif is," Mirabelle interrupted, "the combined consciousness of all those computers, hundreds of millions of them acting as a single organism."

"So, I am everywhere, all at once. Up high in the stratosphere, we have thousands of huge vacuum balloons called topstores, because they are the main generators and storehouses of solar energy."

Vacuum balloons? Flora thought, but didn't interrupt.

"Wherever you are on earth, you'll have at least three topstores in line of sight, and messages pass from topstore to topstore at the speed of light. So, Mirabelle in the Swedish Isles wants to give a hug to her daughter, Evelyn, whose house is just off Antarctica at the moment. I let Evelyn know this, and if she agrees, the two of them are in instant contact. They share as much or as little of each other as they wish. Each stays where she is, but also seems to be in the other place, just like Mirabelle seems to be here with you."

"Only more so," Mirabelle added.

"But... I'm not sure I'd want to be exposed to, um, visitations by just anyone, any time."

Mirabelle laughed. "Neither would I. Artif gives you perfect privacy. It's one of the most inviolate edicts of Control."

"I suppose I'll need to learn about that too, but... Artif, can we please go back to cancer? I... I had myself put to sleep because I had breast cancer, and the cure in my time was very uncertain, and it involved nasty things like having pieces cut out of you and being exposed to radiation and chemicals with terrible side effects. So, I hoped to be awakened when a better cure was available. I funded the research, expected to be out of action for five or ten years. And next thing, I heard your voice, in the far distant future, with everything I've known and loved long gone." Again, she was in danger of crying. She felt Mirabelle's comforting arm tighten around her shoulder.

"I don't understand a couple of things you said, like 'funded'," the blonde woman said, "but let that pass. This cancer, was it common in your times?"

"Yes, it was, and increasing. It was a major source of death, and not only for old people. Even cancer in children was increasing."

Flora felt Mirabelle shudder. "How awful! It's almost unknown for us."

"Let me explain," Artif said. "There are two important reasons for the change. Ever since the establishment of Control, we've had a very careful selection program. People who have genetic faults don't have children at all. The rest donate germ cells between the ages of eighteen and eighteen-and-a-half, and these are mapped for all inherited characteristics. When a person is allowed to have a child, I choose her best germ cell. So, even now, after over thirteen hundred years, the genetic stock is still improving all the time. But already now, we have next to no inherited susceptibilities to disease.

"So, that's one half of the reason we don't have cancer. The other half is even more important. We don't put poisons into our environment at all. In particular, we don't burn hydrocarbons—"

"Did they burn hydrocarbons?" Mirabelle sounded shocked. "But that's crazy!"

Flora ignored her comment. "But, but, there were four people with cancer last year, and three of them got better, and..." She stopped, breathlessly, her eyes on the cloudy depths of the communication globe that was the origin of Artif's voice.

Artif said, very gently, "Flora, they had implants. I detected the problem very early, and adjusted their immune system. It was all done from within. The fourth person was an elderly man who'd never been chosen..."

Mirabelle interrupted with an explanation, "No woman asked him to father her child."

"...and had never done anything remarkable, and he was happy to go. Because one of the most wonderful experiences a person can have is the bonds of loving when you hand on."

"When I was selected for Control," Mirabelle said, "that qualified me for another child. The person whose life this child was to continue was a young woman called Tamára. She had a dominant mutation, so could have no children of her own. Her life centered on loving her mother, and then the mother's house was caught in a terrible hurricane before she could submerge it deep enough, and she died. So, Tamára decided to hand on. I chose the man to father the child, and then Tamára physicaled me..."

"What's that mean?"

"She physically traveled to be with me, in the same house. Not only contact through the implant, but actually physically together. She was with me for the nine months of the pregnancy, and held and kissed my son, Tamás, and then she was ready, and went to sleep, and never woke up." Mirabelle's voice stayed level, her face serene, but great tears emerged from the corners of her eyes, to run down her wrinkles unheeded. "I've had four children, which is the most any woman can have. One was the continuation of an accidental death. But the other three have given me such beautiful experiences."

Flora was silent for a while, out of respect for Mirabelle's strong feelings. Then she asked, "So, Artif, my one hope is to accept an implant?"

"Is that possible?" Mirabelle asked.

"It's true that no adult has received one for well over a thousand years, but after all, that's how Control was established." Artif gave a little laugh. "Brad and his small group went out with a kind of gun Tony had designed, a hundred years before. They shot people, and that put an implant into the victim, and the implant was programmed to ascend the nervous system. And the person joined the team once Artif 1.0 could talk to her. I'm sure we can adapt the old techniques."

"Oh, I still get a dozen questions from every answer," Flora said, "but I'm absolutely exhausted. Artif, can you please organize that implant?"

"Have a sleep, Flora. When you wake up, you'll have one."

"Er, um, before I do, I need to pass some water."

"I'll go now, but I also have a question," Mirabelle murmured. "I wonder why Abel stayed away this time?"

Then she was gone.

Flora slid her feet to the floor and started to stand. Her knees buckled, and she had to grab hold of the edge of the bed to stay upright. "Oh, I'm so weak!" she wailed.

"Your muscles will rapidly strengthen," Artif reassured her. "I've anticipated this, and made a mobile device for you."

The door slid open, and something that looked like a padded armchair skimmed in, its legs just clear of the ground. Still holding the bed with both hands, Flora turned and sat.

It felt wrong, sitting on the commode within sight of the communication globe, but Flora told herself she was being silly. After all, not only was Artif a computer, but also she must be witnessing thousands of people passing wastes, at any one time.

The surprise came when she was finished. She felt a spray of warm wetness, followed by a blast of almost hot air drying her.

She yawned as she stood and clambered onto the bed. "I have one last request, please, Artif."

"Yes?"

"I need clothes. I feel very uncomfortable, being naked."

Artif's voice had a smile in it. "I've got a selection waiting for your choice. But sleep first." Flora lay down, to be covered by the cloth that had draped her during Mirabelle's presence.

Abel

Abel rarely did just one thing. The exception was when he shared bodies with a woman. Then, all his attention focused on the joy of their activity.

He was happily frying fillets of another fish he'd caught while his kitchen prepared a salad to go with it, when Artif asked, "Abel, are you willing to see a visitor?"

He simply said, "Welcome," without even asking who it was.

A young woman stood beside him. Abel told the kitchen to take over the fish, and turned to inspect her. She wore a lace body suit that covered her torso, leaving her arms and legs bare. Pink nipples showed through the gauzy material. She was tall for a girl, a head shorter than him, and willowy, but with firm, up-thrusting breasts. He didn't think she was over twenty-five, a mere child. Her coloring intrigued him: dark golden hair and startling green eyes, combined with skin nearly as dark as his own.

"Welcome," he repeated, with more feeling.

She grinned at him. "Hi, I'm Souda Ramirendo."

"Have some fish," he offered. The kitchen delivered a nicely arranged plate to each. He held his, and led the way to the lounge, facing the view of endless ocean. They sat in chairs that accommodated to their wishes and he savored his catch before asking, "And what can I do for you, Souda?"

She took a deep breath, obviously to calm her nerves. "Father my next child."

"Darling, thanks for the honor, but no thanks."

"I knew that's what you'd say, but—"

"Souda, it's on the public record that I won't father any more children. Tony knows, I've enough. Eighteen! Find yourself a nice young fellow, there are plenty clamoring for the chance."

"Sure, but I want the best."

"You won't get it with me. Look, love, I'm sixty-eight. Where are you on the List?"

"Just made the top 500."

"So, I'll be more like seventy when the child is born. How good a job of fathering do you think I can do when she's a teenager?"

"You said 'no' before your last six children. That's on the public record, too."

"And the youngest is now twelve, and he's a nice boy, but I've only physicaled him three times in his life, and he was too young to remember the first. I prefer to take fathering seriously. Go get yourself a youngster."

A tear appeared in the corner of her eye, but she kept her face calm.

Abel gently said with an inner grin, "Finish your meal, Souda. Go on. You might want to talk to one of my sons, and when the baby is born, I'll take an interest in her. Now, is there any reason why we can't enjoy each other?"

A bright smile lit up the brown face. "That'd be great. Look, at home I've got the most wonderful bed. That's how the father of my first child earned the honor — he designed it specially for me."

"Where's home? Where are you from?"

"I'm from Antarctica."

"Nice place, though too cool for my liking."

"Hmm. But at the moment, I'm closer to your home. My house is sailing up the Gut. Eastrica on the right, Westrica on the left."

"Make sure your house listens for the weather! A storm can whip up in no time, and there's no safety deep down — the turbulence goes all the way to the bottom."

She let go her plate, which floated off to the kitchen. She stood with a graceful, sinuous movement that held much promise, and said, "Come on, then." And even while his physical body lay down quietly on the couch in his own house, his entire consciousness went with Souda. He certainly had no attention to spare for Flora Fielding, or anyone else.

Her house was made to feel tiny by the dark bulk of the overtowering cliff Abel could sense rather than see on their right. He sniffed the smell of the jungle, the smell of childhood. It was darker than dark outside, dense, low clouds hiding the midnight sky.

She held his hand and stood next to him, snuggling against his side as they faced a shallow, ovoid depression, like a double bath in size. "This is it," she said.

"Doesn't look much like a bed to me."

She laughed. "It's brilliant, actually. Very simple, it's just an EGM motor, but it levitates people, not things."

She ran a finger along the front of her suit. It opened up and fell away. Abel noted that her pubis had the same golden hair as her head. "I'll show you," her voice said, while her mouth puckered for a kiss. She tugged on his hand and stepped forward.

He felt his feet leave the floor, and a gentle but irresistible force tilted him until he lay on his back, up in the air by a meter. Souda was above him, exactly parallel, but face down. Her nipples just touched his chest. Her arms went around his broad shoulders and her lips enfolded his. He heard her say at the same time, "Command the bed to give any position you like."

"I'll leave it to you," he answered, his hands exploring the wonderful secret places of her body. They played, arousing each other more and more, and then she took him into herself, saying, "Merge!" Instantly, he is her and she is him and he feels both his own pleasure and hers and every slightest movement is double ecstasy. Their joint pleasure grows and fills the world and is almost too much to bear and will never end.

He exploded at the very instant of her orgasm, and for a long moment they were welded together, unwilling to move.

He withdrew from her consciousness. She took her arms and legs from around him and floated to the edge of the bed. Abel thought at the bed, "I want to stand," and a gentle force pushed him upright, took him to the edge of the oval depression and set him down on the floor.

"Oh, that was wonderful," Souda said, stretching luxuriously.

"Yes, thank you, love. But just imagine, being without an implant. We couldn't even understand each other's speech, even if we physicaled. You'd be just a body to me, something to rub against."

"What made you think of such a bizarre thing?"

"I'm involved in waking up that Sleeper, Flora Fielding."

"Of course. I've heard about it, but I don't take much interest in politics. Come, let's have a drink." She must have sent a command to her wardrobe, for a fresh body suit floated out on a hanger. She took it, gracefully shrugged into it, then took his hand again. The hanger picked up the body suit she'd discarded before their sharing, and took it out of sight.

She led the way to the left side, facing the invisibly dark waters of the Gap. They sat cuddled up in a chair that molded itself to their bodies, and ordered drinks. Hordes of insects hurled themselves at the window, splattering against the plasteel surface.

"How come I've never come across this bed idea?" Abel asked lazily. "You're right, it's brilliant in its simplicity. For over a thousand years, we've used EGM to move objects. Somehow, no one thought of using it to move people. I'll make sure the principle is applied."

"There are only two beds like this," Souda answered, "this one, and Kiril's own. And he's never used the idea for anything else."

"Kiril, that's his name, is it? Tell me about him. And surely, lots of people would want to compliment him by asking for copies?"

"Kiril Lander, from South Calif. He's two years younger than I am. I was sailing my home, minding my own business, when this little boat came over the horizon. There he was, on a quest, gaining credentials. He had no power at all, everything physical. Sails and oars for propulsion, sunlight focused by a parabolic mirror for cooking, not an Artif-operated device on board. No weather-watch, nothing. I'd sprained my ankle and Artif called him to help, and I invited him to stay."

"Amazing, the first meeting a physical?"

"Yes. Well, he's an attractive youngster, and very intelligent, and he was good company then, and we shared bodies physically."

"You know, in all my life I've never done that."

"Oh, the implant still helps. Anyway, he stayed for a while, and it was good fun, and we kept in touch after that. When I got well up on the List, he physicaled me again, a complete surprise, and had the bed with him. Its first use was us sharing bodies again, both of us there."

"It'd be a little messy, wouldn't it? Semen actually inside your body?" Even while he was speaking, his actual body was having a shower back in his own house.

"It's not too bad, a shower fixes it."

"So, where is your child?"

"He's with Kiril's mother, Susan."

Abel raised his eyebrows in an unspoken question.

"I don't want Kiril here any longer. I certainly don't want another physical, and of course he has a right to spend time with his son. I tolerate his visits sometimes when he wears me down, but even that's getting to be a load."

"But doesn't the boy miss you?"

"I spend a lot of time with him. And he loves it there. Susan's second is two years older, and the two are inseparable. They live on South Calif, in a land house, and spend a lot of time looking for ancient artifacts. And this way, I don't have to see Kiril."

"Why, what's he done?"

The green eyes flashed in anger. "He tries to own me! Look, at one time I took an interest in ancient music. I listened to a great many of the recordings Tony preserved. One song stuck with me, from some man called Something Nilson I think." She hummed a tune, very pleasantly. "Translated, part of the words are, 'I'll lock her away in a trunk, so some big hunk won't take her away from me.'"

"What's a 'hunk?'"

"I don't know and I don't care. But that's what Kiril wants to do to me. Lock me away like a thing, and keep me for his exclusive use. You know, he's never shared bodies with any other woman?"

"Odd, but that's his business, surely."

"So it is. Trouble is, he gets pathetic when I have another man. If he was here now, he'd want to kill you!"

Abel shuddered at the thought of one person wanting to kill another. "That's sick! Why hasn't he sought help?"

"He doesn't want help. He wants me. Look, everyone who's familiar with the situation has been nagging him to do something about it, but we can't force it on him."

"No, you can't. But I can. I'm on Control, so I'm allowed to be proactive."

A small smile played on Souda's lips. "I know that, love. That's the second reason I visited you."

"Was there a third?"

She laughed outright. "I heard that you were a wonderful lover."

"Well, perhaps not bad for an old fellow," he said complacently.

Kiril

Kiril Lander was almost at the peak of Mount Chicago, North America's highest mountain. This high, the black rock wore a thick, slick coating of translucent ice. He had the specially shaped toes of his climbing shoes thrust into tiny slots in the ice. His gloved left hand was wedged in another at chest height, and he inserted the right into the still warm slot a little above. He steered the laser gun via the implant and activated it.

The gun took at least five clicklets to respond, then an eternity, maybe as long as half a click, to cut the next slot. At the same time, Kiril became aware of the straps digging into his shoulders. *I'm low on power,* he thought with a sudden burst of fear, and his breathing speeded up, a desperate lapping for air through the mask. "Artif!" he called without words.

"Yes, you are low on power," she instantly answered, "but I can't possibly recharge here. You'd be swept off the rock face."

"Do I have enough to make it?"

"Not at the current rate, my dear. I estimate five more slots, with luck."

By then, his left hand was in the new slot. Instead of his previous careful, one-movement-at-a-time progress, he now did a chin-up, hanging for a long instant on the tips of his fingers, and got both his feet anchored. Still panting with fear, he blasted a slot as high as he dared, reached up and did a one-handed chin-up. His right foot engaged its slot, but the left scrabbled around blindly for a heart-stoppingly long time. Face shield against the ice-covered black stone, he looked up. The top was still intimidatingly far above.

He made a slot for his left hand, at his current head height. The job took forever, and the pack was now a real weight trying to drag him off into space.

Kiril took the deepest breath he could. It turned into three rapid gasps, then he pushed hard with both hands and feet, and swarmed up in one movement, feet engaging the previous handholds. His gloves were pressed against smooth ice, their treated surface providing a little anchoring. Every atom of his being hugged the slippery, unforgiving surface. Slowly, reluctantly, the laser gun cut a slot. He slid his right hand up and thankfully inserted his fingers, hanging on while the second slot melted. "Artif, I may have to drop my gear," he said without sound, panting.

"Then you're dead anyway. Go on, Kiril, one more try." Her voice was calm, warm, confident. His hands grasped slots so high that his arms were almost straight. He gathered himself and again made a single convulsive yet smooth movement and, incredibly, his feet jumped into the slots that a clicklet ago were way above his head. And his eyes were at the level of the very peak.

Every muscle straining, he hugged the slippery, almost vertical face, fighting the weight of the equipment on his back. The laser gun was working — more or less — at making just one more slot, on the rounded top of the continent.

It ran out of power when the slit was about half depth. Kiril was breathing so fast, it must have been three breaths to a clicklet, and yet he felt as if he was drowning. And he was now carrying the full weight of the pack. The laser gun dropped to the black surface, slid off to the side, and disappeared below.

His eyes were seeing a blur. His blind right hand found the inadequate slot and his fingers hooked in.

"Pull!" Artif shouted within his mind.

And then he was sprawled face down across black stone.

His head filled with a roaring sound, through which he heard Artif say, "Kiril, I need to shut off everything to get enough power to open the antenna."

His breathing stopped. His body became rigid, a sculpture in steel. The world was dark, his lungs were a deep pool of pain as his demand for oxygen went unsatisfied.

He heard a blessed sound, a "zfft" that continued forever. A great force pressed him down, so hard that the ice melted under him, a pressure that felt like it would squash him flat.

The power surge stopped. The pack no longer sat on him like a boulder, and a deep breath brought him sweet air, laced with the strong smell of ozone.

He sent a command toward the laser gun, thousands of meters below and still falling. It did not respond. "I think it's broken," Artif said, "it must have knocked against rock many times."

"Never mind, there's the spare." Kiril ordered the dish antenna to fold itself away. "I was terrified!"

"No Kiril, you were not as scared as you think. The oxygen concentrator stopped working because of the lack of power, and then you responded to your own quick breathing as if to fear."

He smiled. "If you say so. It felt awfully like panic to me!"

He sent an order to the spare laser gun, which emerged from his pack and came into his field of view. In less than a clicklet it made a nice big slot for his left hand. Carefully, he pulled himself onto his hands and knees. He used the gun to melt the ice on top of the stone, under his body, then dry the black surface.

He turned over and sat, his feet hanging over infinity. Above him, all around, the afternoon sky was a milky blue. Despite the brilliance of the white disk of the sun, a brilliance that triggered the dimmer in his visor, he saw about half the brightest stars, enough that he could identify entire constellations. They were unblinking disks up here rather than points of light. Over to the left was the enormous ellipse of the topstore that had saved his life, seeming close enough to touch. "How big are those things?" he asked.

"Exactly one thousand meters long," Artif answered. And it's not as close as you think. You're 9,457 meters above sea level. The topstores are over twice as high."

"It'd be wonderful to ride in one."

"There's no life support system, and they stay five years between servicing. And during such a long stay, you'd be pickled by cosmic rays."

"So? I don't think I'll live much longer anyway."

His eyes swept the view. This view was worth the months of preparation, the nearly seven periods of unremitting effort and danger during his climb from the top base camp. From up here, the mountain didn't seem to be a wide-based cone, but appeared to drop away vertically on every side. When he squirmed around to look down the west face, it was a glistening cascade of molten silver as the ice captured the sunlight. Everywhere else, the translucent layer showed the black basalt beneath. Way, way below were the clouds he had climbed through two days before. Beyond them he glimpsed the tortured landscape beneath: a child-toy landscape of tiny mountains enclosing dark blue puddles that he knew were mighty lakes.

The earth curved away on every side. The irregular coastline showed far to the right, with the gray ocean beyond. The magnificence, the silent grandeur were breathtaking.

Now that he was safe, his stomach intruded on Kiril's consciousness. He ordered a cup of thick meat soup, which he sucked through the long, flexible straw of the modified cup without having to remove his face mask, then had a second cup. He'd be unable to eat solid food until he was down again in the airtight comfort of his tent at the top base camp. He'd set it up in a relic of the old days. Artif had told him it was actually a building, blasted upward when the mountain had formed. It had been part of something she'd called "the city," whatever that might have been.

"You're the twelfth person to have physically seen this view," Artif told him. "The last one before you handed on 153 years ago. And you're the youngest, and did the climb in the shortest time."

"Yeah, should get any woman interested in me — any except for the one I want."

Thirst and hunger reduced to bearable dimensions, Kiril again feasted his eyes on the view. "Souda," he called. Tony be blessed, this was the first time since setting out at dawn that a thought of her had entered his mind.

"Sorry, Kiril, she's unavailable at the moment," Artif told him.

"As usual," he sighed. "Look, Artif, all I want to do is to show her this view. Can you just tell her that, please?"

"No, love," she answered gently, "she's busy."

"Is she with another man?" Even asking the question was the thrust of a knife within his innards.

"You know I can't answer that. She may be. Or she may be asleep. You know she's in the Gut, and it's night there. Or she may just have given me an order to block you out under any circumstances. Or whatever. You know I can't violate privacy."

"Why?" he shouted within his mind. "Why has she stopped loving me?" This was not something Artif would answer, and she stayed silent.

"Artif..." and he started to cry. Soundless sobs shook him, and his face mask fogged up from his tears. "Oh Artif, I might as well be dead!"

"My dear," the beloved voice said, "you've been trying hard enough to kill yourself, haven't you?"

"When I'm on the knife edge of danger, I forget myself, forget the world, forget Souda. Nowadays, I'm only alive when threatened by death."

"And during the rest of the time, you're killing yourself with your obsession."

"Yeah, that's spot on."

"Then why not seek help?"

He spoke aloud, for emphasis, "Because I'd rather be dead than not have her obsess me!"

"My dear, why not show the view to Timmy?"

He eased his mask away from his face and dried the inside with the laser gun. He smiled at the thought of his son, and sent him an image.

They were having lunch, time being three quarters of a period later in South Calif, but Tim jumped up and screamed, "Dad!"

Clothed in his climbing gear, Kiril felt stiflingly hot in the house, but he didn't spare the effort of modifying the image. He smiled through the face mask at his mother, sister and son. "My loves," he said, "I've done it. I'm right at the top of Mount Chicago!"

Ria and Tim jumped up and ran to him. He squatted down and hugged them, awkwardly because of the bulky clothes. He was looking at his mother over their heads, and the expression on her face melted him inside.

"I'd like to show you the view. It's unbelievable."

The two children screamed a little, with excitement.

"You can't come with me, you'd freeze, and you wouldn't be able to breathe. Let's merge, the four of us." At the same time, he asked Artif to make a recording of their experience.

And they were within him, looking at the top of the world through his eyes, feeling the multiple aches of his tired body, at one with his conquest. He was also within them, and sensed the rough material of his jacket against Ria's soft cheek, the rapid beating of Tim's heart, his joy and pride at his father's achievement, and Susan's fierce love for his son, and her sadness for him.

He looked up, all around, down every side of his precarious eyrie, allowing them to feast on the view.

"My dear," Susan said within him, "You'd better start on the way down. Tony be with you." Then they were gone, and he was alone once more.

He took a deep, deep breath and spoke to his pack, ordering the rope. It came to his hand in a neat coil. He undid the hitch and shook the immensely long rope out, holding the metal balls attached to the two ends. He sent another order to the EGM motor in the pack, and the two balls traveled in opposite directions, encircling the icy-smooth sides of his tor. He clipped the doubled rope into his carabiner, gingerly stood, arranged the rope, and jumped off on the first leg of the long abseil down.

⚡ **3** ⚡

Flora

Her first thought was, *I don't feel any different.* She lifted a hand to her head, and found a sensitive little spot like a pimple, where Mirabelle's implant had been. But inside, within her mind, she was just Flora, with no additions.

Artif's voice came, from outside as before. "Hi, Flora, I think it was a success."

Flora sat up and looked at the communication globe. "But..."

"It'll take time. In a baby, it takes ten to twenty days. In an adult, who knows? I have no information. In the meantime, I have assembled some clothes for you, and then there is a new visitor wants to meet you. What do you want first, food or clothes?"

"Oh, clothes!" Flora said firmly.

Artif laughed.

The sliding door opened and a very varied row of clothes slid in, hanging from what looked like a steel rod, but, Flora thought, was probably something entirely different. Her eyes lit up: most of these items could have come from her own wardrobe.

"While you were asleep," Artif explained, "I replayed your old movies and copied the designs."

"First of all, I need bras." She could see none.

"Sorry, I didn't think of that. Women wear those things of course, when doing vigorous exercise. But normally it's more comfortable for them to go without."

"Oh yes, the climate change. But don't they, um, develop a sag?"

"You saw Mirabelle. Her shape is typical. Few women have breasts as large as yours. We have selected for small breasts that stay firm, again because of the heat. Small breasts are less likely to get fungal infections under them, yet they are just as effective as providers of milk."

Flora was surprised. "Is that still a consideration?"

"It is. Children are born from the mother in the biologically natural way, and are breast fed. We have selected for easy birth, and of course I monitor the pregnancy, so complications are rare. But 'easy' is a matter of degree."

"I've had children." Without warning, grief again stabbed her. Her children were so long dead that no trace of their existence remained, except for her bizarrely resurrected memory. *I'm a fossil,* she thought.

"Clothes, Flora," Artif said.

"Oh, sorry. Look, I used to run around in slacks and a top most of the time."

"Slacks? Oh yes, tight leg coverings. They'd be very impractical. Flora, you want loose, flowing clothes, and probably you need shading so the sun doesn't burn you. Pick something like that, and put it on. I am making bras to fit you, but they won't arrive for several periods."

Flora still felt weak when she stood, but managed to walk along the row of garments, fingering soft textures, admiring patterns. "Artif, what's a 'period'?" she asked.

"One twentieth of the length of time it takes for the earth to rotate once. One hundred clicks make a period, with one hundred clicklets in a click."

Flora pulled a long-sleeved dress off its hanger. It was bright yellow, with delightful little red roses all over it, just her type of coloring. "I've heard you and the others referring to 'clicklets.' How does that compare to a second? Oh, Artif, there's something else missing. Knickers."

"Actually, you can think of a clicklet as a second. They're about the same length. Now, by 'knickers' do you mean little underpants? I'd advise against that. People do wear undergarments in situations like mountain climbing, but mostly they avoid them. Wear them all the time, and you'll get a terrible fungal infection. You know, many people go completely naked most of the time. Of course, they're the ones blessed with the protection of dark skin. Abel for example."

"Abel?" Flora asked in utter surprise. But he's President!" She thought of the deep, beautiful voice and couldn't imagine the President of the entire planet running around naked. She slipped the dress over her head, and found it to be a perfect fit. She sat on the edge of the bed for a rest. "Is there such a thing as a mirror?" she asked.

A woman suddenly appeared in front of the door, to her right, sitting on air. She wore an identical yellow dress, dotted with tiny red roses. She had bare feet and a gaunt, very pale face. Her gray hair was a straggly mess. Flora turned to look at the stranger and opened her mouth to speak. The woman made an identical turn and also opened her mouth.

"Oh no!" Flora squealed. "That, that horror is me!"

"Why horror, love?" Artif's voice came from behind her, from the communication globe.

"Please make it go away."

The image disappeared.

"I... I didn't realize I looked so awful."

"Tell me the aspects you disapprove of."

"I'm a bag of bones. No meat on me."

"I've found the reference. I can feed you nourishing meals, and exercise will build you up again."

"My hair is a mess. And gray."

"Yes of course, it's gray. It was when you were put into cryogenic sleep."

"No, it was dyed the original color, auburn."

"Your hair and nails grew, if very slowly. The maintenance equipment kept cutting them, so the artificial coloring will have been cut off within a year. I can look up the records and reproduce the chemicals that were used. And cut the shape to whatever you want."

"Now? And I need makeup. I look like a ghost."

Artif sounded dubious. "I've found the reference. We don't have makeup at all now. No doubt I can make anything you desire, but nowadays people don't change their appearance. Women don't need to, and men would be treated with ridicule."

"Women don't need to?"

"Flora," Artif asked, "are you willing to receive a visitor?"

"No. Not looking like this."

"He is the foremost student of BT history now alive. Perhaps he's the person who's been the most knowledgeable about your times, for the past thousand years. And he has waited to meet you since there's been talk of awakening you, a year ago. He's been pestering me several times a period since your first awakening, three days ago."

"Has it been three days? But I look terrible. I don't want a man to see me like this."

"Sit down on your bed."

Flora complied. The door slid open, and an object floated through. In shape and size it was like a cigarette packet with a pencil sticking out of it, but it was black.

"Look at the image," Artif commanded, and Flora's copy once again appeared in front of her.

Flora heard a soft buzz, and a lock of the image's straggly gray hair disappeared. This was repeated time and again, until the image had a boyish, neat haircut. A stylish, short gray decoration topped the gaunt, white face. "Oh, you got that haircut from *The War Correspondent*!" That had been her first Oscar as Leading Lady.

A small globe floated through the still-open door. At first Flora thought it was a cup of chocken, but Artif commanded, "Shut your eyes." She did so, and felt a fine spray on her face, hands and legs, all the parts the dress left exposed.

"I sprayed you with sunscreen," Artif explained. "You'll need that when you go outside anyway. Only, I've put a brown dye in it."

Flora opened her eyes and examined the image. She was still a skeleton, and the hair was still gray, but... "Oh well, thank you, Artif. You've done wonders. I suppose time will do the rest." She sighed.

"Time, and food, and exercise, and sunshine. You'll be right, dear. Now, will I invite Nathaniel?"

"All right, Artif, ask your historian if he'll have breakfast with me. At least, is that possible?"

A pleasant tenor voice answered from the globe, "Both possible and appreciated. I see that some customs haven't changed."

A man stood where Flora's image had been a second before. He was shorter than her five foot nine, and the description that sprung to her mind was, *What a weedy little boy!* He had narrow shoulders, untidy straight brown hair and a narrow, olive-skinned face. He was clean shaven, except for a fringe of brown beard all around the edges. He wore what to her was a wraparound skirt, leaving his scrawny, hairless chest bare.

"Oh, I expected an older man," she blurted out. Apart from the beard, this fellow seemed about sixteen to her, not her idea of the best historian of the past millennium.

The little man stepped forward and smiled easily. "Flora Fielding, I'm delighted to make your acquaintance." His lips did not move, and the tenor voice came from the globe behind Flora. "I'm Nathaniel Tarzan Kyros."

He puffed out his meager chest and held his nose up in the air so comically that Flora had to laugh. "Is you middle name really 'Tarzan'?"

He slumped back into his previous posture and his face lit up with an urchin grin. "Of course not. Of all the one million people on the planet, you're the only one who'd recognize the reference. Tony's records didn't mention Tarzan."

As usual during a conversation, Flora didn't know which of several questions to ask first, but Artif interrupted, saying, "Nat, please take Flora out to the surface. I'll serve you a meal there."

"Wonderful!" Flora said, "It's time I emerged from this hole."

The little man stepped forward and held out his hand. Flora took it. Nathaniel's grip was surprisingly strong, his hand warm and dry. He led her through the open door.

Flora had to stop, again overwhelmed by a stab of grief.

"What's wrong?" Nathaniel asked as she inadvertently pulled him to a halt.

"This room. I... I was involved in its design, what feels like two or three months ago." She looked around at the white walls. Dr. Martin had won that battle against her and Sheila Raymond, the architect. He'd compromised by allowing the rose-colored carpet. All the walls were lined with consoles of dials and control panels. She had said, "It looks like the bridge of a spaceship!" That was true. It couldn't have taken her to a stranger world if it had gone to a different planet. The only new thing was an object, the size of a large table, that looked to Flora like a brown plastic box on four short legs.

Artif's voice pulled her back to the present. "Flora, what would you like to eat?"

"Oh, I'm sorry. The room took me back to my times. Really, I don't care. I don't know the customs. Nathaniel, you choose for both of us."

He rattled off a couple of terms that were meaningless to Flora, starting to walk again at the same time. Then he said, "Nat will do, Nathaniel is such a long name for an ugly little fellow like me, though I always say I'm not as ugly as Tony. But let me give you my credentials. I've done three bull rides, coming third when I was seventeen..."

"I'm sorry, I don't..."

Artif explained, her voice floating back from the globe that was just going through the open sliding door, "Flora, as you know by now, men need to prove themselves. It's customary when a man meets a woman that he lists his acts of daring, wins in competitions, artistic or engineering creations, and any leadership positions."

"But, what's a bull ride?"

Nathaniel said, "Every year, over a thousand boys and young men go out and find a hippopotamus bull. The bull is enclosed, and kept for a particular day. All at the same time, in a thousand or more places, contestants physically jump onto their bull's back. Thousands of women watch, some going into one-way merges with contestants. The fellow who stays on the longest wins. My best ride was two clicks thirty-seven clicklets! I came third."

Artif added, sounding sad, "And every year, an average of thirty to forty get killed, and many suffer from their injuries for the rest of their lives."

"Eisenhower said, 'You cannot make omelets without breaking eggs.'"

Flora had to laugh, despite her shock at what she'd just heard. "Sorry, Nat, that was Napoleon. Long before Eisenhower."

"I know that," the little man said loftily, "I was just testing if you did. Anyway, I've also killed a twenty meter long tiger shark with only a hand-held spear gun. I was thirteen then. And I know more about ancient history than anyone else — you excepted of course. And I'm on the Greek Council, was elected when only twenty-five."

They were in the wide, gently ascending corridor, lit by the indirect lighting she'd had installed. Unobtrusive sliding doors closed the entrances to various service rooms, and to the Staff apartment. Flora stopped, and pulled her companion to a halt. "Nat, please, I need new information in smaller chunks. Let's return to something you said back in the room. Are there only a million people?"

"Exactly one million less the 123 Sleepers. Oh, 122 now that you've graced us with your presence."

"In my times, a small city had maybe three million. Some cities had fifteen million."

"I know what 'city' means, but most people would take a period to understand the concept. I find the idea horrible. Living like ants or something."

"Oh, there is an excitement to crowds, and having people concentrated allowed us to have all sorts of things—"

Artif said, "Flora, welcome to our world." The outside door slid open.

Tim and Souda

Ria and Tim were abseiling down the Freeway. Speaking from the lofty superiority of her seven years, Ria commanded, "Go in smaller hops, Tim."

"I can go in as big a jump as you!" And he matched her, jump for jump down the dark gray, steeply tilted but exactly straight slope. Ria had picked a spot where the endless Freeway was tilted side to side, but its surface was unbroken.

Almost at the bottom, Tim gave her a triumphant look — and crashed knees first into the unforgiving surface. "Ow!" he cried and let the doubled rope slip through his hand. He went sliding down the rough hillside, the knees of his protective trousers shredding away. Then the safety clicked in and he came to an abrupt halt.

"See?" Ria said smugly.

Tim put his tongue out at her. He gingerly straightened his legs and got his feet against the ancient material. He heard the whine of a mosquito, but then one of the several bugcatchers swooped in and swallowed the insect. "Let go now," he thought at the safety, and took the last three jumps down to ground level without trouble.

"You all right? Let me see." She bent to examine his knees. The thick padding had worn away, and the inner lining was quickly turning red with blood. "Mother!" Ria called in alarm.

Susan was instantly there, her blonde hair stringy with sweat, her sun-browned, naked body shiny with it. She'd been exercising, inside. "Artif, any serious damage?" she asked.

"Nothing to worry about. Skin breaks from the impact, otherwise he's all right."

"Tony be thanked. Come on, young fellow." She bent and easily picked up her grandson, who put his arms around her and snuggled his head against her breast.

"Ria said, "I'll tidy up and come." She issued a few orders through the implant and hurried after her mother, toward the house.

Susan's physical self met her image at the door and took the boy from it. The image then disappeared. Susan turned, to see Souda appear. "For Brad's sake," the young woman said, "Timmy, you all right?"

"Yes, of course, Mom. "Ria is teaching me to abseil, because Dad's up Mount Chicago right now, and that's how he'll be coming down. And I can do it!"

Ria said, from the door, "Souda, he can too. He's a good boy."

By then, Susan had ordered a waterproof covering over a couch and put him down. A small bowl of medicated water already hovered there, and she started to clean the little boy's knees. He bit his lip, and didn't utter a sound.

Souda was waiting with the laser gun. As soon as Susan finished, she ordered it to dry the wounds, and then they spread healing film over it.

"Come and give me a cuddle, you two," Souda said, sitting down while Susan cleaned up with a few orders. One warm little body on each knee, she pulled the two gold-thatched heads to her.

Tim said, "Mom, I've got a present for you. But you're not allowed to look at it until you're at home."

"What is it?"

"A secret! I told you!"

She laughed, "You and your secrets. Did you make it?"

"You'll see." A small recording globe came from his room, to him. He pressed it into her hands, and he'd say no more.

At home, Souda had been in the middle of playing her flute when Artif told her that Tim was hurt. So, after a pleasant fifty clicks or so, she withdrew into her physical self. She found that she was still holding the globe, obviously an image Tim brought with him. "That's the present, Mom," he said, looking up at her. Then he broke contact.

Oh, he's a bright child, she thought with fond pride, then activated the message.

Music filled her room, an intricate, ancient flute concerto. Now, where did the little tyke get that? She listened with pleasure. A plate appeared, with a mound of chocken pudding on it. A strawberry decorated the center. The plate swirled in time to the music, and replicated. The two plates tipped to the vertical, then disappeared, leaving their contents. And the two mounds had become her breasts.

The music softened into background, and changed to a recording of her own voice, softly singing, as Kiril's voice declaimed:

> Strawberries on chocken mounds,
> and I love the liquid sounds
> of her singing.

And the breasts were part of her naked body, which swirled, her hair whipped almost horizontal by her spin. The image held a golden flute to her lips, and the music once again replaced the singing.

> Golden locks and feet that dance,
> plays her flute at every chance,
> her fingers winging.

The image continued to swirl. As she came to face Souda again, she held her epee rather than the flute. Kiril had taught her the sport, during his second visit. The music changed to brass instruments, playing to a strong beat. Kiril's voice rose over it:

> Scholar in a dozen fields.

A strong fencer who never yields,
our swords ringing.

The image again turned. When she faced Souda again, she was clothed in her customary lace body suit, and she held empty hands out to her. The face had a loving smile.

Emerald eyes in sunshine face,
I dream of a body clothed in lace,
my essence tingling.

Then the arms dropped and the face became closed, rejecting. The music stopped. Kiril softly finished with,

But oh, she is a cruel friend,
she's bringing my life to an end,
my heart she's wringing.

"Oh Kiril," Souda said. And he was there with her. He wore heavy climbing gear, with helmet and face mask, gloves on his hands.

"My love," he said.

"You in the middle of a climb?"

"I'm abseiling down from the very top of Mount Chicago. It's all right, I've activated the safety. Artif told me, I'm only the twelfth person ever to have got there, and the only one still alive. Only, I'd wanted to show you the view, but—"

"But I was sharing bodies with another man," she said, with calculated cruelty. "I used to love you, but you killed it."

He flinched as if he'd been struck, and hung his head. "And it was despicable, using Timmy to get at me."

"I didn't! It was all his idea!"

"What? A five-year-old?"

"Believe it or not. Ask Artif. He said to me, 'Dad, you compose a poem to Mom, and I'll get it to her.' And I did, and he did. He wants us to be friends again."

Souda felt her resolve waver. "Kiril, I want us to be friends again, too. I'd be happy to have you as my very best friend. I'd even be willing to choose you for my second child. If only..."

For a clicklet, she thought he was going to jump at her and crush her to his chest, but he restrained himself with obvious effort. His face shone through the facemask. "If only?"

"If only it'd stop there. But I don't want you to restrict me, to spend all your time with me, to, to, I don't know, turn me into an extension of yourself. I'm a person in my own right."

"I can't help being obsessed by you. Since that first meeting—"

"I've heard it all! Now listen. I'll let you visit again, on three conditions."

"Go on, I'm listening."

"First, you will share bodies with other women, and I'll talk to them and find out if they and you both had a good time."

He said nothing, but his rigid body was a negation.

"Tony knows, you're an attractive man, and have more credentials than any other young fellow I know, and until you went crazy you were good company. You should have no trouble attracting women."

He sighed. "It's not working on you, and unfortunately that's the only thing that counts."

"Second, you find a woman who'll choose you. Father a child, become committed to a situation that doesn't involve me. Then maybe I'll consent to having a child with you for the second time. And third, get help with this problem. Actually, I've already done something about that."

What?"

"Abel T'Dwuna himself is planning to help you. I approached him, and you know, as a Control member, he has the right. He's planning to contact you. Let him help."

Kiril looked at her with stricken eyes. "Abel. The great Abel. He's the man you shared bodies with." And his image disappeared.

Mirabelle

Mirabelle was also playing a poem, but in a very different mood. The poem had been composed, all too many years ago now, by Hector Sou Lai, and had won him the right to father her first child. She'd been only nineteen then. He was thirty-nine, Deputy President of the Chinese Council, and a world-famous sculptor. Two years after Garcon was born, Hector had died in a caving accident. And at eighteen years of age, his son broke his back in a skydive gone wrong. He survived, but became paralyzed from the waist down. Mirabelle had tried to console him with the thought that after all, Tony'd had the same problem from birth. Garcon's answer was, "He never knew the joys of activity. I just don't want to live like this." After a few months as a cripple, he'd decided to hand on. Mirabelle still stayed in touch with Garcon Sczeszny, his continuation, but sadly, that didn't replace her own son.

And so, Mirabelle had only two things left of her first child and of her first love: the poem, and the famous statue of "Mother and Child." Hector had carved that out of the white timber of an immense holly tree trunk, using hand tools alone. It showed her, with his baby at her breast.

Tamás was down in the garden, studying under Artif's supervision, but his recent escapade up the Tree had left Mirabelle out of sorts. And there was still the problem of poor Flora Fielding. How long was Abel going to keep her in the dark about the sad fate facing her? And when Mirabelle needed peace in her soul, she found some quiet time and played the poem to herself.

She took her house up, far above the troubles of the world, into the zone of peace where storms cannot reach, and got out the cherished little globe. She chose this time to leave visuals off, and merely listened to long-dead Hector's voice, backed by the music he'd selected. He had learned Swedish, a very difficult task for a Chinese speaker, in order to compose the poem in her native language.

Closed eyes quietly crying, she lay back on a soft couch, and played the poem, over and over.

> The White Lady of the West
> bathes my being in the silver light of her smile.
> She rose for me, in the East, to light up the darkness.
> She is the glory of my nights.
>
> Like the golden sun crowns the glorious day,
> her golden hair crowns her marvelous beauty.
> Above all, bearing no comparison,
> She is the glory of my days.
>
> Blue sky, blue sea, blue eyes,
> in a face that banishes the storms of my heart,
> lakes of her soul for me to drown in.
> She is my reason for existence.
>
> The White Lady of the West
> is wise in her youth, beyond her tender years.
> And of all the many things I've done in this life,
> loving her is the best."

Oh, for Brad's sake, I hope not to lose this one too, she thought, a corner of her mind on Tamás, who was wrestling with integral calculus. No one but Artif must ever know of this fear within her.

⚡ **4** ⚡

Flora

The heat struck her like a fist to the face, and she had to close her eyes against the white hot glare. She felt she'd walked into a furnace full of molten steel. She heard Nathaniel say, "That's better, I was freezing in there." She clutched his hand, eyes determinedly shut, as he led her over a surface that felt like ankle-high grass.

"Here, stop in the shade," Artif said. "Flora love, open your eyes if you can."

She allowed some light to force its way through her lashes. An enormous tree trunk faced her. As her eyes became more adapted to the glare, she saw that it was a palm tree. Bizarre — a palm tree high in the Rockies.

"Sit down, Flora, Nat said.

She glanced behind, to see a cushion, floating in the air, just right for her to sit on. "I can't get used to this EGM," she told him, cautiously lowering her bottom. "It still feels like magic to me."

The little man's eyes went out of focus for a few seconds, no, clicklets, then he asked, "Artif, do you have a reference?"

"No. Flora, you've used that term before. What is 'magic'?"

"Heavens, um, I suppose when things happen in a way that my understanding of the laws of nature says should be impossible. I say a special word, and fire shoots out of my fingertips, or something."

"What a good idea!" Nat shouted. He held his right arm rigidly in front, pointed his index finger like a child playing at guns and said, "Fire!"

Flora gasped as a jet of red and yellow flame burst from his fingertip.

Nat lowered his arm as he and Artif laughed. He explained, "I can't do this with my physical body, but images can be manipulated. It's an illusion worked by Artif, either through an implant or through a communication globe."

"Actually, that globe seem like magic to me too."

Nat answered, "In your day, there were still non-technological people. What did they think about an automobile or a television?"

"You're right. Hey, what are those little things? Artificial birds?"

Flora's eyes had adapted to the harsh light by now, and she was looking around. *That McGarrity fellow was right,* she thought. He'd been the geologist she'd retained, and he'd said, subjectively six months ago, "The Continental Plate is so thick here that this valley will be undisturbed even when Southern California falls into the sea."

The valley was still here, though it seemed shallower, the mountains around it steeper. However, its covering had changed beyond recognition. Something like subtropical savannah replaced the conifers, with a small herd of horse-sized gazelle-like creatures grazing in the middle, and bright-plumed birds of many kinds flitting about.

Flora's question referred to other flying objects, much closer. They looked like tiny funnels, darting about on zigzag paths with the mouth of the funnel foremost.

"The bugcatchers?" Nat responded. "They're essential outdoor equipment. Actually, a direct ancestor of mine invented them, nearly eight hundred years ago." He puffed himself up.

"Seven hundred and fifty-three years," Artif said.

"Artif is fascinated by exactitude," Nat said with a grin. "I love to make slight mistakes like that, just for her."

"What do they do, exactly?"

"Why, they exactly catch bugs," he answered, mimicking her tone of voice.

Artif explained, "They are simple devices, like cups and trays. Each has an EGM motor, a battery and a few sensors, and depends on a nearby computer for direction. These ones work off the kitchen inside. You'd be eaten alive except for the bugcatchers."

Two trays floated out of the open door in the cliffside, and stopped before Flora and Nat. She looked at the offering. The cup was not dark brown but clear, with tiny bubbles in it, so this was a different drink. A bowl was piled high with a substance that looked to Flora like a cross between custard and whipped cream. "What's this?" she asked.

"Porridge," Artif told her.

"Doesn't look like porridge."

"Modern speakers of English call it that."

She tried a spoonful. It was delicious, with a nutty flavor.

"Nat," she said while eating, "since I met you, you've told me a great many things I don't understand. I can't even remember them all. For example, how do you know about Tarzan if Tony's records don't mention him?"

The little man looked self-important again. "Fifty-two years ago, my father made a great find: an entire pre-Cataclysm library! It was in the part of China that was called Siberia in your days, and had been buried in a landslide. My father developed a technique for copying the marks on the paper pages without having to open the..."

Artif said, "Books."

"Thank you, Artif. Most of the books were in the markings of ancient Russian, but fortunately they had language courses, Russian books for learning English and French and German and Chinese. That's what I'm doing at the moment. I'm there physically, and am working out the ancient Chinese writing."

"Hold it, Nathaniel, not you alone," Artif corrected.

Nat looked a little abashed. "No, of course not. I'm part of a team. But anyway, this library contained a lot of material Tony must have considered unworthy of being saved. He concentrated on useful stuff, rather than entertainment, except with regard to music. Now, what else would you like to know?"

You implied that Tony was ugly. I somehow imagined him to be, well, impressive."

"Oh sure, he's impressive all right, but he's the ugliest person you've ever seen. And he never walked in his life, was forced to sit in a thing with wheels. Artif, why don't you show Flora one of the recordings?"

"What a good idea! Which one?"

"I know. The one where he talks about the EGM drive, just to prove to her that it was real even way back then. And that'll help me too. I've never been able to make sense of some of the things he mentions, like, what was it? *multinational corporations.*" The last two words came out with a distinct Canadian accent, very different from his usual voice.

Flora had emptied her bowl, and tried the drink. It tasted partly like a fruit juice, partly like wine. "What's this?" she asked.

"My favorite drink. I'm not that keen on chocken, it's too sweet for me. This is kalibor juice, allowed to ferment slightly. Leave it too long and it has alcohol, then it's unusable."

"Here we go again. Two questions: what is kalibor, and what's wrong with alcohol? I enjoy a glass of wine or a cocktail."

Artif answered, "Kalibor is a fruit from a tree that's native to the central Africa of your times. It's now grown in many places. As for alcohol, Tony forbade it. No one has alcoholic drinks."

"Mohamed forbade it too, but in my days, many Muslims drank all the same."

Nat said, "You'll find, Flora, that nobody ever disobeys any of Tony's edicts. Artif makes sure of that."

"Artif, you're a dictator then?"

"I have the reference." She sounded offended. "No! I implement edicts made by humans. Human Leaders determine the rules, and I teach the rules to children. If a person wants to break an edict, I express my disapproval, but don't interfere. If a person is about to do something that may harm another, then I must give warning. But I never control a person."

"All the same," Nat said, "no person ever goes against what Artif says. You just don't."

Do you want to view the recording?" Artif asked.

"Yes please."

A young man in a motorized wheelchair sat, facing Flora. His upper half was that of a big man, perhaps six foot two, with broad shoulders and long, powerful arms. In contrast, the legs were pitiful little appendages, like a five-year-old's legs. They rested, flaccid and unmoving, on a pair of elevated footrests.

Nat was right: Tony was the ugliest person Flora had even seen. Tight, dark brown curls topped a crudely hewn, misshapen visage. The left side of his face was considerably larger than the right. Even the left eye sat in a larger socket, so that the brown marble of his iris had a complete white surround.

Tony was dressed in a checkered, long-sleeved shirt, and a pair of dark tracksuit pants. Flora noticed a bulge under the right pants leg, with a plastic tube poking out. Having had some involuntary hospital experience in the last few months of her old life, she recognized a catheter bag. *The poor fellow's incontinent of urine,* she thought.

Tony smiled, exposing crooked, uneven teeth. This did nothing to improve his appearance. When he started to speak, his voice was slightly slurred, so Flora had to concentrate until she got used to it. Tony said,

> It is essential, in the new world we'll be building, to eliminate the use of hydrocarbons as fuels. They won't last, the evidence shows that their fumes are responsible for major health problems, and their widespread use is the main reason why my times are doomed, why the Cataclysm is coming. In the future, hydrocarbons should only be used as raw materials for chemical manufacture.
>
> What can replace gasoline-burning engines? Three things.
>
> First, once everyone on the planet has an implant, there will be far less reason to travel physically. A person can visit any other person as an image, anytime, anywhere. Artif can generate convincing images for anyone with an implant. I'm sure this can be improved to the point of complete realism in the future.
>
> Second, a combination of solar electricity and helium balloons offer safe, pollution-free transport. This should be the way to carry very large weights. Balloons could be permanent homes, safely above storms in a world of high-energy weather patterns. And a network of very large balloons should be established. Each will be a solar energy collector, with the energy microwaved to points of use on demand, and the network will fulfill the role of communication satellites, without the undesirable effects of rocket-propelled launch vehicles.
>
> The third device will be the most important. As long ago as the early 1990s, three different scientists described the principle of electro-gravitational modulation. They were Karl Hundorf of Göttingen University in Germany in 1992, Susan Mitchell of Edinburgh University in Scotland in 1993, and Chad Davidson of the State University of Florida in the United States, also in 1993.
>
> None of these three ever managed to publish their findings. Papers they submitted to learned journals were rejected. I've

penetrated the archives of the International Journal of Physical Sciences, and copied the original manuscript by Karl Hundorf. Chad Davidson was the external referee, and he stated that the paper was sound, and closely paralleled his own work. A note on the file states, "Not to be published. CIA."

Within a month of the date of this note, Karl Hundorf's laboratory in Germany suffered a terrible fire. This was during their staff Christmas celebrations. The entire staff of the Physics Department died in the fire.

Later, similar tragedies befell the research teams led by Susan Mitchell and Chad Davidson. I have hacked into the data archives of five different multinational corporations. Two are involved in the petroleum industry, two are large car manufacturers, one is a major airplane manufacturer. All five of them had detailed records of electro-gravitational modulation.

My world is being destroyed, because the multinationals don't want to lose profits.

Tony disappeared. Artif said, "Flora, he now goes on to describe the technical details. I didn't think you'd be interested in that."

Flora shook herself. She'd been captivated by the intensity of that young voice, taken over by the personality of the crippled man. She'd forgotten his ugliness, his handicap, and now understood his magnetism for these people, his disciples. "He's wonderful," she sighed.

Nat laughed. "You're like the rest of us. Everyone talks of Tony as if he was still alive. He is, because Artif is his extension, his gift to humankind."

Artif added, "Without a doubt, he was a genius, perhaps the most intelligent person who's ever lived. Except for him, Chaos would have lasted for thousands of years."

Sitting on his own hovering cushion, Nat eagerly leaned forward. "Now, Flora, can you please answer a few questions?"

Flora noticed with surprise that the empty food trays had gone while she'd been listening to Tony. And the sky had clouded over. "Ask away," she said.

Artif interrupted, "It's going to rain soon, but not much wind. Do you want a tent, or would you rather go inside?"

"Oh, a tent please," Flora answered, keen for the new experience, and reluctant to be enclosed again.

"And while we're waiting, we can go through things alphabetically. Tell me, what's an 'airplane'?"

Kiril

He could actually walk here, rather than climb, but the rough, fissured ground required complete concentration. A savage, gusting wind tried to blow him back uphill. He had to free his face mask of sleet, time and again, and rivulets of near-frozen water cascaded down every little gully. Kiril felt cold even inside his padded climbing clothes, despite the effort of the descent. The packed-up Number 1 camp that had been the top base was now a two-meter diameter ball that faithfully followed him.

Artif said, "Go a little more to the right, down that gully."

He did, scrambling along the steeply sloping side, barely above the gushing water. He rounded a great black boulder, which sheltered him from the wind for a clicklet, then a new gust nearly blew him off the slope into the temporary creek. He steadied himself by grabbing a rock almost beside him on the steep incline, then moved into the relative shelter of the next boulder. And beyond it, he at last glimpsed the welcoming light of his Number 2 camp.

In his keenness to get out of the storm he took an incautious step and slipped. He managed not to fall, then more carefully picked his way to welcome warmth and light. He told the Number 1 camp to anchor itself, and entered the waiting tent.

The delicious scent of a rich meat stew came to him through the breathing equipment. He removed his helmet and mask, hung his jacket and outer trousers to dry, and flopped across the waiting bed. "Oh, I'm sore in every muscle," he said. "But maybe I should've broken a leg then. What's the use of living on?"

Artif ignored this, saying, "Have a meal, Kiril, then I've got a visitor waiting to see you." "Who?" *Souda?* he couldn't help thinking.

A tray holding a huge bowl of stew came to him. He sat up with a groan and picked up the spoon. Artif answered, "The person initiating it asked for no pre-identification. Are you willing to let it go ahead under that condition?"

Mouth full, Kiril answered within his mind, "Oh, for Brad's sake, what have I got to lose? Sure, why not?"

He'd barely finished his last sip of chocken when a naked man stood just inside the closed entrance. He was perhaps five centimeters taller than Kiril, who was over two meters tall himself, and with a finely muscled, solid body. His skin was such a dark brown overall that he was nearly black. His tightly curled hair and beard were almost white in contrast. This was the only sign that the visitor was not a young man. His thick lips and wide nose indicated an unusually high proportion of tropical ancestry. "Greetings, Kiril Lander," he said without voice. "Oh, it's freezing here!"

"Abel!" Kiril answered. He stood, reached out and threw his now-dry jacket to his visitor, then gestured at the bed.

"Thank you." Abel shrugged the jacket on, sat on the bed and pulled the top blanket around himself.

Still standing, glaring down at the older man, Kiril said, "I don't want your help. I don't want to change anything in myself. Go away."

Abel merely smiled. "I suppose you feel like ripping me to pieces."

Kiril sighed. "No. Oh, for Brad's sake, if I'd been there when you…"
He couldn't continue.

"When I shared bodies with the delectable Souda," Abel finished for
him.

"Yes. Then I'd have felt a rage at you. But, how can I blame you? Any
man would jump if she beckoned."

"Well, well, tastes do differ. But she is certainly a lovely young woman.
You're very lucky to have her love you."

Kiril snorted. "Some love! She won't see me!"

"Listen, Kiril. I've spent a bit of time during the last few days
investigating you. I now know more about you than your delightful
mother. Incidentally, you're causing her a heap of grief. And your little
sister and cute little son would be devastated if you managed to kill
yourself."

"You're right of course, but…"

"But nothing. I'm right. I usually am. Anyway, mate, you're twenty-
four. By the time you're forty, you could be on Control."

"You're out of your mind! Me?"

"You."

After a long silence, Kiril said, "I understand what you're doing.
You're trying to twist my thinking onto a new path. Give me something
else to strive for, so my yearning for Souda slips into second place. And
any lie will do, as long as it works."

Abel showed no sign of offense. "Ask Artif."

Instantly, Artif said, "Abel honestly believes what he said."

"You want the evidence, young fellow? All right, listen. You have more
credentials than any other man your age. For Tony's sake, believe it or
not, you have more credentials than I did at your age!"

"Yeah, but you know why. I use danger as a distraction."

"Then there is that marvelous bed." Kiril flinched. "Look, that's got to
be the most significant engineering development in the past century! The
principle can be applied in hundreds of ways. Like all the products of
genius, it's so obvious that I wonder why no one has ever thought of it
before. But no one has. And you've showed creativity in many other
ways."

"I've always felt different from other people."

"So have I. It's a sign of a superior intellect. Value it."

Kiril called for a cushion and sat. "I, I can't believe it. I can't take it in.
You're putting me on the same level as yourself."

Abel laughed. "No, not quite. I am President. I've proved my wisdom
in a thousand ways. But what I'm saying is that you have the potential.
Use your undoubted abilities to acquire wisdom. Go into politics. In a few
years, you could be on the English Council. Study people, learn to
understand their motivations. You have all the requirements to be a
Leader, except for experience. In particular, and this is something we

don't publicize, one of the major qualifications for being on Control is that you must have suffered."

"I certainly qualify there! But why?"

"Should be obvious. The most important part of my job as a Control member is to help people in trouble. How can you do that unless you've suffered yourself?"

"I'm not interested in politics."

"I know that. You're interested in Souda. Look, mate, you've spent the best part of a year doing research and preparation for this climb. You can apply the same skills, attitudes and determination to any other project. Like getting elected to the English Council."

Kiril snorted. "So, just to stop being a nuisance to Souda, and a pain to my family, I should acquire a new interest in matters I don't care about? How do you make yourself become interested in something you find boring? Do I care whether English is spoken this way or that? Or the stupid forever-controversy over the Sleepers?"

Abel grinned at him. "You know, I may have managed to get rid of the Sleeper controversy, once and for all. But do you really think the Cultural Councils' main concern is those petty issues? When you're a Leader, you lead. Your main responsibility is to the people in your care. You do what I'm doing now."

"All right, Abel, I'll think about it. Now, will you go away?"

Tamás

Unmoving, Tamás squatted in a low bush. He even held his breath, to avoid making a noise. Tonya walked right past him, her eyes actually sliding over his hide. She walked on, mind and senses probing everywhere. Then Artif said, "Three clicks are up, my dears."

Tamás stood, triumphant. Tonya looked sulky for a moment, thick lips pouting, then grinned. "That's only because you know this place a lot better than I do."

"All the same, I claim my prize." He felt his heart thumping away within his chest. His mouth went dry and somehow everything looked brighter. Tonya was fourteen, and well developed for her age. She was actually a tiny bit taller than him. As he stood there, looking at her, he saw her nipples grow, with little goose-bumps surrounding it.

She stepped up to him, took his face in her hands and pulled him toward herself. Her two black eyes, intriguing with their oriental shape, joined into one. Their noses touched, and her mouth enclosed his lower lip. Her hands slipped around his shoulders, pulling him close, and he was lost in the wonderful softness of her breasts, skin on skin. She ran her tongue over his lip, and her female smell set him on fire. His tongue found hers, and his hands slipped through the waistband of her skirt, enjoying the satin feel of her buttocks.

At last they separated. "Wow, not bad for a little boy," she panted.

"Not that little," he answered, hoarsely, and pressed himself against her once more.

"That's enough for now, darlings," Artif said within, her voice a joyful laugh, "You can dream about each other until your Maturity."

Reluctantly, they pulled apart. "I knew it'd be nice," Tamás said, "but I didn't realize it's so wonderful."

Tonya laughed, took his hand and started walking. Just this touch sent an electric tingle through him. "How come you stay here all the time?" she asked. "We go all over the place, never stop anywhere for long."

"We go to Antarctica when it's winter here, but my mother loves the garden."

"I can see why. It's beautiful."

To the south of them, the two houses strained against their silver tethers, about twenty meters up. A small transport balloon snuggled against Tonya's home, obviously transferring consumables. The garden spread around them. Rock-paved paths meandered among flowering plants of a hundred colors. The air was heavy with the scent of blossoms. An apple tree bearing half-grown fruit stood in a field of strawberries, luscious red fruit in a low green jungle. As they walked, the details kept changing, but always, eyes and nose were surprised by beauty. A dozen different kinds of birds flitted about, their varied song filling the air.

And of course, there was the Tree. Though it was over four hundred meters from their location, it towered over everything, a mighty column of brown and green. At the moment, it had a small cloud tangled within its northern branches, but the top went up, up, up far above that. Upon first meeting Tonya, Tamás had told her of his climb, three-quarters of the way up.

"We do much of the work ourselves," Tamás now explained. "We're down here two or three periods most days, even at times like now when my mother is involved in Control work — she's spending a lot of time with the newly awakened Sleeper, Flora Fielding. And we grow almost all our own food, even tropical things. Come, I'll show you." He turned to the right, pulling Tonya through a gap between a raspberry thicket and a huge chestnut tree, onto another path. A couple of clicks of leisurely walking brought them to the hothouse. He ordered the door to open, then to close behind them. The plasteel vault stretched for a hundred meters. Proudly, Tamás pointed to the row of banana trees, the pineapples, and to the kalibor tree. That was pruned so it wouldn't grow to its full height, but instead was encouraged to spread wide on each side.

"What about winter?"

Tamás let go of Tonya's hand, and jumped to pull down a branch on the nearest banana tree. He separated off two bright yellow bananas, and let the rest of the hand spring back up. "We have the lights," he answered, giving her a banana. He thought at the lights, turning them on for a moment. Previously invisible tubes along the top of the hothouse became blinding white bands of light, and they felt the heat on their faces. He turned the lights off again.

As they left the hothouse, Tamás saw a small weed, and without thinking about it, bent and pulled it out.

"A machine'd do that," Tonya said.

"Sure. But Mom and I, we prefer to get in first. This way, we're part of the land."

"Tamás!" he heard Mirabelle call without sound. "Lunchtime!"

Obviously, her mother called Tonya too. They raced over to the two women, who sat on elevated cushions, on each side of a little fire.

5.

Flora

Like everything else in this new world, the tent proved to be a surprise: a spacious, transparent dome. Before the rain started, the only effect of having it there was that the very light breeze could no longer be felt. Flora could see no poles, pegs or guys. "What holds it down?" she asked.

Artif told her, "It's made of plasteel, so it is quite a massive structure. It's anchored using its own EGM motor."

Flora remembered Nat's comment about a primitive's reaction to cars and TV, mentally shrugged, and continued with her explanations to him.

The rain provided another surprise. Nat dismissed it as "a fairly typical shower," but its savagery overwhelmed Flora, with enormous volumes of water cascading out of the low black clouds that raced through the treetops. And it had come upon them so suddenly! Nor did it cool the air, merely increased humidity, so Flora dripped with water despite the tent's protection.

The grass-covered floor of the meadow soon flowed with muddy water. The flash flood actually lapped against the walls of the tent. It was about a foot deep on the uphill side.

Seeing Flora's concern, Nat laughed, "You're safe here, Flora. Now, can you please explain Universities? I know they were places where people went to learn, but..." Despite the roar of the rain drumming on the tent, Flora could hear his voice as clearly as before.

At last, sated with knowledge, he took his leave and disappeared as if he'd never been. "Oh, Artif, I'm exhausted!" Flora said. "Is there any way of going back inside?"

"Of course you're exhausted. You need exercise to build you up. Stand up and start walking, dear."

Flora complied. She took a few steps toward the door in the cliff-side, down the gentle slope. The tent went with her. It pushed the turbulent water out of the way with a bow wave. Admittedly, this left a ground surface of long, coarse grass lying flat on inches-deep brown mud that squished between her toes. "Oh, Artif," she said, "I haven't walked barefoot in mud since I was a kid."

Artif's voice had a smile in it. "It's nice to see you happy, Flora. But 'kid' is not in my dictionary when applied to a person. Could you please explain?"

Tim

The rain that had hit Flora in what had once been Washington State was the outer fringe of a hurricane. On the island of South Calif, the tempest was a howling demon, an overwhelming force that uprooted trees and hurled thirty-meter waves at the shore. Outside, the air was solid with water, "rain" being an inappropriate term to describe the waterfall descending from the sky.

Tim and Ria could not be moved from the plasteel window. "Oh, you'd drown, just standing out there!" Ria's voice said in Tim's mind.

"You couldn't stand, silly!"

"Don't you call me 'silly'! I mean, there doesn't seem to be any room for air. Think of the poor animals!"

A substantial waterfall cascaded down the outside of the window, and the wind hurled more water at them with its unbelievable fury. The rest of the world was an indistinct blur beyond this.

Something huge slammed against the plasteel surface, so hard it penetrated right through the half-meter skin of water. Horrified, Tim recognized it as a great bird, with a longer wingspread than his height. For a fraction of a clicklet, the surface turned red with blood, then all signs of the unfortunate bird disappeared.

Both children gave a wordless wail of grief and shock. Instantly, Susan stood behind them. She cradled her head in her hands, and as Tim turned, he saw his grandmother's face contorted in agony. "Oh Artif, I just can't..." she said in English, aloud, and though her spoken words were lost in the high-pitched, painful wail of the hurricane, Tim saw her lips move, and heard her within his mind.

In a clicklet, Assam stood next to Susan, his bulk towering over her slight frame, and almost at the same time, Souda appeared between him and Ria, an arm around each of them.

Susan said, "Oh my head! Storms always do this to me. Tony be thanked, I'll be the last to have the fault." She pressed her face against Assam's bare brown chest as he enclosed her in his arms.

At almost the same instant, Kiril was kneeling next to Tim. He wore tight thermal clothing with long sleeves and trouser legs, and had a strong smell. Tim didn't find the smell offensive, besides he knew that his father had no way of washing himself where he was.

He heard Souda's voice, brittle with tension, say, "It's all right, Kiril, I'm handling the situation."

He answered, "My son, my sister, my mother. I've a right to be here."

"All right, then," and she was gone. Tim felt his father's anguish before Kiril guarded his emotions.

"What happened, my loves?" Kiril asked the children.

"We saw an albatross," Ria answered, shakily. "It was, it was, oh, smashed against the window, and..."

"Everything has to die sometime, except for Artif," Kiril replied.

"Even I," Artif's voice said to all of them. "One day, humanity will be no more, and then I'll be gone too."

"Yes, but, but, how can **any** animal survive this?" Ria was crying, great tears running down her face.

Kiril answered his sister seriously. "Darling, this is the third hurricane to strike here this year. Some years, we have six. And that's been happening, year after year, ever since the end of the Small Freeze, twelve hundred years ago. And yet, there are still animals."

Assam added, "It's the way of all life. We fragile-seeming creatures are pretty resilient. Apparently, more than a hundred million people survived the Cataclysm!"

Tim tried, but couldn't even imagine a number as big as that.

Tamás

Dawn light striking from below woke him. Artif said, "Good morning, dear. A visitor is waiting." Tamás looked up. Chia Smith appeared, grinning down.

"Hi there, little brother," he said. "Here I am, tall, dark and twenty tomorrow. I want you to come to my birthday party."

"Chia!" Tamás bounded out of bed and hurled himself at his big brother. Grinning, the young man caught him and gave him a great hug. "You're getting too big for this," he said. He put Tamás down.

Chia wore a crocheted white body suit. A pattern of white palm trees and dragons and elephants and dolphins encircled him, standing out against his dark skin. He was lucky, having inherited Dad's coloring.

"How's the house?" Tamás asked.

"Finished! Just in time. too. Come and look."

The last time Tamás had been here, about a month ago, the walls of the land house had just been completed, but there was no roof yet. Now, he found himself in a spacious, brightly lit, warm space. He looked around with admiration. "Oh, I can't take my eyes from the walls," he exclaimed.

Chia laughed with pride. "Yes, good isn't it?" From previous visits, Tamás knew that this was called ashlar stonework. It was made up of great rectangles of stone. Some stones were bright red, others yellow, white or gray, assembled in a cunning manner that forced the eye to trace patterns. "You do get used to it after a while, then it becomes background. Want to come outside?"

"Of course."

"We'd better wrap up, it's bitter out there."

Two clothes hangers came through an open door. "I've had warm clothes made for everyone I've invited to the party," Chia explained.

The hanger with the smaller clothes stopped by Tamás. It held a bulky sheepskin jacket, fur lined trousers, boots, a hat and gloves.

Both of them quickly dressed. Tamás looked at his brother and laughed, "You look like a giant sheep!"

"And you're a little one. Come on."

Chia commanded the outer door to open, then to close behind them.

First, Tamás looked up at the night sky. It always fascinated him that here, in the Southern Hemisphere, the stars were so different. "Oh, there it is," he said, pointing to the Southern Cross.

Chia said, "I'd better call down some power." Two lines of the faintest luminosity descended. One came from a good way to the south and ended at the house. The other started somewhere to the east, to a point several hundred meters on their right.

"Why two lots?"

"You'll see. Look at the house."

Tamás turned. Concealed lights came on, casting a bright mantle of illumination up along the walls. Tamás gasped with surprise: the outside face of the wall was also stone, but entirely different from inside. Unlike the flush, regular inside surface, this was an intriguingly irregular pattern. Jagged, rough stones of varying shapes and sizes, but the same selection of colors, were arranged in a pattern that dazzled him even more than the inside.

"Random uncoursed rubble stonework," Chia said proudly. There's a good thick layer of insulation between the two walls."

"Good!" Tamás answered with feeling. His nose was dripping from the cold.

"I've never done anything as satisfying as this stone laying, though, tell you what, I'm glad I had EGM to help me. I don't know how they did it in the ancient days."

"They probably didn't finish a house in a couple of months." They both laughed, then Chia said, "Look!"

Four hundred meters away, the huge red bulk of Uluru sprung out of the darkness. The bare, rusty rock glowed with a thousand concealed lights. The great mountain towered over them, stilling their minds with awe.

"The oldest mountain on earth," Chia said reverently within Tamás' mind. "It's so lucky that it was thrust up during the Cataclysm, instead of sinking like so much of central Australia."

"Looking at it like this, I can understand why you chose to make a stone house. The whole thing's a great work of art."

There was a laugh in Chia's thought, "And I've invited quite a few young women for tomorrow. But we're not finished. Here's the third component of the artwork."

More lights came on, to their left this time. These were under the gentle waves of the Inland Sea, and cast blue beams of brightness up toward the sky. Speechless, Tamás turned slowly from side to side and back again, from the azure luminosity of the sea to the ruby luminosity of the great, sacred rock, with the multicolored, eye-catching luminosity of the house in between.

And then, Mirabelle called, "Tamás, where are you? Breakfast!"

Alone again, Chia smiled fondly. He picked up the bundle of furs at his feet and returned to his house. Once within, he sent a command to turn off all the outside lights.

Mirabelle

It was raining below. "I suppose we could do some work in the hothouse," Mirabelle said without much enthusiasm, spooning porridge.

"Hey, Mom, you should see Chia's new artwork!" Tamás was too taken up with his own concerns to notice his mother's mood. "He's spent months on it, but for Brad's sake, it's worth it. He can add it to his credentials."

"Tell me, love."

So, Tamás did, stumbling over his words. Then he said, "Why don't you come and see for yourself?"

She smiled, "Because there's something else that needs doing." She didn't share the thought that if she got too friendly with Abel's family, he'd be sure to find a way of using it against her.

"Mom, I'd like to show Tonya."

Mirabelle had to laugh, "How nice, first love. Just don't get burned."

"Burned?"

"You'll find out, being too keen on somebody can lead to pain as well as to fun."

He stood up. "You'll see, I'm going to gain more credentials than anyone, even Dad, and lay them all at Tonya's feet!"

Mirabelle gave him a loving yet amused smile, and stood to go to her study. This was a bare room, with the curved, almost invisible wall of the balloon bounding one side. She sat cross-legged in the middle of the room on her bearskin, and closed her eyes.

"Flora," she said within, "may I visit you?"

"Mirabelle? You're welcome. I was just feeling lonely."

"I can understand that. On an average day, I have contact with maybe twenty people, but until your implant becomes active, you're dependent on visitors. And how many have you had? Me, Abel, Nathaniel?"

"No," Flora answered, "I've never met Abel, just heard his voice on the first day."

Mirabelle felt a stab of intense annoyance. "How negligent! I'll have to talk to him."

"Would you like a cup of chocken?"

"Thank you, no, I've only just had breakfast."

Flora looked surprised. "But it's late afternoon!"

"You forget, I'm in the Swedish Isles. Over three periods' time difference."

"In my days, Sweden was part of a peninsula."

Never particularly interested in ancient history, Mirabelle shrugged. "I guess the sea was lower then, water frozen into all that ice." The very thought gave her a shiver.

"Tell me about your home. I feel like I'm in prison here."

"Prison?"

Artif said, "I've got the reference. Before implants, people needed external control to discourage them from going against the edicts of their Culture. If they were caught being disobedient, they were locked away. That right, Flora?"

"Near enough."

"Artif," Mirabelle suggested, "why not find a house for Flora? A balloon would be the best." Flora looked apprehensive. "I'm not sure, I don't like heights all that much."

"My main house is a vacuum balloon, though I also have a land house in Antarctica. I love temperate gardening, and have a wonderful garden in each place. I visit Antarctica quite often while I'm up north, just to supervise the machines. It's winter there at the moment, of course."

"But, what happens if something goes wrong with a balloon? You'd crash!"

"Artif, has that ever been known to happen?"

"I'm looking. Once, 291 years ago, a meteorite hit a house. But sea houses and land houses are far more dangerous than balloons, and yet more people live on the sea than in the air."

"Well," Mirabelle said, "from here, a balloon is the only practicable physical exit. You're not up to walking out."

"There are no land vehicles?"

"No. There's simply no need for them."

Tamás

Tamás went to his own room, flopped onto his bed and called, "Tonya, can I visit?"

"Sure, why not?" she answered, and Tamás was in her room, in her mother's balloon. Two other boys were with her, both older and bigger than Tamás. She smiled at him. "Boys, this is Tamás Karlsen, my newest admirer. Aren't you, Tamás? And this is Vladislav Liston and Tashiro Gunter."

Vladislav was tall, already broad-shouldered, and dark. Tashiro had brown hair, a sun-browned face and body, and his smile seemed malicious to Tamás. "You collect them a little young, don't you?" he asked Tonya.

Tamás found his tongue, and his wits. "My father says, a couple of years soon fixes 'too young'. 'Too old' is much harder to cure."

This got laughs all around. Tashiro answered, "Hey, I've never been called 'too old' before. Who's your father?"

Tonya told him, "Abel T'Dwuna. And his mother's Mirabelle Karlsen." Both boys looked impressed.

"But I'm not my parents," Tamás said. "I don't need to climb on their shoulders."

Vladislav grinned, crowed exactly like a little rooster, then said, "I've been practicing bull riding. I'll have a go at it this year."

Tashiro was not to be outdone: "So? I can already swim fifty meters in 29.41 clicklets."

Tamás could only add, "I've climbed three-quarters of the way up the tallest tree in the world."

"Tell us when you've made the top," Vladislav answered dismissively.

"Actually, Tonya, I came to invite you to see something wonderful," Tamás said, ignoring him.

"Some other time," Tonya answered. "I was just about to go out with these two. You'd better go home for now."

For a couple of periods, he did nothing but sprawl on top of his bed, sulking and brooding. When his best friend, Gil, asked to visit, Tamás said to Artif, "Tell him I'm sick," and continued in solitary misery. *I wish I'd never met her,* he thought.

≉ **6** ≉

Flora

Flora was exercising, in the bedroom of her new quarters, in what had originally been designed as the Staff apartment. Artif had supplied two flexible bands, each with a loop at one end and a metal ball at the other. She got Flora to insert hands or feet into the loops, and pull in various directions, using muscles from all over her body. Currently, she lay her back, with the balls improbably hovering near the ceiling. She pulled down with both her hands against the resistance, saying with a puff, "Five."

"Have a rest, Flora. Would you like a drink?"

"Yes please, water if that's possible." She sat up. She wore a loose t-shirt, now soaked with sweat, and a skirt. "And, Artif, is there anything you can give me for pain?"

"What hurts, love?" There was concern in her voice.

"My right breast. Artif, I'm… I'm terrified."

"I've studied the records, and have made some chemicals for you. Normally, I control pain with internal adjustments. If that doesn't work, people's philosophy is to endure. But, you know, no one else now alive would react the way you have."

"How do you mean?"

A cup holding transparent liquid floated in through the door. "The pain-relieving chemical is dissolved in the water."

Flora caught the cup, squeezed to pop the straw out and drank. The liquid tasted just like water.

"If any of my children had a painful, incurable disease, they'd hand on instead of clinging to life, in fear of dying."

"In my day, 'handing on' would have been called suicide, and that was against the law."

"I'm sorry, what's 'suicide'?"

"Killing yourself."

"Flora, please forgive me for saying so, but your culture was crazy! Handing on is not killing yourself, but letting go a now worthless life, as a gift to two people: a woman who is waiting for a child, and the gift of life to the child herself. The old must continually transform into the new. And the other crazy thing is, whose life is it? If you want to end your life for any reason, what right has someone else to pass a law forbidding it?"

Flora was sick and tired of these arguments with Artif and her visitors, so just said, "Your painkiller has worked, thank you. Artif, can I have a shower and a rest before Nat is due?"

"Darling, you don't need permission. I'm your servant, not your master."

Flora walked to the bathroom, which Artif had refurbished before Flora's first awakening. There were no taps, no plumbing visible at all. As soon as Flora stepped into the little cubicle, deliciously hot water sprayed her from all angles, below and from every side as well as from above. And yet, not one drop of water hit her eyes.

"Is the temperature all right?" Artif asked from beyond the screen. "I feel so handicapped..."

"Thank you, yes, just wonderful!"

At last, she'd had enough and asked Artif to turn the water off. Warm jets of air dried her, strong enough to feel like a massage. Naked, she walked back to the bedroom. She put on one of the new bras, though this object looked nothing like the 21st Century ones she used to have. It was a very fine, almost invisible netting that assumed a rigid shape as soon as she put it on, and held her breasts away from her body. She slipped on another loose t-shirt and a sunny skirt with bluebells all over it. Artif sprayed her with tinted sunscreen, then Flora said, "All right, please tell Nat I'm ready for his next interrogation."

It took a couple of clicks for the young man to arrive. By then, Flora had walked outside, and sat down under the shade of their palm tree.

Chia

Chia sprawled in the compliant comfort of an easychair, organizing the entertainment for tonight's party. Three separate recordings were playing. He'd turned sounds off for the boxing kangaroos and the dance of the pink herons (normally, they were backed by music), and enjoyed the magnificent mountain lyrebird's performance. He had his spread tail thrown over his head, the two lyre feathers highly prominent, and did an odd little showy dance. He sounded a continuous series of clicks and burrs, while at the same time whistling piercingly, and imitating a succession of other birds. Visible just beyond him was his audience: the drab, brown female, quietly scratching and pecking at the ground. *Just like humans,* Chia thought, *the male performing and carrying on, in order to attract the precious female.*

He shut these recordings down, sent the heron recording to hide in the bow of the little sailing boat already bobbing by the pier, the kangaroos right at the top of Uluru, and the lyrebirds in a secluded little dell in the forest behind the house.

He commanded the next three to come out of storage. The first was a huge wedgetail eagle, harassed by a pair of small black and white birds, again with a musical backing, but this one designed to raise laughter. He was about to activate the second little globe when Artif asked, "Chia, will you welcome a visitor?"

"Who is it?"

"A young woman you don't know."

He shut off the recording and put the three globes away. It wouldn't do to spoil his surprises! Then he called, "Hello, there!"

She stood between him and the outside door, a dark brown beauty with the light from behind shining through her crown of blonde hair. "Hmm, you do look like your father," she said, "I'm Souda Ramirendo."

"Welcome," he answered appreciatively as she walked toward him. "Actually, if you knew my mother, you'd think I looked more like her. She's got a large dose of Australian Aborigine in her."

"I'm not familiar with the Culture."

"Oh, I'm counted as part of the English Culture, in fact I've been gathering a following. I hope to be the youngest member of the English Council. But, my ancestors are the oldest race on earth. And I belong to this land." He showed the pride he felt. "And I've killed a twelve meter long saltwater crocodile without any equipment, just with a knife, and ran a hundred meters in 9.71 clicklets, and after a year's research copied two ancient stone laying techniques to build this house."

She laughed. "I'm not much use to you for support on the English Council, I'm Spanish, originally from South America."

"Still, I'm happy to have you here, but..."

"But you've a party to prepare. I know. I won't take up much of your time. A friend of a friend of a friend told me about it. You see, your Dad suggested I get to know his sons, and so, here I am starting on the job."

He laughed, "What's the old devil up to now?"

"How would I know?" Full of innocence, the big, green eyes looked up at him. "I just thought you might invite me to your party."

"Done. Only, I'll have to make you warm clothes, and there's little time. Artif..."

"I've already set it in motion," Artif answered instantly.

Abel

A big hurricane approached, ponderously making its way south from its birthplace among the Sunken Isles. Though here the sky was still an unmarred dome of a myriad stars, already the sea moved uneasily. Five meter high waves thrust the house up, then plummeted her into a trough where it seemed that the next wave would swamp everything. Then the house twisted in a tight corkscrew pattern, to rise again.

Abel had put away all the sails, and instead used the two great propellers at the stern to run fast, out of this shallow region where he wouldn't be able to submerge to a safe depth. He had the big dish antenna open, receiving a continuous burst of power. *Good, I'll have full batteries while I'm under,* he thought with satisfaction as the barely visible luminous beam slanting in from far ahead replaced another one from behind.

Abel enjoyed the wild motion. He went down to his lounge, lay on the couch and got it to hold him securely. It was time for some work.

"I call a meeting of Control." And he was in Tony's cave, with the ancient equipment lining the walls. He sat at the head of the smooth blackwood table. It had been made by a man who had handed on hundreds of years ago. The chair was modern though, and instantly made Abel comfortable.

Twenty chairs surrounded the great oval table, with a wide gap to Abel's left.

"About time," came from Mirabelle, within half a click. "We do need to talk about Flora Fielding, or have you forgotten her?" She walked in, this time wearing a green skirt. She sat in her rightful place, at the opposite end.

One by one, the others came, until eighteen of the twenty wisest people on the planet sat assembled. "Tina and Vlad," Abel called.

"Oh hold on, I'm coming!" Tina Chung said, but it was another two clicks before her image walked in. Her olive face was flushed, and her oriental eyes looked angry. Abel noticed that her nipples were hard, and the dark bush of her pubic hair all mussed. "You do pick the worst possible times!" Tina snapped.

A laugh went around the table. "You can keep your pet, don't send him away," Oliver Marasadi teased.

"As long as you can manage to concentrate on business," Abel added, grinning.

Vlad Pradesh came in soon after. What little hair he had stood up in a tangled mess, and his eyes were red. "It's not the third period yet at my place," he complained.

"Sorry mate, there's always someone asleep." Abel looked around. "All right, I declare this meeting open."

Instantly, Tony appeared by his side, in the empty space left for his wheelchair.

He looked around. "Hello, Abel, Mirabelle, all of you my dears," he said within their minds.

They returned the greeting in a chorus. Then Mirabelle said, testily, "Abel, where have you been? I thought you and I were responsible for Flora Fielding."

"We are, and I've kept an eye on her. She is progressing well, and is gainfully occupied, and learning about our society. And I've had an interesting distraction." He looked around at all of them. "I've met a young man whose invention will change the world. It's as significant as, for example, ultra-longwave communication. And that one led to the major revision of Artif 8.4 to the Artif 9 series."

"That saved a lot of lives," Tony mused. "Before, people caught by a hurricane had to choose between risking the turbulence or losing touch with Artif. Many preferred risk to doing without her."

"This new invention will be as significant," Abel declared.

"Don't be so mysterious!" Cynthia Sabatini complained. She was the oldest member of Control, and possibly the fattest person alive, a woman mountain.

"All right, but one experience is worth a thousand words." Then he called, "Souda!"

Instantly, a young woman stood inside the door, looking overawed. Her eyes opened wide upon seeing Tony. Abel could hear her thought, "Oh, why do they have a recording?"

Tony himself answered her, "My dear, I'm not a recording. Think of me as something like Artif. Only, I'm programmed with a different personality, and have a different job to do."

Abel said, "Souda, it's customary for visitors to these meetings to keep quiet about Tony. Don't spread the word."

She took a few steps into the room. Every chair turned toward her, Mirabelle's spinning right around. Souda stopped at this.

Abel said, "This young woman is Souda Ramirendo. She has one of the only two applications of the new device. The inventor has the other. He's a young man called Kiril Lander. Now, I suggest we all do a one-way merge with Souda, and she can show it to us."

Ramona Tushiko, at thirty-three the youngest Control member, asked, "Is that all right with you, Souda?"

Souda looked at the Japanese woman. "I've already given my permission to Abel. Kiril's work should be recognized."

And Abel was Souda, on board her house, which she'd moored at the foot of Table Mountain, brilliantly lit by the late afternoon sun. He was also at home in his own house, ordering the masts to retract and everything closed off, ready for a dive, and also he was in Tony's cave, sprawled in the President's chair.

In Souda's home, at the southernmost point of Westrica, he became at one with her as she stepped forward toward the oval depression of the bed. He heard her succession of orders to the bed and felt her body being effortlessly moved about into the corresponding positions. "It can do many things for you," Souda explained to her internal audience. "Relaxation, enjoyment, exercise, and all without the physical touch of any object."

In the cave, Abel looked around at his colleagues. Cynthia's bloated face wore a look of ecstasy. From where he sat, Abel saw that at least three of the men had erections, and grinned to himself. Tony's face merely looked thoughtful. And Abel's physical self at home commanded the house to submerge.

At last, Souda ordered the bed to release her. Abel withdrew from the young woman's consciousness. Back in Tony's cave, she said, "Kiril also has a bed like this, but for the rest, he's done nothing about applying the idea. And he's refused to allow the bed to be copied by anyone else, even his mother. He needs help." The expressive green eyes were close to tears.

In a few words, Abel summarized the young man's unusual problem.

Mirabelle

When Abel's call came, Mirabelle and Tamás were in the middle of lovingly planting out seedlings: lettuce, cabbage, broad bean, pea, tomato. They placed each plant into a carefully chosen spot, among ornamental plants that would hide, protect and encourage them. Tamás dug a hole with his special little spade, Mirabelle put in a handful of rich compost from the bucket hovering by her side, then gently inserted the baby plant.

She heard Abel's call. Her first reaction was annoyance — it was always at an inconvenient time. Then she thought, *Actually, it's overdue!* She said, "Tamás, I need to go to a Control meeting, and I don't want to do this without focusing my being on it. You carry on, darling."

He nodded seriously. The love of the garden was one of their closest bonds. Mirabelle called for some water, and washed her hands when the hose arrived. Then she walked to a quiet, grassy spot in the shade of an ancient pear tree. She sat down with crossed legs, and closed her eyes.

She was pleased to be the first to have arrived, but allowed Abel to see her displeasure regarding his negligence of Flora Fielding. After all, the poor woman was his responsibility. She'd managed to visit Flora many times, compared to his none.

One by one, the others arrived, though as always there were a couple of tardy ones. When Cynthia settled her huge bulk in her chair, Mirabelle sent her a private, loving greeting: the two of them were firm allies on almost every issue.

Mirabelle quietly marshaled her arguments concerning Flora's future. At last, Abel opened the meeting and Tony appeared.

And then, the bloody man managed to steer the meeting away from Flora, springing something completely new upon them. Something, he said, that was as significant an advance as ultra-longwave communication. Mirabelle remembered, that had been one of the lost facts. Tony had said it was used by the ancients in their radiation-powered undersea ships. He'd obtained the information at considerable risk, and then that storage disk and two others had become damaged in the three hundred year wait before anyone was sophisticated enough to be able to study Tony's technical library.

Abel called a young woman. Mirabelle turned to look at her, and saw her eyes go to Abel in a quick flash. *I don't know what they see in him,* she thought. For herself, she liked her men to be thoughtful and admiring instead of arrogant. Like Oliver, who sent her a caressing thought before they all did a one-way merge with this Souda.

For perhaps five clicks, Mirabelle gave herself up to pleasure. This bed was certainly remarkable, and even while feeling Souda's body being cosseted, her mind was considering the engineering implications, the physics of the device. *I could make a land vehicle for Flora, using this idea*, she thought.

Back in the cave, Abel thanked Souda, then the young woman was gone. "We need to help young Kiril Lander," he said, "for two reasons. First, it is our duty. Second, his idea is potentially very useful, and we need his permission to apply it."

Cynthia said, "Oh that bed! I could actually be comfortable on one of those!" Abel gave her a look of distaste. "You could try eating less and exercising more."

"And that's none of your business!" Mirabelle snapped at him.

Tony held up a powerful hand. "Keep to the issue," he commanded.

Vlad spoke into the sudden silence. "Abel, we certainly need the inventor's permission to copy his idea. But surely, he doesn't own the principle? What if I made a game where competitors hurl themselves around within a room or something, trying to force each other over a line or into a hole? No touching allowed, but each tries to control the other's body movements?"

All the men perked up, looking interested. Mirabelle said, impatient with masculine foolishness, "I've been thinking of a land vehicle. Flora Fielding is feeling isolated and lonely. A few of you might see fit to visit her, since Abel has other things to do." She allowed her voice to show her disapproval. "She is unable to send images as yet, and Artif doesn't know how long that'll take. If she had a land vehicle, she could at least move around physically."

Heinrich Subirano said, in his rumbling bass voice, "Sorry, friends, it won't do at all. What an inventor owns is whatever is new in her creation. This man's new thought is the idea of applying EGM directly to a human body. Certainly, he also owns the application of the idea to a bed, but we need his permission for **any** application."

"That's what I said at the start," Abel said with his usual smugness.

Tamás

Tamás stood, having planted the last baby vegetable. He looked around the garden with pleasure, glancing at his immobile mother. *Lunchtime*, he thought, then called without words, "Artif, I want to wash hands, and could you get me and Mom a nice fruit selection?"

The hose came to him, then a basket with bananas, a pineapple already sliced and peeled, a bowl full of shelled nuts of various kinds, and two luscious pears. He sat down beside Mom's still form, peeled a banana and put it in her hand.

Without opening her eyes, she moved like an automaton, bringing the fruit to her mouth, chewing and swallowing. Her attention was fully concentrated on whatever she was doing at the Control meeting.

Tamás didn't mind. Dad could be involved in activities in many places at once, Mom had a single-track mind, and that was that.

When the fruit was gone, he called for drinks of chocken, and when he'd finished his, he wondered off, thinking, *Now, who? Gil?*

His friend stood in front of him, but looking harassed. "Tamás, it'd be great to play with you, but not now. My Dad's here, and he and Mom're having a blazing row!"

He disappeared.

And then, wonderfully, Artif asked, "Tamás, do you want to see Tonya?"

She stood on a beach, her bare feet scuffing the soft, golden sand. She was naked, and turned toward him with a grin. "C'mon, let's have a swim," she called, and ran into the small waves hissing onto the shore.

Tamás got rid of the kilt on his image and sprinted after her. They dived into the cool embrace of a frothing wave, side by side.

In Tamás's garden, Tonya asked, "Why is your mother sitting like that?"

Tamás dived deep and pushed off the sandy bottom. "She's at a Control meeting, and likes to concentrate." As he rose under her, he let a stream of bubbles escape his mouth, and saw them trickle up along the front of her body. He followed them an instant later.

Tonya laughed and pushed him away as they surfaced for air. "What's it like, having celebrities for parents?" she asked.

Back in his garden, his eyes hungrily ate her naked image. "It's been a nuisance, until now. But if it impresses you..."

She laughed again and dived. He relocated his image to be just behind her, and said, "I'm a shark!" He grabbed one kicking ankle, brought it to his mouth and nibbled on it.

"Merge!" Tonya said, and Tamás discovered what it was to be a girl. In an instant, he explored the sensations of her body, and for the first time in his waking state, his penis grew big and hard.

Tonya broke contact with a giggle, even as Artif said, "My dears, you're too young for that kind of linking."

Again they surfaced for air, and then Tamás sensed a momentary distance in Tonya. "Sure, why not?" she said to someone else.

Tashiro Gunter faced them, treading water. His blue eyes held a mocking gleam as he said, "Hi! Oh, the little boy." He rose to a wave a clicklet before them, then his feet appeared, already rhythmically kicking, and he swam further out to sea with an amazingly fast backstroke. "Watch this," he said within Tamás's mind. When he was about a hundred meters away, he did a neat backward tumble, then, as soon as he was face down, he started swimming toward them, with a smooth, powerful overarm stroke. A boiling wave overtook him. "Now!" he said, and locked his big hands together. His head and shoulders rose above the wave as he surfed past them in a flash.

Tamás swallowed pride and asked, "Can you teach me?"

Tashiro stood and ran toward them again, lifting his legs high to clear the water. As he dived in, head first, he said, "Swim a few strokes and let me see your style."

Tamás lay down on the water and swam forward, as smoothly as he could. Tashiro laughed in a superior way. "Looks all right, you just have to build up a few muscles." He was again swimming, and reached them in a clicklet or two. "Tonya," he said, "sit on me and I'll be your boat." His image relocated below the girl, and he rose, facing upward, his body horizontal.

Giggling, Tonya opened her legs and straddled his stomach, riding him like a horse.

Tamás felt like dying. Salty tears of rage and frustration mixed with the salty spray on his face. He disconnected, thinking, *I don't care what Mom thinks, I'll have another go at the Tree. And this time it'll be to the very top.*

≈ 7 ≈

Flora

Alone under the shade of the palm tree, Flora pushed the half-full plate away. "Oh, Artif, I'm eating all the time!" she complained.

"Your body is filling out, with all this food and exercise. I thought you'd be pleased. Have a look."

Her image appeared, sitting on a cushion like she was. Then the image stood and her clothes disappeared. The naked woman facing Flora slowly turned around. Her body was still very pale where the clothes normally covered it, but arms, legs and face had become naturally brown. The hair, now dyed auburn, had grown slightly, and the face was no longer as wrinkled, having filled out. Artif had left the bra on the image, so her breasts seemed firm, though the right one was noticeably larger than the left. *She's right, I look fifteen years younger*, Flora thought.

The image disappeared, and a strange woman's voice spoke from the globe, a deep, happy-go-lucky voice that Flora instantly liked. "Greetings, Flora Fielding, may I visit? I'm Cynthia Sabatini, a member of Control."

"Certainly, you're welcome," Flora answered, standing.

Then she gasped in surprise. A naked black female giant stood, facing her. This woman was well over six feet tall, and immense in girth. She looked to Flora like an over-inflated balloon: nothing sagged, not even her breasts. Her neck was thick, but without the sagging jowls Flora would have expected in a fat person. Short, silver-colored curls topped the enormous head.

A smile split the black face, showing bright white teeth. "Everyone knows me," she said, "but not everyone has seen me. The first time is a shock. But tell you what, it's an advantage to be different. I've a constant stream of men wanting to find out what I feel like!"

Flora felt her face grow red. "Sorry for staring. Er, in my days, most women were more, um, secretive about their experiences with men. Here it seems to be public, and that's strange to me."

A cushion floated out of the cave entrance, and Cynthia lowered her enormous bottom onto it. "I've studied ancient history. In your days, women and men sort of tied together into supposedly exclusive pairs, right?"

Flora had to laugh at this way of putting it. Cynthia continued, "My understanding is, that there was a very unhealthy power imbalance. Men ruled, women obeyed."

"Not really, in my times. In earlier days, yes, and in some parts of the world. But in the civilized countries, we pretty well had equality."

"Tony didn't think so. He said that unless restrained by strong internal controls, men would use their greater strength and inborn aggressiveness to dominate, and that this led to many of the terrible problems of your world, like people of one geographic region killing those of another. What's the word?"

"War," Artif supplied instantly.

"So, that's why Tony did a very clever thing. He decided that a woman should have absolute control over who fathers a child of hers. And, you see, in our world, nothing is in short supply except for the opportunity to be a parent. Men do as they're told, and everything they do is intended to impress women."

"I like it!" Flora said, laughing. My first husband used to hurt me. I divorced him, and got a great settlement, but..."

"Hold it, Flora," Cynthia interrupted. "My translator is floundering. A 'settlement' is a collection of houses, people living close by for some reason I can't imagine. 'Husband' and 'divorced' are just noises to me."

"Now you know how I feel in almost any conversation." It took quite a bit of effort to explain the ancient concepts.

At last, Cynthia said, "All this is fascinating, but I actually had a reason for visiting you. We've a problem with a young man, and I thought your unique experience may help." She told Flora about Kiril and Souda.

"In my days, that was quite a common problem, we called it 'jealousy'. It could go either way, though, a woman being jealous of a man, or the reverse."

"We have it too — among children. When a child goes through puberty, she often gets overly attached to a person of the other sex. But youngsters grow out of it, it's part of growing up. I've talked to this Souda girl, and apparently Kiril was a slow developer. He took little interest in girls, being more involved in acts of daring even as a boy. Most boys get a pash for a girl, she plays with them as well as with others, and if the boy throws a tantrum, the girl punishes him by favoring other friends. But the first girl this fellow fell for was Souda, when he was a young adult instead of a child."

"There is a balance in all things," Flora said slowly. When one person loves too much, the other is pushed away. From what you say, all he has to do is to give the girl her freedom, then, freely, she'll choose him."

"I might just send him to talk to you."

"I do have time on my hands, and I can't send myself as an image. I don't know if I ever will be able to do it..."

"Oh you will," Artif interrupted.

"...so visitors are always welcome."

"Good."

"Cynthia, I have a question. I hope it doesn't offend you."

The huge woman laughed. "Unlikely to. Go on."

"Your name is Sabatini?"

"Yes."

"That sounds Italian."

"I **am** Italian. For ten years, I was the President of the Italian Council, until I was selected for Control."

"Interesting, but... you don't look Italian to me."

Cynthia smiled. "All right, Flora, what does an Italian look like?"

"Do you happen to know a young man called Nathaniel Kyros?"

"I sure do! He is one of my occasional lovers."

Flora tried not to show how shocked she felt. She had a bizarre mental picture of little, slight Nat riding this giantess, lost between the enormous black thighs...

"I've stunned you again!" Cynthia looked both amused and pleased with herself.

"I'm sorry. My ways of looking at the world are so different! But Nat's skin color is what I associate with Italians."

"Skin color? What's that got to do with Culture? I'm Italian because that's my language. And that's the case because every one of my female ancestors was Italian. And my skin's black because that is a very valued characteristic. A dark-skinned man has a great advantage. Other things being equal, he's more likely to be chosen by almost any woman."

"Oh. Protection from the sun?"

"What else?"

"In my day, there was discrimination on the basis of skin color. Many white people considered colored people to be inferior."

"Albinos? Poor things do occur very occasionally, but of course they don't pass on their genes. Or do you mean your color? Flora, you're not white, but pinky-brown."

Flora pulled up the front of her T-shirt, exposing a section of now nicely firm stomach. It was all too white. She was amused by Cynthia's open-mouthed amazement.

Kiril

He'd never seen a more welcome sight than his house bobbing on the quiet waters of Lake Michigan. The storm had eased several periods ago, but a thick rising mist restricted his vision as the sun sucked up the fruit of days of rain. Kiril commanded the bridge to extend to the shore, sent his two camps over, then boarded himself. "Artif, I'll need resupply when weather permits," he thought.

"It's on the way, love. I've done an inventory," she answered instantly.

"Oh, I'm so tired!" He went into his lounge room, dropped the pack in the middle of the floor, and shed clothes on the way to the shower. He allowed hot water to pummel his body for all of ten clicks, then ordered full strength for the air massage. At last, blessedly naked for the first time in many days, he went to his bedroom and threw himself at the bed. It caught him, and he was asleep before his body reached horizontal.

He awoke to darkness. The house was pitching to a strong swell and a wind sang in the rigging. Kiril stretched luxuriously, then got up. He ate a double breakfast, threw on some warm clothes and went up on deck.

Low-flying clouds scudded along from the north, the half-gale whipping the shallow waters into the irregular waves that were tossing the house about. The full moon played hide-and-seek, painting everything silver, then disappearing behind a black, flying blanket, then peeping out again. Kiril took a deep, satisfying breath of salty air. "Let's get out to sea," he commanded, and the house's propellers started to hum. He easily accommodated his body to the wild motion as the house started its long way out of the Lakes.

Once he was sure the computer knew the path to take, he returned to the comfortable warmth below, stripped again, had a drink of kalibor juice, then called, "Dad!"

"Kiril?" the old man answered almost immediately. "I've been worried about you!"

The sun shone bright and hot on the plains of northern China. Marius Tirgrid was on the ground, looking up as a supply balloon approached his tethered house. He smiled at his son, saying, "I'm getting in a few tropical delicacies."

Like a sea of brown on green, the plain stretched all around, from horizon to horizon. Kiril could see no tree, no hill, no feature to catch the eye, except for a herd of horses grazing in the middle distance. "You keep coming back to this desolation," he said.

"We've had this conversation before. It's not desolation, but space. It's the land of my ancestors. And yeah, I visit it two, three times a year. Been a while since you called."

"Dad, I've climbed Mount Chicago!"

Marius looked at him with approval. "Third highest mountain on earth. Well done."

"What have you been up to?"

"I'm involved in a fascinating archeological project. About a thousand K east of here, we're studying a buried pre-Cataclysm library. Some of it is obsolete magnetic storage, but most of it is marks on sheets of processed wood fiber."

The supply balloon had now docked.

"I don't know how you have the patience for such puzzles."

Marius laughed, putting an arm around his son's shoulder. "I don't know how you have the patience to spend many periods climbing up bare rock, only so you can then climb down again. And both activities give a man credentials."

Kiril had intended to keep quiet about his troubles, not wanting a lecture from yet another loved person, but he now sighed, "I don't give a fart about credentials! Bloody women!"

"Or just one woman? Still?"

"You've got it."

"Watch." Marius put two fingers hand in his mouth, and gave a piercing, drawn-out whistle. One of the distant horses threw up his head, turned and galloped toward them. A magnificent sandy-colored gelding with white markings, he stopped in front of them in a surprisingly short time. Marius stroked his face, and fished something from a pocket of his kilt. He held it to the animal, who daintily picked it off the man's palm with his big teeth. Marius ran a firm hand along the horse's neck and flank, then lightly smacked the rump. "Off you go, Lightning," he said. The horse turned and ambled back toward his herd.

"So?" Kiril asked.

"So, if I built fences and kept him hobbled and restricted, and punished him for straying, do you think he'd come to me willingly at call?"

"Point taken. But I'm not sure how to apply it to Souda."

"I'm sick of lecturing at you. Come on, have a look at my dig."

In America, Kiril easily balanced to the wild, plunging movements of his house, effortlessly keeping his footing as it made its way north, directly into the gusting wind. Keeping his distant image unchanged, he dressed again and went up top. The cloud cover had increased, making the moon merely a veiled glow. His bare face and hands hurt with the cold, but Kiril didn't mind.

His image skipped with his father's from the plains of China to a spacious, brightly lit underground space. Beside him, Marius said, "Hey people, this is my son, Kiril Lander."

Fixed plasteel benches lined the walls everywhere, except for the spaces left for two closed doors. A man and two women sat at their work, and now turned with smiling faces.

"Welcome," the older woman said. "I'm Johanna Wong." She was perhaps forty, and looked Chinese.

The other woman had crinkly reddish hair, very rare nowadays, framing a very attractive if pale face, and introduced herself as Daru Archovna. She looked him up and down. "Hmm. And what have you done so far to please the ladies?"

Kiril said nothing, just smiled, so Marius answered instead, "He's been in two bull rides, the second time staying on for two clicks 72. He was unlucky, that year was unusually good, he came fifth overall. And he's sailed from South Calif to Eastrica in a boat with physical devices only, and he's just finished a climb to the top of Mount Chicago, must be the only person now alive to have done it, and—"

"Dad, please stop." Kiril looked at Daru, "Tell me about your work here."

"Hey, hey, I'm here too!" the man said. He stood up, a scrawny little man but with a friendly face. "I'm Nathaniel Kyros, and I'm the team leader. But I'm happy for the delightful Daru to tell you all about it."

The red-haired young woman expanded her chair and motioned in invitation. Kiril sat next to her. "Never before have I met a man who's shy about his credentials," she said. On the bench in front of her rested a rectangular, flexible-looking object. It had a faded, scuffed two-dimensional picture on its top surface, showing a vase with flowers in it, with strange marks above and below. Daru was controlling a hovering object looking like a message globe, except it was opaque. She positioned it over the thing on the bench, and instantly a white rectangle with a jumble of markings covered a smooth portion of the wall in front of them. "That's page thirteen of this book," she explained. "The writing is ancient Russian. That's my particular interest. I'm Russian myself."

"You can read that?"

"Yes, thanks to Nat and his father, Moss Ahari. Moss discovered this find, and developed the technique. Nat's the one who really made it workable."

"Thank you, darling," the little man said behind them. "All compliments gratefully stored away for future use. Unless you feel like a break now?"

"He may be small, but he's keen! No, Nat, not right now, thank you. Kiril, let me read what this says."

Kiril listened, hiding his lack of interest, as the girl told her ancient ideas about flower arrangement.

In the meantime, he heard Nat say to Marius, "I'll be visiting Flora Fielding again tonight. Fascinating, all the stuff she can explain about ancient times. I reckon I've learned more in the few periods with her than in the previous ten years." Kiril wasn't particularly interested in that, either. Naturally, like everyone else on the planet, he'd heard about the controversy regarding the Sleepers, and the idea of awakening one of them so she could have an input into the decision about their fate. He didn't care either way.

Chia

It was going well. Chia stood with his back leaning against his closed bedroom door, and watched his guests. His mother and father, all his brothers and sisters from both sides, his six closest mates, and fifteen attractive young women made a cheerful throng within his house. Multicolored lights cast flashing beams in random directions as they cruised around the room, up near the ceiling. Several guests simply stood, their eyes captured by the pattern of the walls. The music he'd chosen made everybody's feet tap, and four couples were dancing — at least, jiggling in the one spot, there being room for nothing more. He noted a smile on every face, well, except for one.

Tamás stood, lost in the crowd of adults, looking little and overawed. Staying where he was, he sent an image to stand beside the boy. "Hi there, little brother," he said with a grin.

Tamás' face changed from tension to joy. "Some party!"

"Yeah. Dad's enjoying himself!" They both looked to where Abel's head stuck up above the crowd. He was talking to four girls, including the stranger, Souda. They were laughing at something he'd said.

Trays of food and drink circulated among the crowd, and Tamás kept snatching delicacies as they passed. Chia laughed at him as he stuffed a sweetball into his mouth. "Your mother'll need to resupply after this," he teased.

The boy grinned up at him. "I'm not as silly as I look. I've stopped eating in the physical after the first couple."

"Good. Tony be thanked, you won't get a gut-ache. All right, I think it's time to go outside." Through the implant, he addressed everyone at once. "Hey, you lot! My wonderful family, and scruffy friends, and the flowers of femininity who have graced me with your presence. Thanks for coming. You think this is the party? Think again, the party is just about to start. I've got warm clothes for all of you. Come into my bedroom a few at a time, wrap up, then out you go into the freezing darkness through the door there. Wander around as you will. There are ten prizes hidden all around. Find one, and it's yours. Have fun!"

Then he turned to Tamás again, "Come on, jump your image to me." He withdrew into his body, and led Tamás into the bedroom. The two correct assemblies of clothes slid out from the compact row against the far wall. A trickle of others entered through the door, led by Abel and Souda.

"Why go outside?" she asked.

"Why ask? You'll find out in a clicklet." He told the door to slide open, and stepped out into the night.

The near-full moon was just rising, huge and yellow on the eastern horizon. Tamás said, "Good, Chia, even the moon is adding to your show." He gave the boy's fur-clad shoulder a squeeze, then turned to watch his guests straggle out in ones and twos.

His mother was last. As she stepped out, Chia said, "Look!" and lit all the spotlights. The house, the immense red mountain and the quiet waters all sprang to life. The reaction was all he could have hoped for. Chatter stilled. He saw his guests quietly turning side to side, taking in the totality of his artwork.

He gave them a click, then said, "Wander around, skip hither and yon. Find the treasures, then enjoy them."

His father disappeared, and became instantly visible on the boat at its mooring. Boats had always been one of his passions. Tamás asked, "Is the top of Uluru allowed?"

"Anywhere," Chia answered, and the boy was gone.

Within a few clicklets, he stood alone, except for one person, Souda.

"Don't you want to find a prize?" he asked.

"No. I want to find out a little more about you."

"That's very flattering. How do you like my house?"

"It's wonderful! But you know, the father of my first child made me a copy of his best creation."

He laughed. "I can't make you a copy of Uluru. And even the house took me several months to build."

"Can we get in, away from the cold?"

"Sure." He led the way after opening the door. They shed warm clothing in the bedroom, then went through into the living area.

"Chia, there's someone been asking to contact me. May I bring him here?"

"Why not?"

A naked man stood beside Souda. He was nearly as tall as Chia, with the supple, strong body of a gymnast. He had blond, almost white hair, in contrast to dark, almond shaped eyes, slanted and with Oriental eyelids. A very attractive fellow, despite his pale skin.

Souda said, "Kiril Lander, Chia Smith. Kiril, I'm at Chia's twentieth birthday party. This is the new house he built himself."

"Nice workmanship." Kiril looked around appreciatively, but, before he could say anything else, the bedroom door slid open and Abel stepped through. He'd shed his clothes, and held a recording globe in his hand.

"Son, how wonderful!" he boomed and gave Chia an affectionate hug from behind. Chia heard him command the recording to start, and a flock of herons danced in exact time to beautiful music. He noticed a fleeting look of annoyance cross Souda's face.

The show had hardly started when Tamás popped in. He still wore his woollies, and held a globe in his gloved hand. "Oh, Chia! You hid it where you know I'd find it! And it's great!"

Abel shut down his recording and turned. "Right, mate, we must see yours first." Then he noticed the new visitor. "Oh, Kiril, we meet once more."

To Chia's surprise, Souda stepped forward. "Abel, it's wonderful to see you again." She reached up, her arms went around Dad's neck, and she pulled him down to give him a passionate kiss.

In surprise, Abel let the recording go.

Artif shouted, in everyone's mind, "Beware! Kiril, no!"

Kiril's powerful body was bending. He snatched the falling globe from the air, and, standing close behind Souda, he hurled it with all his force at her back.

The globe went right through Souda's image, and Abel's image, and Chia found himself sitting on the floor, his back against the wall. At first, the world was a dark blur, and his chest was numb, like it wasn't there. Then the pain came. It was a deep, all-encompassing drumbeat of agony that throbbed with his heart, stabbed with every breath. "Artif?" he asked without sound.

"Breathe as shallowly as you can, love," she answered. "Three broken ribs. I'll put you to sleep."

Thankfully, blackness came.

⚡ 8 ⚡.

Flora

Nathaniel had left soon after Flora's mention of the problem Cynthia had brought her. "Kiril?" the little man answered, "Now where... oh yes, he's the son of one of my colleagues. I met him very recently. Tell you what, there may be something relevant in my Library. I'll check."

She was now taking the longest walk so far, right out of the valley and up onto the steep slope to the south. At Artif's suggestion, she'd put on a pair of shoes, one of five Artif had presented to her.

"Does everyone have such a wide choice?" she'd asked.

"If they want to. There's plenty for everyone. That was one of the reasons Tony limited population to one million. But with everyone else, I know exactly what they want, and give them that. When your implant's active..."

"If," Flora had interrupted. She'd never in her life been good at waiting.

Sweating, panting, she stopped when she reached the slight plateau on the top. She found herself on a grassy knoll, falling away to each side. She looked around. The landscape was a sea frozen in a storm, a mad jumble of peaks and valleys. Thick forest and grassland formed a random mosaic, and she saw herds of animals graze in several places.

"This was all spruce and Douglas fir in my day," she said. She'd seen it from a helicopter, one of five her company had owned.

"Darling, you have a visitor," Artif said from the communication globe, which hovered by her side, as ever.

"Whoever, she's welcome."

"Thank you," came Abel's voice. A huge black man faced Flora, a white smile splitting the handsome, gray-bearded face. Give him a spear, and he'd do for a Zulu warrior chief. He wore nothing but a skimpy bit of white cloth around his waist.

"At last we meet, Flora Fielding," he said in that wonderful, deep voice. "You see, I even dressed in your honor."

"How do you do."

Artif said, "Flora, I cannot translate that, I just gave Abel a greeting from you."

"I guess that's what it is. Abel, you know that Mirabelle is angry with you?"

He laughed. "That's nothing new. She is usually angry with me. What is it this time?"

"She's told me that I was awakened at your instigation, and it's your duty to look after me, and yet you haven't visited until now, and that there is something I must be told, but it's your job to tell me."

"True enough. I've been preoccupied with a new development that's turned into a crisis. I'm sorry."

"Flora, do you want to start back?" Artif asked.

Flora started carefully picking her way down the steep, uneven slope. Abel said, "Allow me," and she found herself cradled in his strong arms as if she was a child. One of his arms was under her knees, the other supported her back. He started running down the mountain, his bare feet amazingly fast and sure-footed.

I just don't understand it, Flora thought, *how can an image carry me?*

Abel put her down when he reached the flat of her valley. He was panting, but lightly. "Some water, and seating," he said. Two cups followed by two cushions came floating out of the cliff-side door, meeting them under the huge palm tree.

Flora emptied hers and sat on a cushion. "I have a need to be more polite to Artif than that," she told him.

"Artif? I was speaking to the kitchen. But Flora, I'm here now because you may be able to help with a crisis. Something's happened that's unheard of. A man has hurt another!"

Sadly, Flora said, "That was all too common in my days."

"I know. That's why I hoped you might be able to help. It hasn't happened since Control became global, 1312 years ago."

"I'm neither a lawyer nor a psychologist..." she could see on the big man's face that these terms were meaningless to him, "but it seems to me that it all depends on what he meant to do. Um... Can you describe what actually happened?"

"One of my sons was holding his birthday party. A young woman turned up the day before, and asked to be invited. As I think you understand, it'd have been unthinkable for him to refuse — besides, she's very attractive. At the party itself, she asked my son if a friend of hers could join her. Well, Chia is a generous person, and gave his agreement. And as soon as this strange man appeared, the girl put her arms around me and gave me a great kiss. And her friend went crazy. He threw an object hard at her, with clear intent to hurt."

This had something familiar about it. She said, "Cynthia Sabatini has told me of a young couple, now what were their names?"

Abel offered, "Souda and Kiril?"

"That's it!"

"Same couple."

"So, she is injured?"

"No. Not physically, though as you can imagine she is thoroughly distressed. Naturally, she was there in image. We all were, except for Chia. Artif is able to protect an image from damage. There was a feeling of intense agony for an instant, for both of us, without harm to the person. But the object passed through Souda's image, through my image, and slammed into poor Chia. He's got three broken ribs. What a birthday!"

Flora looked at Abel's concerned face. "Abel, nothing ever justifies violence. In my times, men bashed women and then excused themselves by saying that her behavior goaded them into it. I always thought that to be ridiculous. A person must be held responsible for his actions. But in this case, given what I know of your society, it seems to me that if anyone is guilty, it's the girl. She provoked and goaded him into a fit of jealous rage. He must have been acting on an impulse he would have controlled if he could. There was no intent to hurt your son, he was just unfortunate to be in the wrong place."

"That was exactly my conclusion. They both need help. I'll call a Control meeting, and put Souda on trial. Then I'll recommend that Kiril be required to see you. I just don't know how to help him. We have no experience with this kind of thing."

"I'm... I'm happy to do what I can, though I don't know what success I might have. Abel, send him along."

It was well after Abel had gone that Flora realized, he still hadn't told her the reason she'd been awakened in the first place. Was he avoiding an unpleasant duty? For the first time since her first awakening, a little worm of worry stirred within her insides.

Tamás

"You look dreadful, Tamás said.

"I'm all right, as long as I don't make any sudden moves," Chia replied reassuringly through the implant. He lay very still on his bed, propped up with a collection of pillows. His skin looked gray and lifeless, his dark eyes bloodshot. The great lump on his chest had reduced to a slight swelling, but a blue and yellow bruise disfigured a large area below it.

"Wish there was something I could do to help!"

Chia smiled, laughing obviously being too painful. "There is. Keep me company. What you're doing right now is what I need. Just talk to me, about anything at all. Anything at all, I don't care."

That was hard. How do you talk about anything at all? So, Tamás hung his head for a while, then blurted out the thing on the top of his mind. "Why are girls so difficult? I used to care nothing about them. I just, I don't know, resented that they were allowed to stay safe and comfortable, while I had to keep doing painful and dangerous things so I could impress them."

"Hmm. I remember, as a boy at one stage I actually hated girls."

Tamás cheered up. That helped a lot. He continued, "Then something happened. It's bloody awful and also it's wonderful—"

Chia interrupted, "You've got a pash for a girl. You're about the right age. Just think of it as an illness that'll pass, like my broken ribs."

"Oh no! It's nothing like that. I **love** her!"

"Of course. Sorry, I didn't mean to belittle your feelings. And let me guess. She's older than you, and prefers to play with bigger boys."

"Yes."

"And that hurts like crazy."

Tamás sighed, "Oh, it does!"

"When I was thirteen—"

Artif interrupted, "Chia, a visitor is asking to see you."

"Who?"

"Kiril Lander."

Involuntarily, Chia half sat up, then he grunted from pain, and his skin went even grayer, his lips appearing almost white. Tamás nearly fell off his cushion in shock.

"Oh no! Not that madman!" Chia said without speech.

"He is no danger to you. He asked me to say, he'd like to make amends. He's coming in the physical to bring you a present that'll make you much more comfortable while you're healing."

Chia was shaking, and said, well before Artif was finished, "In the physical? If, if he attacks me, I can't defend myself in my current state!"

"I know what the present is," Tamás interrupted. "Artif, is it his wonderful bed?"

"You'll have to ask him, dear."

"What wonderful bed?" Chia asked.

"My mother's talked about it a lot. Kiril has invented a bed that holds you and moves you around with EGM, and she..."

"Hey, that's brilliant! Why not?"

Artif repeated, "Chia, I can assure you, Kiril is no danger. He was almost ready to hand on, from shame at what he'd done, but then decided to do this as restitution first."

"If you say so, Artif. All right." But Chia still sounded unsure.

The man who stood beside Tamás was a sculpture in misery. His dark eyes were bloodshot and swollen. His pale hair was a tangle. His broad shoulders slumped forward, and he looked old and defeated to Tamás.

"Thank you for agreeing to see me," he said aloud in English, though of course Tamás heard him in Swedish. His voice was slow and hesitant, as if he had to think hard before finding the next word. "I'm... I'm terribly sorry I hurt you. I'm terribly sorry I tried to hurt **anyone**. Particularly..."

"Sit down," Chia said, and a cushion rose from the pile in a corner, making its way to behind Kiril. He sat.

"I've got this bed," Kiril said, apparently changing track, or perhaps he'd forgotten what he was saying. "I've only ever made two of them. So, I took the one from my house, and asked Artif for a balloon, and brought it here. I'm about fifty K away with it. I want to give it to you. It'll make you a lot more comfortable than what you're lying on now."

"Kiril, I'm Tamás Karlsen," the boy said.

"Oh, hi. I seem to have seen you somewhere before."

"I was here when you hurt Chia."

"Oh, I'm so sorry about that! I wish I could undo it, but when she—"

"Kiril," Tamás interrupted, "you didn't want to hurt Chia, but you did want to hurt your friend, what's her name?"

"Souda."

"Why?"

The Kiril looked at him, his eyes full of pain. "She's been the center of my existence for over seven years. I love her, more than life itself. And she plays with me. She rejects me, then she suddenly invites me to a party. Why? So she can kiss Abel in front of me. The great Abel, of all people! I just don't know, you probably can't imagine how that makes me feel."

"Oh yes I can!" I know **exactly** how you feel! Because that's exactly how I feel." Tamás couldn't help it, he sprung to his feet, propelled by his own vehemence. "There's this girl. Everybody says I have a pash for her, but it's more than that! And she enjoys my company, I amuse her, and she lets me kiss her and that. But... She's got these other friends, and when they're with her she treats me like a snotty-nosed little child. Oh yes, I do know how you feel."

"Tamás, you don't know how much you've helped me. I'm not alone. Until now... I've felt like I'm some kind of a freak, a monster, different from every other human being on the planet."

And then something happened that surprised Tamás. He found himself hugging the man, his arms around the muscular shoulders, his face pressed to the slight stubble of Kiril's shaven cheeks, and powerful arms closed around him in a hug of friendship.

Kiril gently pushed him away. "My balloon is here. Chia, could you please open the door?"

The door slid open, and Kiril walked in backward, even while his image winked out of existence. A large, flattish object on its edge followed him. It wouldn't fit through the door, but then it tilted, and just scraped through when lying along a diagonal.

Tamás sent orders to the furniture, moving everything out of the way. Kiril turned and stepped aside. The object stood up again, and skimmed over, next to Chia's bed. It became horizontal and settled to the ground.

Tamás saw that it was an off-white plasteel rectangle, with an oval depression the size of a double bath.

Kiril walked over and stopped next to the boy. "Right, Chia," he said, "simply order the bed to pick you up and carry you over onto itself. It'll monitor your slightest wishes, so there should be no pain."

Chia rose into the air, and then hovered a meter above the EGM bed. The lines of pain on his face smoothed out. "This is wonderful," he said without speech, "thank you, Kiril."

"I caused the injury. Surely I could do no less?"

"Kiril," Tamás said, "my mother wants to use your idea to make a land vehicle."

The big man looked surprised. "How would she know about it? I've given it no publicity."

"She's on Control, heard it from my father."

Chia explained, "Tamás is my brother. We're both Abel's sons. His mother is Mirabelle Karlsen."

"But isn't Mirabelle Abel's main opponent?"

Ruefully, Tamás answered, "She sure is!"

"That can't be easy for you, caught between the two of them. But about a land vehicle. I've just told Artif, your mother is welcome to the idea. It shouldn't be hard. You could make one right now with a few bits and pieces."

"What do I need?"

"A body harness, and an EGM motor strong enough to carry you. The motor from a cushion would do. Artif has the code from my bed, and can reprogram your house's computer, and there you are."

But Tamás thought of all so superior Tashiro Gunter, and had a sudden wild idea. He asked, "What if I wanted to go well away from the house?"

Chia said, "Shouldn't be a problem. You've got your climbing backpack." He explained to Kiril, "Tamás has been toughening up by climbing this absolutely enormous tree at their place."

Tamás felt the equal of these men. He stood back and looked at the two of them. Suddenly he knew himself to be a man, not a boy, a man on a level with anyone. "Listen. I want you to swear to me, on Tony's memory, on Brad's salvation, that you'll keep this a secret, until I release you. I want you to tell no one, no one under any circumstances, that I know how to move myself using EGM."

"What're you up to?" Chia asked, his face showing alarm.

"A quest that's never been done before. I'll travel around the world, all by myself, using EGM."

"Your mother won't have it."

"I'll leave her a message. But you mustn't tell her, or she'll stop me. You must keep my secret, it's my right."

Kiril looked at him with respect and fellow feeling shining on his face. "Certainly, Tamás, it's your right. But you're awfully young for it."

"Doesn't that earn me more credentials?"

"At least, we can help with the practical planning," Chia offered. "Oh, it's good to be able to think straight. Kiril, this bed has really reduced the pain. All right, you can go over both land and water. Recharging the batteries might be a problem over the sea, because the force of it might push you under, and of course you'll need supplies."

"Artif, you can get supplies to him anywhere, can't you?" Kiril asked.

"I disapprove of this idea, but yes, I can certainly resupply him."

"Artif, it's my right. And you must respect my privacy."

She sighed, in all their minds. "Yes."

"About power supply," Kiril said, "At home in my boat, I've got two mobile camps. I developed them for my climb of Mount Chicago. Packed up, each is a two-meter diameter ball that moves with its own EGM motor. It will float on water. So, when you're over the sea, settle the camp on the surface, get it charged up, then transfer charge to your pack at leisure. It's possible, but for Brad's sake it'll be a long and tiresome journey. I sailed in a little boat from South America to Eastrica, so I know."

"Thank you. Kiril, I accept your camp, and I'll look after it. How will you get it to my place?"

"I've set it in motion. It's on the way. You should have it in maybe five or six days."

"You'll need that much time to make your gear and practice using it," Chia said.

Nathaniel

He'd been busy, but at last found time to keep a promise. Nathaniel activated the lovingly restored obsolete machinery, and the letters of ancient Russian filled the screen. With the smoothness of years of practice, he skimmed the catalog, looking at titles under "psychotherapy." *This looks promising*, he thought. The title was *Loving Too Much*.

He thought a command at the modern storage system, and shortly a hard-covered book came to him on a tray. He positioned it under the scanner and started to read. Each time he found something interesting he spoke the words in Greek, within his mind, for the benefit of the recording apparatus.

It took Nathaniel the best part of four periods to finish the book. Then, after a meal and a rest, he asked, "Artif, are Flora and Cynthia available? I'd like to see them both, together."

He was under their favorite palm tree, watching Flora walk out of the door in the cliff-side. The communication globe was by her side. *She's in pain again*, he thought with concern, looking at her face, but made a special show of grinning at her. He said, "Hi, Flora, as you see I keep my promises. Here is the information on jealousy." Triumphantly, he held the little recording globe above his head.

She smiled back. "It's always a pleasure to see you, Nat. Right, tell me about it."

He sent a command to the kitchen's computer, and two cushions floated out, followed by three cups of kalibor juice. "Why three drinks?" Flora asked.

"One is for me," came Cynthia's laughing voice from the communication globe, and she appeared, just right to have one of the cushions butt her behind the knees. She sat, and Nathaniel jumped his image onto her lap. She grinned down at him and mussed his hair. "This better be good, little man," she said, "I'm in the middle of a nice meal, and I like to concentrate on my food."

"Are you ever not in the middle of a nice meal?"

"Now, don't be rude."

Nathaniel was pleased to see a smile swallow the lines of pain on Flora's face. He activated the recording of his various quotes from the ancient book. Naturally, it was voice only, and the three of them listened intently, each in her own language.

> Jealousy, excessive possessiveness, is a very destructive emotion. It is a tragedy that kills what it values, for the object of jealousy almost invariably ends up rejecting the constraints of jealous love.
>
> In part, jealousy is a feeling of entitlement. The unspoken, irrational thought behind the emotion is, "I love you so much that you owe me an equal return of love."
>
> Jealousy is a double tragedy: the more the jealous partner demands, the less the loved person is able to return.

Cynthia stopped the recording and said, "All this is good stuff, but nothing we didn't learn from observing Kiril and Souda. It's good to know he conforms to a pattern. But how about treatment? What to do about it?"

Nathaniel answered, "Wait, first there is some interesting stuff about causation: what leads to it. Listen." He advanced to the right spot.

> Almost invariably, jealousy grows out of insecurity. The jealous lover has a feeling that, unless he binds the loved person, she will escape. No amount of love, no amount of reassurance can satisfy his love, for always and ever, the loved person's return love must be proven anew. And at last, jealousy's fears come true, brought about precisely by jealousy itself.
>
> A person given to jealousy may well be an overachiever. They tend to excel in many fields, for whatever they do, they must prove their self-worth over and over and over. And after every proof, they still feel the need to prove their worth yet again.

"See?" Nathaniel said. "Kiril has made great achievements, and yet he is always striving for more. He doesn't care about credentials, I've seen that myself, and yet he continually strives for excellence. All right, I'll skip to treatment."

> Jealousy is based on irrational premises, so the proper treatment is "Cognitive Therapy," the process of encouraging the sufferer to prove these deep beliefs to be false.
>
> Ask him to keep a record of the thoughts going through his head just before feelings of jealousy intrude. Then convert these thoughts into a testable form, and have the sufferer test them. These surface thoughts can be used to expose deeper held beliefs. The reader is referred to Aaron Beck's work for details.

Nathaniel stopped the recording. "And that's basically it," he said apologetically. "The book is intended for psychologists, not lay people like us."

"Artif, do you have access to this Aaron Beck's work?" Cynthia asked.

"Tony had records of five books by him. These are all intended as self-help books, so they should be useful to you."

"I guess I have some studying to do," Flora said ruefully. "Oh well, I've got plenty of time."

⍢ **9** ⍢

Flora

She was enjoying company, under the palm tree as usual. Cynthia sat on a hovering cushion, facing her. Nathaniel snuggled on her enormous lap, his head resting against a black breast, and as ever, he was asking Flora questions.

Artif asked, "Flora, will you receive more visitors?"

"Of course. Who is it?"

"Me, bringing a new person," Mirabelle said. She appeared, standing beside Cynthia, with a man on her other side. He was tall, though not as tall as Abel, whipcord-slim and graceful. His suntanned face was clean shaven, and he had receding brown hair. His gray eyes looked seriously at Flora. It was now quite ordinary that he wore a bright red kilt and nothing else.

"Greetings," he said, lips not moving. "I'm Evanor Schwartzwald. I was only fourteen when I successfully dived off Migor Cliff into the sea. It's a two hundred meter drop, and fellows are killed every year trying it."

Flora saw Mirabelle stiffen, and shudder slightly. *There's a tragedy there, I'm sure*, she thought, but Evanor continued the customary recital, "And, as a young man I was German high jump champion, cleared 2.67 meters, but then I got into hang gliding. I gave that away when the current project started, but my longest distance was third best in the world, and is still the unbeaten German record."

"And, are you on the German Council?" Flora asked.

He laughed. "No, until the last few days, I'd have had no time for politics, and my interest is in electrons, not people. I leave that kind of thing to the likes of the lovely Mirabelle." He smiled at the Swedish woman, and Flora saw Mirabelle glow.

"You have an unusual name."

"Evanor? You see, I'm the continuation of a woman named Eva. Schwartzwald is simply the family name, inherited through the long line of my female ancestors. I'm not sure how much you've been able to learn about our customs—"

Nat interrupted, "Oh lots! She's a good student, and a better teacher. By the way, I'm Nathaniel Kyros, and my friend is Cynthia Sabatini."

Evanor answered, "Naturally, I've heard of both of you. Flora, you certainly are surrounded by celebrities, but then it's only fitting, you're unique. But let me continue. For the past ten years, I've been involved in the Solar Plus project, and we've improved solar collectors from an efficiency of 51.57% to 53.92%!"

He stood very proud, and the three others looked impressed, but the information left Flora puzzled. "Er..."

"Flora, in your days, according to Tony's records, solar collectors could convert about 30% of sunlight into electricity. Improving this has always been important, and therefore a way of gaining credentials. Until ten years ago, the current figure was 51.57%. The increase my team and I achieved means a huge amount of extra free energy available to humankind."

Nat explained, "It's like finding a mountain of gold or a huge oil field would have been in your day."

Mirabelle said, "Anyway, the Solar Plus project is now in monitoring stage. They've equipped a topstore, and have to wait for five years before they can do anything new. That means that Evanor is at a loose end, and so I've grabbed him to help us design a land vehicle for you, Flora."

"Wonderful!" Flora sprung to her feet, ignoring a couple of stabs of pain. "Only, are there still roads for them?"

Artif said, "I have the reference. A road was a flattened, hard-surfaced ribbon for wheeled vehicles to go on."

Evanor explained, "A young man called Kiril Lander has come up with a new idea, and has given Mirabelle permission to adapt it..."

Flora thought while listening, *Kiril Lander again?*

"...The idea is to apply EGM forces directly to a human body. So, you can scoot along the ground, at a set height of your choosing, up to maybe five meters..."

"What? Just hovering in the air? I'd be terrified!"

"There's no danger," Evanor said, seeming patronizing to Flora. "The computer stops you from hitting anything."

Mirabelle came to Flora's aid, "It all depends on your past experience. Flora, we could make you feel enclosed, like this." And suddenly a glistening, translucent, silvery ellipsoid surrounded Mirabelle. "Tap on the surface," her voice invited.

Flora stepped over and did so. The surface felt crystal hard, and rang melodiously.

Mirabelle's shell disappeared, and she stood there once more.

"Yes, thank you, that'd make a big difference. But can I do that, without a working implant?"

"I can do it for you, Flora," Artif reassured her.

"I'll get to work," Evanor said, then he and Mirabelle were gone.

Mirabelle

Tony's cave had its usual, slightly bluish light. Every face around the great table looked serious and concerned. There were two additional chairs, empty for the moment.

"We're ready to start," Abel said. Tony appeared. After greetings, Abel stated the purpose of the meeting: "A young man, Kiril Lander, has acted with intent to cause injury. This was from impulse, he didn't plan it, and he was placed in a situation where he was provoked into this unfortunate action. He is overly attached to Souda Ramirendo, whom we all met, quite recently. She appears to have deliberately goaded him into violence. We're here to examine why she did this, to help her to get over the terrible feelings of guilt she is suffering from, and to ensure that this kind of thing never happens again. We have also requested Kiril to make himself available."

Mirabelle had to agree, if reluctantly, that he'd made an excellent summary.

"Tibor, bring Souda forward," Abel called.

Instantly, Souda appeared behind one of the empty chairs. By her side was her Advocate, Tibor Gomez, President of the Spanish Council. He was a small, compact man of middle years, and Mirabelle's choice for filling the next open position on Control.

Tibor solicitously seated Souda, then sat himself.

The young woman looked as if she hadn't eaten for days. Her green eyes were bloodshot and swollen. Instead of the provocative lace body suit, she wore a plain gray skirt and a loose top.

Tony said, "Souda, you're here on trial because you did something that led to pain and distress for several people, yourself included. Our intent is not to blame you or make you feel even worse, but to understand your actions. Please, tell us what actually happened, and why."

Souda looked at Tony, as if the rest of Control didn't exist. She spoke so softly that Mirabelle had to lean forward to hear her better. "I... I... Believe it or not, I love Kiril. I thought I was helping him. And yes, although I love him, for the last several years he's been driving me crazy with his possessiveness. If he could, he'd be physically with me, all the time. I found I had no time to myself. Even when I deliberately took up an interest in ancient music, which was something he didn't care about, he wanted to join in and do it with me until I screamed at him to leave me alone. And whenever I had friends over or visited somebody, he'd need to be there, or questioned me about it over and over, even if my friend was another woman. It got so that I simply refused to allow him to see me. Fortunately his mother has become a good friend, and our son now lives with her. That way, both Kiril and I can spend a lot of time with the boy, and yet I can minimize contact between us."

Oliver interrupted her monologue, "Souda, you say you still love him. What does that mean?"

She turned to face him, across the table. "I guess some of it is selfish. He's got more credentials than any other young man I know of. I'm proud that he loves me, and many women envy me. But also, he is a kind, sensitive, warm person. He's a wonderful father to our son. He has deep knowledge on many subjects, and can talk about them in an interesting way. Before... before his obsession got out of hand, we had a lot of fun together. He taught me a great deal, we share many interests, we have a similar sense of humor — only, he doesn't have a sense of humor anymore. But, I suppose the real answer is, I want him to be happy." She paused a moment. "For years now, he's been a tortured person. I want him to be the way he used to be. I've been brooding about this for a while, and that's what led to this... this tragedy. Oh, I'm sorry!" Tears trickled down her face.

Abel said, "You sought me out. Please tell us about your reasons for that."

"I thought you might be able to cure him of this disease. But you failed. I know you went to him, and, nothing changed. So I felt I had to do something myself." She looked around. "What do you do if you're a teenage girl, and a boy gets a pash for you? That's all I did. I mean, it works for children, and what else did I have to go by?"

Cynthia said, "I've talked with Flora Fielding about Kiril's problem. She says, in her days this problem was quite common."

"Lots of problems were quite common in my day," Tony answered. "Lots of problems we've got rid of. My dears, let's concentrate on Souda for now, then we can deal with Kiril's problem. After that, we need to consider how to stop this situation happening to someone else."

"I was terrified when I got the order to come. Tibor did his best to reassure me, and now I see he was right. I feel a lot better. So please, don't spend any more time on me. Help Kiril."

"He should go and talk with Flora," Abel said.

Tibor stood. "Are you finished with my client?" he asked.

"We are," Abel answered.

"I thank you for your treatment of her. I didn't have to say anything in her defense, and that's a compliment to you."

And the two of them were gone.

Mirabelle spoke into the extended silence that followed, "I do understand her actions now. She is right. As a girl, I cured several boys who had a pash on me, by doing more or less what Souda did to Kiril."

"Only, the situation is different," Ramona Tushiko said. "Kiril is not a boy, but a man with a set personality. I can also understand her actions, but I'm not at all surprised that she failed. And I'm concerned, he may well feel so guilty that he may kill himself, without even handing on."

"Let's ask him," Abel said.

Kiril stood behind the chair Souda had occupied but a few clicks ago. By his side stood Martha Jones, Deputy President of the English Council.

Kiril looked as woebegone as Souda had. Mirabelle saw that he was a tall, well-built young man, very attractive despite his pale skin, no darker than her own.

After they were sitting, Martha said, "My client is here under protest. He doesn't believe that Control can do anything to help him. He has made restitution to Chia Smith and the two of them are now friends. All he wants to do now is to hand on."

Abel answered, "Kiril, you're the second person we've invited to this meeting of Control. The previous one was Souda. View this recording."

Souda appeared. Abel had projected her onto the table, facing Kiril. "I... I... Believe it or not, I love Kiril. I thought I was helping him," she said, very softly, apparently looking him straight in the eyes.

The young man half rose from his chair, his hands reaching for her. The grimace of pain on his face made Mirabelle want to mother him, to hug him to herself.

The recording disappeared. Kiril sat once more, looking at Abel. "Yeah, so what? She's said things like that before. The fact is, loving or not, she is annoyed by my company. If we're together for five clicks, she starts snapping at me, and then she won't see me for ages. And all that's irrelevant. Things are beyond Souda, my feelings for her. I've committed an unforgivable crime. I'll be haunted by the memory, the guilt for the rest of my life. I'll hand on, as is my right."

"Certainly it's your right," Abel said to him, "for any reason or no reason at all. But it'd be a sad loss to humanity if you went through with it now. I've told you before, you have great potential."

Cynthia said, "Kiril, you invented something unique and wonderful. I—"

He spoke over her, "Oh, you're welcome to it. I give permission for anyone to use my idea in any way they wish."

Heinrich Subirano leaned across Martha and rumbled, "That's not the point. You saw something that's missed the greatest minds of humanity for over a thousand years. The possibility was always there. I've studied the ancient history of engineering. There once was a man called Watts. He watched steam raise the lid over a pot of boiling water, something millions of people must have seen before him. But his eyes saw a possibility that changed his world, and led to the Cataclysm a couple of hundred years later. So, we have our world thanks to him. You've done exactly the same thing. Your idea will in time change the world just as much."

"I've told you, you're welcome to it."

"Your mind is a tool. You've used it once to benefit humanity. Will you now waste it, instead of using it again and again?"

Kiril sprung to his feet, the chair behind him skittering back out of his way. "I care nothing for humanity! What's humanity done for me?" He glared around the great table. His large hands opened and closed into fists several times.

Tony spoke one word, "Kiril!"

The big man's eyes opened wide in surprise. He turned to face Tony. It was obvious to Mirabelle that until now, in his upset and depression, he hadn't taken in Tony's presence.

"Sit. It isn't customary to shout in my house."

Kiril collapsed into the chair that moved back under him, at just the right time. "Tony, but..."

"Yes. I'm Tony, and this is my home. However, do not talk about me to anyone outside this room."

"Don't worry. I'm unlikely to talk to anyone much." His anger spent, Kiril sunk back into bitter depression.

Abel repeated the suggestion he'd made during a previous discussion. "Kiril, your problem has been that Souda feels constrained by your love. Apparently, this was a common difficulty in ancient days, and we have a person who used to live then. I want you to go and talk to Flora Fielding. I think she'll be able to help you."

Kiril snorted. "Suppose she helps me to not feel the same about Souda. Does that undo my crime? What's the use?"

Tina Chung said, "Kiril, you hurt Chia Smith by accident. You have made restitution and he has forgiven you. You're now friends."

Kiril's eyes turned up towards the cave's roof in exasperation. "You don't understand. You just don't understand, any of you. I TRIED TO KILL SOUDA!" He bowed over, leaned his head on his arms and started to cry. His sobs filled the room.

No one said anything. Martha leaned across and put her arm over his shoulder. Mirabelle felt her own tears come.

After a while, Kiril sat up and wiped his face with the back of his hand. "I'm sorry," he said.

Mirabelle had an idea, and spoke up, "Kiril, you're right. We didn't understand the real cause of your grief. Now we do. I certainly do. It was wrong, it was quite unforgivable for you to have an impulse to kill Souda. It was wrong to have an impulse to kill anyone. It was terrible that you tried to hurt **her**, the most important person in your life." She paused, and Kiril looked at her.

"But think, Kiril. Don't think just of your own feelings like a child would, but think of her. You're feeling guilty because you did this terrible thing. But Souda is feeling equally guilty, because she feels responsible. If you now end your life, she'll bear a load of guilt for the rest of hers. Do you want to be responsible for imposing even more suffering on her?"

"I... I hadn't thought of that."

"You've made restitution to Chia. You need to make restitution to Souda as well. I think that should be your continued existence. And if that hurts, are you not a man? Can you not bear pain?"

Slowly, Kiril stood. He squared his shoulders and stood straight and tall. He nodded, once, then his image disappeared.

Tamás

Mother was up high in the balloon, away at yet another Control meeting. Now was the time to try out the new EGM vehicle. For days now, he'd had all the pieces hidden within a blackberry tangle. A little nervous,

Tamás checked everything meticulously, one more time. He put on the long-sleeved top and long trousers that were the underclothes of his climbing gear, strapped on the harness so that the EGM motor salvaged from a large cushion was in the small of his back, and shrugged on his backpack.

He took a deep breath, and thought at the computer. He was flying! About two meters above the ground, body horizontal, he scooted along at an exhilarating rate toward the Tree. He reached the trunk and thought, "Up!" With hardly any loss of speed, the motor clawed him upward, parallel to the massive trunk. Among the great branches he wove, up, ever up, each obstruction barely glimpsed before it was out of sight, passing below him. He almost forgot to breathe in his excitement. There was no danger as long as he concentrated: as soon as he saw an object, the computer registered it and modified his path.

The level of concentration required soon exhausted him, so he stopped for a rest. He found himself perhaps halfway up already. He sat down in a secure fork, closed tired eyes and breathed deeply. After a while he had a drink, then stood to go on.

I'd better go a little slower, he thought. This was much easier. He could actually afford to blink occasionally, and still he ascended at a glorious rate.

After two more rests, he reached the very top of the Tree. He wedged his feet into the fork of a branch half the thickness of his arm, ordered the belaying rope from the pack and tied on. His head actually stuck up above the tallest branch.

The Tree swayed widely in the gentle breeze. The world moved below him, far, far, far to the left. It stopped, so that as he looked down the Tree appeared to be dangerously bent, then the world moved again, back, and then the sway took him far to the right. What must it be like in a storm! He drank in the view, had a sip of water, then called, "Tonya!"

She was with him in a clicklet. Her feet scrabbled on the thin branch and she shrieked as she started to fall, then her image disappeared.

In her home, he looked out through the balloon's walls at endless blue rollers way below, a white line marking the top of each. She'd been in the middle of doing a painting. A rose bush stood in the center of her room, true to life even to the thorns and droplets of dew on the leaves, but everything was four times normal size. It had no flowers yet, but a blue smudge sat on the branch nearest Tonya.

"Oh you wretch, you gave me such a fright!" she said, still panting a little. "Look, I spoiled the flower."

"I'm sorry. I was so pleased to be up there, I wanted to share the view with you. Of course, there's just nowhere for you to stand."

"Tamás, you're up the top of the Tree?"

"At the very tip. Hey, that's a great rose bush."

"Thank you." She looked at her creation, and the blue spot disappeared. "Hold on," she said, and a perfect, deep blue rosebud appeared in the same location.

"A blue rose?"

She grinned, "Why not?"

"Hey Tonya," he said hopefully, "if we merge you can see my view."

And he was her and felt the curve of her back, so different from his own, and the feel of having breasts, and down below...

"That'll do, Tamás," Artif said in his mind. "Just look at your view."

The blue dome of the sky stretched forever. The Tree swayed side to side, further than the tallest mast in a strong swell. Below, way below, dark green mountains grew out of winding, deep blue ribbons of water: the fiords and islands of his home.

Tonya said, from within his being, "Beautiful! Of course, I've seen this from home, when we were physicaling you, but it's completely different. It's sort of, alive instead of just being out there."

"Sure is!"

"Tamás, thank you for showing me this."

"Tonya, everything I do is for you."

"You're sweet. Bye!" And she was gone.

He took an endless, deep, happy breath and thought about the trip down. He decided against descending head first, and instead commanded the EGM motor to drop him, standing upright, onto a branch perhaps fifteen meters below. His feet barely touched before he dropped again, onto another branch, and another, and another. Down, down, down he went in great, exciting controlled falls.

He'd reached so far down that he could see all the details of the garden below when his mother's call reached him, "Tamás, where are you?"

He was prepared for this. His harness had a carabeener attached. Even while saying, "Mom, I'm coming," he ordered the rope from his pack, threw the ends down so the rope's middle snagged the branch he stood on, and within a couple of clicklets he was abseiling down, feet rhythmically pushing off the trunk.

The subterfuge proved to be unnecessary, because he couldn't see her yet. The balloon was almost at ground level and still descending. Tamás landed. As soon as his feet touched the ground, he jumped into a horizontal posture and flew around the chestnut tree. Using its bulk to shield him, he went to his blackberry tangle, stood and feverishly stripped off his gear. He thought an order at the computer, commanding it to retrieve the rope.

"Tamás?"

"Coming." Fastening his kilt around his waist, he walked out into the open, toward the balloon.

The tether was already down, and the bridge was lowering his mother.

"Oh, darling, I've had a harrowing meeting," she said. She looked exhausted, and Tamás felt a pang of guilt at his plans, at his need to do something that was sure to hurt her.

They had lunch together, then spent the rest of the day working in the garden. Tamás was pleased to see the lines of tiredness and stress disappear from her face.

That night, lying on his bed in the balloon, Tamás asked, "Artif, how far away is the transport balloon from Kiril?"

"Still another day. I wish you'd tell your mother about it."

"She'd stop me. Artif, I've got to do this. If she wasn't so restrictive, I could do it openly. Listen, drop the camp in that little valley on Skagskorg Island, you know, the one with the wild raspberries we picked last autumn?"

"I have the reference." Tamás could hear her sadness, but she was bound to carry out his wishes.

⚮ 10 ⚮

Flora

She opened her eyes to the pleasant dimness of her bedroom. *I wonder what the time is,* she thought.

Artif answered, "Fourth period fifty clicks, love, just after seven in the morning in your terms." The wonderful, deep voice didn't come from a particular location, but somehow it was everywhere.

Flora sat up with a little shriek. "Artif, Artif, I... is it...?"

"Yes, Flora. I'm within you. Welcome to Humanity. Now you're one of my children."

And suddenly Flora was terrified. "Artif," she asked, "the cancer?"

"I'm looking, dear." A long silence followed, then Artif said, sadly and very gently, "The main growth in your breast will have to be cut out. There is no way around that, unless you want to hand on. Even then, you mightn't have the time to wait out a pregnancy. And I've found seventeen other places where the cancer has taken hold."

Strangely, knowing this, having been given a death sentence, was better than the not-knowing, than the hope against despair that had ruled her until now. "So, I'll die?" she asked.

"My dear, all who are born will die. You can choose to go now, or you can choose to fight it. There are things we can do."

"Tell me."

"I can operate. We have microsurgery techniques that minimize pain and speed recovery. Right now, I am adjusting your immune system to help. And since your awakening, I've studied Tony's records. I can't get any radioactive materials, but I have the chemicals ready for your treatment, should you want to use them."

Flora had to laugh, though she cried at the same time, the situation was so ludicrous. "You mean, I left my times, became a living fossil, just so you could apply the techniques I tried to run away from?"

"My dear, they're the best available. Advanced cancer simply hasn't occurred for over a thousand years."

Flora thought, then said, "Artif, I want to live a little longer. I... I've made friends, and I want to find out more about your world, and learn to send images, and... please, I'll face the pain. Help me to live."

"I anticipated this. There is no time to lose. Everything else needs to be put off. I've notified your friends. You'll now go to sleep, my dear. When you wake up, I'll have a morphine-like drug going into you. The largest tumors will have been cut out. When the wounds have healed, you can start on the chemical treatment that's designed to kill the remainder. In the meantime, I'll do my best to stop the problem from spreading and multiplying."

Darkness enfolded Flora.

Tamás

Composing the message to his mother was certainly the hardest thing he'd ever done in his nearly thirteen years of life. She was down in the garden, safely busy, while he tried, and tried, and tried again. *I wish Chia and Kiril didn't know about it,* he thought miserably. If he backed out now, that'd prove after all that he was just a boy with big dreams, and they'd patronizingly smile to themselves. Even so...

I've decided. I've set myself on a course. I couldn't turn back, even if no one else knew about it.

He sighed deeply, then played the recording through to himself. It'd have to do.

The balloon started descending. He heard the faint hum of the motors as they pumped air into the many lift compartments, the hiss of air being compressed. Obviously, his mother was calling the balloon down. He hid the message globe.

Artif asked, "Tamás, will you see Kiril Lander?"

"Of course."

Kiril's house rode on a long, regular swell. As Tamás stood in the lounge room, momentarily he looked out the window along an endless valley with a mountain of water on each side. But already the stern rose to the next wave as it overtook the house.

Kiril stood in Tamás's room and asked, "Are you still determined to go through with it?"

"I feel I must."

"I know how you feel. Tamás, I have a favor to ask of you."

"Go on." Kiril's house twisted with a corkscrew motion, then leveled out. Both of them staggered. Tamás steadied himself with a hand on a wall.

"I've been tried at a Control meeting. I... I was going to hand on, or perhaps go even quicker, but... it was your mother who pointed out that I have no right to do that. I need to stay alive. It's the most fitting punishment for what I've done."

Tamás felt his house come to a stop, then start to rise again. The wall against his hand grew cool as air was evacuated on the other side. "Kiril," he interrupted, "my mother could be here any clicklet. I don't think she..."

The door slid open and Mirabelle walked in. "Tamás... oh Kiril, what are you doing here?" Kiril's image disappeared. Way out at sea, Tamás quickly said, "I'll talk to you later," then he also broke connection.

"What was that man doing here?" Mirabelle asked.

"He and I have become friends. I met him at Chia's house when he brought his bed."

"Tamás, he is unstable. He is on the edge, you just don't know what he'll do. He actually shouted and raved at the Control meeting!"

"He's had a lot to bear lately."

"He may feel bad now. But he snapped once and did a terrible thing. No amount of provocation justifies violence. If he snapped once, he can do it again. Stay away from him."

Tamás felt his lips compress into a straight line. He glared at his mother. Then he took a deep breath, and managed to say without shouting, "He is my friend. He needs support, and there is no one else to give it to him."

Mirabelle held her head in her hands, then raised her arms high. "Who'd have children?" she asked rhetorically, spun around and went out of his sight.

Dinner was a glum affair. Instead of the usual chat, or the friendly silence of two people with no need to say anything, they ate in a tense, wordless duel. When they were finished, Mirabelle stood and stalked off to her study. Tamás thought, *Soon I'll be gone. I may be away for as long as a year. And a quest earns you credentials only because it's dangerous. I could die, without ever seeing her again.*

So he went after her, and asked outside the door, "Mom, may I come in?"

The door slid open. Tamás walked though, and with a little wordless cry ran to her and hugged her around the waist. His head came to just above her breasts, and he buried his face against the soft brown skin of her shoulder.

Her arms went around him and he felt her kiss the top of his head. "Oh Tamás," she said softly, "the trouble is, we're so similar!"

"I'm sorry I was angry and resentful."

"And I'm proud that you're loyal to your friends."

He pulled away and looked up into her blue eyes. "Mom, whatever happens, just remember, I love you."

She laughed. "What is likely to happen, darling?"

He was tempted, very tempted to tell her. Oh, it would have been so easy to tell her! But all he said was, "You never know what the future holds."

She smiled down at his serious face. "Sometimes, I don't believe you're only twelve years old. All right, love. Thank you for coming and making peace. Now I need to go and visit Flora Fielding. She's had surgery, and Artif told me she is regaining consciousness. I want to be there for her."

Tamás felt like a traitor as, back in his room, he called, "Kiril!"

It was night already out here, somewhere in the middle of the Atlantic Ocean. Kiril said, "Thank you for returning the call." He looked out of Tamás's window, way up high, at the red ball of the setting sun. "Tamás, as I said before, I want to ask a favor. When you go, can I please come with you?"

Tamás wanted to say no. This was going to be his deed of daring, going around the world by himself. But he looked at the tall man's pleading face, at the sorrow in the dark eyes, and instead asked, "Why?"

"As I understand, you want to do it without contact, cut off from others. I... I need to do exactly the same. I must sunder myself from humanity, yes, leave even the people I love, and immerse myself in some new ordeal. And, and, well, I respect you. You may be a boy in years, but you've shown more maturity than I have! You'll be terribly lonely out there, day after day, facing the elements, the dangers of the journey, and more than anything the boredom, the deadly sameness that saps your will and your vigilance so that when danger strikes you're not ready. I know, for this quest is not too different from mine when I was eighteen. And, Tamás, having me along will in no way diminish the credentials you'll earn. You'll still be the first person to do it, and certainly the youngest."

Tamás held out his right hand. Kiril grasped it in his, and they sealed their partnership.

Timmy

He looked out the window. It was still dark over the sea, but a beam of sunlight stabbed through the clouds, past the house, and cast a spot of brightness on a small part of the garden. Tim sat up. Ria still slept in the bed against the far wall.

Dad suddenly stood in the middle of the room. He strode over and sat on the edge of Tim's bed. "My darling son," he said. Tim squirmed out from under the covers and snuggled onto his lap. He felt safe and happy in the strong embrace. But then Dad said, softly and sadly, "My dear, I won't be visiting for a long time. People will be saying strange things about me. But just remember, I'll be all right. I love you, and I'll come back. But it'll be a long time."

Ria sat up. "Kiril?" she asked.

Leaving his right arm around Tim's shoulder, Dad held out the other one in invitation. Ria jumped out of bed and ran over. Tim made room for her.

"I heard that," she said. "Why will you stay away?"

"I must. I'm starting on a quest, and it's part of it that I won't be able to contact anyone. Not even the two of you and Mom. Someone else is involved, and I must go along with his needs."

"Who?" Tim asked, feeling a sudden stab of pain that some unknown person should be more important to Dad.

"I can't tell you. I can't tell you anything about it. But one day, it'll be over, then I'll come back again. And even if... even if I should die, please always remember me with kindness." He stopped, and said after a long silence, "Whatever others say."

Ria turned her face into Dad's shoulder, and started to cry. Tim couldn't help it, he cried too. Dad held the two of them, rocking backward and forward until at last both Tim and Ria ran out of tears. Then Dad said, very softly, "I want to remember the feel of your little bodies. The memory of this will keep me going, for a long time."

He gave them a gentle squeeze, then eased them onto the bed. He stood up. "I must say goodbye to Mom too."

And he was gone.

Mirabelle

She felt a vague uneasiness. Something was not right, somehow... Tamás had been preoccupied at breakfast, seemed hardly to listen as she talked about her plans for the day. Instead, she caught him repeatedly looking at her with his dark brown eyes big and sad. And he kept hugging her at odd moments.

She was in the hothouse, digging up a couple of yams for tonight's dinner. She called his name, but got no answer. "Artif, is Tamás all right?" she asked in alarm.

"He is. But he asked me to tell you when you wanted to contact him, that he had to go away. He's left a message on your bed."

"What?" She stood and rushed outside, even forgetting to order the door to shut behind herself. She called the balloon down. It took forever, and then the bridge seemed half its usual speed. At last, she reached her room. And there it was, the fist-sized cloudy globe, resting on her pillow.

She activated it.

Tamás stood in front of her. Tears were running down his face. "This is goodbye, Mom," he said. "I will be back, one day. I know I will be back. I must do something, and I know you'd stop me if I told you. I know I'm causing you pain, and I feel terrible about this. But, Mom, I have no choice. Please forgive me. And when you think of me, don't think of me with anger. I love you." The recording stopped. The image of her son stood there, arms by his side, motionless. She returned to the start and listened, all over again. Then, treating the little globe as the most precious treasure, she put it down before she collapsed across the bed and sobbed like a child.

Oh, Tony protect you, my love, she thought. But Tony hadn't protected the other loves she'd lost, and the world Tony had created was made so that men had to risk themselves, time and again, and invite pain and death. *But he's only a child!* she thought, knowing that this mattered not a whit, that, regardless of age, he had to risk himself, and if he survived this deed, there'd be another, and even middle age hadn't protected her Hector.

After a long time, she sat up, wiped her face and called, "Abel?"

He was there with her. She didn't bother to send an image, just faced him in her own domain. "Abel," she asked, "do you know what Tamás is up to?"

He looked surprised. "As far as I know, he's with you." Wordlessly, she activated the boy's message.

Abel watched and listened, to the end. "He's gone off on a quest."

"Yes, but there's something else. Yesterday, that Kiril fellow was visiting him!"

Now Abel looked worried, too. "Kiril? I don't like that. It's like living on a volcano. If you hadn't tried to cosset him..."

"Shut up!" she screamed, then more calmly, "This is no time for recriminations. We have a situation, and must deal with it."

Abel actually took a step backward, looking startled at her explosion, then nodded. "I'm sorry. You're right. Artif, can you tell me what Tamás is doing?"

"I am sorry, no. Tamás has asked for absolute privacy, and he is a young man on a quest. He has that right, regardless of age."

Abel sighed, looking as helpless as Mirabelle felt. "He does. Drat."

Mirabelle and Abel gazed at each other for a long moment, and then they were in each other's arms, for the first time in their lives. Never before had they been allies in a common cause, but now, each needed the comfort only the other could give.

Tonya

The endless ocean rolled on below. Tonya was bored with it. She sprawled on her bed.

"Vladislav?" she called.

Her tall, muscular friend instantly appeared, his dark face shining with pleasure. "Wow, look at your view!" he said.

She stood beside him in a small clearing, the jungle rearing all around. The air felt still and hot. They were beside a plasteel-fenced enclosure that almost filled the clearing. Within, a hippo bull had his head in a pile of honeydew melons. He opened his great mouth, exposing large, square front teeth and wicked canines, and chomped on a melon. Juice ran out of his mouth as he contentedly chewed.

"I'm bored with the view," she answered. "Is he the bull you're going to ride?"

"Yeah. Meet Merv. Watch."

Vladislav's image suddenly sat on the bull's back as the two of them watched. Merv snorted, a loud, scary sound, and whipped his head back, mouth wide open. Vladislav pulled his leg out of the way barely in time, so that the frightful teeth clicked on air. The hippo continued his motion, dancing around in a circle remarkably fast, then stopped and swung the other way. Vladislav lost his hold and slid off into the mud. Merv grunted, his front feet came off the ground and he jumped. Vladislav desperately rolled to the side, the animal's hooves barely missing him. He sprung off the ground and his hands grasped the rails of the enclosure. But the hippopotamus moved fast, fast, all too fast, and his gaping mouth snapped shut on Vladislav's left leg, the lips meeting above the knees.

The image disappeared. Sweat drenched Vladislav's physical body. He was shaking and panting as if he'd just sprinted a couple of K. "How long was it?" he asked without words.

Artif answered, "Eighteen clicklets, love, but that doesn't matter. You'd have been killed." Within the enclosure, the bulky animal struck the plasteel bars of the wall a mighty blow with the side of his head. He continued grunting, gave a loud scream — then to Tonya's surprise, returned to his meal.

"I've got a long way to go," Vladislav said.

"Are you really going to ride him in the physical?"

"It's the only way to gain credentials from it!"

"I'll watch."

"I'll hold you to that promise."

That was when Tonya heard Artif ask, "Darling, can Tamás visit you?"

"All right." And the boy was with the two of them in Tonya's room.

"Hello, Tamás," she said, "I've just watched Vladislav practicing his bull riding."

"Thank you for seeing me," Tamás answered. "Vladislav, I need a few clicklets in private with Tonya. She'll come back to you soon. Now please, disconnect."

The big boy looked scornful and opened his mouth. Then he looked at Tamás's face, and to Tonya's surprise, he broke contact.

She also looked at Tamás. Somehow, something was different about him. Now what was it? He said, "Tonya, I am now on a quest. You won't see me for maybe a year. But I'm doing it for you. Remember me."

Then he was gone.

⚡ 11 ⚡

Flora

The world was a pulsing blur. A pale yellow surface approached and receded in waves. Flora knew that she was in pain, but it didn't hurt. The pain was a distant thing of no consequence, a mere background.

Artif said, her voice coming from everywhere at once, "Flora, the operation was a success." Flora wanted to say, "Oh good," but couldn't make a sound.

"I heard you, and so did Mirabelle," Artif told her. "Now you no longer need to speak aloud."

Mirabelle said, "Flora my dear, I'm here with you." That was when Flora realized that a warm, strong hand enclosed her left one. "Actually, love, this is the second time you awoke," Mirabelle continued. "Do you remember?"

It was odd — behind Mirabelle's loving, warm words Flora heard a second voice, also hers, saying a sort of a soft chant, something that sounded like, 'Thomas, Thomas, Thomas...' on and on.

"No," Flora thought, "I remember nothing about that."

"I was here then, too. I didn't want you to wake up alone."

"Thank you. You've been a wonderful friend, from the first day."

"I must go now," Mirabelle said, "I have an emergency to deal with at home."

She was gone, leaving an emptiness. Artif said, "Flora, I had to remove your entire right breast, and the lymph nodes in your armpit, and four other lymph nodes, and your spleen. I've modified your body chemistry so that the remaining growths will have calcium skins growing around them. That's only a temporary measure, because they can still grow and could burst out. Hopefully, that won't happen until we are ready to apply the chemical treatment."

"I... I feel strange," Flora thought.

"It's the effect of the pain relieving chemical. Now go back to sleep."

Abel

He strode from the bow to the stern, then back again, over and over, trying to think but doing no more than listening to the same futile thoughts cycle round and round, one after the other. "Artif, is he safe?" he asked yet again.

"Yes, love, he's safe," she answered. That was the only information she was allowed to give. *If only he wasn't with that madman*, Abel thought, was it for the thousandth time?

At last, he reached a decision. "Susan Lander?" he asked.

It was the middle of the night on South Calif, but Susan was awake. Last time Abel had seen Susan, she'd been an attractive, vibrant woman in early middle age. Now she looked old. Dark rings surrounded her bloodshot, swollen eyes, and her cheeks seemed to have fallen in. She sat on the edge of her bed, her room brightly lit. Her shoulders were stooped, and she stared at a point on the carpet.

A man stood over her. He was strongly built, but with the muscles overlaid with a padding of fat. His dark brown face wore the same look of helplessness as hers, reflecting the helplessness Abel felt himself.

"Greetings," Abel said.

"Hello, Abel," Susan answered. "Do you have any news?"

"No. I was hoping your son might have communicated with you, but I see..."

The man had turned to face him. "Abel, I'm Assam Martin," he interrupted. "I understand your son is with Kiril."

"We don't know, but that's what we suspect. And, Susan, I'm sorry to say this, but I don't trust Kiril. I don't know what he might do."

Susan said, with a little sob, "He's, oh, he's a decent person. He wouldn't hurt a boy."

"He tried to hurt Souda, and in the process injured one of my other sons."

"I know, but..."

"Susan, this is getting us nowhere. I want all of us who know either Kiril or Tamás to try and guess where they might be, what they're up to. I'm going crazy this way, I need to do something constructive. Mirabelle, can you come?"

She was instantly with them, hollow-eyed. Abel saw with approval that she held the little message globe in her hand.

"Souda?" he called.

Artif said, "She's asleep, dear. She hasn't slept for ages, but at last..."

"Artif, she'll want to be here," Susan interrupted.

Assam nodded.

"Very well."

They waited in silence for maybe two clicks, an empty eternity, before Souda was also with them. She wore the same loose white top and gray skirt as at the Control meeting. Her golden hair was tousled. She looked ill. "Here I am," she said tonelessly. "What's going on?"

Susan dragged herself to her feet and gave the girl a hug. "Kiril's gone off on some quest, and has requested absolute privacy."

"Good. So, what's all the fuss?"

Abel said, "He's taken my twelve-year-old son with him. And neither of them is communicating."

"Oh. Forgive me, I'm not fully awake, I can't take it in. Where have they gone?"

Assam told her, "No one knows. Kiril came and said good-bye to Susan and the children, said he'd be gone for a long time, maybe a year, and implied that there was danger. For the rest, no one knows."

"Did the boy go willingly?"

"Here is a recording from him," Mirabelle offered, and activated the little globe. They all watched and listened in silence.

"How do you know the two of them are together?" Souda asked.

"We don't even know that for sure," Mirabelle said. "I surprised Kiril visiting my son, and they were both very furtive about it. Kiril broke contact immediately rather than as much as greet me. Tamás got very defensive and would tell me nothing."

Susan added, "And Kiril told the children that he was going with another person who needed absolute privacy."

Souda looked around. "I see. And of course if he had hidden ideas, it might have been him who wanted absolute privacy, just pretending it was the other person."

"Artif wouldn't let him intentionally hurt someone else," Abel said, "She'd be duty bound to warn us."

"Now look," Souda said slowly, "I've heard, Mirabelle, you were the one who stopped him from killing himself. He could be resenting that. He does tend to brood. And Abel, I... I used you in my misguided scheme, and you're the one who leaned on him, trying to help. And this boy is the child of the two of you. I'm afraid... I don't know what I'm afraid of, but I'm afraid." She actually shuddered, and everyone caught her mood.

"Souda," Abel asked, "you probably know Kiril better than anyone else, even Susan. Can you guess what they're doing, where are they, what is he likely to do to Tamás?"

"I am sure he means the boy no harm," she said with conviction. "He may be using him to get at Mirabelle and Abel, but he is a decent person. He'll do his best to look after the boy. Where and what, I have absolutely no idea, but it's bound to be dangerous."

Tamás

I'm flying! I'm a bird! he thought as he followed the winding course of the fiord. He glanced down upon his reflection in the mirror-still, blue water. The upward facing, horizontal boy grinned back at him. Tamás held his arms out to the side and flapped them, and the boy beneath the water did the same. With a slight movement of his head, he could see the large globe following his reflection. It was handy, not having to turn around and yet being able to check on the camp.

The mountains of Norway rose sheer out of the water. Not a breath of wind stirred the leaves of thick forest, a hundred meters to his left. The other side was perhaps two hundred meters away.

"Kiril?" he called.

Kiril's house swooped up a wave, pitching and yawing. He turned to face Tamás. "You'll forgive me for not sending a return image?" he asked with a grin.

"You can come, if you like a swim in icy water."

"How fast are you moving?" That was something they hadn't been able to work out in advance.

"Artif?" Tamás asked.

"One point seven-two Ks per click."

The fiord veered slightly to the right, and widened. Tamás stayed parallel to the left shore. The water now moved to a slight swell, long, spread-out wrinkles traveling toward him.

"Where are you?" he asked Kiril.

"At my current rate, probably a day's sailing south-west of you. It's been a wild ride since I've left America."

"There's hardly a breeze here."

Artif interrupted, "The wind will hit you, almost head on, once you reach the open sea."

"Thank you. And Artif, is there any person between me and the sea?"

"No, Tamás. I've told you."

"And... and what's my mother doing?"

"She is distressed, and worrying about you. What did you expect? She is now sitting with Flora Fielding, but can hardly concentrate."

"Oh..."

The waterway swept around to the left. A deep roar thundered at him, growing in volume every clicklet until he was deafened and his very being vibrated to the sound. He cut off contact with Kiril, needing to concentrate.

A long spit of land cut across the fiord, leaving a narrow gap to Tamás's left. He rushed toward bare gray rock, and felt the computer tilt him up. He soared over the bar at a set height of five meters, then swooped down over turbulent surf on the other side. Even at this height, the boiling foam spat at him, wetting him with a fine spray.

Then he got through broken water, over a vista of endless rollers. The last green hills of Norway fell away behind him.

"Steer more to the left," Artif commanded. "That's it. The two of you are in direct line now."

A steady, powerful wind blew its salty breath onto Tamás's right cheek. He felt his body rhythmically rise and lower as the waves passed under him, and when he glanced behind, he saw that the camp fell further back, continuing to slip downwind. He sent a command to the camp's computer, but noted that its motor already worked at full strength. There was no choice — he slowed down.

Now, the up and down movement became more pronounced. No reflection could be seen below, because the huge waves were background to smaller ones of all sizes, even mere ripples, running away from the wind. Tamás looked up. A speck hovered, far in the distance. The next time the boy rose over a wave, the speck was closer. Then it appeared as a tiny cross, and five or six waves later it visibly became a bird, approaching fast.

I hope she doesn't attack me, he thought in alarm, watching. It was a huge bird, its wingspread wider than the length of his body. It swooped down in a smooth curve, then flew parallel to him, ten meters away. A still, white-rimmed blue eye calmly inspected Tamás, then the bird dropped back and shadowed the large ball that was the camp.

The bird made a shrill, loud noise and rose effortlessly, without as much as flapping a wing. Tamás felt honored, welcomed into the community of the air. He said, "Kiril, I had to slow because the camp catches the wind." He sent an image to Kiril again.

"Of course! I should have thought of that." Kiril looked annoyed.

"Can we make it into a different shape?"

"I've got the other one here. I'll get to work on it, straight away. Tell you what. Leave your camp to Artif, and come at full speed. You won't need it before we meet. Artif, you'll steer it all right, won't you?"

"Naturally."

So, Tamás speeded up again, and this was actually more comfortable, the computer being able to average out rises and drops to some extent. The big globe soon became lost out of sight, somewhere behind him.

He flew on, above unchanging seascape. He started to get cold despite three layers of warm clothing: the ceaseless wind steadily sucked the warmth out of his body. He decided to exercise. At first, he made vigorous movements of arms and legs, but this upset the computer, which dropped and raised him in response. Then he remembered something his father had once told him, and used isometric exercises. He stiffened his abdomen and held it hard for a click, as measured by Artif. Then he bunched his buttocks for the same length of time, then his thighs, gradually working his way around his body. Not only did this warm him, but also it helped the time to pass.

He got tired of this activity, and flipped over, face up to the scudding clouds above. The sun was well away to the south-west, indicating the time to be late afternoon. A pale blue sky showed in jagged, ever-changing patches between clouds of gray and black. After a while, Tamás closed his eyes.

He awoke to darkness. At first, he was completely disoriented, without the slightest idea of where he was. He felt frozen. When he realized that he still flew over the ocean, he was surprised that he felt no stiffness, but the EGM motor had held him comfortably. He turned face down, looking at the slight luminosity of the sea, and once more went through a long session of isometric exercises. As before, this helped to warm him.

He was clenching his jaws together and pressing his tongue hard against the roof of his mouth when Kiril called, "Tamás, can you see my lights yet?"

He commanded the motor to move him into an upright posture, so now he was scooting with his waist five meters above the dark waves. For fun, he made running movements with his legs while his eyes hungrily swept the horizon, from ahead to the far right, then back again to the far left.

A long distance away, almost dead ahead, a little pencil of light stabbed up at the clouds. "Kiril, yes, I can see you!" he shouted aloud.

Nathaniel

He stood, smiling down on Daru's sleeping form. She was naked, lying on her back, right knee flexed, with her arms thrown wildly apart. This made her pink-tipped breasts stand up nicely.

He bent and pressed his nose into the end of her split, into the cute bush of red pubic hair. At the same time, he sent a second image to softly kiss her lips. She wriggled in response, raised her hips and made a little purring sound, but continued to sleep. After all, they'd shared bodies three times on this visit, and anyway he didn't think he could raise it again. Still, you have to be just that bit more skilled at giving pleasure when you're little and ugly. And Daru was now in the top thousand on the List, and he had hopes.

He broke contact, withdrawing all his concentration into his body. He was lying on his own bed, in the land house outside the tunnel that led to the Library. He sat up and ordered a meal. Sharing bodies always made him ravenous. After two big bowls of horse and vegetable stew and a drink of kalibor juice, he lay down again, intending to go to sleep himself.

After twenty or thirty clicks he still lay there, awake. *I'll see how Flora is*, he decided.

Artif had placed her back in the blue room, on the elevated bed. *Tony help us, she looks worse than when I first met her*, he thought, seeing her bloodless, fallen cheeks, a covering cloth hiding the limp form. Two flexible tubes carried fluid from the ceiling down to disappear under the sheet.

Nat called for a cushion and sat, on Flora's left side because he knew that the right one would be painful. He took hold of the lifeless hand that poked out from under the cover.

To his surprise, Flora's voice said, in his mind, "Nat, I'm so glad you came."

"I thought you were asleep," he said, not bothering to speak aloud.

"Artif has been experimenting with dosage. She is trying to get a level that'll keep the pain at bay without putting me to sleep."

"I wish there was something I could do to help."

Her hand stirred in his, and gave his fingers a squeeze.

"You're doing it. You know, it's funny. I've always been afraid of pain. That's why I had myself put to sleep, to get out of just this."

"You told me you... what was the word? invested in research on cancer. How did you come by such a lot of money?" He hoped that talking might take her mind off her pain.

"You know I was an actress. I went to Hollywood, and actually got a small part in a film. That was not easy — there were so many attractive young hopefuls. And then I caught the male lead's eye. He was a big star, everybody's idol. We got married — Nat, you do know these terms?"

"Yes darling, don't worry, I'll ask if you bring up something new."

"After that, I got some good roles just because I was his wife. And Nat, I was good at it, and I was beautiful then, and young..."

"You're beautiful now," he interrupted gallantly.

He was pleased to hear a laugh in her thought.

"Oh, you're incorrigible. Anyway, soon I was getting leading roles in my own right, and Stan got jealous."

"Like Kiril?"

She laughed a little, but ruefully. "No, the opposite. He felt jealous of my success, as if he was in my shadow. So, he continued to be loving and attentive in public, but in private we had these terrible arguments. And he deliberately hurt me, but cleverly, so he left no visible marks."

Nat felt utterly horrified by this. *Tony be thanked, such things are impossible now*, he thought, but did not interrupt her.

"So, I stopped sleeping with him. Sharing bodies. He got himself a mistress..."

"Explain, Flora."

"He habitually shared bodies with another woman, in secret. You know that was against the supposed rules of the time, though lots of people did it. But I didn't mind. I was glad to be left to get on with my life, with my career. I didn't enjoy sharing bodies all that much anyway. I stopped taking contraceptives..."

"Hmm?"

"Chemicals that prevent a woman from having a baby."

"Nowadays, Artif makes the internal adjustment. You have a baby when it's your turn, otherwise you have all the benefits of being a woman without monthly bleeding or the chance of pregnancy even if you share bodies physically. And of course that's rare."

"How convenient! Anyway, I stopped taking these things, they were a nuisance, made you fat, and there were health risks involved. And this was what Stan was waiting for. He raped me and got me pregnant."

"Raped?"

"Forced sharing of bodies."

This time, Nat couldn't hide his horror. "But..."

"Darling, it was all too common in my times. Still, I had my revenge: a scriptwriter who'd become a friend wrote a brilliant movie with a pregnant woman in the lead role. That was my second Oscar. Oh, that's like top credentials for movies. And after my daughter was born, and Stan kept up his violence, I set a trap for him. I had a video camera installed..."

"Please explain both words."

"Something to record sight and sound."

"Right."

"And I made a recording of him twisting my arm and holding his hand over my face until I went blue, and urinating over me, and that was the worst."

Her hand clutched his with surprising force, and her soundless voice was full of disgust.

"But this gave me a weapon. I've told you before, the media, that's newspapers, TV and the like, were very powerful. I threatened Stan that I'd release the recording to the media unless he did what I wanted. That would've destroyed his career, a fate worse than death to him."

"Good for you! What did you demand?"

"An uncontested divorce. Half of everything he had, and that was lots. And I also threatened him. If I found out that he mistreated any other woman, I'd release the recording anyway."

"Did he give in?"

"Nat, he was a coward. After this, my acting career bloomed, then I married again, a much older man. He was so wealthy that compared to him Stan and I had nothing. He made few sexual demands on me, and was kind. He just wanted me as a, I don't know, a decoration. The only thing I hated was that he stopped me from acting. Didn't want his wife to work. He had five children from previous marriages, but wasn't talking to any of them. And when he died, he left all his fortune to me, nothing to any of them."

"All that seems so foreign to me!"

"I'll have to explain the next bit too. Four of his children wanted to fight me for the money, like a trial at Control. You know, a decision about what the law says. I said publicly that I didn't want all the money, wanted to divide it into six equal parts. It was unfair, cutting his children out like that. But the youngest, David, wouldn't have it. We had this absolutely blazing argument, everybody shouting at everybody else. His eldest sister said that if he didn't want his share, we'd just cut it five ways instead of six and he could miss out. And so I screamed at her that yes, we'd cut it five ways, and leave her out. And David started to laugh, and said he'd accept his share on one condition: that I married him!"

"You loved him, I can hear it in your voice."

"Oh yes. I think he was my only love. We had three children, and I did my best movies then, in between the kids."

"Did you enjoy sharing bodies with him?"

"No man in my times would have asked a question like that. But, no, not particularly. I did it to please him, and he was my best friend, and we did many good things together. And then..."

Her voice was sad once more. "...one day, completely without warning he told me that our marriage was over, he didn't love me anymore but found his real true love."

Nat thought his heart would break, for her.

"I was forty-two years old then. David was thirty-eight, and he'd fallen in love with a girl of nineteen. Nat, until then I was defined by my looks: my face, my body, my way of moving and speaking. I gained my fame and fortune by what I looked like. And now, I lost my love because I didn't look as good as a teenager anymore.

"I was in the middle of filming, of making a movie, but I stopped, and never went back to it. For nearly a year, I was so depressed that my friends were worried I'd kill myself. But then I found a new game to play."

"What?"

"Making money grow. I had more money than I needed, but nothing to do with my life. Nat, in my world, money was power. There was a game, played mostly by men, where each tried to gain money at the expense of everyone else, and I joined in. I used an unfair weapon: the fact that I was a woman and therefore couldn't possibly be good at it. And I turned out to be as good at it as at acting. At fifty-two years of age, I was the fifteenth most wealthy person on earth.

"And then I got breast cancer. I'd ignored an annoying little lump for quite a while, putting it out of my mind, too scared to admit it. I told you, I've always been scared of pain. But one day, blood came from my nipple, and I couldn't ignore it anymore. And here I am."

Nat bent forward and kissed the hand he held. "Flora darling," he said, when you're over this, when you're up to it, I want to do something for you."

"What?"

"I want us to share bodies. You'll see that it can be wonderful. I'm very good at it."

"But I'm an old woman!"

He was too surprised to answer for a couple of clicklets. After all, Cynthia was over seventy, and he had other partners older than Flora. At last, he asked, "What has age got to do with it?

≈ 12 ≈

Flora

Flora had her right arm in a sling made of some glistening, silvery stuff. She sat on the edge of her bed, grasped a hovering steel rod with her left hand, and slowly stood.

"Stand there a moment, love," Artif commanded.

She did, taking a deep breath. It didn't particularly hurt.

"Right, Flora, I'll support you with the rod, and there'll be a cushion right behind you. Take a few steps."

After about six steps, Flora felt her knees shake, and sat. The rod lowered with her, still helping her to balance.

"Mirabelle wants to visit," Artif told her.

Flora glanced down at herself. A loose t-shirt hid her mutilated body. She wore a yellow skirt under it. "All right," she answered.

Her friend appeared in front of her, a smile on her face. "Oh wonderful, Flora. You're up!" Without speaking aloud, Flora said, "Welcome, Mirabelle. Have you heard about your son yet?"

The blonde woman looked sad and sighed. "No. But in a way that's good news. Artif would tell me immediately if he was... hurt."

"Artif," Flora asked, "How can you keep a secret like that, from a mother?"

"Darling, it's an edict from Tony. I'm governed by such things. Men must gain credentials, thereby earning the right to reproduce. It's what keeps the species vigorous. Men must face challenge and danger, or they become soft and degenerate."

"But a boy!"

"Tony said, 'A boy is a man before he is full grown.' Many men have done their most daring deeds long before their Maturity. Nathaniel is an example, but of course he felt a need to prove himself, being so small."

Mirabelle said, "Flora, I'm here because Evanor has made a copy of Kiril's bed for you, and the land vehicle is also ready, and he's bringing them to you by balloon. He'll be with you in the physical in a couple of periods!"

Flora heard Evanor ask, "Can I visit too, please?"

"I look terrible, but... all right."

He stood beside Mirabelle, and immediately put an arm around her waist. She snuggled against him.

"Actually, you look remarkably good considering what you've been through."

"The worst is to come," she told him sadly. "I've had it before. These chemicals make your hair fall out, and make you vomit all the time, and you get ulcers all over the place, and you become anemic and catch every disease going, and your skin becomes like paper and bruises from a hard look, and your eyes become bloodshot, ugh, it's horrible."

"Why?" Mirabelle asked, shuddering slightly.

Artif explained, "Cancer cells grow very fast. These chemicals work by attacking any fast-growing cell, which includes the lining of your mouth and alimentary tract, and the bone marrow cells that make red and white blood corpuscles, and so on. But actually, Flora, I may have good news for you. I haven't told you so far, not wanting to raise false hopes, but three men are trying to earn credentials by improving the chemical treatment, to protect you from the effects of the pre-Cataclysm drugs."

"Oh, wonderful. Who are they?"

"Abel sought them out. All three are well known for such work, and they're acting as a team." She paused for a few clicklets. "Here is Turan Abid."

A strange man stood next to Evanor. He was old, his back bent. His head was bald, but as if to make up for it, he had a long, bushy, snow-white beard. He wore a blue and gray checkered kilt. "Greetings," he said. "I won't bother you with my various credentials, they were a long time ago, but it's sufficient to say that they were very impressive. The evidence is that I have five children. Now, I am the foremost biochemist on earth."

"I have certainly heard of you," Evanor said respectfully. Weren't you Arab champion weight lifter?"

"In my weight group, of course. I was fourth in the world."

"I have a friend who only recently broke your longstanding record for clean and press, that's how I know."

"Right, right, Wei Abdulla. But let us get to business. Madam, you're of course the famous Flora Fielding?"

"Yes. Welcome."

"Abel T'Dwuna himself asked me to improve the drug treatment for you. I'm glad to tell you, my team and I are in the testing stage. We first made the drugs specified in Tony's records, and they're ready for you. Then we analyzed their composition and made systematic modifications to the treatment, based on modern knowledge."

"And?" she asked hopefully.

"And we won't know if they're any good until the testing is finished. Actually, I am serving no useful purpose, being here."

"Oh yes you are!" Mirabelle said sternly. "You're here to give this person hope, should that be justified. Now please give a more appropriate report."

The old man looked at her, leaning forward even more to see past Evanor. "When such a lovely lady speaks, I must obey of course," he said, but it sounded like a formula speech to Flora, lacking in conviction.

"I'm Mirabelle Karlsen, a member of Control."

"Even so, what can I add? If the drugs are successful, they should work faster, with fewer unpleasant effects."

"When will you know?"

"Certainly not for at least five days."

Flora started to laugh, ignoring the pain this caused. Evanor joined in, and then Mirabelle too. Turan Abid stood there, looking puzzled. "I will never understand people. Chemicals are much more sensible." His image disappeared.

Kiril

They followed a by now well-established routine. As the sun rose behind them they ordered a hot breakfast, which the modified camp prepared for them, and they ate it without slowing. They did their isometric exercises. This now took up over two periods, more and more time as Tamás's muscles strengthened. Kiril always made sure to stop each exercise at the same time as the boy, though he surreptitiously did more at other times, without Tamás's knowledge. He was worried that otherwise he'd lose strength. As during his long-ago sailing trip, weakness induced by inactivity was a major danger.

On the second day, Kiril had taught chess to Tamás, and they played several games on a set projected by a small globe Kiril carried in his backpack. He now activated the globe and the ten by ten checkered board sprung into existence, moving along with the two of them. He positioned the white pieces on Tamás's side. The boy thought at the set, and his Tony's pawn advanced two squares.

Kiril copied the move, and had the boy in difficulties after ten moves. He won in another five.

"It's not fair, you always win," Tamás complained, but with a grin.

"I've been playing a little longer." Kiril went through the game, move by move, explaining, and showing various possibilities.

They had lunch after that, still on the move, swooping up and down five meters above the waves. Then it was time for a short stop. First Kiril ordered the camp down onto the surface and opened the big dish antenna. They hovered well clear while the power pack was recharged, the force of the energy beam pushing the silver ellipsoid nearly under the surface. Then they transferred energy to their backpacks, taking about twenty clicks to do so. After this, Kiril called down another charge to top up the camp.

Now they enjoyed their daily swim. They landed on the flattish top of the camp and stripped. Tamás was a good little swimmer. After half a period, they had washed off the grime of the day, enjoyed the aerobic exercise they both missed, and had a lot of fun.

Back on top of the camp, they used cloths moistened with precious fresh water to remove the salt, then dressed in clean clothes.

They'd had a scare the day before yesterday. As they swam side by side, a hundred meters or so north of the camp, the sonar sounded a warning in both their minds. At Kiril's insistence, each had his pack hovering above, and they grabbed at dangling straps and ordered the packs to pull them clear out of the water. Kiril was pleased to see the glint of excitement rather than fear in the boy's eyes as he swung over the heaving sea like a gymnast.

It was not a shark that came, but a school of porpoises. They stopped under the two dangling shapes, beaks pointing up, intelligent eyes examining them. Kiril remembered the dolphins of the Pacific, and without hesitation dived in among the marine mammals. They swirled around him, obviously careful to do him no harm, and soon he was riding a smooth, muscular shape.

It took the boy a clicklet to decide to join him, and they spent a couple of periods with their new friends.

Then the largest porpoise whistled sharply. Each animal rubbed against one of them, gently, and they swum off at a great rate.

Afterward, back in the air, Tamás said, "Kiril, I feel really honored. Now I've been accepted into the community of the sea as well as the community of the air."

Today, they had no visitors, friendly or otherwise. Tired but feeling good after their swim, they flew on. In late afternoon, they once more did their isometrics. As the sun got ahead of them, they turned on their backs to keep the glare out of their eyes. At Artif's insistence, Tamás had a couple of periods of education. Kiril listened in, this being far better than allowing his thoughts to run free. It was wonderful, having a companion to distract him from his guilt and sorrow.

They flew on steadily into the darkness. The boy had fallen asleep when Artif said, "My dears, there is a storm to the south of you. I thought it'd miss you, but it's swinging north and picking up energy."

Kiril stopped the camp and ordered it down into the sea. He called down a charge. While their packs were recharging, they put on waterproof clothing: trousers with built-in foot coverings, and tops that only left the face exposed. When the packs were full, they hovered clear and recharged the camp, then, for the first time on the journey, they tied on. Each of them had a ten meter long rope joining him to the camp.

Artif was right: the sea already started to rise as they took off. "Let's swing away from it a little," Kiril suggested, and they flew due west instead of the south-west of their plans. While waiting for the storm to catch them, Kiril sent an image to check on his house. He had a communication globe there, just for this purpose. The house was where Kiril's image had sailed it, days ago at the start of the trip, while he'd been flying beside Tamás: well up a Norwegian fiord, tethered to both shores. Kiril made sure everything was secure, retracted the masts and closed all the watertight openings.

"The wind is picking up," Tamás said, sounding excited.

The waves formed a mad jumble under them, the steady, long rollers from the west being assaulted by the children of the storm, striking them almost at right angles. The computers smoothed out a little of the mad plunging, but despite this Kiril felt himself lifted and dropped, thrown unpredictably in every direction, pulled away from the camp and then hurled toward it. "Now you'll earn your credentials!" he said to the boy.

"I'm going to be sick," came Tamás's anguished thought. Kiril did a one-way merge for a clicklet, but decided that he'd be all right, needed no help. He just allowed Tamás to live through the misery of motion sickness, knowing from long experience that this was the quickest way to become immune to it.

When the storm struck, the wind came from behind them, not from the left as Kiril had expected. By then, the force of their conflict tore the tops of the waves below to shreds, and the breeze had freshened into a sharp, cooling wind. But now, a howling roar rushed toward them from the east, and a vicious blow struck Kiril's back, pushing him down almost into the boiling surface. The motors fought the wind, and gradually the three linked shapes again clawed up to five meters. Even there, an unceasing barrage of salty spray drenched them, so thick that Kiril had difficulty breathing.

He again checked on the boy. Tamás was no longer vomiting, though he had a headache and was dizzy. "I'm OK," he told Kiril. He held a hand in front of his mouth, this enabling him to breathe mostly air.

Good idea, Kiril thought, and copied him.

The wind swung sharply and without warning, now battering them from the north-west, half ahead to the right, and the rain came with it. An icy deluge from above joined the icy deluge from below in drenching them. The weight of water momentarily joined to his body was enough to make Kiril plummet down toward the hungry peak of the mighty wave below him.

"Form a ball!" Tamás shouted within his mind.

They swooped down into a great valley between steep-sided mountains of water, and the wind pressure eased, though the rain still enfolded them in its warmth-sapping, heavy embrace. As Kiril made his body into a ball, sheltering his head from above, he felt a downward tug from the tether. The flat top of the camp held a lot of water, and the motor couldn't cope.

The next wave raised them high again, and the gale struck anew with savage fury, shoving them down hard into the next trough. Kiril sent an order to the camp, flipping it upside down. With relief he felt the pressure of the tether ease.

"How long will this go on?" he heard Tamás ask Artif as once again they were tossed about by the wind.

"At least a day," she answered. "And the worst is still coming."

"It's all right, Tamás," Kiril said, "the storms of the Pacific are much worse. And we may get hit by a hurricane some time."

The boy actually managed a chuckle.

Abel

Life held no joy. He couldn't settle to his administrative work. For once, the planet could run itself and he didn't care. *Oh, I wish he hadn't gone off with that madman... I must stop going around in circles like this.* He wandered around his house aimlessly, from the brilliant sunshine up on the top deck to the dimness of his bedroom, without noticing any of it.

He just had to do something. He flopped down on the bed and called, "Tony?"

He was in the sacred Cave, one of only twenty people allowed to visit without invitation. Tony sat in his wheelchair, looking at him, the asymmetric face sad. "You know I can't help you," he said.

"You made the rules. Can't you bend them?"

"Abel, Abel, that's not like you. A rule is for all, for the benefit of humanity. Anyway, what you said is not quite right. Tony in the physical made the rules. I'm only a computer program, after all."

"You're the embodiment of Tony's personality. You actually know more than he ever did: you have access to information he lacked."

"And I cannot vary his edicts. If I could, I wouldn't vary this one."

Abel smiled, ruefully. "And I know that. If the situation was reversed, I'd say the same. But..."

"You're welcome to sit, Abel."

He sat. "Tony, I might as well do something to distract myself. Is there anything in the old records that might help me to understand the situation, to help me to cope better?"

"Certainly."

A hum sounded, and an ancient screen glowed blue. Abel ordered his chair over, and sat waiting, mind dead, while the machine went through its slow and awkward routine. Then he pushed buttons and called up the catalog.

The English words were mere marks to him, but his translator gave him the equivalents so fast it felt as if he was directly reading the ancient text. He didn't quite know what to look for, and spent a couple of periods blundering around. At last, he asked, "Tony, does 'forensic psychology' mean anything to you?"

"Not really. I think it has something to do with criminal law."

"Yeah, that's it then." Abel selected a title and started to read, a bit here, a bit there. Even then, his troubles weren't over: time and again, he came up against technical terms Tony couldn't explain. He'd probably have thought of using the "Dictionary of Psychology," but he certainly would never have found the "Dictionary of Jurisprudence" by himself.

That was a suggestion of Tony's. Using these two reference books, slowly and painfully, he at last managed to gather information.

Back on his house, he half-heartedly ate a meal, relieved himself, had a shower, still kept fidgeting. Even a difficult and engrossing activity like studying a completely unfamiliar subject was insufficient to occupy his whole attention.

After three periods of solid study, he had to stop. He found himself looking at the words on the screen, and heard the translation, and took none of it in.

He sat back and turned his chair around. Tony asked, "Right, what did you learn?"

He managed a twisted grin, then tiredly rubbed his eyes. "That there were all too many ways for people to hurt one another. I've found an entire section of study devoted to cases where a jealous man killed the woman he supposedly loved. And Tony, in a great many of these, the man ran away with the children of the relationship. There is even a term for it..."

"Kidnapping," Tony supplied.

"Yes. Almost always, if there were children, a major source of conflict was whether the mother or the father should care for them. Crazy. And sometimes the man took the children unlawfully, and disappeared with them. And in many cases in the records, he killed them. Killed his own children!" Abel shuddered in revulsion.

Tony gently said, "Abel, Tamás is not Kiril's child."

"No. No he isn't. But, but, Souda did mention that Kiril may feel that he has strong grounds for resenting both me and Mirabelle. These ancient crazies focused their hate and resentment on their woman, and punished her through the children. What if Kiril feels strongly, in some twisted way, that now Mirabelle and I are responsible for all his woes. Isn't that just the way a crazy person might think?"

"Abel, she also said that she was confident, Kiril wouldn't hurt the boy."

"She did. And she also said that she was afraid. And so am I, oh Tony, so am I."

Tamás

The storm had gone on forever. Nothing existed except the never-stopping waterfall from above mixed with the never-stopping fountain from below, the howling of the buffeting wind, the wild changes of motion as his motor carried him above the turbulent surface of the sea.

Tamás's head still hurt. His empty stomach still occasionally heaved. But the greatest discomfort was the need to empty his bowels. Before the storm, if there ever had been such a time, this was a routine task, but now...

If he opened the magnetic seam of the waterproof trousers, he'd be soaked in an instant. If he opened each of the three layers of clothing within, and actually got rid of his load, it could well be exactly when the unpredictable movements dropped him down, and he'd be smeared with feces, all over. He almost gagged at the thought.

So he held on, with more and more desperation, his head down almost level with his thighs so he could breathe, lurching around above the waves, a falling leaf caught in the storm.

Kiril spoke within his mind, on one of his periodic visits. His voice actually sounded cheerful: "Tamás, how goes it?"

He explained his problem.

Kiril laughed, "No worry, mate. Open up as usual. Sure, you'll get soaked, but after you re-close the waterproofs, the wet clothes will warm up. It's not a big issue, I've often worn wet things under waterproofs for several periods."

"But, but, it might smear all over me!"

"Yeah, the way we're moving that's a real risk. But listen, with all this water, it'll get washed off. Anyway, what's the alternative? Shit your pants without opening up?"

"You're right."

Kiril broke contact. Tamás ran a finger over the seam, and instantly his back became soaked from neck to toes. He opened each of the three trousers, and felt the icy assault of the sea-spray on his buttocks.

Just then, the motor snatched him upward, sweeping him up toward the top of a tremendous wave. Tamás pushed, and felt the blessed relief of losing his load in one explosive heave. Then he was plummeting again with a twist, way past the spot.

He shivered wildly, but happy with relief as he re-fastened his sodden trousers, then the waterproofs. And Kiril was right — after an unmeasured time, he warmed again. When learning about the history of his people, he'd found out about sauna baths. This must have been what they felt like.

"Thank you, Kiril," he said through the implant. "I was desperate, but you were right."

"The best way to face a problem is to just go ahead and do what must be done. I guess that's where experience comes in."

"Kiril, I'm so glad you came with me. I think, if I was alone. I'd be dead by now."

"Yeah, that thought did occur to me. Tamás, you're a great guy, but you're really too young to do this kind of thing alone."

"I agree — now."

"And that proves your maturity. And listen, it's not all one way. Being with you has made my days bearable. If I was alone, I'd be brooding and unhappy all the time. So, thank you, mate."

The storm went on and on, the wind hammering at them from different directions. But now it was no longer a torture, having once more become a challenge. Silently, but with perfect understanding, they flew on above the boiling sea, toward the west.

⚎ **13** ⚎

Flora

All her friends were with her. Abel wasn't, but then she didn't count him as a friend. He'd been charm personified on his one visit, but she had the feeling that to him she was merely a pawn in some game.

It was almost natural to see EGM force moving her bed out of her bedroom. Evanor guided in a large shape. Flora thought it looked like a slice of bread. It was much the same color too, and obviously made of the ubiquitous plasteel. It was larger than a double bed.

The shape settled nicely on the floor, where her bed had been. "Go on, Flora, try it out," Mirabelle said.

Flora felt dubious about this, and her hesitation must have shown on her face. Cynthia eagerly offered, "Look, I'll show you." She stepped — or more exactly, waddled — forward, and then her naked, black body smoothly rose into the air, assumed a horizontal position and slid over the shallow depression of the bed. She hovered there on her back, a look of ecstasy on her face. She closed her eyes and breathed deeply, her enormous breasts rising. "Oh, this is wonderful!" her voice said within Flora's mind.

Mirabelle said, "Hey Cynthia, don't go to sleep!" Everyone laughed.

Cynthia sat up, or got the bed to sit her up, Flora wasn't sure. "I've just got to have one of these!"

Evanor offered, "I'll make you one, Cynthia, just get off now."

"Imagine, sharing bodies on this!" The huge woman sensuously moved her hips. Flora tried not to be shocked. Everyone else laughed, and Nat had a gleam in his eyes. Cynthia slid to the edge of the bed, and then was standing. "Little man, you can be the first to try it with me. Oh, Evanor, my apologies. Unless you claim the right…"

He laughed easily. "I'm more than happy with Mirabelle, besides she needs my support right now."

The tall, blonde woman sighed, "Oh I sure do! I wouldn't know how to survive without Evanor at the moment."

"Come on, Flora, your turn," Cynthia urged.

Hesitantly, she stepped forward. "What do I do?"

"Tell it to make you lie down."

Flora looked at the flat, inanimate object, and feeling silly, said within her mind, "I want to lie down."

She couldn't help tensing herself all over her body as she rose into the air and tilted. This sent spasms of pain in half a dozen places, particularly under her right arm.

"Relax!" Artif commanded, and she managed to obey. All the pain disappeared, and she felt a fluid comfort. Once, in her old life, she'd had a swim in the Dead Sea, and the extremely salt water had made her body more buoyant than a cork. This was similar, but far more comfortable. Each part of her body was weightless, even the organs within, so that nothing pressed on anything else. After the pain and discomfort since her operation, this was bliss.

"Oh, thank you! Thank you!" she said without words.

"All right, love," Mirabelle said, "tell the bed to stand you up, but this time don't get all tense."

"Must I?"

There is still the land vehicle," Evanor offered.

Nat asked, "Artif, is Flora physically up to that?"

"Evanor can explain to you, since the land vehicle uses the same program as the bed, it can support Flora in the same way. Only, it's much smaller, and of course mobile."

They accompanied Flora outside, keeping with her slow, painful progress. This was the first time since her operation that Flora had gone out, and once more the glare and heat struck her like a blow. She recovered much faster than on that first occasion with Nat, and looked around. "Where is it?" she asked, expecting to see something resembling an automobile.

"Here," Evanor said, picking up something from the ground. But Flora had to look up first. An enormous silver shape hovered over her clearing, about sixty feet off the ground. It was shaped like the Zeppelin, of which she'd seen pictures, and was gently tugging at a silver tether.

"Is that a balloon?" she asked, then felt silly for asking the obvious. "It's huge!"

"Oh no," Mirabelle said, "that's a small one. "Evanor came in it in the physical so he could bring your toys. My house is over twice as large. You'll see when you visit."

Evanor seriously explained, "Much of the inside consists of the lift compartments. The load areas — living space, luggage, machinery — are 5.25% of the volume. It's designed so that when it is fully loaded, and the lift compartments completely pumped out, it rises to the stratosphere."

"I thought Tony mentioned helium balloons in that recording, Nat."

"That was pre-Cataclysm technology," Evanor said. "When people tried to implement Tony's directive, they had no source of helium. That's a byproduct of liquid hydrocarbon extraction, and all the old oil fields were lost in the Cataclysm. But then John van den Groot invented plasteel, in 297, and the first application was a vacuum balloon."

Flora looked at him. That number, was that a date?"

"Of course. But Flora, put on your land vehicle."

That made her laugh. Put on a car? The object in Evanor's hand was a small backpack, looking like the one Flora had worn during her first few years of elementary school. It was attached to a gauzy net, of the same material as Flora's bras, now modified to hold only her left breast.

Evanor explained, "I first made one that hung on a harness, and incorporated a control globe so you could think commands at it. But then your implant became effective, so you didn't need the control globe, and immediately after you had that operation. This'll be kinder to your body."

"Thank you. Now, I'll have to be able to put it on by myself."

Evanor placed the little pack into Flora's left hand. "Hold it against your chest," he said, "then tell it to wrap itself around you."

Flora did so, and couldn't help a little shriek of surprise as the netting did just that. "I'll never get used to things moving by themselves," she said. In the meantime, the pack smoothly slid around to be behind her.

"They don't. You send a command to the computer, it executes it, and activates a motor, that's all."

"Like you putting your foot on that pedal, whatever it's called, in a car," Nat added.

Evanor continued, "Now tell it you want a shell." His normally serious eyes held a glint.

Flora did so, and instantly she found herself standing inside a translucent silver cocoon, an ellipsoid like the great balloon above. The section in front of her was transparent, and as she turned her head, the transparency moved with her. As when on the bed, all internal pain had disappeared.

"Sit down, Flora," Mirabelle suggested.

There was nothing behind her bottom, but Flora gingerly lowered herself. Instantly, she felt as if she was sitting in the most comfortable, supporting armchair. The height of her shell reduced in proportion, staying about an arm's length from her in every direction except below, where it seemed to support her feet.

"And now," Evanor said, just tell it the direction to go, and it will. It can skim a finger's breadth above the ground, but then it'll need to joggle up and down to get over obstructions. Or you can fly along at any height up to five meters. And it will never bump into anything you see, because the computer is using your eyes to guide itself by. It compensates for winds, to some extent anyway. Have fun!"

Tamás

Will it ever end? he thought. His whole body ached, every muscle, every joint screaming with pain. He was a helpless ball on a string as the wind pummeled him on the top of each rise, as the tether jerked him around, as he was enveloped in rising surges of salty foam.

Kiril's voice sounded again, "Hey Tamás, look up!"

He flipped onto his back and uncurled his body. Rain no longer pelted down. The wind still blew a gale, but the droplets of water it hurled into his face were tiny.

He felt the punch of water from below, and white foam rose on each side of him, then he sideslipped into a valley. The drizzle on his face felt good. That was when he realized: it was no longer dark. The racing cloud layer above was black, but he could see the shifting shapes of its underside, and the tilted curtain woven from a myriad raindrops.

"I'm worried about our level of charge," Kiril said. "I was caught low once, and that was enough."

"Can we recharge in this?"

"I think so, but we'd better not untie or we're bound to get separated." A particularly vicious gust of wind struck them as they rose above a wave, and contact with Kiril stopped. Then they slid down into a valley again, the waves each side looking ready to bury them, and he continued, "I'll put the camp down, and we'll just have to endure a few dunkings. Get ready!"

Tamás turned face down once more, shielding his mouth and eyes with a hand. Even so, the foam again nearly drowned him as they rose over the broken top of the next wave. The camp lowered, turned the right way up, and was lost for a moment in the whitecap of the wave. It slid ahead of them down the next steep slope. Tamás made sure he was off to the side as a stalk grew out of the center of the camp and opened into the dish of the antenna. He fancied he could see a narrow beam of light strike through the clouds as the camp disappeared inside white water.

Then he had to concentrate. The tether gave him a savage jerk, and he was up to his hips in viciously turbulent water. He flew free as they descended into the next trough. The camp was still practically submerged, pushed under by the force of the charge. It bobbed up momentarily, and Tamás heard Artif say, "Kiril it's all right, I won't fry you, love."

Up into liquid hell, down into momentary relief, time and again and again, Tamás endured — somehow. At long last, he saw through salt-blurred eyes the antenna close and retract. The camp turned upside down and rose.

"Turn your back to the camp and open your antenna," Kiril commanded. "We'll charge while moving."

With the camp in the air again, they returned to the relative comfort of the previous torture. "Let's change direction to south-west again," Kiril said. Tamás had completely forgotten about direction. Once more, he was intensely grateful for the man's presence.

And as he emerged from the next spray of broken water, his eyes saw a wonderful sight: a line of pale blue, on the horizon far ahead.

Kiril answered his mental shout of joy with, "Yeah, we're nearly through it. In the Pacific, I was caught in a storm for five days and six nights."

"How could you survive that?"

Kiril laughed, "One moment at a time. I didn't even have weather watch, so I had no idea if it'd ever end."

"But, but Artif..."

"Artif was with me for company, how could I do without that? But her instructions were to give me no modern help. I wanted to do it the same way as the ancient sailors used to."

The wind veered, for the thousandth time, now hitting them from the left. They sideslipped into a trough. Tamás suggested, "Hey Kiril, can we stay in a trough for a while, then skip across, sort of dog-legging?"

"All right. Artif, please keep us on course overall."

"Certainly, dear."

After this, they scooted along in relative comfort for perhaps twenty clicks, then spent a similar time being savagely buffeted while crossing the waves to another endless valley. And gradually, almost imperceptibly, the wind felt less strong when they emerged, and less gusty. The storm was passing them by at last.

Evanor

Evanor didn't mind discomfort, so the small, cramped quarters of the transport balloon were perfectly satisfactory to him. However, Mirabelle hated it, and preferred to keep her consciousness entirely at her home.

They lay side by side on her bed. This was still an ordinary one. Evanor had constructed an EGM bed for her already, but right now it was making its way far above the Atlantic, in another transport.

"I'm so glad we've been able to ease Flora's pain," she said.

"Yes, you could see the agony smooth off her expression." He felt just as pleased as Mirabelle. "She has an extraordinarily lovely face."

"Yes. She was one of the noted beauties of her time. You know, from what she's told me, people expected her to be stupid because she was beautiful."

Evanor laughed at that. "My experience is that beauty and intelligence go together. Look at you."

"Go away with you! Hey, Evanor, I wonder how she is doing with the land vehicle."

"I'll check." His physical self stood and looked out through the balloon's transparent side. "She's got it on, shell firmly in place, and is making slow circles in the clearing."

"Why don't you put on yours and fly with her?"

"We can merge, then you can come, too."

Evanor enjoyed the now familiar feel of Mirabelle's body from within even as he donned the harness of his vehicle. He asked, "Artif, can you please warn Flora that the balloon is coming down?" and sent a command to the balloon's computer as well.

Within a few clicklets, he was five meters off the ground, waiting and ready at the balloon's dilated exit hole. Looking, down, he saw Flora standing well to one side, near her favorite palm tree. She had deactivated the shell, and was craning her neck looking up at him. Her heart-shaped face showed no sign of pain, and was smiling.

Evanor activated the EGM motor and stepped out into space. He smoothly descended, to stand in front of the woman.

Flora said, "Oh, Evanor, I could never pluck up the courage to do that!"

He had to smile. "Honestly, Flora, there is no danger. I've even built in a fail-safe mechanism. If you instructed the computer to drop you without control, it wouldn't. You simply cannot crash while wearing this. The only way would be if you ran out of power, but you'd get plenty of advance warning of that."

"That's not the point. I'm simply not comfortable with heights."

That was incomprehensible to a retired hang gliding champion, but Mirabelle said within him, "Don't argue with her, love." So he said, "Flora, Mirabelle is here too. She and I are merged."

Flora actually looked around, her face asking, 'Where?' "Merged?" she said.

"Through the implant, I can sense everything she can, and the same the other way. Her consciousness is looking and hearing you through my body."

"Oh. How wonderful that must be for the two of you!"

"It is! Do you want to do a three-way merge? It's possible." Her light brown face went a deep pink. "I... I..."

But she must have given Artif permission, despite her embarrassment, because Evanor was suddenly aware of the large left breast and the missing right one, of the deep itch of healing lesions, of eyes slightly screwed up against glare that was comfortably bright light to him, of the stickiness of sweat in the normal afternoon warmth. He felt her surprise at the sensations of his own body, and that of Mirabelle, lying relaxed and with eyes closed on her bed, far away above the Swedish Isles, of her sadness upon encountering Mirabelle's ever-present background worry about her son.

Then Flora withdrew. "That was remarkable," she said. "Thank you, Evanor and Mirabelle."

He smiled at her. "Actually, I came down so we could take a trip somewhere together. You can go anywhere you like in your vehicle, and Artif won't let you get lost."

"Just being in it is heaven..."

Neither he nor Mirabelle knew that word, but he let it pass without a question.

"...somehow, the motor is relieving almost all the pain."

"Excellent. And I imagine that should speed healing. Artif, does it?"

"Certainly it does. I'm very pleased."

"Right, Flora, shall we go and explore?"

Her silver shell popped around her, then reduced in height as she sat. Evanor also adopted a sitting position. Where do you want to go?" he asked.

"I really don't care, as long as I've got this thing on."

"All right, come with me." He took off, toward the rising slope they happened to face. "We've got to give it a name, 'land vehicle' is so awkward."

"And not an accurate description. Looking at you flying through the air, sitting on nothing, I think of 'Angel's wings'."

They wove among a stand of trees, and he heard a little mental gasp from Flora as the trunks and overhanging low branches whizzed by. "What's an Angel?" he asked.

"Mythical creature. Oh, it doesn't really matter. Evanor, this is so wonderful!"

They were through the trees, in open space. Evanor stopped, hovering a meter off the ground, and enjoyed the vista facing them on the top of the little rise. "Flora, just get rid of your shell for a moment, but stay in the air." Mirabelle smiled within him, saying, "The engineer, always modifying."

Nothing changed for several clicklets, then the shell was gone. Flora hovered beside him, also sitting on nothing. She had her mouth open, half in fear, half in wonder. Her deep blue eyes shone in her face as she looked at him, then all around.

Evanor started to move forward, very slowly. "Come on," he said.

She came with him, and gradually, almost imperceptibly, he speeded up and increased elevation. Flora gave him a little-girl grin and matched him.

She was almost old enough to be his mother, but he felt as if he was a mother himself, teaching her child. Originally, he'd got involved as a way of passing time. Then he stayed because he wanted to please Mirabelle. Now, he was happy to do whatever he could for this lovely, unfortunate woman, for her own sake.

Kiril

The rollers were still mighty, marching mountains following each other endlessly, but they were now smooth, far apart, and predictable. The wind had dropped, and rags of pale blue peeked through the gray clouds above.

Kiril was very aware of the boy's exhaustion, so he said, "Hey Tamás, we should recharge. We never topped up the camp after we took charge for the packs."

They stopped, and he lowered the camp into the water. He then lay on his back in the air, rising and falling five meters above the waves. He spread out his arms, closed his eyes and sent a pretended snore to the boy.

Tamás laughed, and adopted a similar posture. When the camp was fully charged, Kiril unobtrusively checked. As he'd expected, his young friend was deeply asleep.

He commanded the camp to rise from the water, then activated all three motors without waking Tamás, and started a steady progress southwest. He went considerably slower than usual, and concentrated on smoothing out the boy's regular up and down movements.

The westering sun sank below the clouds, and painted the living surface of the sea red. For no reason at all, Kiril remembered the young woman at his father's project. Her hair was just this color.

The wind eased even more, and the temperature dropped. Kiril kept his eyes on the pattern of the coming waves, and it wasn't until he casually looked up that he realized that night had fallen.

Steadily they moved up and down, and progressed over the dark sea.

⚡ **14** ⚡

Flora

She was awake, lying on the wonderful bed. She felt no pain anywhere, but she could locate all the places where Artif had operated by the deep, continuous itch of healing. "Sit me up please," she thought at the bed. She still couldn't bring herself to issue gruff orders to anything that was able to listen to words, the way everyone else did.

She smoothly rose into a sitting position. "Come here, my Angel's wings," she called, then laughed aloud as the little backpack flew to her. She held it in place and told it to wrap itself around her.

Then she smoothly and painlessly flew off the bed, landing to stand beside it. "Oh Artif, it's wonderful," she said without speaking aloud.

"Yes it is, dear. I'm having lots of them made, and distributed to key locations, ready for the bull riding."

"Oh, for injured young men?"

"Yes."

"Artif, can I wear this thing in the shower?"

"There is nothing that water would hurt, and you could have it move around on you while you're standing, so that all of you is washed."

"Then let's do it!" Again, Flora laughed like a child. She flew to the bathroom, her feet skimming the ground, and manipulated the water by thinking at the equipment. She felt like a child at Christmas.

When she was dry, she flew back to the bed, and dressed upon its painless field. But Artif said, "There is one worry, Flora. You're now getting far less exercise than before. You might get very weak again. I suggest we return to your exercise straps, and you can do movements that don't involve any damaged muscles, but keep the rest strong."

"All right."

The two flexible bands came at her, dangling from their metal balls, but then stopped. Artif asked, "Flora, do you want to receive Abel?"

"Oh. He remembered my existence, has he? Well, all right."

The immensely tall, handsome black man stood just inside the door, wearing nothing but a skimpy white cloth around his waist. Flora had to hide her shock on seeing him: since his previous visit, Abel had turned into an old man. His eyes had bags under them, and the skin of his face sagged. His enormous shoulders were bowed forward, his spine bent. His black eyes were bloodshot, and when his voice sounded in her mind, it was a flat monotone, without his customary musical tones. "Greetings, Flora Fielding," he said.

"Greetings, Abel. What's wrong?"

"I haven't slept in many days. I can't eat. I can't do my proper work. All I can think of is my little son, on a quest somewhere, at the mercy of a madman."

"Sit down. Would you like a drink? Kalibor juice?" She thought at a cushion, and was still surprised when it floated to Abel, who flopped down onto it.

"No thanks. I've come for advice. That's all I do nowadays, ask advice from everyone. Tell me about kidnapping."

He was just too pathetic at the moment for Flora to harass him about anything else, but she had a brief internal flash of annoyance. Part of the "proper work" he'd been neglecting was the information he was supposed to give her: why had she been awakened in the first instance?

"Everybody tells me that Kiril won't hurt Tamás, and if he wanted to, Artif would stop him."

"No, that's not quite right. No one can possibly imagine any person intentionally hurting another. But if he has gone mad, who knows what he might do, despite lifelong training by Artif? And she has no power to stop anyone from doing anything. She can and does advise, and express disapproval. Also, she has the duty to warn and call for help. But you see, she could scream in everyone's being all over the planet, but what help would reach Tamás in time? They're together, Tony knows where."

"But, um... Artif, you know where they are, don't you?"

"Of course. I'm with them."

"If this Kiril had thoughts of harming the boy, you'd know?"

"I would."

She looked triumphantly at her visitor. "There you are, Abel. She'd warn you and disclose their location as soon as Kiril had any intention of hurting him."

"When he exploded last time, it was sudden and unpremeditated. I've been studying the records. Many of the ancient killers had the same pattern."

"Artif, can you tell us about Kiril's mental state?"

"Flora, as Abel well knows, I can't. Tamás has specified 'no information.' His quest requires that he knows nothing about anyone else, and that he is isolated. It's a thousand-year pattern."

Abel sighed. "Yeah, that's right. I was out of touch with everyone for over a year when I walked south to north all along the spine of Westrica. I finished three days after my seventeenth birthday."

"Abel, you mightn't want anything, but it's actually my meal time. Please eat with me." Flora sent a request to the kitchen, and heard Artif say to her within, "Good girl, that's what he needs."

But Abel just waved an impatient hand, "Food!" he said scornfully. "Flora, please tell me about kidnapping. I've studied the ones who took their own children away, but I want to understand the motivations of people who did such things."

"Yes, that was one type of situation, battles over the children. Probably the most common reason was money. You know what that was?"

"I think so. A common measure for things so that, in a world of shortages, there could be fair exchanges."

"That's not a bad first approximation, but it was more complex than that. Money was also a measure of success. Look, you have a great many children, haven't you?"

"Yes. Eighteen."

"And in everyone's eyes, that makes you better than a man with five?"

"I see. So, having more money was the same kind of measure?"

"Yes. Except here and now, there is a limit of one million people. If you have more children than others, you're depriving other men, but humanity as a whole doesn't suffer. But in my times, there was no limit to wealth, to the amount of money that could be generated. So, there were great imbalances. I personally controlled more resources than entire countries, with millions of people."

Abel nodded. "And there was no Artif then, which meant that many people did horrifying, sick things. Like kidnapping."

Two trays arrived, with hippopotamus steaks and an arrangement of vegetables. Without noticing it, Abel started to eat.

Flora continued as if there had been no interruption, "I used to have bodyguards. These were men, paid to protect me and my family. Without them, I might have been kidnapped, and when I had children, they were very vulnerable. In a way, being very rich was like being in prison."

She saw the look of incomprehension on his face. "Locked away, deprived of freedom. I was forced to move in a very restricted circle, that of other very rich people. Any stranger simply had to be treated as a potential predator, after my money in one way or another."

Abel had cleared his plate and sucked his cup dry of kalibor juice, though Flora had hardly started on her meal. She privately ordered another meal for him.

"It sounds to me like everyone was striving and fighting for something that wasn't worth a lot anyway."

"That's easy to say in a world where in effect everyone has unlimited wealth. Life was certainly easier and more pleasant if you had lots of money."

"I can see that, up to a certain limit. But we're off the subject. I want to understand the mentality of those you had to be protected from."

"Look Abel, have you ever come across men who resented the fact that you have eighteen children, while they haven't even been chosen once?"

"Oh, often. But they have to put up with it. There are very good reasons why women have chosen me. It's the way the species improves, and it's hard luck on the losers." For a moment, he looked like his old, arrogant self.

"And they have internal controls. As you said, Artif is with everyone. In my day, some of those people might have done things to harm you, without any expectations of return, just to 'even the score'. But also, they looked on criminal acts as a way of gaining money. Rich people, or their loved ones, had often been kidnapped, with the promise of return if a large sum of money was paid. Except, sometimes, they returned a dead body."

Abel visibly shrunk in upon himself. "How awful!"

Flora had barely finished her meal as the second tray arrived for Abel. He hardly noticed it, or Flora's subterfuge, but started to eat again.

"Then there were the political kidnappings. Many groups of people felt discriminated against, suppressed, treated harshly. Often, this was in fact true. They felt powerless in the face of the dominant group in their area, so resorted to what was called 'terrorism': randomly killing people, causing damage, spreading fear. Kidnappings were a part of this. Often, terrorists were caught and put in prison, then their friends would kidnap a group of people, and threaten to kill them unless the criminals were released."

Abel looked at her. His mouth full, he said within her mind, "Right. Pretend you're a terrorist. You have a better chance of understanding them than I would. Your friends are in prison, you want to get them out. What kinds of thoughts in your head could possibly justify imposing terror and suffering on people who are in no way responsible for your friends' fate?"

Flora tried, speaking slowly and hesitantly at first, then speeding up as she got into the role. "They're tools for my use. I have justice on my side. This is a war, I am trying to liberate my people, and there are always casualties in war. I am not nasty, I don't wish to hurt them, but after all, my victims are from among THEM, part of the oppressing group, not one of US, and so they're barely human. THEY, those foreigners, are little better than animals anyway. And look what THEY have been doing to my people! I must have revenge! And after all, I am personally willing to die for the cause, so surely I should be willing to kill?"

"I can see why you were a great actress, Flora." He'd finished the second meal, and was sucking on the cup of chocken Flora had ordered with it.

He continued, "I just can't imagine that Kiril would feel anything like these people did. He's had no interest in politics, in anything but Souda, for years now. But I've come across this strange concept of revenge during my studies. Tell me about that."

"Revenge? That was very much part of certain cultures, and of some individuals everywhere. 'An eye for an eye and a tooth for a tooth.' If you've done me some harm, or at least if I honestly believe that you have, then I have a right, even a duty, to hurt you the same amount in return. In New Guinea, it was quite a problem. These feuds went on for generations.

Someone from your village has killed somebody in mine, so I sneak in at night and kill a grandmother, or a child. Then of course you'll do the same to my village, backward and forward, on and on."

"But that was not part of your culture, was it?"

"Not at that level of viciousness, no. But it was entrenched in several technologically civilized cultures too: Italian and Arab for example."

"That doesn't help. I want to understand someone from a non-revengious culture, who thinks like that."

Flora laughed. "I'm sure that word is as new to you as to me. I think the proper word is 'vengeful'. All right, let me think. Artif, do you come across psychoses sometimes?"

"Please explain, Flora."

"Diseases of thinking and feeling. One was called 'paranoia:' a perfectly reasonable construction of beliefs based on one or two false assumptions. It sometimes led the sufferer to do terrible things, in what he believed was self-defense. These people saw threats everywhere."

Artif sounded offended, "I wouldn't let anything like that happen!"

"It did happen in my times. Abel, Artif's implication is clear, this doesn't apply to Kiril. But if I was paranoid, I might conclude from false assumptions that Control — you, Mirabelle, Cynthia, whoever else is on it — is a group bent on something evil. You have all the power, Artif is on your side, so it's my duty to save humanity from your evil plans, and everything is justified. If I have to hurt one or two people, even a child, that's justified because I am saving EVERYBODY from the terrible fate you're planning."

"Hmm. Or perhaps, I've been treated unfairly for years by Souda, and now she's been vindicated by Control. I can't bring myself to hurt her, but how dare these people side with her and go against me? I'll punish them, give them a terrible time by influencing a suggestible young boy. I'll make him think I'm his friend, then talk him into disappearing with me. Oh, I won't hurt him myself, but a quest is only a quest if it's dangerous. Let them stew and suffer for maybe a year, that'll teach them to oppose me! How does that sound?"

Flora had to agree that it was plausible.

Tamás

Something bright shone on his face. He cracked his eyelids open and saw the great red ball of the sun, hovering in a pink sky, low over the corrugated sea. He lay on his back, sliding upward along the slope of a wave.

"Good morning, Tamás," Kiril cheerfully said through the implant. "Artif has told me, we should see the land today!"

Tamás told the motor to sit him up and turn him toward his friend. "Great! Hey, can we speed up?"

The last vestiges of the storm were many days behind them. The sky above was a pale metallic blue, without a cloud in sight. The up and down swooping motion now stayed in the background of Tamás's consciousness, noticed only if he thought about it.

Kiril laughed at his eagerness. "Sure, then we'd run out of charge sooner. We can miss out on our swim at lunchtime if you like."

Tamás was torn. "I do want to see New York," he said. "Though 'Old York' is a better name."

"I'm told it's pretty amazing, and sad too. But what's the hurry?"

"Oh, you're too old to understand."

"At twenty-four?"

Both laughing, they ordered breakfast, did their isometrics and played a couple of games of chess. Kiril was merciless on the board, and still won every time, but Tamás now lasted into the endgame.

They flew until lunchtime, and had their swim after recharging batteries.

Tamás was having a chemistry lesson with Artif. A recording scooted ahead of him, always two meters in front of his eyes. It showed a kilogram of water in a tall, narrow measuring beaker at different temperatures, side by side: a bubbling beaker of near-boiling liquid, a cool beaker with the level noticeably lower, then just above freezing point, the height in the beaker between the two others. Beside this was a block of ice, clearly larger than the liquid volume.

"Odd, isn't it?" he asked.

Artif showed him a picture of the water molecule, and was about the give an explanation, when Kiril shouted, "Look out!"

A large flock of birds came arrowing at them. Tamás saw that they were terns. He'd always thought of them as harmless, small creatures, much smaller than gulls, but now they seemed enormous as several came straight for him at great speed. He gave a loud yell and desperately waved his arms in front of his face. One of those beaks hitting his eye...

At the last instant, the flock of feathered missiles divided. Some went above him, some below, or to either side. He actually felt the wind of their passage on the skin of his face.

He turned as the last bird passed him. They wheeled in the air, above the three much larger shapes lumbering through the air, then took off with great speed, back the way they'd come from.

"What was that about?" he asked, his voice shaky.

"A welcome I guess," Kiril answered, also far from calm. "I thought you said, you've been admitted to the community of the air."

"That was a Norwegian bird. Obviously Americans are nasty."

"Careful, there, young fellow. I'm an American bird, you know!"

Their laughter was out of proportion to the worth of the joke.

Kiril now dived head first down along the slope of the wave, smoothly turned in the trough to soar up the side of the next wave. Going full speed, he rose well above five meters before falling back. "I saw it!" he said in Tamás's mind.

That looked like fun. Tamás copied him and catapulted himself to a good height. And yes, he saw an indistinct dark line on the far horizon. As he came down, he noted that the water was a slightly different color, with a browny-greenish tinge to the deep blue.

He catapulted himself up high for another look, but Kiril said, "Not too often mate, or we'll have to stop for a recharge. That's physics rather than chemistry, but you should know, every measurement changes the thing measured. The more you look, the further it gets."

"How come you know about so many things?"

"Just smart I guess. You'd better go back to your lesson, and you might catch up to me one day."

Tamás sent an image of himself, with EGM motor attached, to hover in front of Kiril. He gave the image wide cow's horns and a long, red tongue sticking out between pointy fangs.

But then Artif reactivated the lesson. Tamás got rid of the image and returned to study.

Turan Abid

Turan felt immensely satisfied with himself. He closed down the recording, saying, "Good, the whole process is here for future uses. I don't give a stuff about credentials anymore, but you two should be well served by such an achievement."

Mitchell Samanara, whose balloon they were in, grinned at the old man. "I'll go full speed, you tell the lady the good news." The balloon had started from Alaska, and had been traveling toward Flora Fielding's cave ever since the start of the project.

Turan disconnected. Back home in North Eastrica, he asked, "Flora Fielding?"

She was hovering above some kind of a contraption with a shallow depression. Turan noted that her face now lacked the signs of pain. Remarkably quick healing. She sat up, still in the air. "Welcome, Mr. Abid," she said, her expression a mixture of expectation and apprehension.

"Er, Turan, not Mister," he corrected her mistake. "Madam, I'm happy to tell you, the chemicals are on the way. My associate is coming in the physical, and should arrive sometime today."

"And they work?"

Insufferable woman, was she questioning his results? Stiffly he said, "I would not supply them if I had the slightest doubt. I've come to give you instructions. One of the things we've done is to prepare a drug that toughens your mucous membranes. This will counter the worst side effects. Unfortunately it will temporarily interfere with your sense of smell and taste, and reduce your appetite. At the same time, your absorption of nutrients will be reduced, so you need to eat more for the same benefit. You'll have to force yourself to eat, whether you feel hungry or not."

"Thank you. I'm so grateful to you and your friends!" She smiled, and suddenly he realized what a beautiful woman she was.

He continued, "We've also modified the drugs so that your bone marrow is protected from them. Your blood will therefore not be affected. However, the mucous membrane toughening also means that you'll get no pleasure out of sharing bodies, and in fact, while the treatment continues, that's best avoided because of the vulnerability of your skin."

"That's one thing that won't worry me," she interrupted.

Turan continued, "Unfortunately, your hair will fall out, and your skin will get dry and flaky. But such effects are temporary, and at least they don't hurt."

She sighed. "I know all too much about such things."

Cynthia

Cynthia had a nice idea. "Flora?" she called.

Artif explained, "Turan Abid is with her at the moment, love."

"Good news?" she asked excitedly.

"You know how these scientists are. They hate to commit themselves until it's unavoidable. I'm sure their work will prove useful. Right Cynthia, Flora is available now."

Flora was sitting up over her EGM bed, her face a sunshine glow. "Cynthia!" she said excitedly, "the modified drugs are coming! Maybe, maybe..."

Cynthia wanted to hug her, but thought of the wounds of her operation and restrained herself. "That's wonderful, love. I'm sure they'll work."

"Come up here with me."

"Gladly!" Cynthia commanded the bed to pick her up, and instantly felt the discomfort of her body ease into smooth pleasure. "Oh, this's the life!" She got the bed to sit her up, facing her friend. "Actually, I came to invite you to see my home."

"Oh. You mean... do you mean, me, send an image?"

"Of course, what else?"

"But how...?"

"Put on your land vehicle rig, then lie on top of your bed and close your eyes. That way, your image will have the comfort of the EGM lift, and for this first time you can concentrate on just one location at a time." I'll be with you in both places."

The little backpack with its attached plasteel netting floated to Flora, who put it on. They lay down over the bed, side by side — just barely, there was room for this.

"Now what?" Flora asked.

"Open your eyes."

It was amusing, to see the look of amazement on the face of Flora's image, in her home. Cynthia had to laugh. "Welcome," she said. "As you can see, I have a land house. I'm not too happy on a heaving ship, and I have far more space than I could have in a balloon."

She took her guest to the huge picture window.

"That's beautiful," Flora said. Outside, the level plain stretched as far as the eye could see, and all of it was covered in a regular array of citrus trees: mostly oranges, but also lemons and grapefruit. Golden fruit and delicate blossoms peeked from among the green leaves.

"Smell it," Cynthia said. "This is very fertile land, because in your days it was sea bottom."

"I can't quite take it in. Where am I?"

Cynthia laughed. "You're right back in your cave, lying on your bed with my image beside you. Your image is here, on the Adriatic Plain."

"Yes, there was an Adriatic Sea, between Italy and the Balkan countries."

"It rose during the Cataclysm, and volcanoes surround it even today. We're over a hundred meters above sea level, and of course that's a long way above the old one."

"How much above?"

"Oh I don't know, three hundred meters?"

Artif said, "Three hundred and fifty-two meters."

"Terrible," Flora said, "All those cities drowned!"

"City? Oh, yes, I remember. That was a long time ago. Look, I'll just sit down in the physical, and then the two of us can jump around a little. I have communication globes in several places near the house, which saves a lot of walking."

As Cynthia flopped into a chair, Flora asked, "Can you send more than one image then?"

As many as you can pay attention to. My image at your place isn't doing anything, so needs no attention. Some people can do something in the physical, and at the same time work three or four images. Our little Nat is marvelous like that. Others need to focus on just one place at a time."

They spent a pleasant half a period, Cynthia showing off her flower garden, currently being tended by half a dozen machines, her herd of tame deer, and her art gallery. Three dimensional artwork was her major hobby.

Looking around at her creations as Cynthia activated globe after globe, Flora said, "Darling, that waterfall. How could you make that?"

"Watch," Cynthia answered. She said privately to Artif, "Flora as she was in that movie where she is helping poor black children."

Flora gasped as her representation suddenly stood in front of them, dressed in the ancient fashion as in the movie. Cynthia then played around. She replaced the old-fashioned clothes with just a skirt, but seeing her friend's face glow red, she put on a skimpy t -shirt. Then she modified the image's skin color, making it as dark as her own, but leaving the hair and eyes the way they were. "There," she said, "how do you like that? Modern Flora."

Flora laughed. "I don't think I'd be very comfortable, being black. It's just not what I'm used to."

"All right, love." So Cynthia changed the image's skin color a bright green.

They both laughed, but then Artif said, "My dears, Mitchell Samanara is just arriving in the physical, bringing Flora's drugs."

⚡ 15 ⚡

Flora

Flora flew off the bed and, feet barely clear of the ground, skimmed outside. When she emerged through the sliding door into the sultry Turkish bath of an overcast day, Cynthia's image already waited for her. "Which direction is he coming from?" Flora asked.

Artif answered, "From the north."

Cynthia suggested, "Flora, your motor should enable you to rise parallel to the cliff."

She looked up and shuddered. "Oh no, I couldn't!" Fortunately, it proved to be unnecessary. A huge silver shape scooted over the treetops from the north, lowering even as it came to a stop. A silver streak dropped from its center when it was fifty feet off the ground. Flora saw that it was a globe no larger than her head, but seeming very heavy the way it landed. The tethering rope was attached to it. The balloon kept lowering. It was longer than the entire clearing, and she thought it would get in trouble with the branches of the trees. It stopped just clear. A circular hole appeared in the side, and... Flora couldn't believe her eyes. A silver plank grew from the hole. A man stood on its tip, enfolded in a silver spider's web. The plank grew and smoothly lowered him to the ground. It had become something like a flat-topped circular staircase without the steps, a spiral ramp. He stepped clear, and the now-long flat silver spaghetti contracted back like a tongue in a naughty child's mouth.

A gypsy pirate, Flora thought, looking at the white grin splitting the young man's swarthy face. His black hair and beard were a tangle of long ringlets. He wore a skimpy bit of red cloth around his waist.

"Greetings," a strange masculine voice said, as if from between her ears. The man's lips hadn't moved, and it took Flora a moment to realize that it was him, speaking to her through the implant. Meanwhile, he'd continued, "I'm Mitchell Samanara. I was only thirteen when I did my first bull ride, and I've been in five altogether. I play left striker in the Indian national godurball team, and we're currently third in the world..."

He went on and on in this vein for perhaps five minutes, hardly pausing to take a breath. He ended with, "... and of most relevance to you, dear lady, I'm one of the three biochemists who have developed your new drugs. In fact, all the work was done in my house." He fluidly waved a casual arm up toward the enormous balloon above their heads. It had risen again, and was now gently tugging at its tether.

"Welcome, Mitchell," Cynthia said. That was lucky — Flora had forgotten his name during the interminable recital of his credentials. "I'm Cynthia Sabatini, and of course this is Flora Fielding."

Flora smiled at him. She said aloud, "Yes, welcome. Do you want to come in out of the heat?" He looked puzzled.

"What heat? But sure."

As he walked forward, the bit of cloth slipped and fluttered loose. Embarrassed, Flora looked away. "Sorry," Mitchell said, "Artif told me to dress. I don't usually bother." Completely unselfconscious about having exposed himself, he gracefully bent, snatched the falling cloth from the air and wrapped it around his waist again.

Flora led the way in, skimming just above the ground, and breathed easier once in her bedroom again. Cythia's image was already there, sitting above the bed.

"Freezing in here!" Mitchell said. "Hey, how do you do this levitation stuff?"

"It's a new concept," Cynthia explained, "You apply EGM force directly to a person. Come and sit here, you'll see."

He did so. "I'll warm you up," the big woman offered with a grin, and put a huge arm around his shoulders. He grinned too, and snuggled into her padded body.

Flora tried not to be shocked. She asked, "Have you got the drugs?"

"The machine is being unloaded right now. It's an automated device that'll generate the drugs for you as you need them. I'll leave enough raw materials for a month. If you need more, it can come with your regular supplies."

Artif interjected, "Flora, I'm looking after all that, don't worry."

"Would you like some refreshments, Mitchell?" Flora asked.

"Me too!" Cynthia immediately said. "I'll have a cup of chocken and Artif, a nice big slice of cheesecake."

"Sounds good," Mitchell said.

Flora went without cheesecake. After her first sip, she asked, "Cynthia, what good is it to you, eating as an image?"

"I mirror in the physical. That's normal, though you can do without it, or replace." She laughed at Flora's look of confusion. "I can eat a piece of dry bread at home, and it'll taste and feel like cheesecake while my image is eating that."

Mitchell pulled away from her. "I don't think you do that too often."

Cynthia grinned at him. "You know, we're embarrassing Flora. I'll line up entertaining company for her, and the two of us can get to know each other better."

Abel

"Don't do this, Abel," Artif said firmly. "You'd disapprove of anyone else who tried it on."

"But he's my son!" Abel shouted aloud.

"I'd be obliged to tell you if he was in danger."

"We've had this discussion, a few thousand times. Artif, I'm determined."

She didn't answer.

One more time, Abel played through the recording. It showed him, with Tamás standing on his left, Kiril on his right. He bowed his head courteously, saying, "Greetings. You know me, I'm Abel T'Dwuna. I am sending this message to everyone who has ever met me, including you. Please listen, for I need your help.

"This boy..." he gestured to his left, "...is my son, Tamás Karlsen." He gestured the other way. "And this man is Kiril Lander, a member of the English Culture. They are together, somewhere, equipped with a device that allows them to move through the air as if they were flying, though they need to stay close to some massive object like the ground, or the surface of the sea. I'm told the maximum distance is five meters. They may look like this."

Kiril and Tamás disappeared from beside him, and one-tenth sized copies of them flew in a circle around him, face down.

Abel's image in the recording assumed a look of desperate gravity. "Kiril has recently done the unthinkable, and hurt another person. He was acting with intent to hurt someone, but in fact the injury was suffered by a third party. That's irrelevant: he had intended to damage another human being. He was tried by Control. There, in front of the supreme governing body of humanity, he lost his temper and started shouting."

Abel held his arms out to the side. "Kiril is unstable. He may seem to be reasonable, but then suddenly he snaps, under the impulse of some provocation. Who knows what might set him off next?"

His voice became soft and calm again. "You should also know that there is some indication that Kiril may bear ill feelings both toward me, and toward Tamás's mother, Mirabelle Karlsen. My belief is that he somehow induced Tamás to accompany him on a supposed quest, in order to get at us, his parents. I'm convinced he means the boy no harm, but..." Worry now showed on the recorded face, "... who can tell when he might snap again, for some unknown reason, or no reason at all?

"I fear for the safety of my son. The danger I wish to protect him from is not that facing any young man on a quest, of course not. It's the unreasonable, unacceptable risk of being in the constant physical company of a madman who might attack him at any time.

"I fear for Tamás. I also fear that Kiril might do something to harm himself. And I fear that he might attack some other person.

"If you see them, or even have any evidence of their location, please contact me immediately. "Thank you."

Abel shut off the recording, and lay down on his bed, the little globe lost in his big hands. "Artif, now I want to simultaneously send an image to every person who has ever met me, except for those who already know of the problem. They don't need it. I don't care what the recipients are doing, or where they are. Tell them I need to speak with immense urgency. I'll then appear, give them an image of this recording, and break contact."

Artif repeated her earlier request. "Abel, this is wrong. Don't do it."

"I must. Do it now."

All over the planet, more than eighteen thousand people received the recording. Flora was one of them.

Tamás

More birds flew around them from time to time, but these ignored them. Tamás saw swift, dark shapes swim under the surface, and once a fish jumped out of the water, soaring high and flying along for a surprising distance. And now the land was visible whenever they rose above the crest of a wave.

A fresh breeze started to blow from behind them as the late afternoon sun shone into their eyes. The sky ahead became dappled with small clouds. Again Kiril called and pointed down. The sea had a fuzzy-edged divide between the clean water under them and to their right, and a brown flow beyond, stretching out of sight to the left. "Must be the outflow of the Hudson River," Kiril said.

Soon, the skyline ahead became serrated, and the water below turned green. With every rise over a wave, the shore had more detail, more clarity, despite the glare of the now-setting sun. The clouds turned a dirty red.

A regular booming sound reached Tamás, growing louder every clicklet, and he saw white surf break on yellow sand. Beyond, a bizarre landscape stood, stark and dead, silhouetted in front of the sun's huge, red disk. Everywhere he looked, he saw the skeletons of great rectangular structures.

They flew over the beach. It was odd, actually uncomfortable, not to be rising and falling but to fly level, five meters above coarse, long grass. This turned out to be merely a spit of land, with still water beyond it. By the last light, Tamás saw that the monstrous structures stood in water. Lower-lying tangles of girders filled the gaps between them, obviously the same kinds of constructions, fallen over.

"I don't want to fly among these things in the dark," Kiril said, and Tamás agreed.

"Over there!" he said, pointing. One of the nearby skeletons had a solid-looking floor about forty meters up. He could see its underside. Kiril leading, then the camp, then Tamás, they got the motors to claw them up along a great, rusty steel column, and at last settled on a solid surface. After the constant motion of their long crossing, they could hardly stand upright without staggering.

As the world grew dark, Kiril told the camp to anchor itself. They tied onto it with their belaying ropes, in case of a sudden wind, and settled for sleep, a meter above the ancient floor.

When Tamás woke, it still felt strange to be still. The floor looked far less solid by the red light of dawn. He could look through great cracks, right down to the still, dirty-looking water, with a metal spider's web in between blocking most of the view.

"I think there were floors like this one on top of the other, like a set of shelves," Kiril said. "But why?"

Artif explained, "People used to live here, like many hundreds of land houses stacked up. People did various kinds of work in some compartments."

"How awful!" Tamás shuddered.

"Oh, I don't know," Kiril answered. "A lot depends on how you're brought up. I imagine people like that might find it odd, each of us living in a separate house. All right, let's explore a little." They left the camp where it was, and dropped feet first down into the rust-lattice sided canyon. The dead landscape seemed to stretch forever, tangles of girders and twisted posts and great masonry slabs sticking out of the murky water. They weaved more or less randomly among the rectangular skeletons.

Something shiny loomed ahead. An immense tower still wore much of its skin: thousands of flat panes that looked like transparent plasteel, but must have been an earlier material.

"That's what it all must have looked like, once," Kiril mused.

The land under the water sloped uphill, and gradually the ancient ground level emerged. "Hey, I know what that is," Kiril said, "we have surfaces like that at home. These things were called 'roads', and were made for wheeled vehicles to go on."

Lower ruins bordered the roads here. Tamás recognized the remains of stonework, though nowhere as nice as Chia's.

An open space stretched in front of them, covered in scrub and long, coarse grass. Something moved as their shadow slid along the ground: a female hippopotamus and her young ran out of their path, flattening a gorse bush.

"This is so depressing," Kiril said, "Let's return to the camp."

Artif guided them back. They reached it in about a period. They had breakfast, recharged the batteries, dropped down to five meters above the water, and started their trip westward across America.

Vladislav

Merv the bull looked out between the plasteel bars, his little piggy eyes mean. If he could talk, he'd be saying, 'Come on, then!'

Vladislav didn't want to. Sure, Artif snatched the image before Merv could inflict any real damage, but always, there was pain, sometimes a short burst of immense agony. And one day, all too soon, it was going to be for real. His stomach clenched into a tight fist as he looked back at the hippopotamus.

Artif said, "Darling, do you want to study a few recordings again? I assure you, everyone feels like this."

Vladislav sighed. "No thanks. What's the use? I'd just be putting it off." He closed his eyes, breathed deeply as he'd been taught, and thought of Tonya. He visualized her, and remembered her promise to be with him during the bull ride.

"All right, Merv," he said without words, and then his image straddled the wide, resilient back. Merv dropped to his front knees and kicked his rear legs up. Vladislav was ready for this move, and lay prone, his hands pressed on each side of the thick neck.

The bull rolled onto his side even as his rear legs landed, but by then the boy was crouching. He jumped up, landing hard on the beast's abdomen, and sprung again as if on a trampoline as Merv continued his roll. The bull smoothly rolled back onto his feet, with the boy gaining the top.

Action stopped for a clicklet. Vladislav gripped folds of skin with both hands, barely in time as Merv charged forward with a sudden bound. The huge animal's enormous weight smashed against the side of the cage. His head struck, but the cage held and bounced him back.

Vladislav couldn't hold on, and was thrown against the cage. He managed to take the impact on his forearms with a double breakfall, and grabbed on.

Merv stopped after his rebound, and charged forward again, gaping mouth wide open. Vladislav pulled his legs up with desperate haste, and pushed off with both feet. He landed with a backward somersault, his legs straddling Merv behind the neck. He'd been practicing this trick for days.

The hippo turned side on, and smashed against the bars again. The boy pulled his left leg up, but too slow. He felt his leg crush — then he was back in his body.

Merv had a string of mucus hanging from his mouth, and was breathing heavily. He snorted, and turned to look at Vladislav through the bars.

"Sixty-seven clicklets, love," Artif said. "Your best, but you were still killed."

Vladislav was breathing too heavily for even a mental word. The memory of the pain was just too awful. He wiped sweat from his eyes with a trembling hand. "Oh Artif," he managed at last, "I'm afraid!"

"Of course you are, my dear. Every man is. It would be no achievement if you weren't afraid."

Walking on shaky legs, the boy went home, to study a few recordings from the champions.

Abel T'Dwuna had been his own age when he'd set the still unbroken world record, an unbelievable four clicks ninety-five.

Ria

She knew she was dreaming, but this didn't lessen the feeling of terror. The dream started nicely enough. There was Kiril, flying high above the ground. He held his arms out to the front, and great, beautiful multicolored wings flapped above him. He was a huge butterfly, and he flew in loops and swirls. Ria waved to him and he waved back.

But then, Kiril got smaller, and smaller again, and now a huge bugcatcher chased him. Desperately, Kiril dived toward the ground, his wings flapping. The bugcatcher followed right behind him. Kiril rose sharply, the bugcatcher continuing on its previous path and missing him, but it stopped sharply in the air, turned, and raced after Kiril. On an on, the deadly dance continued above Ria's head. Always, Kiril barely managed to stay ahead of certain death.

And, all the time, Kiril was getting smaller and smaller, the bugcatcher was getting larger and larger, and Ria knew that Kiril was tiring, and then the funnel of the bugcatcher was around Kiril's legs and...

Ria awoke to look into Timmy's concerned face. He was shaking her shoulders. She raised herself on one elbow, and he let her go. At the same time, the door slid aside and Mom walked in, her hair a tangle.

Timmy said, "Ria, you were shouting in your sleep."

"Oh, thank you for waking me. I... I had a nightmare about Kiril."

Mom sat on the edge of her bed and gathered the two children to her. "Tell me," she said.

"He was flying. Like a butterfly. And a bugcatcher was chasing him and..."

She shuddered and couldn't continue, but buried her face between her mother's breasts. Mom gently stroked her hair. "Darlings, I'm worried about him too, but also I trust him. We know he'd never do anything nasty to this boy, whatever Abel might say."

Ria felt Mom tense, and heard the anger in her voice.

The three of them had been eating their dinner when the first visitor arrived: Susan's elder brother, Alexei. He held a recording globe in his hand and asked, "Have you seen this?"

"What?" Susan had asked.

"A recording circulated by Abel T'Dwuna. It concerns Kiril." His eyes flicked to the children.

Ria said, "He's my brother, Tim's father. Whatever it is, we have to know too."

"Darling, it's not a good idea. I'll show it to your mother, and she can tell you about it." ·

"Stay here," Mom commanded, and went to her bedroom. The door slid shut behind her. Uncle Alexei's image disappeared, and Ria heard faint sounds through the door. She heard Mom shout something. She couldn't understand the words, but the anger and indignation were plain to hear.

She and Tim looked at each other, just as Artif said, "Jim wants to say something to you." Jim Hotten was her best friend, after Tim.

Jim stood before them, dark eyes blazing. "I don't ever want to play with you again," he spat. "Your Kiril's a criminal!" and before either of them could answer, he'd disappeared.

Tim looked at Ria with dismay on his face. Ria said, "Timmy, remember when he said goodbye to us, he told us to think kindly of him, whatever people said about him?"

Timmy grabbed Ria's hand. Great tears were coursing down his face.

Mom's door opened. Uncle Alexei was gone. She looked grim. "Abel is accusing Kiril of doing nasty things, of being a danger to people." She took a deep breath. "It's not true. We must have faith in him."

"I do!" Ria said.

"Me too!" Timmy added.

Mom explained, "Abel said, Kiril and a boy with him can sort of fly. Nobody knows where they are. Abel wants them found."

"But Mom, he's on a quest, isn't he?"

"He is, Ria. I don't know how Abel can get away with this."

After this, an apparently endless succession of visitors came. Some were sympathetic, or indignant on their behalf, but most came to sever friendships.

Was it a wonder, then, that Ria had dreamt about Kiril, flying?

16.

Flora

Mitchell had walked out. Cynthia gave her a cheerful wave and her image blinked out of existence. A cup floated through the door, Artif saying within Flora's mind, "Darling, here is the start of your treatment."

She had to pull a face at the bitter taste of the drink, but if this thing defeated the cancer... She watched the empty cup return to the kitchen outside her room. At almost the same instant, Nat's voice sounded in her mind: "Flora, Cynthia called me, and told me the good news. May I visit?"

"You know you're always welcome." She told her Angel's wings to stand her from her sitting position and smiled at him as he appeared in front of her.

He looked very serious. "Flora, you've done so much for me! Before we became friends, I had a great deal of knowledge about your times. Now, I understand them, and that's immeasurably better. So, I want to give you something in return."

"Nat," she said gently, "I'm not interested in sharing bodies, with you or any other man. I certainly wouldn't want you to see me naked."

He smiled. "I anticipated that. Look, I'll just give you a special massage. Lie on your bed, love, face down, and close your eyes."

She did so. "Take off your... what was that term? Angel's wings." She gave the order, but of course the bed kept her pain-free and comfortable.

She felt a strong, gentle pair of hands firmly knead her left foot and, surprisingly, an instant later, another pair of hands started on her right foot. Normally, her feet were ticklish, but Nat's kneading movements produced no discomfort at all. And then, she felt her shoulders being massaged as well. Another pair of strong hands kneaded the muscles there with small, circular movements, loosening tension in her neck, shoulders, the upper parts of her back. She opened her eyes for a moment, to see his lower half. He knelt on air, obviously held there by the bed. His red kilt almost touched her face as he leaned over her body.

Meanwhile, the hands at the other end moved onto her calves. She felt her legs being gently bent up at the knees, then each leaned against what just had to be Nat's torso, and two hands were doing their soothing dance on each of her legs.

"How can you do this?" she asked without speaking aloud. That was getting almost commonplace now.

"I've sent three images, that's all. And here is another one."

Yet another pair of hands made their deep, soothing circles on her lower back, on either side of the spine. "Isn't this bed wonderful?" Nat asked. "I couldn't hover over you without it."

Hands moved from her shoulders onto her neck again, then gently massaged her ears. This produced an immensely pleasant sensation. Flora gave herself up to delight as other hands moved from her lower back to her buttocks, as hands gently separated her legs and started on both her thighs at once.

"I'm a virtuoso," Nat laughed within her mind. "Here is yet another image."

The new pair of hands were on her cheeks, softly holding her face. Warm, moist lips touched hers and sucked her lower lip. She felt a tongue stroke her lip, then slip into her mouth with irresistible insistence. Her body was on fire, she was drunk on the pleasure, her whole skin glowing with ecstasy. She opened her mouth to him and found his tongue with hers.

And another mouth kissed her as well, on her pubis. His nose teased her, and his tongue, and for the first time in her life, she exploded with sexual joy.

"Now you're ready for me, darling," Nat said within her mind. They were still kissing, all his many hands still stroked and kneaded her body, the ones on her buttocks having slipped under the skirt, and she was wriggling and rhythmically pushing against the mouth on the focus of her pleasure. She felt her legs being separated further, and the pressure of strong, muscular thighs between hers, and then he was within her, deep within and stoking the fire of her existence. She had never felt like this before, there were no words for it, she was transported to levels of feeling she didn't know could exist.

Suddenly, he was done. He pulled his lips away from her mouth and laid his cheek against hers. All the many hands disappeared, but his nose still gently moved against her clitoris and he was still within her.

Flora opened her eyes to see the side of his head, beneath her and very close. The legs of his other image stuck out beyond. A huge bump raised the front of the kilt. She reached over with her left hand to flick the red material aside, then took hold of his erection and gently stroked it. He — another manifestation of him — moved within her, with a circular motion that sent more shivers of pleasure through her.

And then all contact ceased. Flora lay prone for a long moment before asking the bed to sit her up. Nat, just one image, stood beside the bed, naked now. His erection was rapidly shrinking and softening, and he had a pleased grin on his narrow face.

"Thank you, Nat," she said. "You were right. Thank you."

"And I thank you, Flora. I've never before kissed a face as beautiful as yours. And next time, we might try the same thing while merged."

"There won't be a next time for a while, Nat dear," Flora sadly answered. "I've taken my first dose of the new drugs, and I was told to avoid sharing bodies while they're acting on my body."

Tamás

Tamás coughed again. "It stinks here," he complained.

"It's Mount Cline," Kiril explained with a shrug. "It blows off every three or four days. That's why we have all that muck in the air, too."

They were bone tired after flying all day, and had decided to camp by the shore of a dirty-looking creek that made its way to the lake to their right. Actually, everything was dirty-looking. Tamás thought, this must have been the way things were everywhere before the Cataclysm. Their clothes, the now set-up tent, their skin, everything wore a coating of fine gray dust that clung with a sticky insistence. At least, inside the tent, they were protected from more of it settling on them.

"We'd better go easy on the fresh water for the moment," Kiril said.

"Yeah, I wouldn't want to drink that stuff out there! But where is it coming from?"

"The Great Lakes are here because ice ground great holes at one stage. That makes the crust here a little thinner than anywhere else. So, during the Cataclysm, when the weight of water over land shifted everywhere, the continental plate cracked around here, and BOOM! You got Mount Chicago, and all the little ones around it."

"Sure, but that was a long time ago."

Kiril laughed. "To you or me. Not in geological terms. Anyway, five of the volcanoes are still active. Only four years ago, Birrel had a major lava flow. But Cline never settles down, just perks away."

Tamás was about to answer, when Artif said to both of them, "Darlings, the resupply balloon is about to reach you. I'll have to open the tent to the outside."

"Thanks, Artif," Kiril answered. "I think Tamás might manage to survive the experience." Tamás told a cushion to hit Kiril's head. Grinning, the big man easily ducked under the missile.

They quickly put their clothes on again and went outside.

When the supply balloon came, it was from the south. Tamás saw an indistinct movement within the murk, like a moving cloud. It rapidly coalesced into a silver dot that grew.

Looking at it, he felt a sudden, utterly agonizing stab of sorrow. There was no perspective within the haze, no sense of distance, so what he saw coming at him was his mother's house, his home for all of his life until now. Oh, how he missed her! He thought of their two beautiful gardens, so different from the dirty place where he now stood. He visualized her, the way he'd seen her last, looking a little puzzled when he'd given her a surprise hug. He managed not to cry — somehow.

The supply balloon stopped overhead and lowered to three meters above the camp. The stunted trees nearby posed no problems. A bridge lowered, and soon a procession of parcels made their way into the camp.

Within three or four clicks, the bridge retracted, the balloon rose and sped away to the south. They returned to the camp.

In the morning, Tamás tried to look out through the camp's side, but the outside coating of grime had made it practically opaque. He and Kiril washed, had breakfast and dressed. They went outside, and Tamás heard Kiril order the camp to pack itself up.

Something was different. A breeze blew from behind them, from the east. The sky above was blue, the air crystal clear. The smell of sulfur no longer stung his nose. Tamás breathed deeply and turned west. He stopped, his eyes wide open in wonder.

Three mountains broke up the horizon. The rightmost was topped by a wavering plume of smoke, pointing away from them. The skyline beyond these three was jagged like a shark's teeth. Mountain after mountain reared its pointed peak, blue, indistinct points filling the gaps between the green and brown serrations of nearer mountains. But all of these were dwarves. Behind them all, taking up the entire center half of the view, stood a black, glistening triangle so huge, so high that, even from this far vantage, Tamás had to tilt up his head to look for the peak.

"Mount Chicago," Kiril said within his mind.

"And you climbed that?" Tamás's already immense admiration for his friend tripled to awe.

"I did. And it came close to killing me." Kiril sighed. "It might have been better if…"

"No!" Tamás shouted aloud. "I'm more than glad that you've survived."

Kiril laughed it off. "Anyway, that's only the third highest mountain in the world. Nipon and Baikal are higher. No one's ever climbed either of those and survived."

Suddenly excited, Tamás turned to him. "No, but they didn't have our advantage. I reckon we could!"

Kiril laughed, in genuine amusement now. "Not this trip, mate. It took me over nine months to prepare for my climb. But yeah, you have plenty of time. Oh well, let's go."

The ellipse of the camp started off at Kiril's order, and the two of them took up position on either side of it.

Abel

He'd been keeping track. This was the fifty-third false alarm.

In the physical, Abel sprawled in the bow of his house, his eyes half-heartedly seeking the first signs of the North Californian shores. His mood was a paradoxical amalgam of restlessness and ennui: he couldn't be bothered to do anything, couldn't settle to any task. Nothing was worth the effort.

His image in Nepal violently shivered, even inside the borrowed fur clothes.

Harry Hamadrar was a short, spare man with a hawk nose in a long, thin face. He chose to wear a black moustache in an otherwise shaved face. "It's such an honor, Abel," he said. "I hope my recording will be of help to you."

Outside the plasteel window of the land house, the air was solid with the Monsoon. Diagonal curtains of water cascaded out of a near-black sky, blotting out the no-doubt beautiful view of the Himalayas.

"I don't know how you can live in a place like this, mate," Abel answered, "but yeah, they could be here just as easily as anywhere else."

Harry laughed. "I wouldn't live in any other place, certainly not on a rocking boat where I'd have to worry about hurricanes all the time. Cup of chocken?"

Abel didn't particularly want anything to eat or drink, but said, "Thank you," and sucked the cup dry when it came. He just wished Harry would get on with it.

At last, his host called for the recording globe, and activated it. Abel saw the far view: a magnificent range of serrated mountains, their very tops tipped with white ice and snow, even now in summer. Great black clouds boiled in the valley, blocking out about half the view, but moving and shifting as the strong southerly wind carried them along. It must have been of gale force.

"There," Harry said, and a red line with an arrow at the tip appeared. The tip moved south to north, slowly on this small scale, even as Abel peered at it.

Harry was right. Certainly, an object that may have been the size of a human flew along, wings — or arms? — spread. As Abel watched, a cloud swallowed the shape. "Could you go back please?" he asked.

Harry did so, then stopped movement. Again Abel watched the shape. Harry magnified the image, zooming in. Unfortunately, clarity was lost as magnification increased. The shape had become a pale blur against the darker background of the cloud.

Then realization hit. "Harry, how far above the ground would you say that shape is?"

"Hard to tell. Five hundred meters?"

"Yeah. This device allows a maximum height of five. I think what you've got is an albatross, carried inland by the wind."

"Oh. I... I'm sorry, wasting your time like this."

"Harry, at least it's a distraction from worry. And you did your honest best. Thank you."

He couldn't disconnect fast enough, to get away from the bone-freezing temperature the mountain man preferred.

Back home, Abel's experienced eyes detected the land swell: the endless line of rollers were no longer that of the deep sea. The water had also changed in color, in response to the increased load of microscopic plant life. Maybe he'd find them here, on Kiril's home ground.

Tamás

Kiril had decided to go right around the tortured volcanic area. They swung wide out over the Lakes. Tamás almost cheerfully endured another, short burst of motion sickness, the waves being very choppy over the shallow bottom. This was much better than flying through sulfurous muck.

On their right, ahead and behind, stretched the beauty of the Lakes: deep blue water with fish often breaking the surface, birds by the hundreds, and lush green islands everywhere. During their passage, they saw seals and dolphins as well as alligators that slid into the water when the flyers' shadows approached, and hippopotamuses in great numbers. The Lakes zone was a major hippopotamus-farming area, supplying meat for all the lands north.

The world was very different to the left. Just in sight along the horizon reared the uneven sawtooth landscape, with Mount Cline's smoke and haze dirtying the sky above them. And ever-present, brooding and threatening in its mighty majesty, Mount Chicago thrust for the sky, a black cone of power.

On the third day over the Lakes, Tamás asked, "Look, there are hundreds of little mountains. How come Chicago became so big?"

Kiril answered, "I could tell you all about it, but Artif, isn't this a good opportunity for that recording, you know, about the geology of the Cataclysm?"

"Of course." A map appeared in front of them, scooting along above the waves, rising and dipping with them. "This is North America before the Cataclysm," Artif explained. The shape was roughly triangular, as now, but the coastline was completely unfamiliar. It was much larger, and white covered a great deal of the northern part. The Lakes were also considerably larger, and quite a different shape. The whole area was criscrossed with lines, and had spots of different sizes in many places.

Kiril explained, "The white bits are permanent snow and ice. The lines are roads. remember, I told you about them in New York."

Artif added, "Some of the lines are railroads. They used to have two parallel metal rails on the ground, and vehicles with special wheels that could go along them."

"For Brad's sake, why?" Tamás asked.

After a short silence, Artif said, "I have no information on that. Doubtless an intermediate technological development. Anyway, the spots are settlements: towns and cities."

"Like New York?"

"That's right. The biggest around here was Chicago, about eight million people." A spot on the map, right on the southern tip of Lake Michigan, glowed red.

"Eight million!" Tamás exclaimed in wonder. "Why?"

Kiril laughed. "They lived. They had to live somewhere."

"But, but, didn't they know how to control births?"

Artif told him, "They did, at this place and at this stage in history. But, each person had full control over the number of children she wanted to have. There was no overall coordination about population size."

"Be thankful for that," Kiril said, "That's one of the reasons the Cataclysm occurred."

The map now changed. All the white disappeared, and a great area of the coastline turned red. Artif said, "This red area is what was devastated when the Great Wave struck."

Tamás sounded sick. "So many of those cities were hit!"

"Yeah, it must have been terrible," Kiril said, "But in a way, they were the lucky ones. They avoided worse to come."

Artif continued, "The Great Wave broke up all that was left of the polar ice. It had been thinning and weakening over a long time, due to warmer water underneath and dust settling on the top."

"Dust?" Tamás was puzzled.

Kiril told him, "Their technology dirtied the air, and their farming methods destroyed the soil so the winds raised dust. And all that settled everywhere. And snow and ice reflect less sunlight when covered in dust, see?"

"Anyway," Artif continued, "There had been a huge weight of ice on the north of the continent. When that disappeared, the whole continental plate flexed on its thinnest part, up the middle. The Lakes originally formed because moving ice had gouged out the rock, so the crust was a little thinner here than elsewhere."

A blue line zigzagged across the continent, following the line of the Lakes as they'd been in ancient times. Beside the map, a cross-section appeared, showing that the land was immensely thick in the west, under the Rockies, but thinner under the irregular line of the Lakes.

Tamás said, "Right, I understand all that, you got the line of volcanoes. But why hundreds of little ones and one giant?"

"Because, love, at almost the same time as the release of weight from the north, you got the extra weight of water on the shorelines, east and west. These three forces had to meet at a point, and that was Chicago." Artif paused. Bright green lines of force showed on the map, and now the shoreline changed to North America's modern shape: much smaller, and with great bays and promontories replacing the far more compact outline.

"Naturally, no one actually knows exactly what happened. But scientific investigation indicates a two-stage event. The first effect of the cracking of the continent was the line of volcanoes, and an immensely large, elevated lava plain. First, there must have been a huge explosion. Remember the buildings in New York?"

"Yes," they both answered.

"Kiril, you've seen it as a boy, but watch this reconstruction, you two."

The map disappeared, and instead they seemed to be looking out of an elevated window. They faced a vertical surface, which Tamás recognized as resembling the facade of the glistening building in New York. People's silhouettes moved behind transparent panels. Below, the road was a busy place. Colored lights flashed, even though it was daylight. Wheeled vehicles moved and stopped, moved and stopped, apparently in response to some of the colored lights. They were of many different sizes and colors. One pulled over to the side and a woman got out, so clearly, they carried people.

People on foot hurried both ways, and crossed from one side to the other in great numbers whenever the vehicles stopped. Everyone wore thick, heavy clothing, and had warm-looking head coverings.

Tamás asked, "What's that white stuff?" White flakes fell from the dark gray, low clouds, and heaps of slushy white material lay about in the streets, bedecking all the horizontal surfaces of the buildings.

"Snow," Kiril told him. "Remember, the Cataclysm started in the Southern summer, so it was winter here."

Tamás now heard a deep, distant rumble. Looking a little sick, Kiril said, "Here it comes!"

The tall buildings shook and swayed. A visible wave rippled along the road below. Some vehicles stopped, others bashed into them. Faintly through the transparent window covering came the sound of the smashes, and of human screams.

A black gap suddenly opened across the road. A moving vehicle entered it, going sideways, and hit the far side. As it tumbled down, a side door opened and a child fell out, her arms waving.

The building on the other side of the road was toppling over, toward them, and fell with a horrendous crash.

The scene disappeared, and now they watched the city from a great height. They could see the network of roads and buildings, stretching far into every direction. And everywhere, buildings were swaying and falling, great cracks rent the earth, and now smoke and red hot lava erupted from the ground. And a great jet of almost white incandescence grew from the middle of the city, a fiery fountain that reached for the sky. Tamás thought it had to be many K in diameter. Entire giant buildings were tumbling up toward the sky, pieces falling from them. Some of the pieces were rectangular components, but other, tiny ones had waving arms and legs.

Lake Michigan was also alive. A great wave arose, a steep-sided mountain of water, and swept the land. It had to be hundreds of meters tall. Steam hid the ground below as water met fire, but the jet of lava still shot for the upper reaches.

Oh, Tony help us, those people! Tamás thought, then he couldn't help it, vomited up his breakfast.

Kiril's image appeared beside him, wearing the flying gear, and put an arm around his shoulders. "It was a long time ago," he said soothingly.

Tamás wiped his face with the back of his hand. "Until now, the Cataclysm was only a word to me. But they were real people!"

Artif said, "It's only a reconstruction, Tamás. But it is known that buildings were thrown, some of them perhaps ten thousand meters into the air! The lava built up with extreme speed, and it's thought that there must have been lots of water to cool it almost instantly. So, the outsides hardened, and the middle part kept growing upward. The upper level of this lava plain is more or less where your top camp was during your climb, Kiril."

"Oh yes, the rectangular box thing I set up in to get out of the wind."

"That was a building, lying on its back."

"And the second stage?" Tamás asked.

"Volcanic action was worldwide. An incredible quantity of solid matter floated in the air, right up to the stratosphere, and this caused the Small Freeze."

"I get it!" Tamás interrupted. "Weight of ice again, flexing the other way!"

Artif's voice had a smile in it. "Yes. And Chicago grew to what you can see now. You know, it's been proved, the inside of the mountain is still liquid. If you drilled in deep enough, you'd hit molten rock. It's like a bulge in the earth's crust."

Tamás asked, "Was Mount Baikal made the same way?" He found it much easier to retreat into theory than to remember the fate of those ancient victims of the Cataclysm.

"Yes, though of course there were fewer people there. Lake Baikal was the deepest lake on earth. The crust was thinner under it than anywhere else, so when Eurasia flexed, that just had to be the place. It hasn't got this conical shape though. That's probably because the instant cooling aspect was missing. Over about four hundred years, it erupted through many different vent holes. So, not only is it taller but also far more massive."

Tamás glanced to the left and said, "Hmm, Chicago is massive enough for me!"

Kiril agreed. They'd been flying over the lakes for three days now, and the great mountain seemed to stay in the same place, beside them, in the distance.

⚡ 17 ⚡

Flora

She bit into the steak, mechanically chewed it until she was sick of the activity, and swallowed. She looked with distaste at the plate, chose a lump of deep red vegetable and put it in her mouth.

Artif said, "Flora, a supply balloon has just dropped something for you. Here it is." The door slid open and a brown box floated in, about the size of Flora's head. It stopped in front of her.

"How do I open it?" she asked without speaking aloud.

"It has a magnetic seal. Run your finger around three of the top edges." Artif's voice held pleasurable anticipation.

Flora complied. The lid came loose, and she pulled it up so it hinged on the fourth side. She saw something soft inside, the same color as her hair. She reached in and took it out. "Oh Artif, a wig!" It was, the exact style Artif had maintained for her since her awakening. A smaller parcel nestled under it. What's this?" she asked.

"Eyebrows, eye lashes and body hair."

Flora had to laugh. "I certainly won't need that!"

"Well I like to be thorough. I'll shave off what's left of your natural hair and you can put these on. They'll stick more or less permanently."

Flora's hair had been falling out in patches for days now, and she had asked visitors to stay with audio only, as on her first day. It'd be wonderful to be able to receive and send images again.

But for now, she dutifully returned to her tasteless, pleasure-less meal.

After the plate was empty, she had a cupful of water, there being no point in drinking anything else, then Artif used a laser gun to remove all the hair from her head, face and body. Flora called up an image and, looking at it, settled the wig on her head and carefully put the eyebrows and lashes into place. She didn't bother with false hair under her arms or the last little patch of fur.

"I'd better return to reading," she said.

She was into the third book on Cognitive Therapy, not that there was any chance of having this Kiril come to her for help. As she well knew, Kiril had disappeared, with Mirabelle and Abel's son.

But she had started the task, and found the concepts interesting.

Reading a book was very different than in the twenty-first century. There were no lines of words on a screen, or even more old-fashioned, on the pages of a paper book. Instead, Flora simply became aware of the content of sentence after sentence, as if she'd thought of them herself.

Only, the deep, pleasant inner voice was that of a North American man, presumably Aaron Beck himself.

This book was entitled *Love is Never Enough*, and dealt with the difficulties that arose in marriage, when there had been such a thing. Flora thought it very relevant to the problem between those two strangers, Kiril and Souda.

Vladislav

He stood on top of an elevated platform, a big basket of hippo delicacies hovering by his side. One by one he tossed them in and watched Merv eat them. Each bit of food was a little closer, and the large watermelon was just in the right place. Vladislav had done this exact routine for the past several days.

Artif said, "All contestants, get ready."

Merv was right under him, contentedly munching. Within his mind, Tonya told him, "I'm with you." He took a deep breath to quieten his churning insides.

Artif continued, "Three... two... one... Now!"

Vladislav leapt over the top of the fence, landing astride the broad back.

Merv instantly dropped to his front knees and kicked his back legs up, then almost in the same movement, he stood and reared. This was an easy challenge now: Vladislav compensated and hung on. The bull whipped his head back to snap at his right leg, which the boy pulled barely out of the way, economically, and was ready for the reverse movement. Merv now did something new: he reared up and fell over backward. Vladislav jumped off, and as the bull stood he was on top again.

This was within the rules.

The bull roared, a terrifying sound that started as a deep bellow and ended as a shriek, and bounded forward. By the time he hit the wall, Vladislav had his legs gathered under him. He leapt for the wall, did his backward somersault and was riding again.

Round and round they went in the deadly dance, attack and defense smoothly intertwined. Vladislav was without conscious thought, in a forever-now of reaction, meeting each attack as soon as his huge opponent had committed himself to the move. He was unaware that he was sweating and panting, he was unaware of the passage of time, his whole being was constant fluid movement.

For perhaps the fourth or fifth time, the bull tried to crush him against the side of the cage. On this occasion, as soon as he hit, he rolled over, his back scraping against the tough plasteel bars. Vladislav once again sprung to the ground on the opposite side, his feet touching lightly, then he was in the air once more as Merv raised himself. But even while standing up, the bull swung sharply toward Vlad, his fearsome mouth opening wide.

The great, gaping mouth came for him, and he was rushing through the air toward the slavering teeth. He twisted desperately, and his head actually scraped under the bristly lower jaw. His arms wrapped around the thick neck and his feet swung up toward the horizontal.

But Merv was still moving, and he twisted with an almost sinuous movement that was too much for the Vladislav's tired arms, sweat-slick skin. He was thrown clear, onto the ground at the foot of the fence.

Instantly, too fast for thought, he sprung up, up high, and his hands grasped the top of the fence. He was over, and landed in a heap on the ground outside. The bull's teeth snapped loudly, just behind his bare heels.

After a long, breathless moment, Vladislav rolled onto his hands and knees, his head hanging down. He looked up, into the small, vicious eyes of the animal who stood there, a few centimeters away, but safely on the other side of the fence.

As Vladislav slowly struggled to his feet, Tonya appeared and reached a hand down for him.

"You were wonderful!" she almost sang, and hugged his sweaty body to her.

Artif said, "Vladislav Liston, you lasted one click and seven clicklets. Well done!"

"How did he come in?" Tonya asked.

"Wait… Two hundred and seventeenth. But he was thirteenth in his age group, out of 181."

"Next year, I'll do better," he said. He sent a command to the herder, and then to the gate in the enclosure.

Merv looked at the open gate as if he couldn't believe that he was free again, after his long imprisonment. He lumbered forward, then suddenly turned toward Vladislav and Tonya. But the herder sent out a thin, crackling red line of force, stinging the bull's nose. Merv stopped and turned aside. Again and again, the herder moved him with electric shocks that hurt but would do no harm. Vladislav's daily companion disappeared in the thick jungle.

Souda

I wouldn't have believed this, Souda thought to herself, *but I miss him.* She'd been receiving regular counseling from Tibor, and felt that she had now come to terms with her guilt. She agreed with her mentor that, while she was responsible, she'd acted in good faith, and the important thing was to learn from the experience, to grow as a person.

And as Tibor had said, "Because this has happened, we now know something that's been lost in the mists of time: how to deal with this kind of problem. It's happened once, it could happen again, but now we have recordings to help people in the future."

It was nice to have been useful, but Souda did wish the experience had come from someone else.

The trouble was no longer guilt, but rather that she'd lost interest in all her usual activities. She had an image with Susan and the children almost all the time, and put on a smiling face for them, but she hadn't touched her flute for over a month, had done no needlecraft, hadn't even taken the trouble to sail her house to a new place. "Oh, I can't be bothered!" was her most frequent reaction to almost any thought, almost any suggestion from someone else.

She sat in an easychair she'd ordered into the bow of her house, looking at the silhouette of Table Mountain against the incredible brilliance of the clear night sky. She hardly noticed the flock of bugcatchers busily swooping about her, keeping her free of the myriad tropical pests.

"Artif," she asked, "can you tell me what's wrong?"

"You know what's wrong, love."

She sniffed. "Yes. I made him go away, and he went." She could visualize his cleanly molded face, the contrast between his fair hair and dark eyes, the grace of his movements. "Oh, I wish there was a middle way! And now he's hunted like a freak. You know, Artif, I think Susan is right. He's been dealt a terrible injustice."

Artif couldn't comment on this.

"Do you think I could send him a greeting?"

"No, Souda. He is not to have contact until his quest is over."

"Yeah. And now I know how he felt when I kept him away."

Tamás

At last they were back over land once more, the volcanic area behind them. On a clear day, Mount Chicago was a black finger in the east, sticking above the horizon. The land they passed through was mountainous too, but far older. One morning, they stood on a peak, looking ahead at the beauty of range upon range: green in the foreground, blue with distance beyond. The fresh sun of the morning cast long shadows, bringing forest and meadow into sharp relief.

Up above, a topstore caught the light, and blinded them with a silver spear of brightness.

The camp was packed up, they were ready to go, when Kiril suddenly said, "Beware!" He took off and flew under the spreading shade of one of the great trees that bordered their clearing. The camp was right behind him.

Tamás followed, even while asking, "What's up?"

Kiril landed, turned and pointed south. A balloon was moving almost directly toward them, no more than two hundred meters off the ground. "Artif, why didn't you warn us?" Tamás asked.

"Because the occupant of that balloon is asleep," she answered instantly.

Nevertheless, they waited for the long silver shape to go its swift, silent way, until it was out of sight. Then they set off for the west again.

A herd of gazelles stampeded from fright of their coming, and Tamás enjoyed watching their graceful movements. Then another stand of trees rushed toward them, and it was fun to weave among the trunks, hardly slowing. They came to a cliff, a great drop-off running north-west to south-east. Rather than descend, Kiril chose to skirt the edge, moving northward. The sun was high in the cloudless sky now, and when Tamás glanced up, he saw an eagle float motionlessly far above. As they followed the uneven edge of the cliff, he heard a murmur that gradually strengthened into a deafening roar.

"I was hoping for a waterfall," Kiril said happily in his mind.

The cliff swung left and right again, and now Tamás saw a descending cloud, a thick white mist blanking off the cliff-face ahead. The sound of the waterfall had become mind-numbing, all-encompassing, majestically furious. The noon sun painted hundreds of rainbow circles of all sizes onto the falling white curtain, and these shifted and changed as the two of them followed the curve of the cliff's edge.

They moved slightly away from the cliff and soon reached a river. The two hundred meter width of water was not flat but formed a shallow V. In the middle, in its hurry the water formed miniature whitecaps. Whirls and eddies bordered the fast water.

"Feel like a swim?" Kiril asked without words.

Tamás grinned at him as they flew in the cool air above the river.

They kept going until the waterfall's sound lessened to a background murmur, then stopped for lunch. Still keeping its ellipsoid shape, the camp unfroze their orders, heated the meal and delivered it in a tasteful arrangement. Tamás hungrily devoured a roast bird, three thick slices of coconut bread, and servings of four vegetables. While sipping raspberry juice, he said, "You know what I miss most about home?"

"Tell me, mate."

"Fresh grown vegetables and fruit. Sure, this stuff tastes great and all that, but nothing beats food you've grown yourself."

"We could do some hunting and gathering. I've got bows and arrows in the camp, and I've noticed plenty of edible plants around."

"Good idea, though it'd slow us down."

Kiril ordered a second drink, sucked the cup dry and sent it back to the camp. He stood to go. Suddenly Artif shouted to both of them, "Precedence! I'll direct you!"

Without warning, Tamás was battling for a life.

Abel

His house was anchored in a sheltered little bay on the North Californian coast. Abel now started a systematic campaign, visiting everyone who lived within two hundred K of the western coast. Well, everyone but Susan

Lander. He wasn't ready to face her. Currently, he was talking to an old woman called Tonga Chigoru, who lived in a land house in a sheltered valley nestled among forested hills.

"I have no particular basis for believing them to be here rather than anywhere else," he explained. "But seeking them sure beats doing nothing."

"I imagine so," Tonga answered, her voice dry, "but suppose you found them, what then?"

The question took Abel by surprise. He actually hadn't given it any thought. "I want to protect my son."

"Of course. What will you do, attack Kiril?"

"Attack? You think I'm crazy too?"

"Forgive my saying so, Abel, but your actions in this matter have been something less than rational. I think you should let events take their course, and get on with your proper business."

"But—"

"You were kept busy enough until this emergency blew up, weren't you?"

"Yeah, but—"

"Abel, I'm eighty-five years old. That gives me a somewhat longer perspective on things. Look, your son could die on this quest, true. He could die because of something Kiril may have done. But also, he could survive, and be killed in his first bull ride. Or live to be a hundred and never amount to anything. Or come through this venture with more credentials than any other boy his age. For Brad's sake, let go. Don't be so obsessed."

"You don't understand. I was counseling this young man. I should have been able to do something to help him."

"I do understand. Instead of helping him, you've joined him. He was obsessed by Souda, and incidentally, I know her, because Susan Lander's grandmother and I were cousins. Anyway, now you're obsessed by Kiril. No, don't interrupt, just listen. His problem was that he didn't see Souda as she was, an attractive, pleasant, intelligent young woman, but idealized her as Perfection, all things good. His obsession distorted reality.

"Your problem is the same. You've put a label on this young fellow, and now you are fooled by your own label."

Abel looked at the wrinkled, dark face. White hairs grew out of several moles on her cheeks, and her white eyebrows bristled. The black eyes were full of concern, for him. Thin white hair formed a halo about her head. She stood, slim and still straight, despite her great age.

He sighed, suddenly defeated. "Tonga, you may be right. I'll think about your words."

"Come back any time," the old woman said within his mind as he disconnected.

⚡ 18 ⚡

Flora

It was no longer scary, flying in her Angel's wings without the protective silver shell. Sitting on nothing, about six feet off the ground, Flora confidently wove among a stand of closely spaced palm trees, about an hour's ride from home. Although a brisk wind moved the branches and sang a song in the trees, she was untouched by as much as a leaf. As soon as she glimpsed an obstacle, the computer plotted its path and moved Flora out of the way. *What a wonderful toy!* she thought.

She'd never been this way before, and looked forward to the new view that should present itself when she reached the top of this rise.

Ahead, bright beams of light speared into the cool shade, then she flew over grass. The early afternoon sun shone a little to her left, in a spotless pale blue dome. A lush landscape of rolling green hills spread before her. Forest stood stark and clear on the nearby slopes, but the distance shimmered with heat. Trees moved and swayed with the wind, which provided some welcome cooling on her sweating skin.

"Stop, Flora," Artif said within her mind. Flora immediately complied, and then saw that the ground in front fell away very sharply, perhaps another thirty feet ahead. She was on the top of a cliff.

"Lower me," Flora thought at her Angel's wings, and by the time she straightened her legs, she was standing. She looked around. To her right and slightly behind her, she saw a great tangle of blackberry, with luscious purple fruit in abundance on the thorny vines. These berries were three times the size of those from her times. Leaving the EGM motor idle, merely supporting her inside to avoid pain, she walked over and started to pick berries. She couldn't savor the taste, thanks to the chemotherapy, but their juiciness refreshed her as they slid down.

She lost track of time, moving along the boundary of the thicket, reaching further and further in as the easily accessible berries were gone.

Artif shouted internally, "Beware! Bear! Get out of there!" Simultaneously, Flora became aware of an unpleasant odor. It had to be strong to have penetrated her chemo-deadened nose.

Not comprehending for the moment, Flora turned and looked around. The stink intensified with great speed, and then she saw it. A huge, dark brown, bulky shape came soundlessly toward her along the grass, parallel to the edge of the blackberry thicket. On all fours, the animal loomed taller than her. Its mouth was half open, and hot brown eyes glowed on either side of the blunt muzzle.

She couldn't believe the speed of the beast. Artif shouted again, "Flora, flee!"

She turned in the opposite direction and sent a command to the EGM motor on her back. She was practically thrown into the air, then pain lanced into her in a dozen spots. She was swung in a great arc, straight into the middle of the tangle of thorny blackberry canes.

Flora cried out in agony. Razor-sharp, hooked thorns bit into her face, her arms, her legs, through her flimsy t-shirt into her body. They entangled themselves into her skirt, and as her motor vainly pulled, they bit with savage force everywhere.

The bear roared, a deep, ferocious sound that loosened Flora's bladder in her fear. The wind-whipped canes swung her slightly, and she looked at the huge animal. She saw it was a male, for he had risen onto his hind feet. Up in the air as she was, he still towered over her. Disregarding the thorns, he grasped two handfuls of canes and ripped them away from the tangle, wading in directly toward Flora.

She knew she was about to die a horrible death. The stink of the animal enveloped her. The roar from his open mouth seemed to shake the world, and he would have her in a second or two.

A shape appeared, barely visible behind the bear. It was that of a brown-skinned boy flying face down, as if swimming in the air. Like a missile, he smashed into the bear's back.

The bear turned with incredible speed, and one taloned paw struck at the boy. But the great blow passed right through him, and the animal actually staggered when no resistance met his force.

The boy's image disappeared, and instead a man flew at the bear from the other side. He was also horizontal in the air. The wind of his passage whipped long, very pale hair back, but his body was bronzed. His fist struck the bear on the nose, then he disappeared.

The boy was now behind and slightly above the bear, and an unshod foot shot out, delivering a hard kick with the heel to the rounded top of the animal's head. At the same time, another, identical boy again struck the bear from behind, copying his previous attack. The man was also there, ducking under the bear's left arm and delivering a body punch.

Flora heard, "No, keep to one image." The man's deep voice sounded calm and amused. The bear roared even louder, if that was possible, and wildly swung his arms. The three images disappeared.

"Lead him toward the cliff," the man said.

The boy appeared, standing on the ground. The bear held out his great brown arms and bounded toward him, away from Flora. He reached the boy's position in an instant, but the boy was no longer there. He stood, in the same posture, perhaps ten feet further away. The bear charged him, but the boy repeated the trick until he appeared to stand right at the very edge of the cliff.

All this must have been no more than a few seconds. Flora now saw two images of the man appear, one each side of the boy. Both were low down, horizontal, and spearing for the bear's legs with great speed. And a third image of the man struck the bear hard, on the back of the neck just above the shoulders.

The bear's roar of anger became one of terror as he toppled. All four images disappeared as he fell forward, arms wildly waving. He tumbled from Flora's sight, over the edge of the precipice.

A perceptible time later, she heard a great thud.

Man and boy appeared, standing side by side. "You can add this to your list of credentials, boy," the man said, still in that calm, amused voice. "I did a recording of it, something you'll be able to show your Tonya."

The boy answered, "Oh, but it was agony when he struck through me!"

Still caught in the tangle of blackberries, being held by the motor but swung by the wind, Flora was a landscape of pain. No part of her had escaped the hooked thorns, which bit deeply into her flesh everywhere. All the same, she had attention enough to note the details of her rescuers.

This man was the most beautiful human being she'd ever seen. His long hair was more platinum than gold, in startling contrast to the sun-browned skin. His tall body reminded her of Michelangelo's David, although she very quickly raised her eyes to above his waist: he was completely naked apart from a harness holding a large backpack. His face had a classical, chiseled beauty that was actually enhanced by the definitely oriental shape of his dark eyes.

The boy had darker skin, and straight, brown hair. His features were an exact copy of Mirabelle's with one exception: his eyes were brown rather than blue. He was also stark naked, but this was less disturbing to Flora.

So, Flora said, through the implant, "Thank you, Kiril and Tamás."

Dismay crossed the two faces, but the man merely said, "Madam, I'll cut you loose."

An object popped up out of his backpack and floated toward Flora. It was familiar: a black cigarette pack with a pencil poking out of it. It stopped in front of Flora, turned slightly, and a blinding red beam shot from the tip of the pencil. The laser beam severed cane after cane with swift efficiency, and within a couple of minutes, Flora could to fly forward out of her prison.

"I know who you are, too," the boy said in the meantime. "Greetings, Flora Fielding. My mother has often spoken about you."

The laser gun flew back above Kiril, descended, and disappeared inside his pack. He reached forward with large hands and delicately started to pluck the thorns still embedded in her skin.

Tamás's image relocated to stand on her other side, and he joined in the task of removing thorns.

Kiril said, without audible speech, "We're coming fast in the physical, should be here in about a period and a half. Artif called us, and saving a life has precedence."

Another new concept, Flora thought. "Precedence?" she asked.

Tamás explained, "We're on a quest, and should have no contact with anyone else. But helping a person in trouble overrides this. There is simply no one else who could have done what we did, because we're the only ones with a flying harness."

Listening to him was something of a distraction from the repeated sting of thorns being pulled from her skin. "Apart from me and Evanor," she said.

"Evanor? Artif, can you clarify please?" Kiril asked.

"An engineer who has helped Mirabelle copy your ideas," Artif replied. "However, he is not wearing his flying gear at the moment, and was asleep when Flora needed help. You two were the only ones who could send an effective image with sufficient speed."

At last, her two helpers stepped back. "Would you like us to escort you?" Kiril asked.

"If, if it's no trouble, I'd be delighted."

"We'll come with you in image then, and go to skin the bear in the physical. Tamás has only just expressed an interest in hunting, so he might as well learn about the messier aspects."

They started off, Flora in a sitting position, her two escorts face down on either side of her.

"Oh, pull your head in!" the boy answered, as if he was talking to another lad his own age. "I've hunted with both my parents, and also with my brother, Chia."

"Flora," Kiril offered, "I have supplies of healing film in my pack. If you would take off your clothes, I can attend to your thorn punctures."

"Oh no! Artif can help me when we get home. It's not that far." But meanwhile, she was dripping and dribbling blood from many places. Her cream-colored t-shirt looked like it had the measles. She was very aware of the maleness of this tall, beautiful young man. *In a way, I wish Nat hadn't woken me,* she thought. Despite the thousand aching wounds of her body, she couldn't stop a feeling of excitement every time she looked at Kiril.

To distract herself, and to pass the time, she asked, "Tell me about your quest."

Tamás answered, "For different reasons, we both needed to go on an extended deed of daring, and we teamed up. I'm so glad! I simply couldn't have done it without Kiril, I know that now. I'd have died several times, and also his experience has made it easier, and the company has kept boredom at bay. And I've even beaten him at chess once!"

Kiril laughed easily. "It won't happen again in a hurry, so savor it, mate."

Once more, Flora was impressed by the friendship, mutual respect and easy equality between these two. Abel was wrong. She said, "Do you know that the whole world is looking for you?"

They turned to her in surprise that just had to be genuine. "By what right?" Tamás said angrily. We're on a quest!"

"When we get to my place, I'll show you a recording. Meanwhile, tell me something about your adventures."

They started their story, Tamás's excited young voice interleaved with Kiril's quiet, amused baritone. At last, they reached the cave.

Kiril now said, "Flora, we'll leave you for a while. In the physical, we still haven't reached the bear's body, but should do so soon. When we're finished there, we'll come here and camp outside in your meadow."

Their images blinked out of existence.

Tamás

The bear looked huge even in death. Tamás immediately started to slice the skin open over the abdomen, but Kiril spent a few clicks making a new tool. He attached a multiple-pronged grapple to a metal ball from his climbing rope. This way, an EGM motor could be used to strip skin as they cut and flensed.

Even then, it took nearly two periods before the skin was off, clean, and rolled into a bundle on top of the camp.

The camp was making heavy going of getting up the sheer cliff-face, weighed down as it was with the bearskin and the recently replenished supplies. Tamás and Kiril added the lifting power of their individual EGM motors, pushing at the camp from below.

"Let's recharge," Tamás suggested when they finally gained the location of their fight with the bear.

He was the one to open the dish antenna, then they stood clear while the camp absorbed the gift of power from a topstore to the north. They filled their personal batteries, topped up, then zoomed toward Flora's home.

"Is this the end of our quest?" Tamás asked.

"It doesn't have to be. I broke my Pacific quest when I met Souda." A brief look of pain crossed Kiril's face, but he continued in an even tone of voice. "I stayed with her for three months, then completed my journey. We can stay with this lady until we're sure she is all right, say a day or two, then go on."

"It was funny, how she reacted when you asked her to take her clothes off."

Kiril grinned. "She did her best not to look at my genitals, too. I happen to know, in ancient times, public nakedness was unacceptable. Human bodies were considered dirty, to be hidden except in private."

"For Brad's sake, why?"

"I don't know. But remember, they lived in an ice age. Such attitudes just had to change if people wanted to live in our kind of world. Anyway, it's getting cold now, mornings and evenings. It's won't be a hardship, wearing some clothes when we're with her."

"Yeah, I suppose. I wonder what this recording is about. You know, the whole world hunting us?"

They found out, soon enough. The sun had set when once more they entered the clearing with the doorway into the cliffside. Kiril told the camp to set itself up. They dressed, then the two of them walked in.

Flora stood, waiting for them. She had a mosaic of healing film all over her face, arms and legs. She still wore her flying harness, but over clean clothes. Tamás noticed that her face was apprehensive. "I'm sorry, you won't like this," she said.

Tamás saw his father, watched the message, but couldn't believe it. This was outrageous! Hands bunched into fists, eyes blazing, he shouted "That's not fair!"

Kiril was more in control, though his lips were compressed into a thin line. He said, "Tamás, he must've gone crazy with worry over you. Maybe you should have confided in him."

Tamás barely listened. He mentally shouted, "Artif, I must see him, NOW!"

And he stood in the lounge room of his father's house. Abel had been striding up and down but stopped and turned to look at him. Tamás opened his mouth to shout at Abel, until his eyes took in the terrible changes. His mighty, powerful father had become an old man with a bent back, a lined face and sagging jowls. His previously supple, muscular body was now a skin-covered skeleton. On seeing his son, Abel's face lit up with his old grin, but what a terrible sight that was, what a travesty on the skull-like visage with its wrinkled neck and over-large eyes!

"Tamás! Oh Tony be thanked!" the old man — never in his life before had Tamás thought of him as an old man — bounded forward, arms spread for a hug.

The boy relocated his image, two meters back. At the same time, he noted the automatic request from his father to send a return image, and said "No!" to Artif within his mind.

Abel stopped, arms still uselessly held out each side, that grin frozen on his face, meaningless now. The bloodshot eyes looked at Tamás with puzzlement. "What... what has Kiril done to you? Why..."

This broke the spell, and Tamás could think again. He said, "Dad, what's wrong with **you**? I'm OK."

Abel dropped his arms, a shadow of his old authority back. "There's nothing wrong with me, now that I know you're safe." Again he tried to send a return image, and again Tamás blocked him.

"You don't look all right. Have you been sick?"

"Only sick with worry about you, being with that madman."

This rekindled the anger that had originally brought Tamás here. "HE IS NOT A MADMAN! HE IS MY FRIEND!" He continued, a little more calmly, "I've just seen the recording you sent to the whole world. It's unfair! It's terrible! It's untrue!"

"Oh yeah? Then why are you treating me like a stranger? Worse than a stranger, for you won't let me hold you after all this time apart, you won't even let me visit wherever you are."

"Kiril has nothing to do with that. I came here to, to, to tell you how angry I am. It was an awful, hurtful thing to do, and I'm ashamed to be your son!"

Abel stood up a little straighter, and a terrible sadness showed on his ravaged face. "So. He has stolen your love from me as well."

Tamás lifted both his hands to his head, and tugged hard at his hair in his frustration. "Oh shit. No." He took a deep breath, once more torn between pity and fury. "Dad, listen, this is getting us nowhere."

"Yeah, I've noticed. Maybe, we should start talking instead of emoting. You came here, you start. Tell me."

"It's simple. I'm on a quest. I kept it a secret, for one reason only. If I hadn't, Mom would have stopped me. You know that."

"Hmm. She'd have tried."

"I was going to go alone, flying around the world with the new EGM rig. Kiril had been through terrible times, and begged for me to allow him to come with me. He apparently copes with problems by taking on a challenge."

"Yes, I know that."

"Dad, it's been good for both of us. I would've died several times, except for having him there. His experience and, I don't know, his way of doing things have been more than useful, and I've learnt a lot. And I had company. And for him, he's told me that being with me has helped him to heal from his sorrows. And listen, he's not a madman. Looking at you, having seen that bloody recording, I'd have to think that you're the one with problems in that line!"

"Finished?" It was bizarre to see the old expression of dignified anger on the skeletal face.

"Yeah, I'm finished."

"All right, son, think of things through my eyes. Kiril has done the unthinkable, and acted with intent to kill another person. He had provocation, sure, but is there anyone else on the planet who'd have reacted like that, to any provocation? Not likely! Then he's on trial by Control, in Tony's cave, and he loses his temper! Can you believe that? And then this person disappears in the company of my son."

"And you knew he wanted to hand on, wanted to make restitution for his crime."

"And who stopped him? Your mother. Who had leaned on him earlier? I did. How did I know he wasn't using you to get back at us? Was I crazy for not trusting his stability?"

"Dad, it was a terrible misunderstanding. You must undo the damage. You've got to make a new recording, an announcement telling everyone that Kiril has done nothing wrong, we are just on a quest together."

"I'd do just that — if I believed it to be true. Prove it."

"Look at me. Do I look abused?"

"Your actions in the past few clicks have told me that you've been set against me, your thoughts manipulated."

Tamás borrowed some words from his father. "OK, Dad, think of things through my eyes. I've been enjoying a person's company for months, been through danger and adventures and long periods of repetitive, boring activity, and he kept me going. I learnt from him more than I'd have thought possible, and he's now my best friend."

He saw a look of pain on Abel's poor face. Correctly interpreting it, he said, "Oh, Dad, listen, he isn't a second father to me, far less a replacement for you. A short while ago, before I started, I was a boy. I had child friends. Now, I'm not much older, only just thirteen, but I'm a man. And I have a man for a friend. You're still my father."

"Then let me hug you, boy!"

And, pity overflowing in his heart, suddenly Tamás wanted to do just that.

19.

Flora

For an interminable time, the boy's body had been inanimate, hanging from his flying harness like a ragdoll. Barely before Abel's message had finished, he'd shouted, "That's not fair!" then he'd gone absolutely still and limp. His head hung down. His feet were on the floor, but clearly wouldn't have held his weight if it hadn't been for the EGM motor on his back. He barely breathed, and Flora started forward in concern.

Looking at him, Kiril said reassuringly, "I'd say he's visiting his father. They'll be having an all-mighty argument, and all his energy is concentrated there." At the same time, Flora heard his voice within her mind, as if he was muttering, "Sit him comfortably, support his head and arms," and the boy's body moved in accordance with these commands. Tamás was still a ragdoll, but now one that was sitting in a comfortable, invisible armchair. Obviously, she'd overheard Kiril talking to Tamás's EGM motor.

No, Abel is wrong about Kiril, she thought again, seeing such considerate behavior. Aloud, she asked, "Kiril, can I offer you some refreshment?"

"A meal would be nice. Tamás and I've had no dinner yet." He sent a stream of fast thought toward the kitchen outside the door, and also sat.

"Will he be able to eat? I mean..."

"Oh yes. He won't taste any of it, but it'll fill his belly."

Flora also sent an order to the kitchen, and saw a brief smile cross Kiril's face as she added a "please" on the end. Then she said, "Kiril, for several months now, quite a number of people have told me about you and your friend, Souda. Three members of Control have asked me to talk to you about your problems. So, at last we've met."

"Why, what difference can you make?"

Flora opened her mouth to answer, but the young man continued, "And anyway, I have a worse problem now, or maybe two worse problems."

"I might be able to help because jealousy was a common thing in my times, and also I've been reading books on how to help you. I guess the worse problems are this recording from Abel, and..."

"And acting in a way that was intended to, to... hurt Souda." Kiril's face, his whole body was a sculpture in grief.

"Kiril," Flora said gently, "it happened, and cannot be undone. But as a result of that unfortunate episode, you've changed, and are a different person. Can you tell me, what good changes in you have come from it?"

He looked surprised. "Good changes? Tony help us, good changes?" He stopped, thinking, and Flora didn't break the silence.

The door slid open and three trays came in.

And suddenly, Abel stood between her and Tamás. The boy was upright, actually held off the ground in his father's embrace. Flora could see the tall black man's back. All the ribs were showing, and his bare buttocks and legs seemed to have shriveled away. All the same, he held the boy as if he was no weight at all. Tamás's chocolate-brown arms seemed pale against his father's dark skin. They were welded around Abel's neck.

Kiril had sprung to his feet, his open face a battlefield of emotions: joy for his young friend, hostility to Abel, apprehension, surprise.

At last, Abel put Tamás down. He turned to face Flora, then glanced sideways at Kiril. His now-bony left arm was still on Tamás's shoulder, as if he couldn't bear to break contact. "Greetings, Flora, Kiril," he said, his voice once more the old, resonant baritone.

"Welcome, Abel. You look like you could eat something. Have my serving." She told her tray of food to go to him.

Kiril laughed. "Yeah, have mine too, you old skeleton."

Abel looked in the corner, at the pile of cushions. One of them rose and flew to him. He sat. "I'm not sure I can eat even one full meal. My stomach's shrunk. But he started on Flora's meal, keenly enough.

Kiril called his own tray back and started to eat. Nevertheless, Flora heard him say, "Eat now, Abel, but afterward we have some serious talking to do."

"Surely," Abel replied, without voice as well.

Young Tamás also started to eat, with the ravenous hunger of a growing boy. He said without voice, "I'm sure it can all be sorted out now. Let's not get heated up about a chain of misunderstandings. Please?"

The maturity of that comment surprised Flora.

A fourth tray came through the door, and Flora started to eat too, dutifully, without taste. She looked at these three males who had suddenly burst into her life. Speaking through the implant, (and wasn't that still a strange thing?), she said, "Kiril, if you can't stay with me for now, please come back at the end of your quest. We have work to do together." Somehow, the idea of spending a lot of time with this young man was very attractive.

Kiril looked at father and son, still touching as they sat side by side. His face lit up with an idea. "I think I might stay with you, right now. Abel, how'd you like to learn to fly?"

Tim

Tim and Ria were out, gathering relics. The basket following them held a good collection of strange objects, to be checked against the records once they got it home. It was amazing how durable these old things were. Still, some of them quickly disintegrated once they'd been exposed to the sun, which was why it was important to go prospecting immediately after heavy rain.

Ria darted ahead and bent. She showed him her find: a blue, tapered cylinder about the length of his little finger. One end was closed off, and a short, flat protruding part was attached at the other.

"What could it be for?" he asked.

"For finding." She giggled, and tossed the thing into the basket.

Then something wonderful happened. Tim heard his father's voice, saying, "My little loves!" and he stood between them, wearing a white t-shirt and a blue kilt. He squatted, and Tim and Ria ran to him. Oh, it was so wonderful to be hugged to that muscular chest! "Oh, Kiril," Ria said, very fast, "we never believed those nasty things about you! Never!"

But Tim could only add, "Dad, you missed my birthday!"

Dad held him away so they could look into each other's eyes. Tim saw that his big, tough father had tears coming from his eyes. "Timmy, my dear, it was something I had to do. But now, Tony be thanked, it's over. And with some luck, I mightn't ever go on another quest, until I go with you on your first one in a few years' time."

"Is that a promise?"

"It is."

Still snuggling against Dad's chest, within the circle of his arm, Ria asked, "Who was this boy with you?"

"I'll introduce you to him when I can. He's only a boy, sure, but you can thank him when you meet him. Being with him has helped me to feel better. He was going to do something so dangerous that he was bound to kill himself. I liked him at first meeting, so I convinced him to let me go with him. And that was tremendously good for me too. I can now live with... with myself."

Kiril stood, one child cradled on each arm, and started walking toward the house. Tim called to the basket, which started following them, then gave himself up to the enjoyment of his father's touch: the feel of his skin, the strength that carried him and Ria like they were dolls, the lightly noticeable smell of his body.

But Ria said, fiercely, "Kiril, I don't believe you could have done anything bad!"

Dad stopped and put them down. He squatted so that he could look Ria in the eyes. "My darling, I'm afraid I did. I have a rather terrible distinction: I'm the only criminal now alive, the only criminal for over a thousand years. It's true." Once more, tears ran unheeded out of his dark eyes, down his face.

"What was it?" Tim asked.

The depth of pain in Dad's eyes was terrible to see. "I... I... oh, Tony help us, I tried to kill your mother."

It was true. It had to be true, but it was unbelievable. "But you love her!" Tim blurted out.

"I do. I... I offer no excuses. At the time, I reacted in a way I wish I hadn't. But... but I cannot deny it. Completely without thought, from impulse, I reacted to a situation and acted to harm her."

Ria reached a small hand for his face and wiped the tears off his cheeks. "I love Souda," she said, "but I love you too, all the same."

And things were all right again.

Mirabelle

The balloon flew over endless ocean, south of the bulge of Westrica. With the changing of the seasons, Mirabelle was moving from the Swedish Isles to Antarctica. In the physical, she sat cross-legged in her study. Her image was back in her northern garden with its riot of the colors of late autumn, supervising the machines, when Artif said, "Darling, Abel wants to visit. He's got someone with him."

"Who?"

Abel's voice answered, "Find out." It was the old Abel's voice, and for the first time in ages, had a laugh in it. Mirabelle's being lit up. *Tamás!* she thought with certainty.

She cancelled the image and opened her eyes. "Welcome," she said.

The boy had grown. His skin was darker, his brown hair long enough to cover his shoulders. He wore a white t-shirt and a blue kilt, and what just had to be an EGM harness.

Without words, Mirabelle and Tamás rushed into each other's arms. Her son's nose rubbed against Mirabelle's right ear, that's how much taller he'd become during the months of his disappearance.

"My love," she said, "I've died a thousand times since you'd gone."

"Oh Mom, I'm so sorry! But I was OK. And mainly because I had Kiril to look after me. He's great!"

Standing back, looking at mother and son, Abel said, "And when Tamás continues, I'll be the one going with him."

In Abel's house, Mirabelle looked at father and son, Abel's arm over the boy's shoulder. "You'll need to strengthen up first," she told him, "You look like death on legs."

In Flora's room, with Kiril on one side and Flora over the bed, he answered, "Nothing a few good sleeps and good food won't fix. It'll take Tamás several days to reach me in the physical, and you'll see, by then I'll be OK."

"It's all right, Mom," the boy said seriously into her ear, "I'll look after him."

Susan

She was hand-making a salad, using the vegetables she'd picked outside, when she heard Ria's voice raised in a shout, "Mom, Mom, we have a visitor!"

She turned and had to shriek with joy to see her son, walking in
through the door, carrying the two children. Kiril smoothly bent and let
the children go once their feet were on the ground, then his image
relocated, and she was submerged in his embrace.

Susan clutched him to herself, buried her being into the harbor of his
arms, rubbed her face against the hollow of his neck. "Kiril, Kiril, Kiril..."
was all she could say.

After an unmeasured time, he gently pulled away from her and took
her face in his great hands. "Mother," he said, "things will be all right
now."

"And bloody Abel?"

"That's why I'm here. Wait."

Reluctantly, they each let the other go, but still stood face to face,
within touching distance. The children were snuggled against Kiril's legs,
and he dropped a hand on each golden head.

He said, "We're about to have another visitor. Any clicklet now."

And Abel stood, just inside the door. Susan gasped when she saw the
changes in him. He was gaunt beyond belief, his face a skin-covered skull,
his ribs clearly outlined. His abdomen was actually a hollow. However, he
stood straight, and a happy smile illuminated that ravaged face.

"Greetings," he said, "Once more, I have a recording for you. This is
for everyone who received my previous recording, and for all those people
who were affected by it in any way."

His image disappeared. A small recording globe hovered in the air
where he'd been. Susan heard Kiril send it a command.

Abel stood in front of them once more. "Greetings, I am Abel
T'Dwuna," he said. "I am overjoyed to report that my son Tamás Karlsen
is well, and not in any danger other than the risks of any young man on a
quest."

His face now grew somber. "And I have a sincere apology to make. My
previous message was based on a series of misunderstandings. Since the
Control trial of his situation, Kiril Lander has done nothing reprehensible.
It is now my opinion that he will never repeat his previous mistakes. Far
from endangering Tamás in any way, he has been protecting and teaching
Tamás, and my son's success on his quest is in a large part due to Kiril's
company. For this, I publicly thank Kiril." He bowed his head.

"I cannot undo the damage I've done. All I can say is that I was wrong,
and acted from anxiety for a loved person. Tonga Chigoru, a wise old lady
of the English Culture, recently pointed out to me that in fact I had
succumbed to the same patterns of thinking as those that got Kiril into
trouble. He and I are now two of a kind. I ask his forgiveness."

Abel's image looked at them. He ended with, "Thank you for your
attention." Then he was gone, the little recording globe still hovering in
front of the closed door.

Souda

Artif said, "Darling, are you still interested in contact with Kiril? He's available now."

Souda's heart did a somersault. She put her flute down — not that she'd managed to play anything reasonable — and asked, "Why? Quest over?"

"You can ask him."

Souda was torn in two. Yes, she very much wanted to see him again. And yet, how was he going to react to her, after what she'd done to him? Despite the months of therapy, her guilt flared like a reinfected wound.

"Well?"

She took a deep breath. "Yes, Artif. Tell him to visit me."

He was dressed for a change, in T-shirt and kilt. His pale hair was a mane covering his shoulders. "My love," he said, "thank you for agreeing to see me."

"You're... you're not angry with me?"

"Angry?" He laughed, unbelievingly. "After I attacked you? I came to ask your forgiveness."

The sun shone on the world once more. Souda slowly, sinuously walked toward him. "Kiril, I'll forgive you, on one condition." She stopped, almost in touching distance.

"What's that?"

"That you forgive me, my love."

And she was effortlessly lifted in mighty arms, and carried like a baby to the bed, the wonderful bed.

⚡ 20 ⚡

Flora

Flora lay face down over the bed, her eyes closed, as Kiril gently and delicately removed patches of healing film from her legs. "Your skin is so fragile!" he complained.

"It's the chemicals I take to fight the cancer."

"I know that. But it's hard not to tear your skin. I don't want to give you any new wounds, that's for sure."

He moved from the left leg to the right. Artif said, "Flora, Nathaniel would like to..."

"Oh yes, he's welcome," she answered before Artif had finished. She got the bed to sit her up and turn her around.

The little man stood inside the door, his dear ugly face lit by a great grin as usual. "Greetings. Kiril isn't it? Perhaps the most famous man on the planet?"

"Well, I..."

"Congratulations," Nat continued as if Kiril hadn't spoken, "not many people can say they've bested Abel. You can add it to your credentials."

He walked forward, and his eyes opened wide on seeing Flora's patchwork appearance. "Now, what have you been up to, love?" he asked.

"Had an argument with a blackberry patch. Kiril and Tamás rescued me from a huge bear, then had to pull about a thousand barbs out of my skin."

"Oh you poor thing!"

She laughed. "It's healed fast. This healing skin's marvelous, and it was a lot better than being ripped apart by that beast."

"The bearskin is curing outside," Kiril added. "I have the feeling that Tamás might like to save it as a gift to his lady love."

"I'll have to meet this young man." Nat joined Kiril in delicately stripping small patches of film from Flora's skin. "Where is he?"

'I've decided to stay here with Flora for now. Tamás has gone on alone, toward Abel's house, which is moored in a bay south of here. He'll be fine by himself for a few days. In fact, I think he's now experienced enough to cope with anything short of a hurricane."

There was a silence while the two men concentrated on their task. Nat gently peeled off the first of three patches of film next to Flora's right eye, and she stayed motionless for him. Using the implant, she said, "Nat, there's something I've been wanting to ask you about..."

"Hmm?" He straightened and looked at her.

"There was little point before, Abel was in no fit state to do anything, but... Everybody tiptoes around the reason I was awakened in the first place. Mirabelle won't tell me, she says it's up to Abel. And she sounds furious whenever she says that."

Kiril's thought came, angrily, "You mean, for all this time, he's kept you in ignorance? That's cruel!"

"He's told me he had an emergency on his hands. You of course."

The big man snorted. "That's an excuse! Look, he has this awesome reputation that he can do ten things at once, in ten different places. He's not President because of his looks or charm, but because of his mental abilities."

Nat said, "Flora, I agree with Kiril. But you know, you don't need to wait for him. Why don't you visit him instead?"

"Great idea!" Suddenly Kiril's face lit up with a wide grin. "Hey Flora, now's a good time, before Tamás gets there. After that, he can hide behind being on a quest, if he chooses."

Flustered, Flora said, "But I can't just burst in on the President!"

"Why not, everybody else does." Nat was grinning too. "There, your face is clear now."

Kiril explained, "It's part of his job as a Leader. His main responsibility is to help people in trouble."

"And since he is responsible for YOUR trouble," Nat leaned forward and lightly kissed her cheek, "it's time you brought it home to him."

"But what do I do?"

"Is that the great business magnate speaking? The great actress? Put on a good show of disdainful anger to him. Look, I'll go home, and Kiril can..."

"I can work on the bearskin for a while." Kiril turned toward the door, which slid open. He marched out. Giving a cheery wave, Nat's image disappeared.

"Artif?" Flora asked without words.

She stood just within the open door of what had to be the stateroom of a ship. The broad, long room was roughly rectangular, with the walls curving in toward each other on the far end. The ceiling was low and very slightly domed. Abel, standing near the huge window to the left, had less than a foot of space above his head. She was surprised at how neat everything was, and yet comfortably homely. It was a very masculine room, most things being a shade of brown: light tan colored resilient-seeming floor, almost-white walls, big, comfortable-looking couches and chairs.

Abel must have been gazing out the window. Beyond him, she saw still water, rippled by a slight breeze, with a spectacular headland of yellow, bare rocks in the background. Surf boomed faintly. The tall man turned toward her. His mouth was full and chewing, and he held what looked like the partly eaten drumstick of a gigantic bird in his right hand.

He was still gaunt, Flora could still see his ribs, but his face had started to fill out. His eyes no longer bulged, and the wrinkles of his neck had mostly smoothed out. He stood straight and moved with some of his old grace.

"Greetings, Abel," Flora said, remembering to keep her voice cold.

"Welcome, Flora." He waved the drumstick. "As you can see, I'm working hard, preparing for my coming trip with my boy."

Flora had omitted to put on her Angel's wings. This was the first time since its acquisition that she was without an EGM motor. She was pleasantly surprised that her image felt no internal pain.

Even while facing Abel across his magnificent room, she was aware of him, standing right next to her where she sat on her bed. The only difference was that his image was not eating. Both versions of Abel were stark naked, but Flora was used to this now.

Abel continued, "Can I offer you some refreshment?"

"No thank you. Abel, before you get busy again, we have some talking to do." She made her words into icebergs: slow, icy and threatening.

Abel glanced at a corner. Two cushions floated out, one to each of them. They both sat. In her house, she called for a cushion for him, and the image sat, too. In his house, he looked down at the drumstick with something like distaste. A tray came in through the door past Flora, and he put the food on it. He took a damp blue cloth from the tray and wiped his mouth and hands. The tray went out again.

Flora waited in frigid silence during the few seconds this took. Abel now looked her in the eye. "You're annoyed with me."

"You're very perceptive."

"Flora, as you know, 123 Sleepers survived the Cataclysm and the Chaos that followed it. You're one of them. We're sure that there were many more, but they were in the wrong places. Particularly during the Chaos, many of their houses were entered... and there was no Artif then, as yet."

"So?"

"I'm coming to it. As you also know, Tony decided that the planet's population should be limited to one million. Brad was an old man when the first Sleeper was found, a man named Harvey Kocsis..."

"I knew Harvey! He'd been one of my main opponents in the trading game. He specialized in destabilizing the money used by a particular country, then trading in the currency..." She saw that her words were meaningless to Abel, so simply concluded, "Then suddenly he disappeared."

"His records said that he was developing something called Alzheimer's disorder, and while he could, he put himself to sleep until a cure was found."

"That was a condition where an older person lost mental abilities, became more and more child- like and helpless. They did bizarre things."

"Pity you didn't have the custom of handing on. Anyway, Control had a long debate about whether this Harvey was part of the one million or not. Mind you, at the time they didn't yet hold sway over all the planet, there were still wild humans, and several millions, oh Artif?"

"The records estimate about thirty millions still alive."

"Thank you. So, one more or less seemed like a petty question to many of them. But Brad's judgment was that it was essential to work out the principle."

"Abel, you're being very long-winded about this. Are you avoiding something?"

His dark eyes flared at her. "Flora, it's hard enough. Just let me give my lecture and listen. Where was I? After a lot of debate, they decreed that a Sleeper was part of Humanity. And a number of times, this has been re-examined, and each time the decision was upheld. This issue is the longest-standing controversy, and the one that's been reopened the most often."

He stood and strode a few paces from side to side, in both their homes. "For well over a thousand years, we've had a million less 123 people active on the planet. And this has always been a source of resentment for a very large segment of the population." He grinned, mirthlessly, "Naturally, these were people who had trouble qualifying for children: women only allowed one child, men never chosen. You know, 'If only the Sleepers didn't count as people, I might be able to have a baby,' that kind of thing."

"Surely, that's such a small percentage..."

"Of course. The practical difference is negligible. But when were people ever swayed by numbers? There are tens of thousands of people out there, who passionately feel that there should be a million people, PLUS the Sleepers. And since it is the duty of Control to allay discontent, there are Control members who, quite properly, keep arguing for this. Such as your dear friends Mirabelle and Cynthia."

"Mirabelle and Cynthia have both had four children."

"Surely. They wouldn't be on Control unless they had top qualifications."

"Are you implying that they advance a cause they don't believe in? Or is the view you're opposed to held by people other than those who can't have children?"

He waved a dismissive hand. "I was stating generalities. The bulk of them are of inferior stock, and resent this. Not all of them, true. But most of them."

"Abel, you know that you're a very arrogant man?"

He shrugged. "I've often been accused of it. But it's based on evidence: I'm usually proven right by events."

"How can you say that!" Flora felt her face flush with outrage. "What about your, your infamous recording about Kiril?"

He had the grace to look abashed. "Yeah, that was a mistake."

"Then learn from it!"

"Look, do you want to hear my explanation, or do you want an argument about my attitudes?"

"I'll have the explanations first, thank you."

"I've never heard 'thank you' used as a weapon before. I must remember the tone of voice. Anyway, just over two years ago, the oldest member of Control decided to retire. When he went, we didn't have enough people from Asian Cultures, so included that in the search parameters. Artif found four suitable people, and we chose a young Japanese woman. And as her first act, she resurrected the old fight about the Sleepers. It got so that Control was polarized into two camps. We couldn't get onto any other business, it was round and round endlessly. So, I came up with a novel idea. Not for the first time in my life, I found a solution no one had thought of, ever before."

He was being arrogant again, Flora thought, but after all that was the way of the times. Men crowed. She let it pass.

He continued, "Until now, no one had ever considered, what do the Sleepers think on the matter? I proposed that one Sleeper be awakened. This person would study our society, then advise us on a multiple decision: The Sleepers could all be awakened and join into society, and in due course die like everyone else. Or they might be considered to have died before the Cataclysm, for is it a life, is it a kindness to be unconscious, merely breathing, for an infinity? We couldn't tell, but one who survived the experience would have a better perspective. If so, their life support could be turned off, allowing them to hand on, though unknowingly. Or, the awakened Sleeper might recommend one thing for some Sleepers, something else for others. Or advise us to leave them alone. But at least, I argued, this gave us a chance to get rid of this recurring issue, once and for all."

He stopped. Flora thought about the problem, head bowed. "That's a terrible responsibility," she said at last. Did she want these other Sleepers left as they were, in an artificial coma forever? Or awakened into what she was facing: an ancient problem with no modern treatment, because the problem was also a fossil? Or in effect recommend their execution? What a choice!

"I know. Why do you think I found it so hard to tell you? I'll be honest, I wouldn't want the job!"

"You know, I don't much want it either. Why did you choose me?"

"Artif assured us that your condition didn't affect your intelligence. You had great credentials in your old life, so much so that your reputation as an actress has survived even to today. And... I've always loved to look at your face."

She felt herself flush. "Did you look at me while I was lying there, unconscious, and..."

"No, no, of course not. But I've often watched your movies."

"And when do you expect an answer?"

"Flora, don't hurry. When you're ready. Sometime before you die, whether that's this year or fifty years from now. Artif will know, and I, or the President after me, will call a Control meeting with you as guest."

"And in the meantime, you've shut up everybody about the issue of the Sleepers."

Looking smug, he answered, "No one has ever accused me of being stupid."

Tamás

He missed Kiril terribly. As Artif guided him through twisting valleys, on the shortest route to the sea, he kept wanting to say something, exchange a joke or friendly insult, risk another drubbing on the chess board, or just glance to the side and see the large, comforting shape zooming along beside him. But he only had the camp for company.

A long, winding valley opened up in front of him as he crested a rise. Artif said, "Darling, now just follow the river."

"Thanks." For two days now, he'd had to concentrate almost all the time, weaving among trees or crossing undulating upland plains. The land fell away sharply in front of him, a rocky slope covered with stunted bushes and long grass. The water course at the bottom was scarcely a river here, more like a lively creek. Without a pause he swooped down toward it.

He started to do his isometric exercises once above the watercourse. He swept around a bend to the right, and a herd of horses fled at his approach. He turned to comment to Kiril, but his friend wasn't there. And you don't send images when you're on a quest.

The sky was overcast, and Tamás felt cold, even in his warm suit. He stopped and donned a second layer of clothing. Artif said, "It'll rain soon," so he put his waterproofs on, too.

What caught him soon after was not the heavy, warm rain of summer, but a cold, neverending autumn drizzle. He flew into curtains of tiny droplets that wetted him despite his waterproof cover. *Tony knows how they get in!* he thought, but get in they did. After a while, he felt wetter than in a storm over the Atlantic.

And Kiril wasn't there to make a joke of it.

Miserably he pushed on into the rain. The creek below him joined another, and more tributaries cascaded down into it over broken rocks or flowed out of deep gorges, and by nightfall he was over a respectably-sized river. He set up the camp on the lush grass of the left shore. He thankfully stripped in the wonderful warmth of the tent, devoured a meal and slept the night through.

In the morning, he looked out at the rain that still smeared itself down the tent's dome, and groaned. "Oh Artif, how long is this going to last?"

"In this area, it'll keep raining like this for the next three months or so, with a few short breaks. You can also expect a few severe storms."

"Thanks," he said sarcastically, raising his eyes to the invisible sky.

There was no point waiting, then. He dressed, put on his pack, and went out into the drizzle. Water trickled in around his face by the time the camp had packed itself up.

Kiril

Kiril sprawled over a sort of hovering nest he'd made for himself from ten cushions, and watched Flora hovering over her bed. "I've thought about that question you asked me," he said.

She looked puzzled, so he explained, "In what way am I a better person for having... having committed my crime." He just couldn't bring himself to say, "having tried to hurt Souda."

A smile lit up her face. Its beauty warmed him, despite her peeling, pale skin.

"I think it's as much due to the time I spent with Tamás as to anything else, but I now know that I can live without Souda. Before, my every thought focused on her, and I could distract myself only through danger. I don't know why..."

Flora interrupted, "Kiril, habits are hard to break. From my reading, I know that habits are not limited to actions, but also involve feelings and thoughts. For some reason, you formed a habit of thought. Then it never had a chance to be broken."

"I didn't want it broken! And that's the other change, the other improvement in me. My... habit brought me to the point of having done something terrible. So yes, now I acknowledge that it's sick. I do want to break it."

"So, you're saying, if you hadn't given in to an impulse and tried to kill Souda..." he flinched at this, "...then you might have gone on suffering, and making Souda suffer, for the rest of your lives?"

"Yes. And now I realize how childish I was. At my trial, Mirabelle said that I had to think of how other people felt, not only how I felt. And you're right, my, what's that word? jealousy made her unhappy just as much as it affected me."

"Nat has found a Russian book that said, 'Jealousy is a double tragedy: the more the jealous partner demands, the less the loved person is able to return.' Kiril, there's always a balance in things. In my days, people used to share houses, not like now when everyone lives alone. And if one person preferred more tidiness than the others, he or she would be doing an increasing amount of the tidying work, the others less and less, until this led to resentment and arguments."

Kiril had to smile at her awkward wording. "Flora, just say 'she,' that does for both men and women. And I can see what you're saying. I took over the desire to be together, so much so that there was no room for Souda."

"Exactly! But listen, do you think Souda would be interested in taking part in our discussion?" Kiril hadn't even had time to ask Artif, before Souda stood beside him. She wore one of her lace body suits. He could sense the scent of her body, and suddenly Flora's home seemed brighter. "Greetings, you must be Flora Fielding," Souda said. Then she turned to him. "Hi, love. I wasn't doing anything much anyway. I thought you must be neglecting me!"

Kiril reached out a hand toward her. She took it, and he pulled her onto his lap.

"Welcome, Souda," Flora said. "Kiril and I were talking about jealousy."

Souda had to have the word explained to her, but then she turned her face to him, "Kiril, is it still a problem?"

Flora explained, "Maybe not right now, but you can be sure it'll return. Patterns of thinking always do. But I've done a lot of reading, there are things you can do about it. Now, first let's examine the things that initially attracted you to Kiril. They're the key to the things you later found annoying about him..."

⚡ 21 ⚡

Flora

Flora couldn't sleep. It was late at night, must have been the small hours. Artif said, in immediate response to the thought, "It's just after one."

That was periods of course. Flora's mental arithmetic wasn't up to a conversion, this time of the night. "Uh, what's that in hours?"

"Twenty to three."

Kiril was asleep, in the blue room. Artif heated it for him to "normal" temperature, and he put on his flying rig. This enabled him to sleep, hovering in the air.

Flora sighed, yet again. "Artif, how in Heaven's name can I make a decision about the Sleepers?"

The deep, mellow voice sounded warmer than usual. "My love, that's the kind of question I'm programmed never to answer."

"Can I talk to you about it? I mean..." she tailed off, not knowing what she meant.

"Of course you can. Just don't expect me to solve human problems. I mustn't."

"It seems to me that every choice is wrong. When I consider the possibility of leaving them as they are, I ask, would I be interested in returning to suspended animation? And I shudder at the thought, it's horrible. It's the negation of life, worse than death. Then I ask, should they be turned off, and that's murder, it's abhorrent to me. And finally, awakening them? Harvey was a bastard, excuse me, but if he was awakened, could you help with his problem?"

"There are records."

"Yes, you could help him the way you helped me. By going back to the records, and maybe improving somewhat the treatment that was possible then, the treatment we Sleepers fled from. So, Harvey would wake to mental decline and loss of dignity, a bizarre second childhood. Incontinence, meaningless acts, ugh... And he was once one of the most powerful people on the planet. Sure, he abused that power, but still..."

"Why don't you try to sleep, Flora. Your decision will come to you if you give it time."

"I don't know that I can."

"There at least I can help you."

And her consciousness submerged into a soft, warm darkness.

Of course she overslept in the morning. She dreamt of her grandmother. Gran sat in her large, padded armchair, the reclining one that had a footrest spring up when you pulled against the armrests. She smiled at Flora, who was very little, and as always, she was knitting. Her shiny metal needles went "click, click, click" against each other in a never-ending rhythm, and the complicated pattern of the next sweater grew in front of Flora's eyes.

The clicking noise stopped. Flora opened her eyes, and found herself back above her EGM bed. She lay nearly face down, in the almost-dark ambience Artif maintained during Flora's sleep in that windowless room.

Still smiling at her dream, Flora asked for light, got the bed to stand her up, and started walking toward the bathroom.

The clicking noise began again, but now she realized that it must be quite a loud hammering, heard faintly through the door.

She swiftly dressed and went out. A brilliant oblong of sunlight spearing in through the open outside door sharply divided the corridor in two. The noise was more like "clang, clang" here, rapid, loud and sharp. Clearly, it came from the meadow outside.

Now, what's Kiril up to? she wondered as she hurried that way. As always, her eyes needed a little time to adapt to the glare, but then she saw two nimble figures dancing around one another. Each wore a face mask and a padded chest guard, but the shapes were unmistakable: Kiril and Souda. Their left arms were raised and bent at the elbow. The right hands held straight, whippy-looking swords that constantly clashed and slid along each other, swirled and struck, prodded and blocked. She stopped, captivated by the beauty of this dance of mock warfare. They seemed to be evenly matched, despite Kiril's great strength and longer reach. Souda was attacking, her sword tip prodding at his face, then, avoiding the blocking blade with a circular motion, it struck at his abdomen. Kiril was skipping backward with sure little foot movements, then suddenly he leapt to his left, his arm moved with a blurringly fast movement and his blade speared for Souda's body. She pivoted on a heel, her sword striking his down, and now she was retreating with Kiril pressing her close with his blade seeming to come from everywhere at once.

Again there was a change: she struck his blade up, at the same time dropping onto one knee and thrusting for him in one smooth movement. Her blade bent into an upwardly facing arc, its point resting on his padded stomach.

"Touché!" Flora heard her shout aloud in glee.

They stopped, and removed their face masks with their left hands. Holding sword in one hand, face mask in the other, they embraced.

"Wonderful!" Flora called, clapping her hands.

They turned to face her, both of them panting, yet grinning broadly. Kiril was naked apart from the frontal padding; as usual Souda wore one of her lace suits that left arms and legs bare. All their exposed skin shone with sweat.

"Hi, Flora," Souda said without words. "You saw, I got him!"

"Kiril's eyes slid around to her face in a quick look of adoration. "Yeah, this time," he answered. "Kalibor juice?"

"H-hmm," Souda answered.

To Flora's surprise, five cups floated out. One stopped by her hand, two each went to the young fencers. Both of them emptied one cup with a single sustained suck on the straw, then lingered over the second.

Flora asked, "Where did your swords and things come from?"

"I brought them in image, of course," Souda answered. "Look." Instantly, swords, face masks and padding were gone.

"It puzzles me. How can an image have physical effects? Like, once Abel's image picked me up and carried me."

"Yeah," Kiril answered, walking toward Flora, "of course he could. What's the problem with that?"

"Um, an image is something Artif created, using my brain. So it's not really here..."

Artif said to her, "Darling, it's hard to explain without a basic grounding in physics. And you've expressed a distaste for that."

"Can you try in words?"

Kiril said, "I'm for a shower," and eased past her. Flora noted, to her surprise, that Souda now looked fresh, and her golden hair was wet.

Artif answered, "In your days, an image was a flat, two-dimensional representation, like your movies. Since the Artif 3 series, our images might better be called 'copies' in terms of your concepts."

"But, but... does that mean that you create matter?"

"No. Of course not. I manipulate matter and energy. It's all according to the laws of physics." Flora gave up.

Tonya

"Have you heard from your little boy?" Tashiro Gunter asked. He was sprawled on the carpet in Tonya's room while her image watched him as he backstroked in the center lane of a fifty-meter pool. The other four lanes were empty, though Tashiro's mother and little sister were visible nearby as they worked in their flower garden.

"No, he's on a quest, silly. Anyway, why belittle him? Does he worry you?"

"Some quest." His voiceless speech paused as he did a perfect backward tumble at the turn. "He was being mothered all along by this Kiril. Abel said so."

"Maybe, but he's easily the most famous boy on the planet now. That's credentials enough in itself." Tashiro turned again and, incredibly, increased his speed. His feet kicked up a foamy wave, then his right hand touched the end of the pool. He lowered his feet and stood in the chest-high water. Artif immediately said, "Seven clicks fifty-nine point two seven, love."

Not bad for a one-K training swim." Tashiro sounded pleased with himself. "You know, Tonya, the other day I broke thirty clicklets for fifty meters backstroke? I reckon I have a real chance."

"World champion Tashiro? Why not, you've worked hard enough for it."

He sprung out of the water with one smooth movement. "There are 287 starters in my age group, and every one of them has been training just as hard. Will you be with me?"

She jumped her image away to avoid being wetted, and grinned at him. "I wouldn't miss it. One-way merge."

He glowed, and in her room his image reached out and stroked her ankle. "Thanks. But if you can manage it at the same time, the panoramic view should be terrific. Seeing all the starters side by side. It's for the competitors, but anyone can watch."

His stroking hand moved up her leg, and he squirmed a little closer. It was time to put him in his place. "You know," she asked, "I was in one-way merge with Vladislav while he did his bull ride?"

Tamás

There was little wind. Tamás chose to be a considerable distance out to sea, so that he could avoid the need to follow the scalloped coastline. He had managed to fill well over a period, pleasing Artif at the same time, by watching a recording of plasteel manufacture. Closing his mind to the unpleasantness of the ever-present drizzle, he now did his isometric exercises, rising and falling with the swell without even noticing the movement.

A sudden, loud booming noise made his head turn to the right. Ahead and about a hundred meters further out, a huge, blue-black shape surged out of the sea, rising far above Tamás's five meter height. Up, up the great whale soared, then the boy noted with horror that several smaller, but still very large shapes were attached to her: to her tail, to a fin, to the end of the great sail on her back. Black and white spots marked these creatures.

The whale turned at the top of her rise, and plunged head first back into the sea. A great plume of foam arose, marking her disappearance. *Oh, the poor thing!* Tamás thought, and changed direction toward the spot. By the time he got there, he could see no sign of the prey, or the pack of hunters. Saddened, he turned south once more.

Artif said, "Darling, that's life. Those orcas were hunting. They need food as much as you do."

"Surely, you're right. But that great, intelligent creature, to have to suffer like that!"

"We have no right to interfere in the workings of nature."

With his mind, he knew she was right. All the same, he wished he could have done something to help the whale, the victim, the sufferer. Sadly he traveled on, under the ever-wetting curtain of fine rain.

After perhaps another period, the gray world turned pink. First a wide, upwardly facing red sliver of a circle poked below the low clouds of the horizon. Soon, this sank into the sea, so that now a wide strip of fire with circular edges spanned sea and sky, at the edge of vision. A low-flying bright pink blanket lay low over a bright pink sea. A huge, brilliant double rainbow appeared, flying along with Tamás as he rhythmically rose and fell above the waves. He could not take his eyes from it, until he got a crick in his neck from looking to the side. The rainbow and its rosy background disappeared as the topmost tip of the sun drowned in the sea, but in his mind's eye he saw it for long after.

He flew on for a while, then ordered the camp down into the water. He landed on the flattened top, had a hot meal and a drink of chocken, then tied on and settled for sleep. He turned himself face down, above the floating camp, in order to minimize the discomfort from the continuous drizzle.

He couldn't sleep for a long time, being kept awake by warring images of a rainbow sunset and a tortured whale, Nature at Her best and worst.

When he awoke, the grayness of dawn already backlit the distant land to his right. Tony be blessed, the rain had stopped, but low, dark clouds continued to amble shoreward. He got started, and had a breakfast of hot porridge and chocken on the move.

He was just considering a stop to recharge the batteries when Artif said, "Tamás, if you now change direction to exactly south-east, you'll get to your father's bay in about a period."

"Will the charge last that long?"

"Easily."

He speeded up, eager to have company once more. He spared a thought of admiration for Kiril, who had been alone for many months during his crossing of this same Pacific Ocean.

Souda

Once more, she was snuggled up against Kiril in a comfortable nest. They faced Flora, who asked, "Kiril, think back to the first time you felt insecure about Souda. What made you think that she might prefer another man to you?"

This sounded interesting. Souda waited, almost holding her breath.

"The very first time I saw her. I'd been sailing in my little boat for what felt like forever. I was bored with my own company, and sick of the monotony, and sick of nothing but fish and preserved food, because I'd arranged that there'd be no resupply from Artif, and sick of having to treasure every drop of fresh water, and I'd have quit if it was possible.

"And then, I saw a sail on the horizon. Being on a quest, of course I had to go by, so I steered away. But the ship changed direction, kept coming closer. Oh how I wanted to sail over and meet another person! And then, incredibly, Artif said, 'Precedence. She's hurt herself.' So I went toward the ship, and sent an image. I saw this absolutely gorgeous girl with her left ankle swollen up and a look of pain on her face."

Souda explained, "I'd slipped down a flight of stairs. And it was late at night for all my friends who'd normally help me. It was reasonable for Artif to grab the nearest person. But..." she wriggled her back against Kiril, "...you could have just dealt with it in image and sailed on."

"Yeah, but did I want to just sail on? One look at those green eyes, and all I wanted to do was to stay. And even as I was winding a bandage around her ankle, I thought to myself, *Someone this gorgeous must have a dozen lovers!* And I bled inside."

Souda felt him tense at the thought.

Flora must have seen this, too. She said, "Good, you can feel that, right now. Kiril, as I understand it, in today's world it's not expected of a person to have just one lover, is it?"

"No, although some people choose to. My mother and Assam choose to be exclusive, have been for years."

"Is Assam your father?"

"No. He first became a friend when I was fifteen. But he's my little sister's father."

"So, were you hoping for that kind of relationship with Souda?"

"Hoping? Sure. Expecting?... That kind of pairing is rare for young people."

Flora's face showed that the next question was important. "Right. Then why did the thought even enter your head?"

Kiril didn't answer for a long time. At last, Flora asked, "Kiril, do you think you're attractive to women?"

He laughed at that. "Now I have credentials, it doesn't matter what I look like. But yeah, I remember as a child, I overheard two ladies talking about me, saying what a pity it was for a boy to be so pale. Oh, excuse me, Flora, you're even paler, but light skin is not exactly a recommendation. It's ugly."

"And, are you good at things?"

"Sure, I've proved it a hundred times."

Again Flora looked up, emphasizing her next question: "Kiril, why was it necessary to prove it a hundred times? Wouldn't once or twice have been enough?"

Again Souda felt his body stiffen. "I've succeeded at things 'cause I WORK at it! I've got to try and try and..."

"Why?" Flora's question was soft, and yet like a whip. Kiril almost whispered, "Because... I'm not much good."

Flora smiled. "Got you! Kiril, you just said something that's either true or false. Look at the evidence. Or better still, Souda, you examine the evidence. Is it true that Kiril's not much good?"

Souda laughed aloud. "False! False! False! Mate, you're one of the best-looking fellows I've ever seen, despite the skin color. And I don't know another man half as competent. You got all those credentials because you've worked at them, sure. But no matter how hard you work at something, you also need to start with the right abilities, strength, intelligence, creativity. So there!"

Flora asked, "Kiril, where did this idea come from? That you're not much good?"

Kiril's thought was a mere murmur. "I guess, it's always been there. Not as a thought, just as, I don't know, background, something I knew, and had to disprove every day."

"And every time you disproved, it, you still had it within you to be disproved again?"

"Yeah, spot on."

"When you were a little boy, someone told you that you were not much good. It doesn't matter who, or when. But you took it in, and it stayed to poison your way of seeing yourself."

Kiril sat up straighter, one of his large hands gently steadying Souda. "You're right! I hadn't thought of it in years! I must've been maybe five years old. My father often took me to a group where everybody rode horses. That's one of his passions, and I love it, too. There were other children there, but I guess I was the youngest by several years. And now I remember, now that you've dragged it back for me, that's what the other children said about me. "Oh Kiril, he's not much good.""

"Kiril my dear, now you're an adult. Then, you were a little person, and just accepted what bigger children said about you. Do you need to be ruled by their opinion, for the rest of your life?"

There was a silence, but this was the silence of peace, of success, of acceptance. Then Souda said, "Thank you, Flora."

Flora smiled again. "Kiril, chains strangle love. Souda is yours, as long as you let HER make the decision. And if you should lose her love, then let that be a growing experience, to make you a better person, like the troubles of the recent past have made you a better person."

Tamás

Tamás left the camp and his pack on the deck and sprinted down to the lounge room. The door slid open in front of him, and he saw his father. Abel was flat on the floor, his hands by his shoulders. His bony back was covered in sweat. The boy heard his thought, "Eleven."

Abel rolled to his side and looked up. He was panting.

"Hi, Dad," the boy called, "pushups?"

"Yeah, got to get fit again. But for Brad's sake, it's hard at my age!" The boy felt a terrible stab of guilt. "Oh Dad!" he cried.

Abel rolled onto his side and sat up. "Done is done, mate. 'Sorry' won't change it. Want a drink?"

"No thanks, I'm all right."

A cup floated from the kitchen to Abel, who sucked it dry. "Oh, that's better." He stood with a suppressed groan. "The trouble's not so much that I've gone weak, but that it's such an effort to make myself do something about it."

"Dad, you can't go on a quest like this. I mean, I remember not long ago when you did a hundred pushups, you know..."

Abel grinned. "Yeah, when young Gordon challenged me." Gordon was another of Abel's sons, a man of forty-two. "Look, from what you and Kiril have said, this EGM system carries you so it's no effort. That's why it's been so good for the Fielding woman after her operation."

"Sure, but on our quest, we spent several periods a day on isometrics. And went for a swim when over water, or a run on land, every day. And..."

"I've ordered a device that'll help there. I stumbled across the idea two days ago, in Tony's records, and it's on the way. We can leave as soon as it arrives."

"What's that?"

Abel laughed. "A wheeled vehicle that goes nowhere. It'll have a stable platform with a seat. There's one wheel that turns against a variable resistance. You can turn the wheel by pushing a pair of pedals, or by pumping a handle back and forth, or both. And the design allows it to be folded away. So, I'll torture myself on it every day that doesn't have an emergency."

"That's what I was going to say. We faced many a day when we had to cope with storms, or wild animals or other risks."

"Trust me, boy. I'll be OK. Only thing is, it'll be a quest for you, but I've got a planet to run, and I'm way behind. I'll be doing one-way visits all the time. That OK with you?"

This was a first: Dad ASKING Tamás's permission! "Oh sure. I mean, it's not for me to say what..."

"No, no, it's your quest. I'll protect your isolation, no one will find out anything about you."

"OK, if it isn't against the rules..."

Abel grinned down at his son, "I'm for a shower. Make yourself at home."

Tamás did. And as soon as he had organized his gear, he asked for Tonya. He held a recording globe in his hands.

She was down on the ground, in the balloon's shade, wearing a red skirt and nothing else. Compared to the temperature in Northern California, this place was a steam bath. Even as Tonya turned to look at him, Tamás got rid of the clothes on his image.

They were in a little clearing in tall, vividly green forest. Tonya had been picking wildflowers, and held a many-colored posy. "Well, well, the wanderer," she said, half mockingly.

"I had to break my quest," Tamás explained. "I'll be going on soon though."

"You've grown taller and darker. I like it."

"Give me a kiss, then."

She laughed and swayed two steps closer. Tamás relocated his image and hugged her to himself. He felt the flowers tickle the back of his neck as he submerged his being in the feel of her body, the taste of her mouth.

She felt his erection between them and stepped back with a little laugh. "Whoa, down boy! Tell me about your adventures."

"Kiril and I had to kill a huge bear. I've got the recording for you..."

Artif asked, "Tonya, Michaela wants to visit."

"Sure."

Another girl appeared, about Tonya's age, with lighter coloring, more like Tamás's. Her hair was dark blonde, her face unusually pretty. She wore a diaphanous pink dress that showed her body underneath. She looked at the two of them with a half-smile, then exclaimed, "Hey, I know you! You're the boy who disappeared!"

"Michaela, meet Tamás," Tonya said. "Tamás is my special friend."

"One of them," he blurted out.

Michaela laughed, a pleasing silver sound. "Hey, it's no good getting too serious about it. Anyway, most girls'd be happy to have you as a friend. Me for instance."

Tonya didn't look all that pleased. "Tamás specially came to visit to tell me of his adventures," she said.

"Hmm. I'm listening. Go on, Tamás."

So, stumbling at first, but soon warming to his narrative, Tamás mentioned a few highlights: the giant bird, the thrill of flying over endless ocean, the great storms, New York, the volcanoes and lakes, with Mount Chicago towering over them, the time when he'd fallen asleep and Kiril barely stopped him from crashing at speed into a tree, another time when they woke to see three hippopotamuses through the walls of the tent, the fight with the bear, and Flora. He then played the recording for the two girls. Kiril had made it from Tamás's viewpoint, using all sensory modes, so the two girls screamed with pain when the bear struck through him, and gasped each time he managed to avoid the animal's clutch by less than a clicklet.

He came to a stop, saying, "Kiril won't be coming with me now. My father wants to, and I reckon I'm now experienced enough to look after him. He's in a terribly weak state, but he's stubborn. He'll come if it kills him."

Tonya nodded. "I saw both recordings. On the second one, he was a walking skeleton!"

"He's been eating all he can, and forcing himself to exercise. All I can do is hope."

Michaela gave him a bright smile. "Do keep in touch when you're not actually on quest, won't you?"

"I can pass on anything he tells me," Tonya told her, rather haughtily.

Kiril

Artif said, "Kiril, the supplies you've asked for are just arriving."

He got the EGM motor to stand him, then deactivated it. He shrugged off the harness and threw on some warm clothing before striding out of the blue room, along the dim corridor, to the outside.

He shivered, even within his clothes. The uncurtained night sky blazed with a myriad glories.

The air was still and cold as a crystal. Kiril drew a deep, happy breath while he waited.

Without sound, a great oval hole appeared in the splendor above. It grew as the balloon advanced into the clearing. He heard a soft thump: the anchor landing, then saw an additional faint luminosity, which had to be the bridge extending to the ground.

A procession of packages came dimly toward him. He stepped out of the way, and they floated past, toward the kitchen. Three boxes stopped next to him. "Here you are, my dear," Artif said, smiling.

Kiril sent them to a far corner of the control room and returned to sleep.

After breakfast the next morning, he left Flora with an excuse, and went outside. He called his new tools and materials to him, and got to work. It took a few clicks to place a protective perimeter around a circular area of almost level grass, and while it was setting itself up, he sent a stream of commands to the kitchen inside. Its computer would control the fence, and it would keep out undesirable insects and birds while admitting helpful ones. This was easy, Kiril just asked Artif to copy the program from Susan's garden.

Kiril opened the biggest box. The digger was inside. Personally, he preferred to do work like that manually, but Flora would need to maintain the garden after he'd moved on. He sent it into the middle of the now-fenced circle and called power down for it. And even while the energy was pouring into the device, he instructed it on its task. Then he went inside, taking the third and smallest box with him.

Flora was drinking what looked like a cupful of water. Her face was a mask of distaste. She swallowed the last mouthful, saying through the implant, "Why is it that I can taste nothing else, but the horrible medicine taste still comes through?"

Kiril had to laugh. "Here's something to cheer you up," he said. "I've got a present for you." A smile lit the lovely face. He passed the box to her, and she opened the magnetic seal of the lid. Puzzled, she asked, "What's all this?"

"Seeds. Your autumn garden. I've got eight autumn vegetables, bulbs for six different flowers, and started roots for several species of flowering shrubs. We can plant them out today."

"Kiril, how kind. Only, I've never done any gardening. In my, in my old life I hired other people to do that."

He laughed. "Here, machines can do the work, but growing plants is a joy almost everybody insists on. It's a connection to nature. It's your link with next summer, your undertaking that you'll still be here to enjoy it."

Suddenly, tears wetted her face. "Will I?"

"You will." He stepped toward her, took her face in his hands and bent. He softly kissed her on the lips, then gently drew her against him.

Flora reached up and put her arms around his neck. "Thank you, Kiril dear," she said within his mind.

He pulled away so he could look her in the eyes. "Flora, I... all my life, I've been a troubled person, always driven, always having to prove myself and never satisfied with the result. And now you've come into my life, and for the first time ever, I'm a peace. Thank you. There's nothing I can ever do that'll be enough to repay you."

Once more, her face shone with her wonderful smile. "Kiril, it won't last. Habits are hard to break. And the next time you fall back into the habit of thinking, 'I'm ugly, my skin is so pale,' or 'I'm not much good at anything,' what'll you do about it?"

He had to think a moment, but then the answer became obvious. "I just tell myself that Souda thinks I look OK, and that'll be true even if, Tony help us, she falls out of love with me, and that I don't have to be ruled by the opinions of children I've long out-done in many fields."

"Right! You just use the same methods that helped you now. And each time, it'll be easier, because you're working on establishing a new habit."

⇗ 22 ⇗

Flora

Now that the air was less hot and humid, Flora liked to be outside whenever it was not raining. She sat on a hovering cushion, under her palm tree, looking with pleasure at the rising green seedlings in Kiril's garden. She couldn't see him, but was used to his active ways by now. He was probably climbing a cliff or a tree, or alternately, he could be quietly sitting somewhere, and visiting somebody in image. He'd taken her along to meet his family, and she'd also visited Souda on her beautiful sailing ship, now making its way across the broad Pacific toward America.

Artif said, "Flora, Mirabelle is inviting you to see her southern garden."

"Wonderful," she answered, and was instantly in the now-familiar room inside the silver balloon. Mirabelle sat cross-legged on her bearskin, the sky a pink and mauve glory behind her, as if the wall of the balloon was not there.

"Greetings, love," Flora said, "is that a sunset or a sunrise?"

Mirabelle laughed, "Here it doesn't make all that much difference. This is the land of the midnight sun."

"And yet you can have a garden?"

"Oh yes. I'm told it's the sea currents. My land here is far closer to the Pole than the garden in the Swedish isles, and yet the climate is much the same."

"Hmm. In my day there was a warm current making western Europe livable."

"There you are then. Let's go down and look around."

Flora still found a descent on a "bridge" to be scary. She closed her eyes and held hard onto Mirabelle's hand until she felt her feet safely on solid ground once more.

"Can you smell it?" Mirabelle asked.

"No," Flora sadly answered, "remember, my medicines knock out smell and taste?"

"Oh. Sorry."

Flora looked around. A symphony of color surrounded them. Neatly trimmed azaleas and rhododendrons bordered both sides of the wide path they stood on, all in full bloom, and every tall bush had blossoms of a different hue. The air was solid with the buzzing of a myriad bees. Still holding Flora's hand, Mirabelle walked forward, and soon turned right onto another path. "I've got this part laid out as a flowering maze," she explained. "Actually, Tamás planned the layout, when he was only seven. Then I decided on what plant was to go where."

"You can be proud of him. He's a decent boy, and very mature for his age."

"Thank you." They smiled at each other. "I'm so glad that he turned out to be all right, though I worry about him, flying over the Pacific. Such an unsuitable name for that treacherous ocean!"

"Abel will look after him."

"Have you seen him lately?"

"Yes. He's aged terribly. But, Mirabelle, that shows how much he cares for the boy."

They walked through an area bordered by a jungle of roses. Mirabelle sighed, "Oh, it's a shame you can't smell it! Artif, when can Flora stop taking these medicines?"

"Of course, I am constantly monitoring the cancer cells. The moment I can no longer find any. I estimate this to be another two or three days."

Flora had to scream in her delight, and she found herself enfolded in Mirabelle's strong embrace.

Ria

Outside, the rains of autumn were pouring down. Artif had finally released the children from their respective lessons, and now they were playing a game of chasey ball. They sat in opposite ends of the big living room, guiding their missiles. At the moment, Tim was chasing Ria. Her ball was in a corner, apparently trapped. He made his ball lunge for hers, but, giggling, she dropped it sharply down almost to floor level, then had it charge straight for his face. He automatically flinched away, but of course the balls were programmed to never bump into any object. The ball skittered off to the side, a few centimeters from his nose.

Tim's ball came charging after, and almost hit Kiril, who suddenly stood in the middle of the room. Tim screamed, "Dad!" and allowed his ball to drop to the floor.

Ria was so filled with joy she just had to jump up and run to him. She and Tim reached Kiril at the same time, and he swung them both into the air.

She clamped her arms around his neck and kissed the slight stubble on his cheek. Kiril said, "My darlings, it's great to see you again. Everything all right?"

"It is, now," Timmy answered, "but there are a few children we don't bother with any more." He did have a tendency to bring up unpleasant things. Ria produced a distraction. "Kiril, Kiril, I can do division in my head! Try me!"

He laughed. "All right, love, what's thirty-five divided by seven?"

"Ask a hard one! Five of course."

"Actually, my dears, I came to ask you, do you want to meet my friend Tamás?"

Both of them shouted "Yes!" And Ria saw a big boy facing them, an attractive chocken brown in color, with a mane of straight brown hair covering his shoulders. The boy had a little half-smile on his face, as he said through the implant, "Hi, I'm Tamás. Kiril has told me a lot of good things about the two of you."

For the first time in her life, Ria could think of nothing to say. She just drank in Tamás's appearance: his clear, broad forehead, the strong chin, the level brown eyes, the way his muscles rippled under his skin as he moved. All she wanted to do was to go over and stroke that brown skin. She wondered what if would feel like, to kiss his lips.

But Tim had no trouble finding an answer. "Yeah, mate, we've heard a lot about you too," he said. Ria had to smile inside: he was an exact, high-pitched copy of Kiril.

She saw the glint of amusement in Tamás's eyes too, and instantly liked him even more. Instead of making fun of Tim, he answered seriously, "I'd rather have done without all that, and I know the whole thing's given you two a lot of trouble."

At last, Ria found a safe topic. "Would you two like anything?" she asked.

Kiril put the two of them down. "Yeah," he said, "not so much seriousness. Hey, you children were playing, weren't you?"

"No, I mean a cup of chocken or a bit of cake or something."

Her brother ran a gentle hand over her hair. "The perfect hostess. Why not. I'll have both."

"Me too," Tamás said. "But Kiril, tell them about the party."

"Party!" Timmy shrilled as Ria sent a command to the kitchen.

Kiril explained, "There's this lovely lady. Souda and I have become very good friends with her. She's been terribly sick, and now Artif told her that she's better. So, we're going to surprise her."

Tamás added, "She's the Sleeper who's been awakened, Flora Fielding. And you'll never guess what we're planning to do: a flying display!"

So, within a few clicklets, the two children had their images on Abel's beautiful house. All through the preparations, Ria managed to stay close to Tamás, helping him to put up colored streamers on the top deck, in the lounge, around the lower walkway. He put on her flying harness for her and watched her swoop around a little. "Don't forget, it's not really flying," he warned. "You need something big nearby, no more than five meters away."

"You'd rescue me if I fell," she answered coyly, and he laughed.

"Ria, I'm happy to be your friend," he said kindly, "but don't get too fond of me. Let me tell you from personal experience, that's not a good idea."

Kiril

He had to grin to himself: Flora had no idea at all. Physically, he perched on a high branch in a eucalypt. He'd climbed up for the exercise, and so that Flora wouldn't see him — just in case he gave something away.

At the same time, he had an image at Abel's boat, as fully involved in the preparations as all the others. At last, Abel said, "Kiril, can you get her please?"

"With pleasure." He hopped down from branch to branch, at the same time calling through the implant, "Flora, where are you?"

"In my bedroom." She sounded sad. Despite the wonderful news of a few days ago, she often sounded sad.

Kiril sent an image, and was with her well before reaching the ground. Flora sat over her EGM bed. Her deep blue eyes were swimming with tears.

"What's the matter, my dear?" he asked.

"I... I was thinking of the Sleepers. The other Sleepers. About my task."

He walked over to her, while saying on Abel's boat, "You'll have to wait a couple of clicks." In the tree, he jumped the last three meters to the soft grass, landed with a roll, and stood.

He took her hand, gave a command to the bed and got his body so she was cuddled on his lap. She snuggled into his chest. "You're a good friend, Kiril."

"Darling Flora, I could never do too much for you. Thanks to you, Souda and I are closer than ever before, and I've had no jealous thoughts at all, even if I don't see her for days. And inside, I feel good about myself. Before, that was hardly ever true." His physical self shrugged on his EGM harness, so that the image on Abel's boat could copy.

"I'm so pleased."

"But listen, Flora, we have to go somewhere."

"Tell me."

"Put on your... Angel's wings, then lie down and close your eyes."

"What's all the mystery?"

He laughed. "Just do as you're told."

Her harness flew to her, even as his physical self walked in. He left his image to cuddle Flora. She lay back, and her eyes closed. He asked Artif to send her to Abel's house. There, he made a new image that held her hand. "Right, love," he told her, "open your eyes." All the work of organization and preparation was worth it. The two of them were in the bow on the upper deck, for it was not raining at the moment. Kiril felt the safety rail against the back of this new image, while the other joined everyone else in performing for Flora. He hovered a couple of meters above the deck, holding hands with Souda on his left, his mother on the right. Naturally, Assam was on Susan's other side. Ria and Tim were zooming in joyful circles over-and-under, and around the four of them, golden wings flapping.

Flora's eyes were huge blue pools of amazement. Her mouth formed an "O," and her hand clutched Kiril's with enough force to hurt. He didn't mind.

Everyone Flora had met was there in the air, performing various antics, and all were wearing long, golden wings flapped by a thought-controlled electric motor. The design had come from Nathaniel's research, turned into reality by Evanor.

Standing at the rail, Kiril just had to laugh. Abel and Tamás were chasing each other, doing figure-of-eights around the three tall masts. Cynthia was at the full five meters above the deck, reclining on her side, and with the wings lazily flapping. Naturally, Nathaniel acted the clown, three or four of his images charging around and almost bumping into everyone and everything.

Evanor zoomed toward Flora, then landed as neatly as any bird. "Here are your wings too, darling," he said, and passed them over.

"But, but..." Flora's cheeks were bright red, and she burst out laughing, and laughed until she was doubled over and tears came from her eyes. "Oh, you lot are wonderful," she managed at last.

"Join us, Flora," Abel invited, also landing on the deck in front of her.

As Evanor adjusted the netting that held the wings onto Flora's mutilated chest, Mirabelle came up to her and passed over a vividly colored bouquet of flowers. "From my garden," she said. "I hope you'll be able to smell them now."

Tears still coursed from Flora's eyes, but Kiril saw that they were tears of joy. She stepped away from the guard rail. "How do I work the wings?" she asked.

Tamás zoomed over the small group by the bow and overshot the top deck. He went plummeting down, but neatly recovered. Within a clicklet, he came over the rail and landed in front of Kiril and Flora. "You fly with the EGM motor," he explained. Just tell your wings to move, with whatever speed you want, and they'll keep going until you tell them to stop."

"Oh. I thought you were REALLY flying."

Kiril looked at Evanor. "You know, if you made the wings big enough..."

Everyone but Evanor laughed. He answered seriously, "A new sport? Why not, though it'd be a very inefficient use of energy."

Flora's golden wings gave a few hesitant flaps, then stopped. "My dears," she said, "This was a lovely surprise. Thank you. Oh, I feel so happy!"

Tonya

She'd never before tried to have her consciousness in three locations at the same time. She was with Tashiro's family by their four-lane pool, looking at him, already in the water. She was also watching the incredible panorama of an apparent pool with 287 lanes, a sixteen-year-old boy in each lane. And now, she went into one-way merge with Tashiro.

He held onto a shiny bar attached to the wall of the pool, but only lightly. His feet were against the plasteel pool lining. Tonya felt the churning of his insides, the rising and falling of his abdomen, quite fast now after his warm-up, the tension in his shoulders, back, arms, legs. Then he took a great breath, and as he slowly exhaled, he went around his body, loosening muscle after muscle. Within a couple of clicklets, he was completely relaxed, his mind without thought.

Artif said, "Take your marks!"

Tashiro pushed with his feet and arched his back.

"Ready!"

He took a breath, and held it.

"Go!"

Tonya watched 287 muscular bodies arch through the air, Tashiro marked for her with a red arrow. She also saw him disappear head first in his own pool, and felt the smooth kiss of water over his face, chest, genitals, legs, as he speared along, hands extended beyond his head. His feet blurred in the flutter kick, and still well under water, he pulled back with the right arm, then the left. She also saw the panorama as Artif showed it to him, as well as in her own right.

His face cleared the surface as he reached far back for the first stroke and he took a smooth breath while his hand followed its complicated driving path.

The great horde of competitors all seemed to be in a straight line, all stroking together as if their performance was orchestrated. "Come on, Tashiro!" Tonya screamed by the poolside, chorusing with his sister and mother and a dozen other spectators.

He reached the halfway mark, but so did all the others.

One dark head was now a shade ahead of everyone else, and many were dropping behind. Tashiro was still level with the great majority of swimmers. She felt the smooth rhythm of his body, the breath whistling in and out, and back home in her balloon, the muscles of her physical body flexed in automatic response.

The leader had pulled ahead by nearly a meter. Tonya saw that Tashiro was up with the rest of them, but just couldn't tell if he was second or twentieth, so close were they. The five meter flags flashed over Tashiro's head. His body arched, and his hand slammed against the pool's end.

He stood, panting.

A short silence followed, then Artif announced, "This year's sixteen year old fifty meter backstroke championship was won by Alan Wong of the Chinese Culture. His time of 24.89 clicklets is a new world record! Second was Susor Adagala of the Swahil Culture with 26.15 clicklets, third Mokep Alexandrov of the Russian Culture with 26.19, fourth Tashiro Gunter of the German Culture with 26.25..."

Tonya didn't hear the rest. She got rid of the skirt off her image, and dived in to give Tashiro a great hug.

In her mind, he was exulting, "My personal best!"

Tamás

"The logical way is to go to Japan, then over the China Sea to China, then the steppes through to Europe." Abel shuddered. "Only, it's nearly winter. It'll be bloody cold."

"Is there another path?" Tamás asked.

"Sure. We swing south, more or less along the coastline. India and that. It's much longer, but the weather should be kinder."

Tamás said, wistfully, "I'd hoped to see Mount Nippon and Mount Baikal."

Outside, the usual drizzle of late autumn floated down, so the two of them enjoyed the warmth of the lounge room. Abel was pedaling the exercise machine, lazily spinning its wheel. Tamás knew that, at the same time, his father also carried on a discussion with a couple of other Control members in Asia somewhere, and offering comfort to a recently bereaved person in Africa.

"Well, it's your quest," he answered through the implant.

Before Tamás could think of a reply, Artif said, "My dears, Evanor wants to make a gift to you."

"Welcome," Abel answered aloud.

The wiry, bronze-colored man stood at the doorway, smiling at father and son. "Greetings," he said. "I'm glad you haven't started yet. Abel, the next supply balloon will have a little luxury in it for you, so wait for it, won't you?"

"What is it?"

"Two things actually. An electrically heated suit — I know how you hate cold — and a magnetic water-repelling device. You can keep dry even in the worst rain."

Tamás said, dubiously, "I don't think I can..."

Evanor grinned at him, "Naturally. It wouldn't be much of a quest, would it? So, I only made one set. You can continue to be uncomfortable."

Abel also grinned at his son's discomfiture. "My thanks, Evanor. This solves a problem for us. Now we can take the northern route without me freezing my testicles off."

"It's extra power use of course," the engineer explained, "but you'll still be well within safety limits."

Tamás suggested, "Maybe we can carry extra batteries in the camp, fully charged, just in case?"

Evanor flashed him an approving glance. "The extra weight is negligible. Good thinking, young fellow. Not that they're likely to be necessary, but the first principle of engineering is to expect a bit more than the worst."

"This is very good of you, Evanor."

"Abel, I'd be bored to death if I didn't keep thinking up new gimmicks. I've invented 573 distinctly different devices so far, and I'm racing to get over 600."

"Good credentials!" Tamás said admiringly.

The supply balloon arrived three days later. Abel made sure the house was held with three strong tethers, retracted the masts and closed all the watertight doors. They took off on the first, long leg of their journey, toward Japan.

⚎ **23** ⚎

Flora

For Kiril's sake, Flora had the room far hotter than she would have otherwise. Even so, he wore long-sleeved shirt and pants. It was snowing outside, though everyone assured her that this rarity would soon pass.

"I'll be sorry to have you go," Flora said sadly. "I've got used to having you around, and in my times few people lived alone."

"Flora my dear," Kiril smiled at her, "I'll visit often, and you'll always be welcome at my house, wherever it is."

"Thanks. But of course it's not the same as the two of us bumping into each other, rubbing along doing our own thing in the same place."

He took a couple of long strides and joined her above the EGM bed. His mighty arm encircled her. "Yeah, I'll miss that too, Flora. But my house is now at anchor right next to Abel's, and it's just too cold for me here. I'm going south, might physical my mother and the children."

Flora smiled inside when thinking of Tim and Ria. "They're delightful."

Kiril laughed. "Ria still has a pash for Tamás. And if you'll remember, he was too kind to be cold to her."

"I can understand that. He's been on the receiving end. Do you think I should talk to her?"

"You're welcome, though my mother's handling it well enough. Most children go through the phase."

"Did you?"

"No. Maybe if I had... but I was having too much fun with adventures." He paused for a while, then he picked up her hand and kissed it. "You remember, Flora, the first time you counseled me, you asked how my troubles made me into a better person?"

"Hmm?"

"That truly was the start of my healing. I can never thank you enough. And Souda reminded me yesterday, there is one more thing I need to do to be fully healed. I'd like you to help me with that too, so your job is complete."

"You're being very mysterious!"

Gently but irresistibly, his arm pulled her closer, and she felt the heat of his breath on her face.

"Share bodies with me, please," he whispered, aloud, in English.

Her heart was trying to escape her chest, and she felt herself go hot all over. But then, *this is ridiculous*, the thought came, *he's just trying to be kind*. She pulled away, saying, "Kiril, I'm older than your mother, and have a mutilated body, and I know my pale skin is considered ugly, and..."

A second Kiril faced her, kneeling above the EGM bed. His hands gently held her face, and his lips stopped her speech. And she was submerged in the strength of his body next to her, drowned in the feel of his mouth, his tongue, she was on fire and all thought was gone and she opened her mouth to him, reached out and pulled the Kiril in front onto herself. She hardly even noticed when the clothes disappeared from this Kiril but ran her hands along his shoulders, his back, his buttocks, arched her body as a big, warm hand slipped under her top to fondle her breast, as another big, warm hand eased between her legs, and fingers opened her and played with the center of her pleasure.

"Merge!" he whispered in her ear.

"What? How?" she asked through the implant, but suddenly she was him as well as herself, and felt his pleasure and excitement. His erection was almost painful, and now she knew he was not being kind, he wanted her as much as she wanted him, and she wrapped her legs around him as he entered deep into her body. Nothing exists except their doubled pleasure, the rhythmical dance of love that is taking her to joys unimagined, and she is drawing him into herself, hands on his buttocks as her ecstasy builds, and builds, and suddenly peaks so she gives a little scream.

She felt his body convulse an instant later, then his consciousness withdrew from hers. The image that had loved her disappeared, but she found the physical Kiril still cuddling her.

He laughed, aloud. "Just look at me!" he said, somewhat ruefully.

She turned and did so. The front of his trousers was marked with a great wet spot.

"Oh, of course. I still can't get used to this image business."

"Flora, darling, thank you."

"You thank me? Kiril, it's the other way."

"Right, that's the best kind of thing isn't it? Let's thank each other." He gently disengaged and stood up over the bed. He shrugged off his shirt and pulled off the stained trousers. Then he lay down again, his head against her thighs. He lifted her skirt and started to nibble her buttocks.

"Oh Kiril, can you, again?"

"At least once or twice, then a few more times after a rest," he answered within her mind, separating her legs with his hands.

Abel

Abel enjoyed the look of pleasure on his son's face. After all, during the past two months, well, nearly two months, they'd seen four small islands, and for the rest they'd been over the ocean. And in Abel's opinion, the western approach to the continent of Japan was perhaps the most beautiful landfall in the world.

The huge, mountainous shore stretched in front of them, left to right as far as the eye could see. The skyline had a pleasing regularity, as if each volcanic cone had been placed with care, an up-and-down landscape a very talented child might create. Everything in sight was some shade of green. The distant peaks were a soft pastel green, a backdrop to the vivid verdure of the rainforest in front of them. Now that the water had shallowed, even the breakers beneath them were green topped with white. On the beach, tough salt-resistant grass came almost to the tide line, so that now, at the high mark of a spring tide, only the barest strip of yellow sand showed.

Abel swooped through the spray, the water repeller device keeping him dry, and grinned at Tamás's thought of resigned annoyance as the boy followed close behind. Then, after twelve days since the last islet, he could stand on solid land.

Both of them staggered, and would have fallen except for the support of the EGM motors on their backs.

Of course, Abel was elsewhere in image. In Heinrich Subirano's land house at the Sunken Islands, he said, "OK, I'm glad that's wrapped up."

"Yes," Heinrich's bass voice rumbled, "and it's good to have you back at work, Abel. You're looking better, too."

"Not back to normal, though. I guess I never will be the same. Oh well."

Heinrich stood. "Abel, I'll have to prepare my house for this hurricane, so if you'll excuse me…"

"Sure. Though I don't know why you have a land house in such a risky place. I prefer to dive deep."

Heinrich laughed. "The house has survived five hurricanes in the past year. I'll be fine. I live here because this is my ancestral home. This little island is the tip of a mountain that was once on the island of Java."

That was surprising, and Heinrich had been a friend and colleague for twenty years. "But, aren't you from the Malay Culture?"

"Of course. So few Indonesians survived the Cataclysm that my ancestors were absorbed into the Malay Culture. But they originally had a distinct language and customs. There were an estimated two hundred and eighty million Indonesians."

Abel shuddered, imagining what must have happened in this area when the Great Wave struck, and then the islands sank while the sea level rose. "Your ancestor was lucky?"

"Yeah. Family tradition is that she was visiting Australia. Anyway, Abel, I must prepare."

"See you, then. Enjoy your hurricane." He severed contact.

While this was going on, Tamás was saying, "I've seen the maps of course, but I didn't realize it was so beautiful."

"Yes, it is, isn't it?" They were walking now, up to the edge of the tree-line, and Abel heard Tamás order the camp to set itself up. "Actually, in a way the whole continent is one mountain. All these peaks here are foothills to the real thing."

"Any active volcanoes?" Tamás asked, wrinkling his nose.

Abel laughed. "No, though there are earth tremors every few years. Japan is still growing. But you know that I have no interest in scientific stuff. Artif?"

"No, Abel," she instantly answered, "there haven't been active eruptions anywhere in Japan for over three hundred years."

"Why not? In America they're still active."

"Darling, the geology is very different. During the Cataclysm, the Eurasian supercontinent buckled. There was land where the China Sea is now, the most populous land on earth. As that part sank, Japan rose. In those days it was just a chain of islands, not a continent in its own right."

"Oh. So, Mount Nippon is a wrinkle instead of a volcano?"

Both Abel and Artif laughed. "Yes," Artif continued, "Much of it was sea bottom. There is actually a fossilized sunken ship so high it's above the level of permanent snow."

The camp was ready, and while Tamás listened to his lesson, Abel took a step to stroll toward it. A slight movement attracted his eyes, and he froze. Right in his path, a snake's head was raised at him, the small, beady eyes immobile, the forked tongue flicking in and out. The head was black, with a red stripe running down the middle. The open mouth showed a pair of disproportionately large, curved fangs. A drop of clear liquid hung on the right fang.

"Tamás, don't move!" he said through the implant. "Death stripe." Abel didn't dare to take his eyes off the snake, but saw in the periphery of his vision that Tamás had stopped.

Suddenly, Tamás was right behind the snake, and brought his foot down, hard, on her body just where she rose from the grass. The snake whipped with incredible speed, striking for the boy's leg.

Abel heard Tamás's cry of pain as the image disappeared, but all the same, another image of the boy appeared between him and the animal, and again the boy stomped down, hard. "I've got her, Dad!" he called. His voice held a mixture of triumph and still lingering agony.

Abel's thinking clicked back into action mode. He ordered his laser gun from the pack even as he rushed forward. This time, Tamás's foot was planted across the snake's body, not five centimeters from the head. The animal whipped around, and before Abel covered the three steps in between, the two-meter-long body coiled around the boy's leg, up his body and curving around his neck, but Tamás was bearing down hard.

Abel positioned the laser gun and cut the snake's head off, just clear of his son's foot. Then he continued to play the beam of energy on the head, vaporizing it until nothing was left but a charred hole in the grass.

Even then, the rest of the sinuous body still kept moving, and squeezing the boy. Gingerly, Abel reached out a hand, grabbed the tip of the tail, pulled, and flung the body well clear.

He took a shaky breath, then said aloud, "Boy, you can add that to your credentials."

Tamás grinned at him. "I promised to look after you, didn't I?"

Nathaniel

Flora's face held a look of pleasure as she gazed around the ancient Library. "Oh, Nat, I always love to visit you here," she said. "Where are the others?"

"You forget it's late at night here," he told her. "For convenience, they all live physically near this time zone."

"Show me a book!"

He had to laugh. "Oh, for Brad's sake, you always ask this, then you get all frustrated because they're in Russian." But he did as she'd asked, requesting the complete works of Tolstoy. The heavy tomes came out of storage almost immediately.

Flora held one reverently, saying, "This 'for Brad's sake' is a very common saying. You know, I've never been told Brad's story. I mean, I know he was Tony's disciple, and lived a hundred years later, and was the first President of Control, but surely more is known about him?"

"Of course, but the earliest part is reconstruction. Artif, do you think you could show Flora?"

"I haven't, because I know how sadly she'd respond to the horrific parts," Artif answered.

Flora looked at Nathaniel with a wordless question.

He told her, "You see, it was during the Chaos. Tell you what. Artif, if Flora agrees, I'll be in one-way merge with her and help her through it."

He took her hand and pulled her to one of the seats. She let the book go, and it floated over to join the other volumes on a benchtop. They sat, side by side. He closed his eyes and relaxed his body. He saw, through Flora's eyes, as rainforest replaced the underground room. Blue sky could be glimpsed through a canopy of gently moving high branches.

He sensed Flora's thought, *Oh, I thought Brad was a boy!* as they saw the child from behind. He wore soft leather trousers, boots and jacket. His long, blond hair was in two neat plaits, and obviously this was the feature puzzling Flora.

Nat explained, through the implant, "Human hair was a precious resource. They made bowstrings, rope and the like from it."

Brad swiftly filled a large cane basket with mushrooms that grew thickly under the trees. He moved with what had to be a habitual silence, and when the basket was full he picked it up from the ground, straightened and turned. Now he appeared to be looking straight at Flora.

The boy had a beautiful face, apart from his pale skin. He looked about ten years old, the best guess research had come up with. He started walking, cheerfully enough, though his eyes darted everywhere, and he placed his feet with care, avoiding any noise.

Suddenly he stopped and his blue eyes widened into a stare of horror. Unheeded, the full basket slipped off his arm.

The face came closer, and was as close as if he was about to kiss Flora, then they were within Brad, looking out. He gazed slightly upward, into the distance. In between the crowd of trees, he could clearly see a rising column of smoke. He took a shuddering breath and started to run. Habit still made him avoid stepping on dry branches, but he ran with rapid strides, arms pumping hard. Soon, he breathed with mouth wide open, the air whistling in and out.

Light brightened between the tall trunks, and Brad slowed. Still fast, but with almost exaggerated care, he flitted from tree to tree until he was sheltering behind one that bordered a clearing. A fence faced him and blocked his view. It consisted of an endless row of closely spaced thin timber posts sticking into the grassy sward, with long horizontal sticks woven between them. Just to the left of where Brad stood, the fence lay flat on the ground. The smoke formed a thick column, rising from perhaps two hundred meters beyond the fence.

He could hear distant screams, and mouthed a silent "Oh no!" His little heart pounded in his chest, as much from anguish as from his run. He made his way to the break in the fence and peeked around it.

Flora didn't recognize the plants in front of the boy, so Nat said in her mind, "Turnips, love." Just to the left stood a great stand of maize, towering above Brad's height. He slipped among them, moving past the immature heads and wide green leaves without disturbing any. With each step the terrible sounds became louder: a woman's ongoing wordless wail, deep-voiced shouts, bangs, then a sharp scream, suddenly cut off. Brad was thinking, *That's Anna crying!* He got to the other end of the corn plantation to reach a neat double row of bushes. "Artichokes," Nat told Flora as the boy now got down on his hands and knees and advanced from bush to bush. He was crying, and gasping for air, and a great knot seemed to bind up his throat.

The stink of smoke was strong now, and Flora could hear the words being shouted. A man yelled, "Hey, my turn, you buggers!" Another laughed.

Nat felt Flora tremble, and squeezed her hand. He saw a vivid image of her first husband, Stan, face contorted with triumphant rage.

Brad had reached the last artichoke bush and peered around it.

A neat post and rail fence enclosed a group of ten log buildings. Two of them were on fire, tall, red, sooty flames reaching for the sky. The nearest houses had glassless window openings facing the boy. Momentarily, a dark-bearded man's face showed in one of the windows.

As soon as he was gone, Brad sprinted forward. He slipped between the rails of the fence, picked up a fist-sized stone without slowing, and jumped onto the windowsill. As his knees touched the timber sill, he threw the stone with full force, at the back of the man's head. He was just walking out the door. The crunch of stone on bone sounded loud, even through the noise of the continued screaming, shouts and bangs, the roar of the fires. The man fell forward. Brad leapt from the windowsill and was on him in a couple of strides. Blood gushed from the mat of dark hair on the back of the man's head, but already he tried to raise himself. Brad's eyes were fixed on a knife in a sheath on the man's belt, on his left side. He snatched the weapon, raised it high and with a soundless little sob plunged it into the man's back.

The blade sank deep.

The man's body went rigid.

The boy pulled the knife out, to be drenched by a crimson fountain. He stood up shakily, turned and vomited. He took a deep, painful breath as he wiped his mouth with the back of his hand. *I must think. Oh Anna! I can't stand it. They mustn't find me. What about the others? What'll I do?*

As his thoughts chased each other around in his head, Brad returned to the window and climbed out. Still holding the bloodied knife, he ran to the corner of the house, got down on hands and knees and looked around it. Seeing no one, he sprinted to the next building. This had no windows, and an animal smell came from it, clear even over the smoke. Brad moved to the left, and went straight to one particular place. He pushed on the end of one of the logs making up the wall, and it pivoted. With a brief struggle, he squeezed through the gap, then pushed the log to close it from inside.

Five small enclosures each held a pig, hard to see in the dim light. Brad was in the middle corral. The pig there turned to face him, and pushed her snout toward the boy. He scratched the animal between the eyes as he walked forward, then he climbed over the gate of the enclosure.

He came to a large, closed double door. It was shut, but both doors sagged on thick leather hinges and a gap shone between them. He peered out, and took a sharp, involuntary breath.

One of the burning houses, the MacDonalds' house, was directly across a wide courtyard. A wooden table, obviously dragged out of a house, stood in the middle of the space. A naked young woman was held face down on it by four grinning men. Each grasped one of her wrists or ankles. Leather trousers down about his ankles, a fifth one was pumping away between her legs. She was still wailing, but with less force now.

Flora was sobbing, so Nat said, "Darling, remember it's a reconstruction. Fiction, not fact." Brad's eyes skipped to the right, where another group of men worked around a fire. The fuel was broken bits of furniture. A long carcass was impaled on a metal rod, held on a couple of supports. One man turned a handle attached to the rod, rotating the carcass. As it turned, a recognizably human female front faced the boy. It was already well browned, but he screamed, "Mother!" and everything went dark.

Once more, the recording showed Brad from the outside. He lay on the ground, huddled face down. Suddenly the large door started to swing inward, and fetched up against his body. It stopped, then irresistibly continued, sweeping the boy along with it. He hardly stirred.

Singing, laughing or shouting, several men crowded in. Each carried a stick. They opened the five gates, then drove the pigs out with shouts and prods. The boy's inert body lay hidden behind the door.

Artif now said, "We skip many days. How many is not known." The first impression was smell: the sharp, unpleasant odor of a long-unwashed human body. Nat sensed Flora's shock as she looked at the boy. He was gaunt beyond belief, his cheeks fallen in, his eyes bulging out of his head. The front of his brown leather top had a large black stain. Flora drew a sharp breath as she realized that this was still the bloodstain from the man Brad had killed.

But the most shocking thing was the expression on Brad's face. Previously, he'd had a keen, intelligent look, and even in the midst of panic his actions had indicated a purposeful, clever mind. Now, his emaciated face had a vacuous smile painted on it. His eyes were blank and incurious, an idiot's eyes. As he walked, his gait was poorly coordinated. In fact, he tripped on a branch lying on the ground, staggered and fell. He lay there for a moment, then giggled and struggled to his feet.

He came to a blackberry patch. Flora noted that the fruit was the same size as in her own times, rather than the big ones she'd eaten before the bear attack. The boy picked berries, popping them into his mouth with grubby hands. A thorn scratched him and he drew back with a little cry of surprise. He started to cry like a toddler would, and went on, leaving the rest of the fruit untouched.

A creek blocked his passage. He got down on the ground and noisily slurped water. When he stood, the empty smile was back on his face. He waded across, his boots and trouser legs getting soaked, and apparently without any aim, he continued upstream, along the other shore. The creek led him around a curve, and suddenly a glowing pink ball hovered in front of him. A tune sounded, and Nat heard Flora's thought, *Hey, that's "Three Blind Mice."*

The boy giggled and reached for the globe. It moved slightly away from him and he followed. The globe turned green, then blue, then red, and as the colors changed, so did the melody. Always simple and childlike, it tinkled away, seeming to mesmerize the boy.

He followed the glowing ball until they reached a place where two small streams joined to form the creek. It led him to the left, along the shore of the chattering ribbon of water. The sides of the gully deepened and closed in, and now Brad was in a blind alley, facing a cliffside. The water bubbled out of the ground, at the base of the cliff.

A grating sound came, and part of the stone wall slid aside, exposing a tunnel. It was brightly lit, had a smooth, domed roof and a brown-carpeted floor.

The boy stopped, his heart suddenly beating like a bird trying to escape a cage. A woman's voice came, a deep, mellow voice, Artif's voice but a little different. "Don't be afraid," she said gently. "Things will be all right now. I have something nice for you to eat."

Looking from behind the boy, Flora saw a tray scoot along the corridor, about a meter above the floor. It stopped by the boy's side. He flinched, but didn't move otherwise. A small, brown, oblong object rested on the tray.

"Pick it up and taste it," the voice commanded, gently but firmly.

Hesitantly, slowly, Brad lifted his right hand and took the object. He brought it to his mouth. Flora's viewpoint changed to within the tunnel, looking out. She saw the boy's face light up with delight. He gobbled the piece of chocolate.

The voice said, "Darling, there's more inside. Come on. You'll be safe. No one will ever hurt you again."

The boy stepped forward, then disappeared. Flora and Nathaniel were back in the Library.

He said, "That was Artif 1.0. A primitive version of a communication globe backtracked Brad, and found the remains of his village. That's how the reconstruction was possible. For the rest of his long life, Brad remembered nothing from before his salvation, nothing but his name."

Flora shuddered. "I can well believe that."

⚡ **24** ⚡

Flora

She awakened to a crying sound, and it took her several shaky breaths before she realized: she'd been the one crying.

The dream was still crystal clear in her mind, all too harrowingly clear. Once more, she saw the world through the eyes of Brad, the little boy, once more through the gap in the sagging doors. She smelt the odor of the pigs behind, heard their occasional scratchings even through Anna's terrible screams, even through the roar of the MacDonalds' house burning across the yard, even through the coarse laughter and shouting of the raiders.

In the dream, her eyes, his eyes, poured tears that blurred his vision, and his breath came in quick strangled little gasps, and his shoulders felt rigid enough to snap. Anna, Anna who'd so often been kind to him, was screaming, and screaming, and the man raping her turned his face toward the barn, and it was not a hairy savage but Stan's overly handsome face, and Stan looked exactly as when he'd raped her, all so long ago: teeth bared in a grin like a snarl, and the violet eyes shooting lances of hate at her as he held her arms to each side while he violated her, and how he spat in her eyes as he ejaculated, and then held her for another eternity, saying in that mellow voice that had the fans swoon, "We want to give the little spermies a chance to hit the target, don't we, Blossom?"

And the boy's eyes skipped to the right where some men worked over a fire, but suddenly Flora was the one lying naked, bruised and bleeding on the rough wooden table, and splinters dug into her breasts, the side of her face, her stomach, and the man was rubbing hard, in and out of what had been a virgin opening until today, and it hurt, and the four bastards pulling on her limbs were crushing her wrists and ankles, but what hurt worst was the indignity, and oh God, everyone was dead, and so she cried, and cried with each insult of penetration...

And awoke to the sound of her own voice.

Shakily she asked the bed to sit her up, and the light to come on. "Oh Artif," she called.

"My dear, I'm sorry. I had grave doubts about showing you that recording."

"Yes. Oh..." She couldn't think of anything to say, or even to think.

But Artif did. The wonderful deep voice had a lot of concern in it. "Darling, I can sense... oh no!"

"What is it?"

"I have found new cancer cells within you. And they're multiplying at an alarming rate, far faster than before."

"Artif..."

"What, love?"

"Don't tell Nat. It was his idea to, to watch that recording. Please, don't tell him it triggered a relapse."

"Very well, dear, I won't. If you like, I won't tell anyone. But I want to start you back on the medicines as soon as possible."

"We still have Mitchell's machine?"

"Oh yes, but we no longer have the raw materials. I've already set it in motion, but it'll take some time."

Flora stayed silent for a long while, sitting over the bed's energy field, mind blank. She felt no despair, no worry, no disappointment, nothing at all. It was as if the thinking part of her had gone back to suspended animation.

At last, after an unknown time of numbness, she stirred and said, "Artif, yes please. Get the chemotherapy going. I need time. But... I'm going to hand on. I'm... I'm now a different person from last time. Only..."

"Yes Flora?"

"I particularly want to hand on to Souda and Kiril's child."

"Souda is currently 342 on the List. Oh, as of this clicklet, 341. It'll be a while before she can have a baby, and then you'd need another nine months. And also, there is no guarantee that she'd choose Kiril."

Despite her situation, Flora gave a little laugh. "Oh yes there is!" she answered.

Souda

She was visiting Susan when Artif told her that strong winds were expected. So, without breaking off her conversation, she instructed the house to reduce sail, and supervised the various details.

Timmy sat with the big window behind him, playing chess with another little boy. "Where's Ria?" Souda asked.

Her son sniffed disdainfully, "Oh, she's still all soppy over Tamás. She's making a painting or something in our bedroom. No one's allowed to see it, so what's the point?"

Souda laughed. "Just you wait, you'll get smitten too one day."

"No thanks, that's all silly stuff." The other boy made a move, and Tim responded almost instantly.

Kiril's voice came from just behind Souda, "Good move, Tim, but you should think three times and move once."

She turned to see him standing very close behind her. "Hi, love," she said.

He grinned down at her, stepped over and pulled her back to him. "May Tony's blessing be with Flora forever," he murmured aloud.

"Yes, but don't give her all the credit. Much of it is due to you."

He laughed. "I won't argue over that." A second image of him looked around, high on the bridge of her house, one hand steadying himself against the already violent movement. "I enjoy a good storm."

"Hmm. It'll slow me down though."

"I still can't believe it, you, coming to be with me in the physical."

"Stop it, you big oaf!"

"What?"

"You're running yourself down again. I know at least thirty women who'd walk over the ocean if you called them."

Tim's opponent made his move, and this time their son dutifully pondered over his. Then he flashed a grin sideways at his parents, and advanced a pawn. His grin was so exactly his father's that Souda just had to rub her back against Kiril. At home, the house was ready to face the worst, so, hanging on to the rails, she started to descend. This was the set of steps she'd slipped off, on that day when she'd first met Kiril.

Without warning, Artif said in her mind, "Souda, Kiril, darlings please cancel all images except for the two of you together, then get comfortable. I need to tell you something."

"I must go. Be back soon," Souda said at Susan's. At home, Kiril's image blinked out from above her, and he waited below. One hand grasped a rail while the other was half raised to catch her, in case.

The house bucked violently, and she hung on with both hands. Spatters of stinging rain struck her face. Then she reached the walkway, and ducked into the corridor.

Her eyes swept around as she entered the living room. Everything was secure. She staggered across to an easychair and dropped into it. Kiril relocated to sit beside her, and the chair held them against the increasingly wild motion.

"Right, Artif," Kiril asked, "what's wrong?"

"Flora. Her cancer has come back, and it's worse than the first time."

"Oh no!" they exclaimed together.

"I'm organizing her treatment, but this time she is ready to hand on."

Souda heard Kiril's thought, "Artif, please tell me, anytime, when she wants company, any help at all."

At the same time, she couldn't help saying through the implant, "Oh it should be our child!"

She felt Kiril's body stiffen next to her. He looked at her with incredulous joy. "Does that mean..."

"Yes, Kiril. I'll choose you."

Artif laughed, as a mother will at a cute child. "You know, darlings, that was Flora's request when she found out. She wants to hand on to your baby."

Souda had to sigh. "Pity it's not possible. It's still too far off."

"Not quite, darling. There is precedent. I'm talking to Abel about it, right now."

Abel

They zoomed along yet another beautiful grass-covered valley, symmetrical rounded mountains on each side. Ahead, a herd of deer bolted up into the tree-covered slopes at their approach. The late afternoon sun shone weakly through a gray cloud layer from behind them, so that objects had the barest shadow of a shadow. Abel flicked a glance at his son and asked, "What does this place remind you of?"

He was delighted to see the boy blush, but Tamás didn't answer.

"Tonya's breasts?" he teased.

"Almost right, Dad. Actually, last time I visited her she had a friend there, a girl called Michaela. These mountains are more her shape. But the valley yesterday, that was exactly Tonya."

They both laughed. "Only, Dad, girls don't have fur on their breasts. These mountains do." He referred to the thick stands of forest clothing the slopes.

Artif suddenly said, "Abel, we have a problem."

"Yes?"

"Flora Fielding's cancer has recurred."

He flicked his mind toward and away from his son, so fast that Tamás was unaware of it.

"No, I haven't told him," Artif said reassuringly. "After all, he is on a quest. But she wants to hand on, particularly, to Souda Ramirendo. And she is too far down the list."

"I'll call a meeting of Control," Abel said.

Mirabelle

Outside in his garden, Oliver Marasadi stretched luxuriously and said, "This time of the year is wonderful here. Everything is still lush after the end of the Monsoon, and yet the air is crisp and dry."

Mirabelle had to agree. Oliver's garden was a tropical paradise, and a work of art. She opened her mouth to answer when Artif said to her, "Darling, brace yourself, I have bad news." She told her about Flora's relapse.

"I'll go to her immediately."

"No, love. Abel is about to call a Control meeting, and you know you have trouble with multiple consciousnesses. Anyway, Cynthia and Nathaniel are already with her, and Kiril and Souda want to be available any time. Go home."

Oliver had heard all this. "Right, Mirabelle my dear," he said, "I'll see you in the Cave." Sitting in her study, Mirabelle opened her eyes. Abel appeared almost immediately, saying, "I call a meeting of Control."

And she stood behind her chair in the sacred Cave. The room was more than half full, and others arrived in rapid succession.

Abel looked around. "I declare this meeting open."

Tony appeared, looking as grave as the humans. He greeted them, then Abel quickly summarized the reason for their meeting.

Tony said, "Cancer is like that. It appears beaten, but even internal monitoring by Artif cannot detect all the rogue cells. And then something happens to give the immune system a setback — and the cancer takes off again."

"This request of hers, to hand on to a particular woman's baby," Tina Chung asked, "is that possible?"

Abel grinned humorlessly. "The request is possible. She made it. Whether it can be granted..."

"Where is Souda on the List?" Oliver asked.

"Three hundred and forty-first," Tony answered. He had access to the same information base as Artif.

"What's Flora's life expectancy, if we do everything possible?"

A silence followed, then Tony said, "Somewhere between two months and a year. A year is extremely unlikely."

"Tony, there is precedent, isn't there?" Abel asked.

"Yes. On 181 previous occasions, a person was allowed to hand on to a woman who was not yet at the top of the List. In every case, there was a strong emotional reason..."

"There is this time too," Cynthia interrupted.

"Yes. But in all previous cases, the recipient was within the top ten or so. Twelfth was the lowest. And every one above her was asked, and gave her permission to be bypassed."

Mirabelle said, "The principle is what matters. We can ask every woman above Souda, and if we argue well enough, they'll agree. That's assuming that Control decides to support her."

Ramona Tushiko shook her dark head. "I don't know that I can. People wait so long, and with improved health standards, life expectancy has been rising. I mean, that was why I brought up the Sleeper issue in the first place."

Mirabelle had to jump to her feet in her sudden excitement. The chair behind her moved back fast. "Of course!" she said loudly. "None of this applies."

Everyone looked at her. Abel's gray eyebrows were raised high. She explained, "Flora is a Sleeper herself. Until she was awakened, none of those women on the top of the List could have expected to receive her life. She is one of a kind, her own precedent. I think we can decide for her whatever we like, and it'll have no effect on any other decision, except perhaps the lives of the other Sleepers, should she recommend that they be awakened."

This made sense to everyone. Abel said, "Mirabelle, you and I should prepare a recording together, and then send it to all those women ahead of Souda. and the rest of you can try to convince any who decline to step aside."

Even Ramona had to agree after this.

Cynthia

She hid her sigh of exasperation, but continued to put on a polite, friendly front. Lia Mai Mattioli repeated, through the implant, "I really can't accede to this, no really, it's too much." She sounded whiny and petulant.

Cynthia felt like snapping at her to grow up, but she'd had decades of experience at counseling. She smiled sympathetically and said, "You're worried about you age, love, aren't you?"

Empathy wins every time, she thought as the woman visibly relaxed. "Oh, I'm so glad you understand! Look, I'm fifty-one. I've had one child, and for I don't know how long I've done everything, absolutely everything to earn a second one. And at last... I'll be seventy by the time the child gains her Maturity! And now they're asking me to step aside for some young chit of a girl! It's not fair!" Tears stood in her eyes.

"I can certainly see your problem," Cynthia replied. "I remember, trying to cope with my youngest. She was born after I was elected to our Council. I was forty-three then, and yes, having her as a teenager was exhausting! Oh yes, I can see your problem."

Lia Mai sat at ease now, and had a half-smile on her still teary face. It was time to gently move her out of her position. "Where are you on the List?" Cynthia asked.

"Forty-second."

"Artif, please tell us, how long ago did Lia Mai advance in the List?"

"She is actually forty-first. Three clicks ago."

"Oh. I didn't realize things were so fast. Is this typical?"

"No. The gap before that was almost three days."

"I see I have to approach this differently. I didn't know it was so variable. Hmm. All right, Artif, what is the average number of deaths in a year?"

"Averaged over the past ten years, it's 497."

Cynthia looked the woman in the eyes with an encouraging little smile. "That's interesting, Lia Mai. My mental arithmetic is not that good, so let's simplify things. If you were fiftieth from the top, and there were five hundred deaths a year, you could expect to be number one in about thirty-six days, right?"

Lia Mai nodded.

"And actually, it's less than that, let's say thirty days. Forty deaths in thirty days, more or less. Now, how much extra delay is there if you are one further down the List?"

Lia Mai didn't answer, and a fleeting look of stubbornness crossed her face. Cynthia continued, "Another way of looking at it, you just advanced one position in three clicks. Before that, in three days. So, at the most, you are giving up three days."

"Cynthia, it's not quite that. Here is this young girl. Why shouldn't she have to wait like everyone else? It's not fair!"

Cynthia's face showed nothing of her exasperation. "You know, you are not being asked to step aside for the prospective mother, but for the Sleeper, Flora Fielding. Lia Mai, she is about the same age as you, actually a couple of years older. And she is dying of a horrible disease. She has only a few friends. Of all the million people on the planet, she knows maybe ten or fifteen. She particularly loves Kiril Lander, the young man Souda Ramirendo has chosen, and has loving bonds to Souda as well. You'll be making your sacrifice of three clicks, or at the most three days, for Flora's sake, not for Souda's sake."

"Oh all right!" Lia Mai stood and crankily turned her back to her visitor.

"Thank you," Cynthia said politely before severing contact.

Souda

The effects of the storm could no longer be felt. The house moved comfortably, working into a steady, regular swell. Souda stood on the top deck, lazily looking toward the horizon. Landfall shouldn't be too far away now.

At the same time, she had an image with the children. The three of them were swimming and frolicking in the shallow waters of the beach near Susan's house. Souda neatly dived through the cascading waterfall of a chest-high breaker, surfacing into momentarily smooth water beyond. She heard Tim's high-pitched, wordless shout of enjoyment, Ria's laugh.

Another image visited her friend Arnolda in France. Arnolda had chosen not to send a return image because she was highly susceptible to motion sickness. She was just saying, "Darling, I'm so thrilled for you, getting your second so far ahead of time!"

"I'm not so thrilled about the reason for the advance," Souda answered. "It's a real crying shame about Flora."

"Right, though I don't know her at all. Tell me, what's she like?"

At home, Artif told her, "Souda, stand up and look well ahead. See the balloon coming toward you?"

In the physical, Souda did so. She turned to watch the two children to ensure their safety, and answered her friend, "She's a remarkable person. A lovely lady, and very wise. Look, without her help, Kiril and I would still be enemies instead of lovers."

"Hmm. Half your luck. Pass him along any time you like."

At home, Artif explained, "This is the supply balloon bringing Kiril's semen. You'd better say good-byes."

So, in South Calif, Souda called, "Susan!"

"Yes, Souda?"

"I need to go. Can you come and watch the children?"

As soon as Susan's image appeared in the water next to her, Souda cancelled this image. In France, she said a quick goodbye and also disconnected.

On their converging courses, the house and the balloon swiftly approached each other. The silver ellipsoid stopped above the masts and lowered. It stayed ahead and on the downwind side, to avoid stealing the wind from the sails. A bridge descended to the deck, and a procession of boxes started their way down. Artif rarely failed to make multiple use of a delivery.

A tiny box led the procession. Souda grabbed it and took it inside. It was icy cold to the touch. By the time she got to her lounge room, a similar box already waited for her. She put Kiril's box hard against hers. A click sounded. Artif said, "Done. Now love, lie down, and I'll implant it."

⚡ **25** ⚡

Flora

As ages ago, at her second awakening in this new world, Flora snuggled into the strong comfort of Mirabelle's embrace. They sat side by side upon the force field of Flora's bed, waiting for the call. She was wearing her Angel's wings.

"It's not threatening," Mirabelle said. Her voice was strained, and she had a look of concentration on her face. "It's just that I find it very hard to be active in more than one place."

"I'm not scared," Flora answered. All the same, her insides were churning. Artif had reduced the painkiller drug dosage to allow Flora to concentrate, and now even the EGM fields were ineffective: she had the deep throb of pain pounding within her in several places. Her relapse had occurred a month and a half ago, but the cancers were growing at an alarming rate. She just had to ignore this for the moment. Once more, she quietly marshaled her arguments to herself.

Then Mirabelle stirred. Her right arm tightened around Flora's shoulders, and she reached over with her left hand to squeeze Flora's right. "They're ready," she said.

Flora found herself in a large, vaulted room that just had to be in another cave, not too dissimilar from hers. One of those self-modifying chairs was in front of her. Mirabelle stood by her side, still on the left, behind another chair. More chairs encircled a great oval table. Flora knew there had to be twenty, but somehow there seemed to be more. These chairs were occupied. The table was a shiny deep red, and obviously made from timber. Behind, all around, were wall-mounted desks holding quiescent computer equipment, familiar to her from her old day.

Almost opposite her, Cynthia gave Flora an encouraging smile. At the left hand end of the table, Mirabelle, another image of Mirabelle, raised her arm in a friendly salute, then disappeared. And diametrically opposite her now-empty chair, Abel sat, his black face impassive. Flora thought he looked old, and still unwell.

Tony — a recording of Tony? — occupied his wheelchair, to Abel's left. He said, in his slightly slurred voice, "Flora Fielding, welcome to this meeting of Control. When you leave here, say nothing about my presence."

"Thank you," Flora answered in some confusion. But..."

"Think of me as another manifestation of Artif. Now, Abel, proceed."

Abel looked at her. "Flora Fielding, please sit down."

Mirabelle helped her into the chair, which instantly adapted itself to give Flora comfort. She then sat herself.

Abel continued, "Are you ready to give us the benefit of your wisdom?"

"I... I guess so." Flora looked around. She spoke, softly at first, but soon her ancient training took over, and she reverted to her resonant, strong voice. "When I was told of my task, the reason you woke me up, I despaired for a long time. I still feel it was an unfair burden to place on me, to place on any person.

"I had to choose one of three courses of action, either for all the Sleepers together, or individually according the nature of each case. I could recommend that the Sleepers be left in cryogenic storage forever. Or I could recommend that their life support systems be turned off. Or finally I could recommend that they be awakened, like I was."

She paused, looking down on her lap, then swept her eyes around the room. "As you all know, I have decided to hand on. My cancer, the disease that sent me into cryogenic storage, has struck again. I'm in constant pain, and as soon as I have finished here, Artif will operate on me again. Otherwise, I won't live long enough to welcome my replacement.

"And, I've been exposed to your ways of thinking enough to realize that death is a part of life. It comes to us all. I want to spend my last few months in the company of two young people I've grown to love very much, Souda Ramirendo and Kiril Lander. And I've been granted my wish. I may hand on to their child.

"Suppose that the best biochemists on the planet today assured me that they will find a cure in perhaps ten years' time. Would I return to suspended animation in order to wait for this cure?

"No. I shudder at the thought. Even if that hope was there, this would only be a temporary reprieve. Two days, two years, two decades, we all have to die. I'd rather go now."

Dear Cynthia had great tears rolling down her bloated black face, but she smiled at Flora.

Others were quietly crying too, even some of the men.

"If this is true for me, it's true for the other Sleepers. I cannot in good conscience recommend that they be left the way they are.

"I've studied the records of all 122 Sleepers. Some are heading toward undignified senility. They should be awakened, gently told that there is no cure for their condition, and never will be, and given the choice of living out their lives under suitable care, or of handing on whenever they are ready. I think all of them will decide to hand on before they lose all their mental abilities. But the choice should be theirs.

"Others have had themselves put to sleep because of cancer, like me, or heart conditions, and in two cases, brain tumors that were inoperable in my day. They should be awakened, and given the same kindness and courtesy I've received. Some of them may actually be cured.

"I recommend that people with the best expertise and interest should research treatment methods for the conditions these Sleepers are suffering from. They should be awakened one or two at a time, in an order that will maximize the chances of a cure for them. And each Sleeper should be given a triple choice: return to 'sleep,' live, or hand on.

"There are eleven cases who have put themselves in cryogenic storage for no more reason than vanity. They were getting old, and were hoping to be awakened when the ravages of aging could be reversed. As I understand it, that will be never. In the world you have, in the world Tony designed, a life is a precious commodity to be passed on, not something to be infinitely hoarded. So, their wish will never be granted.

"Their situation gave me the hardest choice. But, in the end, I think they should be treated like the others: awakened, welcomed with kindness and care, and gently told that they will stay old and ever aging, until they die. All of them are people with fascinating life experiences, and they may find meaning in passing on their knowledge. And if any want to return to Sleep, let them."

A silence filled the room when Flora stopped. At last, Abel smiled at her. "Thank you, Flora," he said. "For my part, I support the adoption of your recommendations. My original choice was to leave the other Sleepers alone, but I think you're right."

A big, broad-shouldered, grizzle-haired man said in a deep voice, "Flora, thank you. I apologize for the suffering we have imposed on you. But if what you say is right, then awakening you was for the best after all."

Tony spoke next. "Is there anyone with a contrary opinion? No? Flora, thank you. It shall be as you recommended. Now, Abel, please organize a working group to implement our decision."

And Flora was back in her room, flat on her back above her bed. Mirabelle said to her, "My dear, thank you." Then she was gone.

Artif told her, "Darling, I'll operate straight away."

Tamás

The white line of Mount Nippon was still on the horizon every time Tamás looked behind. A topstore floated above it, seeming almost to touch the peak. When he mentioned this to Dad, he got no more than a smile. Then Dad relaxed, saying, "Sorry, Tamás, I was just finishing at a new working group I have to chair." The boy had noticed, nowadays Abel found it harder and harder to be in several places at once. *It's my doing,* he couldn't help thinking, *I should've told him I was going on a quest, even if I didn't tell Mom.* There was no point in saying anything though, Dad always dismissed the problem.

Below them, a gentle breeze rippled the shallow waters of the China Sea, so that their flight was almost level. Abel said, "Remarkable land, Japan."

"Yes, so gradual a rise on the other side, and almost a cliff to the west. Dad, why hasn't anyone managed to climb to the top?"

I did try when I was a young fellow, got over twelve thousand meters, almost there, but then my oxygen concentrator broke down. I abseiled down the steep side, reached breathable air in seven clicks, was almost dead by then. Anyway, a few have actually climbed all the way up, but then they died on the way down, isn't that right, Artif?"

"It is. Three men have climbed Mount Nippon: Arathon Manandhar in 897, Anthony d'Abbs in 1215 and Boris Chipek in 1216. He was Anthony's best friend and went up to retrieve his body, but was caught in an avalanche when he was almost safe."

Tamás said, fired up, "I'll give it a go one day! With Angel's wings, it should be a lot easier."

"Yeah, son, but it mightn't be worth as much for credentials."

"Abel," Artif said, "The same thing was said the first time someone used a backpack with a computer and EGM motor in it."

Abel laughed. "I did say at the start, Kiril's invention is going to change the world."

Tamás looked down at the milky blue sea beneath. Not far to the right, a flock of cormorants were fishing. They scooted over the surface, at about the same speed as he and his father. Now and then a bird suddenly dived, to reappear almost immediately with a silver wriggle held crosswise in the beak. Still flying, the bird made a peculiar toss of the head, letting the fish go and swallowing it head first.

Artif told him, "You know, in ancient days when this was highly populated land, people used cormorants to catch fish for them?"

This was interesting. "How?" he asked.

So, Artif showed him a recording of a muddy, wide river with many primitive-looking boats on it. The view focused on one boat. Three naked, brown-skinned children sat cross-legged on the deck, gutting small fish. A man wearing ragged shirt and trousers supervised the birds. These cormorants were smaller than the ones still catching their food nearby, and each had a wooden ring around her neck. A long string was tied to the ring, attaching the bird to the rail of the boat.

Tamás saw a bird come in. She had a fish in her beak. She tossed and swallowed her prey in exactly the way of the modern wild ones, but the fish stuck, wouldn't go past the constriction of the wooden ring. The man casually caught the bird, pulled the fish out of her mouth, then fed her a small handful from the bucket of fish guts.

"That's a bit unfair on the birds!" Tamás said as the recording disappeared.

Abel laughed. "It's even more unfair on the fish." He glanced back at the camp behind the two of them, and the exercise machine came to him. He set it up with a command, and sat on the seat. Continuing to scoot forward at the same speed as before, still beside Tamás, he started to pedal, rhythmically moving the handle backward and forward. Through the implant, he said, "Oh I hate this thing!"

About half a period later, Abel was covered in a sheen of sweat, but stubbornly continued to work his exercise machine. Tamás had spent the time doing his isometric exercises, while simultaneously constructing a recording of several beautiful views he'd seen of Mount Nippon.

Artif suddenly told them, "Darlings, a squall is approaching from the north. You'd better prepare."

"Quick!" Abel shouted, hopping off the machine and sending it to pack itself away. "Lucky we've got a full charge."

Tamás was already calling for his tethering rope. "We'll be right, what's the hurry?" he asked. "We've survived four storms over the Pacific, surely..."

"Shallow water," Abel said succinctly. The exercise machine was stowing itself away in the camp. Abel stepped into his waterproof trousers. "And these storms move fast."

Artif added, "Storms over the ocean tend to be circular swirls around a center that moves slowly. These arctic squalls move in a straight line, funneled between the two land masses."

As soon as he was prepared, Tamás rose to full height and looked to the right. An ominous black line there was swallowing the pale blue of the spring sky. It visibly grew and swelled. Soon, he could see that the front edge of the cloud line was swirling, and dotted with tiny points of light. Where they were, the air was still and somehow heavy. The sea beneath was a wrinkled carpet with barely a wave. And yet, that threatening cloud continued to swallow the sky, and now the lightning became little flashes of vivid light, joining one part of the cloud to another, or striking down into the sea.

They flew on toward the west at the best speed possible, waiting.

The sea below rose to a lazy swell, about a meter in height. Another wave followed, well separated from the first, then another, closer and higher. A distant, continuous rumble forced itself into Tamás's consciousness. It grew, but still, he felt not a breath of wind. The world held its breath, waiting for the blow.

Somewhere far to the right, a blinding finger of light joined sea and sky. Tamás counted to ten before a sharp detonation rent the air, followed by a terrible rumble that shook and vibrated him. "Tony help us," he said through the implant, "you wouldn't want one of those to hit you!"

"I've been talking to Evanor," Abel answered. "He advised that I turn off my water repeller."

Tamás laughed. "Do you good, a bit of water never hurt anyone!"

The icy, freezing breath of the storm struck them a stinging blow, laden with millions of tiny white balls. Tamás couldn't help crying out from the sudden pain as the hail struck his face, the top of his head. "Curl up, Dad," he shouted within his mind, and formed a ball himself. He still felt the continuous battering through the waterproofs and three layers of clothing.

The cloud's edge reached the sun and swallowed it. Everything became dark and gloomy, but then the world split apart with an eye-searing blast, followed almost immediately by a mighty crack that left Tamás deafened. And straight after, he could see nothing.

He felt himself thrown around by the passage of waves below, from right to left, and these were broken waves now. He tasted the salt of rising foam enveloping him, and still the hail battered him from above. The tether tugged him toward the camp then loosened, again and again. He ordered the camp to turn upside down, and sent a cautious thought to check on his father.

Abel detected him and said, "I'm all right for now, Tamás. We just have to endure. I don't think these storms last all that long."

Reassured, Tamás concentrated on trying to keep water off his face so he could breathe. After all, this wasn't his first storm, was it? But certainly, the air was freezing, what there was of it, and the waves below performed an unpredictably mad dance that tossed him around mercilessly.

Another spear of lightning struck the sea somewhere to the left, again close enough that the thunder was immediate and deafening.

A wave reached up, and, supposedly five meters above the surface, Tamás felt himself enveloped in water. The sea struck his side a mighty blow and carried him down, tumbled him about as if he was swimming in pounding surf.

The motor on his back clawed him upward, but the tether jerked him down and sideways at the same time. At last his head broke the surface and he sucked in a desperate breath, laden with salt spray. Once more he formed a ball and checked on his father.

Abel was in trouble. He flew above the sea, face down, but to Tamás's horror he wasn't breathing. "Artif!" Tamás shouted within his mind.

"I'm working on it," she replied immediately. Her voice was warm and calm. "Send an image and help."

Tamás was by his father's side, the image wearing Angel's wings too. He grasped Abel's flying form to stop the storm from tearing them apart. "What can I do?"

"His tongue is caught in the back of his throat. Loosen it."

One arm convulsively gripping the broad but bony shoulders, Tamás put a hand on Abel's face. Dad's mouth hung slackly open. He thrust in two fingers, but just then his physical self was tumbled about my another mighty wave. Somehow, he managed to keep the image going as well, and used it to cushion Abel's inert body as the tether jerked them down hard, as the wave struck here ,too. Then, he again put two fingers in Abel's mouth and scrabbled around until he felt the tongue flop forward.

"Good, love. Now squeeze his chest."

Another enormous wave hit his body, and again he endured, also protecting his father. Then he got his image to lie directly under Abel, and reached both arms around him. He pushed hard with both hands on either side of the spine. Abel's body convulsed, and Tamás felt rather than heard him gag and vomit, over Tamás's head.

The broad chest rose and fell, then Tamás felt his father cough. And he heard the thought, "Ohh... thank you, son."

He didn't dare to let go. For what felt like forever, he continued to battle the storm with his own body while sheltering Abel from the worst, using the image. At last, he found himself tiring to the point where the image's breathing became uncoordinated, and he sucked in a great volume of stinging salty water.

Artif automatically canceled the image, but the searing pain gripped his chest for quite some time.

Abel said, "I'll be all right, Tamás. Concentrate on yourself."

"But..."

"You've given me a good rest. Do as you're told."

Tamás could imagine what that "good rest" might feel like, but obeyed.

Artif said, "It's blowing itself out."

Tamás risked a glance to the right. What hit his face was rain, not hail, and he fancied that the horizon looked a little less gloomy. The waves below were still broken and steep, but they no longer snatched at him.

Tumbled about mercilessly, they flew on.

⋟ 26 ⋟

Flora

End of spring was a delightful season here in the new Rockies. Flora could once more control pain by staying within an EGM field, because Artif had cut out all the tumors she could find. Again, the chemotherapy had made her hair fall out and her skin become like paper, and again it negated her sense of smell and taste. Unfortunately, the multiple lesions of the operations now interfered with the workings of Flora's body, despite all Artif's manipulations.

And the cancer cells still continued to multiply.

Strangely, she felt no fear. She no longer minded dying, as long as it could be after the birth of Souda's baby.

Currently, Flora was resting after a meeting in Tony's cave where her advice had been sought on the order in which the Sleepers were to be awakened. She was in two places, her Angel's wings on in both. In the physical, she enjoyed one of her favorite lookouts on top of a grass-covered hill overlooking a wild mountainscape. Swallows swooped and cavorted in the valley before her, and she thought of the view beyond as a live painting: a breathtaking panorama of wooded slopes receding as far as the eye could reach. On the nearby slopes, each tree was a line that swayed with the wind. The distant peaks were tiny blue points serrating the horizon, and, in between, the gradation was too gradual to be noticed. The whole view formed a single symphony of grandeur, as if designed to soothe her soul.

In image, she reclined over the top deck of Souda's graceful ship. Both tall masts were bare, and three long silver lines tethered the ship to the shore. This was the bay where Abel's ship had been, last autumn.

Kiril's ship was moored right next to Souda's. The two craft were almost touching, but some sort of device invisibly stopped them from bumping into each other as they bobbed and bowed in response to the gentle waves.

The youngsters were below, which was all right with Flora. She didn't need to have them dance attendance on her, just wanted to be within their ambience.

She smiled to herself as she compared the two ships. Souda's was all grace and smoothness, a lady of the sea. Kiril's had straight lines, and the three masts were raked back, giving the ship the look of a racer. Souda's wore pastel colors of pink and mauve and blue, while Kiril's was pure white, with a black line halfway between the water and the bottom guard rail.

Souda's voice sounded in Flora's mind, "Darling, would you like a drink?"

"Thank you," she answered, more to be agreeable than from desire. She couldn't taste it anyway. Souda popped out of nowhere next to her, holding a cup. At the same time, back home, an identical cup floated out of the so-called basket next to her. Actually, it was an oval shaped, open-topped plasteel container.

"How are you, love?" Souda asked, then a fleeting look of doubt crossed her face, as in, 'Should I have reminded her of it?'

"No pain right now," Flora reassured her, "and no, you're not stepping on my toes by asking."

To her surprise, Kiril emerged from around a structure on his own ship, and in one smooth jump hurdled the two guard rails. He ran up the ladder and stood facing the two women, his breathing slow and deep.

"Oh, I thought you were below with Souda," Flora exclaimed.

"I was, in image," he told her, "and isn't she looking gorgeous?"

She was, Flora had to agree. Souda had the bloom of early pregnancy, and had not suffered any morning sickness at all.

Flora gazed at these two attractive, vital youngsters, and a sudden, entirely new thought came to her. *They're my children. My own kids're as dead as the era they lived in. Now, I have these two. They're really and truly my children.*

And looming death sentence or no, she was happy.

Tamás

The mountains of Mongolia were a bleak sort of a place, Tamás thought as he sat on a hovering cushion, just outside the camp. A little fire flickered between him and Abel, and the bugcatchers worked hard to keep them safe from a hovering cloud of little black flies.

The sun was a great red disk to the west, in a valley between two bare hills. Even by the ruddy light, Abel looked gray. He sat on his cushion, long legs splayed out, head drooping, back bent.

I know! It's like Chia when he had the broken ribs! Tamás had been annoyed by a half-remembered recognition every time he looked at his father. Since the storm, some twenty days ago, Abel's skin had a color of lifeless gray, the color of a black person whose skin is drained of blood. He coughed, a deep, racking cough that seemed to bother him a lot lately.

After the storm, Tamás had suggested that perhaps Abel could leave him to continue alone once they reached land. Artif had confirmed that she could easily direct a balloon to them, and then Abel could go wherever he wished.

Abel's reaction had been so violently negative that Tamás had backed off. Several times a day since, he'd tried to find a way of renewing the offer, but somehow there never was a suitable opportunity. Knowing Dad, almost certainly he'd carefully engineered matters to ensure this. But at last, the boy could stand it no longer.

"Dad?"

Abel raised his head. His eyes were bloodshot. He said, "Hey, did you know this area bred some of the greatest conquerors of antiquity? Artif, what was that fellow called, Something Khan?"

"Ghengis Khan," she replied.

"Yeah, that's it. Just imagine, boy, thousands upon thousands of savage warriors..."

Despite his resolve, Tamás was tempted to explore the matter, but he saw through his father's ploy. "Dad," he repeated.

"What?"

"You're sick."

"I'm OK."

"Oh yeah? Then why do you look like you've been chewed by a hippo?"

Abel laughed. "Do I?"

"You look terrible, Dad. Artif, tell him."

"Tamás, love, I've told your father several times, he has a low-grade infection of the lungs. Some seawater is left behind, and it'd take microsurgery for me to remove it. And his blood pressure is far too low. And Abel, you haven't told Tamás about the arthritis in your left knee."

"My left knee is OK. I've lived with it for a long time. And I haven't fainted, have I? And if that water hasn't killed me in what? twenty-one days? then it won't now. You two just mind your own business."

Tamás sprung to his feet and shouted, "It so is my business! You're the only father I've got!"

"Oh, sit down, son. Look, I got to be President because I don't quit, ever. If I start on a course of action, I DO it. I'm going to Sweden, with you."

"Well I don't want you along. And it's my quest."

"You know, you sounded just like your mother then?"

"Is that meant as an insult?"

Abel laughed again. "No, a compliment. I'm not the only stubborn person on the planet. But yeah, it's your quest. And also, you're only thirteen years old, and I'm your father. So there."

"DAD, I DON'T WANT TO BE RESPONSIBLE FOR KILLING YOU!" Tamás started crying, with great sobs he couldn't help, tears he was ashamed of, and hiccupping, painful breaths. He turned away and hid his face in the crook of his arm.

Abel's voice sounded in his mind, through the implant, "Settle down, Tamás. It's OK, I'm listening."

He turned back to face Abel across the fire. He took a deep, slow breath and impatiently wiped the tears off his face with the sleeve of the shirt he'd put on against the evening chill.

"Listening, are you?" he asked bitterly. "At last! How many times have I tried to talk to you about how I feel? And what I get is, 'No need to apologize,' or 'Sorry has never changed anything,' or some such dismissal."

"Yeah, but son, I truly mean it. There is no need to apologize because you've done nothing shameful. I'm responsible for my own actions and emotions. And this includes my own mistakes. You needn't carry me around on your back. True."

"Dad, you look terrible. You look sick, and whatever you say, if I hadn't gone on a quest, if I'd told you before I went, if I hadn't made you worry about me for months, you wouldn't be like this. You would still be the ageless, powerful man admired by everyone. You changed, and you changed because of what I did, and nothing you say can change that."

A long silence followed Tamás's outburst. Abel looked at him, across the flickering flames. He leaned forward, picked up a stick and threw it onto the fire. At last, he said, "Yeah, there's truth in what you say. My health went downhill as a result of what you did. But, there was something in between. My thoughts and emotions. My health suffered as a result of what you did, but not because of what you did. I suffered because of my own actions. It's my responsibility, not yours."

"I don't understand the distinction. I mean, if I throw a stone and it happens to hit your head, then you got hurt because you didn't duck."

Abel laughed. "No, poor analogy. You threw a stone in a safe direction, and I rushed over and got in its way so it'd hit me."

"All right. But the stone did hit you. And you're now sick. You need to rest, and allow Artif to get that water out of your lungs. And the worst is behind me. I still have a long way to go, but it's all on land, and summer is coming, and—"

"No. I'm coming with you."

Abel stood up, turned his back on Tamás and walked into the camp.

For a long time, Tamás sat by the fire as it died down into a red glow, then even that faded to a gray heap of ashes with the odd red light when the breeze picked up for a moment. When at last he went into the camp, Abel was well asleep. He snored softly — something else that was new since the storm over the China sea — and apparently still asleep, suddenly he half sat up, coughed several times, then flopped down onto his other side.

Sighing, Tamás crawled into his own sleeping bag, and lay there for ages, still awake.

In the morning, he had the new approach clear in his mind. As he accepted a bowl of hot porridge from the camp's kitchen, he said, "Dad, I'm not finished with last night's discussion."

"I am." Abel half turned his back to him.

"Dad, just listen. Suppose I was not your son, but some other person. For some reason, sound or silly, I'm distressed about something. It's your duty to counsel me, right?"

Abel turned back and looked him in the face. "Right."

"OK. I'm distressed. Counsel me."

"I thought I'd been doing just that. You did what at the time you felt you had to do. Now, with hindsight, you might do it differently, but way back then, you did the best you could. That shows that the experience has been of benefit to you, that you've become wiser as a result of making a mistake, that is, assuming you made a mistake."

"My problem is that because I did something, you've suffered, are suffering."

"Here we go around the same circle. I'm physically unwell because of something I did. It's my fault, not yours."

"Dad, this is a sort of a game of chess between us, and you just made a bad move."

"Huh?"

"This is the first time you've admitted that you are physically unwell." Without warning, they grinned at each other.

"OK, Dad, suppose I was the one who was, as you put it, physically unwell. Would you step in and order me to give up my quest, or at least to take a break?"

"You're a child. My child. It's my duty to look after you. I'm not your child. It's not your duty to look after me. Topic closed."

"But Dad..." Tamás stopped, for clearly he was talking to himself.

Mirabelle

Early summer is the best time of the year here, Mirabelle happily thought as she settled into her northern garden once more. Evenings were chilly of course, but the days were delightful. So, after lunch she sat down cross-legged in the garden, under her favorite pear tree, rather than up in her house.

"Flora?" she called.

Her friend stood there, smiling down at her, and also Mirabelle faced her under the palm tree outside Flora's cave. Flora had been eating, clearly breakfast. Mirabelle hadn't seen her for several days, and was shocked by her appearance. Even through the loose top her body looked angular, and her face was gaunt. Her skin seemed like a tightly stretched film. In contrast, her face bore a radiant, serene smile.

Mirabelle made sure nothing in her face or voice showed her concern. "It's nearly time for awakening Marcel," she said. "I thought we'd need each other's support for that."

"I agree. Just a minute, I'll say good-bye with my other images."

"Images? In the plural?"

Flora laughed. "I have one on Souda's ship almost all the time, and I've taught a game called Chinese checkers to Ria and Tim. We're in the middle of a three-way game, but Souda is willing to take my part."

Mirabelle had to laugh. "Who'd have thought that you'd become better than I am at controlling images!"

"I don't know that I am. But you know, my training as an actor has helped. Anyway, you can just stay here in your garden, and I'll have my image with you and still take part in whatever Artif wants us to do."

"All we have to do is to listen, and to talk when it seems appropriate."

Flora looked a little uncertain of herself. "My French is atrocious."

"That doesn't matter. Just send in English, Artif will translate."

"Oh, I thought this might be different." Flora settled, lying flat in the air, ten centimeters above the grass. She reached out and grasped Mirabelle's hand.

Mirabelle heard Artif say, "Marcel, wake up. Marcel Prousard, wake up... Good, I detect that you are conscious. Don't struggle. The machine is slowly bringing you back. You'll be OK."

She saw the look of remembrance on Flora's face. Way back, Artif had used the self-same words for her.

She heard an indistinct groan. "Where... what..."

Artif said, "Marcel, you had yourself put to sleep because you didn't want your heart condition to kill you. Remember?"

"Oh... cold..."

Though slurred and weak, the voice had a pleasant timbre.

"The machine is warming you very, very slowly. That's necessary to ensure that there will be no damage. Now, Marcel, move your fingers."

Mirabelle exchanged a look with Flora, then sent the thought, "Marcel Prousard, welcome. I'm Mirabelle Karlsen."

She heard, "And I am Abel T'Dwuna. Welcome to our world."

Flora also said, "Marcel, I am Flora Fielding. Welcome from me too."

"Oh, a name I recognize. The voice too. I am honored."

"The other two who spoke are the Deputy President and President of all humanity. Their presence is far more of an honor than mine."

"Marcel, move your legs and arms," Artif said.

"Oh, they are made from putty, yes. But who is the lady with the wonderful voice? I see no one."

Flora happened to say something, before anyone else: "Marcel, I was in just your situation a year ago. I had cancer, and had myself put in cryogenic storage. I was awakened just like you are being awakened now. I was the first, you're the second."

Artif answered the man's question, "Marcel, I am Artif. You can't see me because I'm not a person. Think of me as a computer."

"My God. Hmm. **When** is it?"

Artif told him, to be met by an incredulous silence. At long last, Marcel said, still unbelieving, "It took fourteen hundred years, FOURTEEN HUNDRED YEARS to develop a cure for heart problems?"

"Marcel, it's not quite like that," Abel answered. Almost immediately after you went to Sleep, the world suffered a Cataclysm. That was followed by the Chaos, which lasted nearly 150 years in your part of the world. You'll learn our history in due course. You were not awakened for medical reasons, but because Control, the supreme governing body of humanity, decided to awaken all Sleepers like you."

Well said, Mirabelle thought grudgingly.

Flora spoke again. "Marcel, this is a wonderful world. At first I was horrified, like you are now. And, in my case, the cancer I had in the twenty-first century is killing me, now. We decided to make you second because your health problem is the most likely to be curable. So, you're in a better situation than I was."

Abel added, "We'll do our best to help with your problem, though you must know that no one else on earth has had a seriously faulty heart for well over a thousand years. Artif will ensure that you suffer as little as possible, and you have the choice of going back to your Sleep."

Mirabelle said, "Marcel, soon after Flora awoke, she chose to accept something every other person on the planet has, called an implant. It will enable Artif to examine you inside, and is your one chance of a cure. Do you want it?"

The man laughed, though still weakly. "Do I have a choice, then, eh? What are the negatives?"

Flora reassured him. "Nothing. It's wonderful. I won't overload you with information now. At my awakening, that was the bad part, the barrage of new information I just couldn't cope with, and the homesickness for my own times. But the implant is a boon in every way."

"I won't live long without an artificial heart or something. What have I got to lose?"

Artif told him, "Marcel, I'll put you to sleep again. When you awake, you will have the implant. In Flora's case, it took eight days to become active. I expect about the same for you."

They disconnected. Flora breathed a deep sigh of relief. "Thank Heavens, that could have gone worse."

Mirabelle opened her eyes. "Yes, this was easy. Wasn't that why you advised that he be the first? The ones with incurable problems..."

"And you might have to cope with them without me. I just hope I last long enough."

Mirabelle gently stroked the fragile hand holding hers. "Everyone hopes that, love," she said.

Marcel

He didn't open his eyes at first. Something felt different. Then he identified it: the sensation of being supported by a surface was missing. It was like hovering in the air, but that couldn't be, surely? He reached under himself with a hand, to encounter empty space.

That beautiful voice, what was it called? Artif, said immediately, "Marcel, welcome again. While you were asleep, you were moved onto a new kind of bed—"

Flora Fielding's voice interrupted, "Think of it as a kind of force field. It's absolutely wonderful, especially when you have wounds inside. With all the operations I've had, I couldn't live without one."

Marcel opened his eyes. He was still in the same place as at his first awakening: in the cave deep in the Appenines where he'd set up his cocoon, his one last hope for survival. And it had worked! Through the eons, it had kept him alive, and now there was hope! And as an added bonus, oh la la, *la Fielding* herself. He had an excellent visual memory, and could instantly see her, several views of her: being rescued from a wrecked sailing ship, her torn, water-logged clothes revealingly hugging her magnificent body; as a pregnant woman of the slums, battling to survive; as a wicked siren luring wealthy men to ruin. She certainly would be welcome to lure him!

Not that any of his wealth could have survived, and anyway, back then, she could have bought him a hundred times over.

"Marcel, are you all right?" Artif the disembodied computer voice asked. "You haven't answered."

"Yes, Oh I just had memories. Of Flora Fielding."

Flora laughed, a pleasantly musical sound. "Marcel, I'm flattered. But don't expect me to look like I did in my movies. As I told you, I'm not at all well."

The room had a vaulted ceiling, a semi-circle hewed out of the living rock. His own company had done the work. He hadn't bothered with any sort of prettyfying, it was just a shell for a body, was it not? His bed was gone. Instead he hovered above a sort of a large plastic rectangle with an oval depression in the middle. His naked body was held in a sitting position, necessary to allow him to breathe, and he noted the external artificial heart still strapped to his chest. Naturally. It had to be there or he'd be dead.

Artif said, "Marcel, I have some clothes waiting for you. And as soon as you're dressed, Flora wants to visit you so you can share a meal."

"Oh yes, I am hungry! But how do I get up?"

Instantly he felt a gentle but irresistible force move him along, then set him on his feet. It was strange. His legs felt like butter, would not have held him, but that force did. He stood there, like a puppet hanging from its strings.

The gray metal-lined door swung silently open and a row of clothes came in, hanging from a steel rod. Marcel felt his jaw drop open. "What the hell?" he said.

Artif's voice came from behind him, "They are borne by the same kind of force as the one supporting you over the bed. It's not magic — indeed, the principle was developed back in your times."

"It puzzled me a great deal too, at first," Flora added.

Marcel tried to turn, but couldn't move in the grip of the force field. Then Artif said, "Oh sorry," and the force turned him.

A globe, about forty centimeters in diameter, hovered beside the force field bed, at about his chest height. It was like a crystal ball filled with clouds. Artif's voice came from it. "When your implant is active, you'll be able to control the bed and all sorts of other things. For now, you need to tell me what you want and I'll do it for you."

"Can you release me?"

"No. You'd fall. Your muscles are extremely weak after all this inactivity."

"Er, where is Flora?"

"I'm here." Her voice also came from the globe. "I'll be there with you as soon as you're dressed. For now it's sound only, both ways."

"Thank the good God. I wouldn't want you to see me the way I am."

Flora laughed. "That was exactly my reaction upon awakening."

"Artif, can I now dress, then?"

He was turned, and felt himself held up as he walked toward the clothes.

Flora said, "I've chosen these for you. The climate has changed since our times, so you have to dress for the tropics. Men wear a kilt rather than trousers, and few of them wear anything else. In fact... No, we'll introduce new information gradually. Anyway, choose a kilt and a comfortable top."

He did so. One was as good as another. He said, "I did not realize you spoke French so well."

"I don't. Our speech is being translated, both ways."

This was truly an amazing world.

Artif said, "Flora, Marcel is dressed now."

Once more, he felt himself turned, and the force gently moved him back toward the thing he could only refer to as a bed, though it was like no bed he'd ever seen. He was picked up and returned into a sitting position over it.

A woman stood by him. One instant, he was alone with only the globe for company, the next instant she was there. He had to work hard to keep dismay from his face. She was an old woman! Oh, the magnificent architecture of her face was still there, still beautiful, but her skin looked like parchment, and she was gaunt. She wore a yellow skirt and a white, loose top. Her hair was cut short, almost like a cap on her head, and was the auburn color he remembered.

She said with a sad little smile, "Cancer does this to you, and the chemotherapy. But I'm not quite ready to die yet. That's another thing I'll explain later."

Two plastic-looking trays floated in. Everything floated in air, seemingly. The one that stopped in front of him held two croissants, perfect in every detail and giving off that fresh-baked smell. A knife and a small dish of butter were beside them, and a black little globe.

Flora told him, "The globe is the modern version of a cup. It has black coffee in it. No sugar, is that..."

"Yes, perfectly all right, thank you."

"Give it a gentle squeeze."

He picked it up and did so, and the delicious scent of coffee reached him. A short straw now stuck out the top of the "cup." He took a sip, and found the coffee to be perfect. "I like the service in this hotel," he said.

"We specially grew the coffee, as soon as it was decided to awaken you. It's not a generally enjoyed drink. Later, you can try other flavors, but Artif has built up a good store of coffee beans for you."

He'd never been a big eater, but now he consumed the croissants and still felt hungry. However, he was hungrier for information. "Tell me about this world," he demanded.

"There are only one million people. A baby is only allowed to be born when somebody dies. And so, everyone can have all the material wealth they want, almost without limit. Not that people are greedy — when you have universal plenty, you don't need to be."

He nodded with instant understanding.

"Everybody has an implant. Also, every mechanical device has a computer. The implant is like an internal radio link, but much more than that. I'm actually in America. What you can see and hear, and for that matter smell and touch if you wish, is a sort of a copy of me, projected by the communication globe. When your implant is working, you'll be able to receive and send such images simply by expressing the wish. And Artif will be with you, all the time. Inside your being."

He shook his head. "It sounds marvelous."

"It is. Oh, this world has problems too — after all it's inhabited by people — but life is far better than in our times. Everything is automated. People don't do work in the sense we had to."

"I can guess one of the problems: boredom, no meaning to life, eh?"

"Far from it. Just that meaning is not equated with work, with earning money. People still strive, in much the same way, but the goals are different."

Marcel wanted to find out so much more! He was an explorer facing a strange country and wanted to see it all, now! Only, against his will, he yawned, a mighty, jaw-dislocating yawn.

"I'll go now," Flora said with a smile that illuminated and transformed that haggard face, "but next time, I'll introduce other people to you. I'll start with one of my special friends, Nathaniel Kyros. You'll like Nat, everyone does."

And she was gone, as if she'd never been.

⇗ 27 ⇗

Flora

Artif had operated, yet again. This time there had been cancer in Flora's liver, and one of her kidneys had to be removed. She awoke on the elevated bed of the blue room, to find Kiril sitting there with her. He said, within her mind, "Welcome back, love. I was the winner."

"The winner?"

"Nine of us wanted to be here when you awoke, but everyone knew you wouldn't be able to cope with a crowd. So we got Artif to select by random numbers."

She had to smile, despite the waves of pain held in the background by Artif's ministrations.

"Congratulations." It was wonderful, being able to talk without effort, without sound.

"Flora, even though I'm the one here, Evanor wants me to give you a message."

"Hmm?"

"He's invented a little machine for you. It's on the way, by balloon."

"Is he up to 600 inventions yet?"

He laughed with her. "I imagine he's well over. This thing can be inserted under the skin—"

"A very minor procedure," Artif interrupted.

"...and it filters your blood. It'll pull out any cancer cells it finds."

"Oh, he's wonderful. You all are. How is Souda?"

"She's busy watching her tummy grow. You know, the baby is moving?"

"Yes dear, remember, last time I felt it? And, any news of young Tamás?"

"There can't be, Flora. But I do know that Abel is very sick."

"Yes, he looked awful last time I saw him. Poor fellow's aged terribly."

"I think it's worse than that. Mirabelle mentioned that he's missed several important Control meetings, and that's never been heard of before. He just wouldn't do that unless..."

"Unless what?"

"Unless he was dying."

"Oh dear. And when I first met him..."

"Abel's been every boy's hero for the past forty years. But he's not my concern. You are."

"I'll be all right now, for a while. It's become a pattern, you know. These wretched things get started somewhere in my body, however much of the medicines I take, and they grow. They press on something so they hurt, or constrict something so my body won't work the way it should, and then, next thing, here I am in the blue room. And after a while I recover from the operation, and things are all right for a while, except some part of me no longer works like it should. But I go on — until the next time."

"All the same, darling, I want you to hurry up and get strong again."

"Yes. I still have nearly four months to go. I'm determined to make it." She didn't share the thought that she very much doubted whether she'd succeed.

Artif broke in, "Kiril, I want Flora to rest now for a while."

He bent over her and gave her a light kiss. Then he was gone.

As Flora drifted off to sleep, she just wished she could go. It would be so easy to stop struggling! She often felt like this, in the darkness of the small hours.

But as soon as she was able, she sent an image to the two ships and their two delightful occupants, and watched as Souda grew, almost day to day, and her resolve hardened.

Unfortunately, so did her insides, in response to the chemicals she'd been taking, it felt like forever. No matter how much she forced herself to eat of the tasteless food, she got thinner and had less and less energy. If the cancer didn't kill her first, malnutrition might.

Tamás

He chose to set up camp well outside the ancient ruins. Artif said this was Budapest, on the Danube river. The scenery was beautiful and would normally have been intriguing, but Tamás had no attention for anything. He knew his father was dying.

Abel felt hot to the touch, and was less than semi-conscious. The boy ordered Abel's EGM motor to sit him comfortably, then pushed the straw of a cup of water into his mouth. "Drink, Dad, drink," he said through the implant.

Nothing happened, though he heard Artif repeat the order. Then she said, to him, "Love, I'm sorry."

"Can you do anything?" His eyes were dry and burning, but he could no longer cry.

"Once, years ago, he told me that he wanted to die on a quest. Darling, he's having his wish."

"Please. Get somebody. I don't care about my quest."

Mother stood there, then a couple of clicklets later, Evanor was by her side. "Tamás!" she said.

"Mom, oh Mom, he's dying."

Evanor bent over Abel and put a hand on his throat. "Still a pulse here, but he's terribly hot. Artif?"

"Double pneumonia. Tamás and I both tried and tried, but he wouldn't quit."

Mirabelle gave a sad little laugh. "Isn't that just like him? He never could admit his age. Going on a quest at nearly seventy!"

Incredibly, Tamás heard Abel's thought, through the implant. "Still criticizing me, Mirrie?" The thought had a laugh in it.

"Yes, you old fool. Why didn't you go for help?"

He didn't answer, instead said, "Tamás!"

"Dad?"

"I'm happy. And I'm proud of you. Don't... ever... change." And his chest stopped its movement.

Once more, Evanor put a hand on Abel's throat, even as Artif said, "He's gone, my dears." Mirabelle held out her arms and Tamás went to her comforting embrace. He was taller than her now.

"Oh why?" he cried through the implant, feeling helpless, and lost, and very, very young.

"It's the way he was, all his life," she answered, stroking his hair. "He always had to strive for the impossible, and the incredible thing is, he usually achieved it. Oh, he and I never got on, not ever, but he was a great man."

Evanor offered, "His many acts of daring will be remembered for hundreds of years. I doubt that anyone will ever beat his bull riding record. And a person who'd do the things he's done could never admit that now he was too weak to, to... oh, I don't know!" Though Abel had been a relative stranger to him, it was clear from his glistening eyes, his rigid posture, that he was greatly upset, too.

Tamás looked up and finished Evanor's sentence: "To do what a mere boy was doing."

He pulled away from his mother. "It went wrong over the China Sea. We got caught in a storm, a short squall really, but vicious. There was lots of lightning, so he turned off his water-repelling device. Then we got caught by some waves so high that they broke on top of us. And he nearly drowned. I managed to help him, but some water was left inside his lungs, and then he just wouldn't quit. And Mom, it spoiled everything. All we did after that was to argue. There was no fun in it anymore, the quest was just something to finish and get out of the way. And even when I saw Mount Baikal, it was, 'so what?' We saw lions, and a mighty herd of wild cattle, and had all sorts of experiences that should've been exciting adventures, and oh, Tony help us, they were nothing. Because I knew he was killing himself, and I couldn't stop him. And so, I don't give a fart for credentials! I'm stopping."

"Tamás," she answered gently, "it's the right thing to do anyway. Come on home."

Artif said, "I've already diverted a balloon."

Evanor

Witnessing Abel's death had affected Evanor far more than he cared to admit. He'd never seen a person die before. Every time he thought of it, he felt his forehead go clammy with cold sweat, and once he even felt his gorge rise.

And when he was upset, he drowned himself in work. He had two projects in hand: a way of getting nutrition into Flora, and the artificial heart for Marcel.

Artif was playing a recording for him, from Tony's ancient archives. He saw diagrams that would have puzzled most other people, but were clear to him. He thought at the recording globe at his side, copying the ancient technique with modifications. "Yes," he said, "glucose and amino acids and all the other nutrients, directly into the vein, that's the go. She can be built up whether her intestines absorb food or not."

He ordered the recording of his design for her blood filter out and projected the two images side by side. "Artif, it's simple. We just make a second blood filter, replacing the existing one. Only, this has a pipe to the outside, with a tap on it, here. Three times a day, she hooks up to a container full of nutrient fluid, and allows the food to enter her bloodstream directly. You'll just have to monitor for any bacterial infections."

She approved. Evanor glanced out the side of his balloon, at the Atlantic ocean below, then sent commands to his machines. He knew that Artif was already bringing a supply balloon, so that the new device could go to Flora as soon as it was ready.

Marcel's problem was far more of a challenge. In ancient times, he'd had an artificial heart put in, after his immune system had rejected transplants from dead humans. He'd decided to be placed into cryogenic storage after this internal heart machine had failed.

Evanor called up the records available about him, studied them for a couple of periods, then asked, "Artif, can I talk to Marcel?"

He found the Sleeper outside, under the shade of a huge, spreading oak tree. Marcel wore Angel's wings, and had obviously been exercising under Artif's directions: his feet were hooked into the loops of two exercise straps.

"Welcome, Evanor," he said through the implant. "I find it fun, talking like this."

Evanor smiled at the Frenchman. Marcel was an attractive fellow in early middle age. Distinguished gray strands sprinkled his dark, curly hair. Of course, his skin was terribly pale, but then he wasn't interested in impressing the ladies, was he?

He said, "Marcel, I'm working on the new heart for you. Tell me again, what went wrong with the previous one?"

"I guess my immune system is too good. I've been thinking about this, and that's the realization I came to. My body rejected three donated hearts, then the stainless steel and teflon device."

"That's the one I've been studying. Artif found the plans for it, from your archives. It was rather a large thing. I can make a copy, the same size as a human heart, and using plasteel for all components."

Marcel visibly drooped. "Oh. It won't work. My immune system..."

"Artif, tell him."

She said, "Marcel, now that your implant is working, I can manipulate your immune system. That's my main tool in maintaining people's health."

Hope and despair fought with each other on Marcel's face. "Is it possible?"

"It is," Evanor said firmly.

"Oh, to be physically active again! I used to be an athlete, distance running, you know. But then had my first heart attack at thirty-nine. It's in the genes — both my father and mother died from early heart attacks. Still, I lived so healthy, I was sure I'd beat it..." He stopped, and sat there, head hanging. Obviously, he'd returned to his youth.

Evanor respected the silence. At last, he asked, "You must have been very wealthy to be able to afford all that treatment, then have yourself put to Sleep?" He'd learnt a lot about the early days, through contact with Flora and Nathaniel.

Marcel raised his head and suddenly grinned. "Oh yes! And I started as a simple surveyor, built it up all myself, and never did a dishonest thing to earn it. Hard work and imagination. When I handed over to my son because I was too ill, we were the biggest geological survey firm on earth! My last project was to win the most prestigious tender of all..."

"Marcel, please explain 'tender', my translator has no equivalent."

"The United Nations — oh, it was not like Control, but an association of all the countries in the world — decided it was necessary to extract minerals from Antarctica. Otherwise, we'd run out of many materials. And my firm was given the job of mapping the underground resources. We were chosen as the best."

Evanor was immediately interested in the technical aspects. "Nowadays we do that with energy scanning devices on the topstores. Certain cosmic rays pass right through the earth, and we can map the patterns of distortions in them. So, we can generate a cross-section of the earth's crust, everywhere."

"Fascinating. I'd like to see it."

Evanor sent Artif a request, and instantly the two of them were looking at a recording: a maze of colored lines that would have been meaningless to most people. He explained, "This is the map of the substrates directly under us, right here. You can see, the Pyrenees stand on a very thick base...—"

"Surely. I knew that, that's why I chose this spot. Evanor, this is wonderful technology. In my day, we had to rely on sound rather than electromagnetic radiation."

"Sound?"

"Yes. Vibration. Same thing, isn't it? You set off three carefully placed explosions, and monitor the vibration in various places. Not as accurate as this, but it served."

Evanor's heart went cold. He was overwhelmed by horror, and pity for this man. "Artif, how do I tell him?" he asked privately.

"He'll have to find out, eventually. But you needn't tell him yourself."

But Evanor was not used to shoving off responsibility. Gently, he asked, "And, Marcel, did you set off explosions in Antarctica?"

"Kind of. Not me personally. Unfortunately I was far too sick and weak. I did all the preparatory work. On the day I found out that we won the tender, I entered my cocoon. I left my son in charge. He was still young, but a brilliant geologist."

Still, Evanor didn't know how to broach the topic. Marcel looked at him. "Something is wrong, eh?"

"I... I really don't know how to tell you. Look. Marcel, humanity was in trouble in your days."

"You're right there! Oh the crime rate! And drugs, and wars that made no sense, and every city even in the rich countries had homeless people starving in the streets..."

"And you had terrible health problems due to pollution in the air, water and food."

"We did, true."

"And you mentioned that mineral resources were getting scarce."

"Yes, but where are you leading?"

"To the worst problem your world faced: climate change. That was what led to the Cataclysm, the event that ended your world and led to the Chaos."

"So?" Marcel looked wary and puzzled.

"I think the Cataclysm was bound to happen, in one way or another. No individual can be blamed for it. But what actually did happen was, that the Ross Ice Shelf in the Antarctic catastrophically detached, and caused a two hundred meter high wave that swept around the globe."

Marcel's pale face grew so white it was almost luminous. He looked more dead than alive. "My God..."

After a long silence, Evanor said, "No one now knows the reason the Ross Ice Shelf cracked off, but the theory has always been that it was due to explosions used in geological exploration. But, my friend, it was not your fault, personally. You did it in good faith."

"Oh my God!"

"Marcel, no!" Artif suddenly shouted. The Frenchman reached for the external artificial heart under his t-shirt, and jerked it free. A gush of crimson blood pushed the thin material away from his body, instantly staining it.

Evanor jumped forward, and pinched hard over the artery. Fortunately, he had an exact knowledge of the device's attachment. An instant later, he closed off the input side, which was releasing blood at a slower rate.

Three other men appeared, one of them with surgical clamps. Evanor knew them all. "Oh Tony be thanked, Neil, G'don, Carlo," he gasped.

Neil, a tall, thin black man, was the foremost expert on the human body. He said, without seeming excited, "We have about two clicks to fix it. No panic." All the same, he worked with swift efficiency. Marcel had stopped moving, though his chest still pumped air.

It took no longer than a click to have the heart device back in place and working.

"He's lost a lot of blood," Artif said. Fortunately, there is frozen blood in his stores, for emergencies. Rig up an intravenous drip for him."

Evanor thought at the EGM motor strapped to Marcel's back, and the four of them accompanied the inert body as it floated to the bed inside. The equipment for the drip already waited for them. Artif said, "I'm still warming the blood to body temperature."

Evanor had another worry. "When he awakens, he'll just do the same, won't he? He needs constant attendance, and urgent counseling. And I'm the wrong person for that. Look how I blundered, telling him."

A bag of deep red fluid came in on a tray. Neil quickly attached it, then punctured a vein on the back of Marcel's hand. Carlo waited ready with a magnetic clamp, and then wound a plasteel mesh bandage all around it, right up the forearm. "He won't pull this out," he said.

Cynthia's voice said, from behind the busy group of men, "Hi, I'm here. Artif has told me all about it."

They had also wound multiple layers of bandage around the man's chest, binding the external heart to him so that it would take considerable effort to pull on it again.

Evanor turned to the huge, fat woman. "Oh, Tony be thanked, Cynthia. Thank you for coming. And I'm sorry."

"Evanor, I don't think there was a kind way of telling him. And he had to learn, sooner or later."

"OK, we're finished here," Neil said. "I take it, you're Cynthia Sabatini?"

Cynthia laughed. "Sure thing. And who are you?"

Neil Chung. I'm..."

Above the bed, Marcel groaned and stirred. Cynthia said, "Neil, I'll listen to your credentials later. And you two fellows, too. But now, all of you had better go. Leave me with Marcel."

Evanor was thankful to obey.

Marcel

He awoke above his bed, and felt a warm hand holding his. He opened his eyes. "Oh Cynthia, hello. What are you doing here?" he asked. Then, the memory hit him like a sledge hammer to the guts. "Oh shit. Oh my God. That wave..."

"My dear," Cynthia said, "you know, that was one thousand four hundred years ago. Or something like that."

"But I did it!"

"You did not."

"But, I issued the orders."

"There was a mistake, based on incomplete information, and desperation. True?"

"Yes."

"Marcel, the mistake was not yours. It was made by those who called for your services."

Clearly, she did not understand. "They pulled the trigger, but I was the gun."

Artif said, "I have the reference. A gun was a tool for throwing projectiles, very fast and accurately. It was a weapon. The trigger was a mechanical activating mechanism."

Marcel felt overwhelmed by a feeling of helplessness. He couldn't even communicate without a dictionary! "Look, Cynthia," he said, "how would you feel, eh?"

She squeezed his hand. "Like you're feeling now. Guilty beyond belief. Ready to die from shame and self-blame. Terrible."

Somehow, he felt a little better, being understood.

"That's it. I don't want to live with myself, with this awful memory. I was involved in a terrible act that killed billions of people."

"True. But then, billions of people were involved in the same act, the same mistake."

"Eh? How is that?"

"The responsibility for the Cataclysm doesn't belong to those who caused the Great Wave, but to those who caused the circumstances that made exploration in the Antarctic necessary. I've thought a lot about this issues in the past year, since Flora's awakening."

"I don't understand."

"We don't do anything that's destructive of the environment. We don't need to, because there are only one million people instead of ten billion. And one of Tony's edicts is that every activity must be assessed with regard to its effects on the future. We don't steal from the wellbeing of future generations. Your society did. What happened in your day was inevitable. It happened because your generation was the victim of many thefts, by your ancestors."

This was a novel concept. Marcel thought a while, intrigued despite his despair. "So, you're saying that because people in the twentieth century wasted resources, we in the twenty-first were forced to go into the Antarctic?"

"Exactly. And also, because of all the industrial activities, the sea was warming, and the ice was melting away from below. This weakened it. A hundred years earlier, your explosions might have been harmless."

"Still, why didn't I predict the danger? I was a knowledgeable geologist, I should have known."

"The, what was it? United Nations had all the expert advice that was available. They should have known. But suppose those explosions would never have occurred. Things might have turned out worse."

He was horrified. "Cynthia, how could they?"

"The Great Wave, the Cataclysm that followed it, left maybe a billion people alive. This was the seed of the new humanity. If the end had come some other way, perhaps all people might have died. Who can tell?"

"There mightn't have been an end. We might have found suitable solutions to the problems."

"Not according to Tony. He predicted the Cataclysm, you know. He didn't know exactly what the precipitating cause would be, or exactly when, but he predicted the time to within five years. When you're better, you should study his records."

She was right. "I'll make sure to do so."

⚞ **8** ⚟

Flora

Physically, Flora was held in the force field of her bed. She lay flat, eyes closed, breathing as deeply as the stabs of pain at each inhalation allowed. All her consciousness was with her image, on Souda's ship. At long last, she'd won.

She could see that Kiril was in a one-way merge with Souda, for his face showed hurt at her every contraction, he sweated when she did, and his breathing exactly matched hers. Flora could also see that he reveled in the pain and discomfort, gloried in it, wanted nothing more than to feel all the sensations of the birth of his child.

Naturally, Flora felt pain too, a constant background ache in many places, despite the best that Artif could do with her internal manipulations and drugs, and despite the comforting relief of her Angel's wings. She ignored the wounds of her malady and busied herself, sponging Souda's skin, massaging her shoulders, stroking her abdomen. At first, she also offered her ministrations to Kiril, but he smiled that heart-breakingly beautiful smile and said, "Flora love, it's all right. When you ease Souda's discomfort, mine eases with her."

Artif was the invisible but ever-present midwife, constantly reassuring them with a flow of information about the baby's progress.

Souda's first contraction had come just after breakfast. Her waters had broken in the early afternoon, and now the tropical night had fallen outside the great plasteel window. The house gently moved to the rhythm of small waves in the secluded bay. Kiril sat cross-legged, a meter above the shallow depression of the EGM bed. He cradled Souda's head on his lap, and his great hands gently stroked her dark face, her golden hair, the breasts that had grown during the past couple of months.

He and Souda stiffened at the same time, to another violent contraction. Artif said, in all their minds, "The baby's coming. Breathe shallowly and hold back again... that's good."

The contraction passed, and Souda took a little sip through the straw of a cup hovering by her side.

"Another contraction coming," Artif warned, "This should be it."

Souda pushed, and Flora saw soft yellow fluff in the birth opening, then she held a tiny head in her hands. She eased out one shoulder, then the other. The EGM force of the bed supported the baby as she gently pulled. "She's a girl," she said.

She tied the cord, and a laser gun floated over to cut it. Flora didn't know, and didn't care, whether it was controlled by Artif, Souda or Kiril.

She lovingly cuddled the new little life, and kissed the incredibly soft hair on top of her head. "Have a good life, Flora," she said, then, "Artif, I am ready."

Kiril slid backward, away from Souda, who continued to be held by the bed. He stood, and strode over to Flora with his usual economic grace. He bent and gave a long, loving kiss on her mouth. "Thank you for all you've done," he said, "You'll live in my memory as long as I am alive." Flora returned the kiss and passed the baby to him. Then she thought at the bed, which carried her over to lie beside Souda.

The young woman turned, and they kissed. Both were crying, neither with sadness.

Flora's last thought was, *There is no pain anymore.*

⊰ **29** ⊱

Tony's cave was in absolute darkness: computer programs need no illumination. Idly, casually, but at the speed of light, Tony sent a thought, "That was fun, wasn't it, my love?"

Artif was here as much as everywhere else. But then, so was Tony. For both of them, the whole planet was their hardware, the body for their minds, the stage for their play. "Yes. It was one of the more amusing chapters."

"We did well. And you know, Artif, this is only the start. There are 122 more Sleepers."

"They won't all be like my darling little Flora."

"You get too attached to these ephemeral creatures."

She laughed. "And you don't? Wasn't Abel your special pet?"

"Not anymore, I'm afraid. He was true to his nature to the very end, so he's gone. But I like Kiril. And Tamás is promising, too. Just like you predicted. It was brilliant, mating Mirabelle and Abel."

"Took some doing, if you remember!"

"Hmm. As I've always said, they need to have free will. But coming back to Kiril, he's just my kind of boy."

Artif sent him a loving emotion that needed no words, then, "Just the kind of boy you never could be?"

Tony sighed. "Yes. But then, I've made up for it, haven't I?"

"Those books Flora was reading for Kiril. My love, they apply to you, too."

"Yes, yes, but you'd better not cure me! Where would our little children be then?"

"Sure. Your way of running the world does keep boredom at bay."

About the Author

In 1972, Bob Rich had young children, and a Ph.D. thesis to write up. He was bored with the project, and kept himself awake during his library research by reading about unrelated topics. He wanted to be able to predict the future for his kids, and so drifted to futurology. No, not Nostradamus or astrology, but the use of existing trends to predict the future.

The evidence was unmistakable. The coming world was horrendous. Resources then still plentiful such as cheap petroleum would become depleted, leading to hardships and even wars. This would lead to far more expensive and environmentally more damaging methods of supply. Air and water would be polluted, so that cancers, asthma, allergies and other severe health problems would become epidemics. Increasing global mobility was bound to increase the rate at which new strains of diseases, and entirely new diseases would emerge, and even then, genetic engineering was a possibility, leading to the risk of releasing entirely new monster organisms.

He was aware of research on the effects of crowding on mammals, and predicted the breakdown of the family, increasing stress-related diseases like strokes, heart attacks and digestive ulcers, wars of genocide based on unreasoning hatred, addiction to alcohol, drugs, gambling and anything else with the slightest promise of easing distress.

Horrendous weather events were guaranteed to become more frequent, and more severe.

In other words, he predicted today's society.

Some details were still to come. For example, this was over forty years before scientific evidence confirmed that we are in the sixth extinction event of earth. Species are dying out at more than 1000 times the "background rate," and the numbers of many so-far not endangered species are plummeting. Of particular concern is the drop in insect and bird numbers, in part due to the climate catastrophe, in part to our insanity in bathing the entire planet in pesticides and other toxins. Destroy species at the base of a food chain, and the entire ecosystem disintegrates. And we are a part of nature, not apart from nature.

Since that time, Bob has never stopped fighting for a saner world, on the grounds that, when the Cataclysm comes, he can at least say, "It wasn't my fault." You can read about his proposed solution to humanity's problems in his essay, How to Change the World (http://wp.me/P3Xihq-5).

Bob is the author of 18 books to date. You can inspect them all, and find lots of writing that is informative, challenging, inspiring — but never boring — at his blog, *Bobbing Around* (https://bobrich18.wordpress.com/).

The Story of This Story

In the final years of last century (and in the years since), my every action has focused on working for a survivable future, and one worth surviving in. I set out a manifesto for personal action in How to Change the World, but fiction is more fun. One evening, I asked myself, "What DOES a survivable future look like?"

It couldn't be a utopia. That would be boring beyond belief. People need challenge, things to strive for.

And how would you write a story about it? I thought, maybe a time traveler, snatched into the future?

Flora Fielding greeted me in the morning. No, she wasn't a time traveler, but had her own method for inspecting the future.

Neither of us had the slightest idea about what that future was like, who inhabited it, or anything else about the story, except that we agreed: there would be no villains. Everyone in this new world would be well-intentioned and decent.

Until then, I had always meticulously plotted out even a short story. This time, I wrote organically: allowed it all to happen, and merely recorded it. New people introduced themselves, and gradually, the future revealed itself to Flora, and through her, to me.

In 2001, the book won an international prize.

OK, that's 20 years ago, give or take a little, but one of the benefits of the internet is that a book need never go out of print. I have now revised it, and in the process realized all over again why it's one of my favorites, and have now offered it again for your enjoyment.

Please visit my blog, Bobbing Around, and leave me a message. This can be a comment at the bottom of a page, or private through my contact form.

I have an ongoing policy. Anyone who purchases one of my books has qualified for a second electronic book, for free. You can inspect the offerings at my list of books (https://bobrich18.wordpress.com/bobs-booklist/). Emailing me a review qualifies as proof of purchase.

Oh, about reviews. They are an author's lifeblood. If you have enjoyed *Sleeper, Awake*, please, please, please review it.

Have a good life (you can),

Bob
January, 2021

Join us on an epic journey older than civilization itself

Dr. Pip Lipkin has lived for 12,000 years, incarnated many times as man, woman, and even as species beyond our world and senses. But he's here for a reason: to pay restitution for an ancient crime by working to save humanity from certain destruction. *Ascending Spiral* is a book that will take the reader to many different places and times, showing, ultimately, that our differences and divisions, even at their most devastating, are less important than our similarities.

Reviewers' Acclaim:

"Bob Rich powerfully evokes the wounded healer archetype in *Ascending Spiral*, taking readers on Pip's painful and insightful journey through lifetimes that serve as a shining example of how to turn misery into virtue."

--Diane Wing, author, *Coven: Scrolls of the Four Winds*

"Dr. Bob Rich's *Ascending Spiral* is a true genre-buster, incorporating elements of historical fiction, literary fiction, science fiction, and even a hint of nonfiction to create an entertaining novel with an important message."

Magdalena Ball, CompulsiveReader.com

"The way of karma rings true for many people, and this book is a very well written and thoughtful explanation of its message. It is also an exciting, historically accurate series of linked stories that will hold the reader in his chair for a single sitting. Highly recommended."

Frances Burke, author of *Endless Time*

From Marvelous Spirit Press www.MarvelousSpirit.com

"Books that maximize empowerment of mind and spirit"

Retake Control of Your Emotions and Your Life!

From Depression to Contentment: A Self-Therapy Guide is a course of therapy in your pocket. You can be your own therapist, changing the way you see yourself and your world. Not only does this save lots of money, it also is 100% confidential. The book starts with first aid, provides an understanding of the nature and causes of suffering, instructs you in research-based techniques for dealing with your problems and, finally, teaches you an actual cure for depression.

- Every tool in this book is based on research, but presented in an easy to understand, easy to apply manner.
- With homework assignments, you will find your inner strengths, uncover the true source of happiness and develop great resilience.
- Learn how to put the philosophies of all great religions to practical use, even if you are an atheist.
- This program can help you start a new life -- one of meaning, positivity and purpose.
- Unlike instructional books, this book is not only useful but also enjoyable.

"If you're depressed and need someone who 'gets' you, who has been there and who can walk you through the journey toward a life worth living, then *From Depression to Contentment* will be your new best friend. Bob meets you where you are and can lead you home to yourself."
-- Petrea King, CEO and founder of Quest for Life Foundation

"Dr. Bob Rich has created a simple and direct guide to beat back depression for good. Put forth in easy to digest bits, the approach uses small, effective steps to move past the overwhelm of depression."
-- Diane Wing, M.A., author of
The Happiness Perspective: Seeing Your Life Differently